Always

LIZZIE MORTON

Edited: Black Quill Editing

Adeen Print
978-1-7391175-5-9

Abby and Jake.

You were the best start to the most incredible journey.

This book is yours.

Always.

Chapter One

Abby

Everyone screws up in life, no matter who they are, and often they screw up multiple times. It's normal. No one bats an eyelash because screw-ups, more often than not, are easily rectified.

It's the fuck-ups that are problematic and they're the ones everybody notices.

And I, Abby West, have fucked up.

Well and truly.

I'm wandering around Leeds Festival, avoiding everyone and everything, searching for space in the one place I'm least likely to find it. Thousands of people bustle around me in a uniform of rubber boots and aviator shades, laughing and dancing like they don't have a care in the world. I struggle to swallow over the lump in my throat as I take it all in, knowing I might never look or feel like them again.

The drama of the summer has come back and bitten me in the ass and even without the evidence in front of me, my gut is telling me nothing will ever be the same.

Accepting that I can't stay away forever when exhaustion kicks in, I make my way back to S.C.A.R.A.B.'s tour bus and climb into bed, praying no one will bother me. It's a wasted effort even trying to sleep because I'm hardwired to Jake. I spend the whole time listening, waiting for him to get back, which ends up being hours later. Peeking from under the cover, I watch as he gets on the bus after the rest of the group. Electricity fills the air. My body starts to hum the way it always does when he's nearby.

I ache for him to climb into my bed, wrap his arms around my body, and make everything feel right. He won't though, because I told him not to.

We can't pretend everything is fine when it isn't.

I've done this to myself.

The others call it an early night in preparation for the final set of the tour, and fifteen minutes pass before everything goes silent. Only the sounds of the festival can be heard, filtering through the thick metal walls of the bus. I spend hours staring into the darkness, sleep refusing to come. Instead, I lay, replaying Six Seconds to Barcelona's performance over and over, each painful, heart-wrenching moment. It's the early hours of the morning when I eventually drift into a restless sleep. Images of Jake and Dan, two sets of eyes, brown and blue, full of pain and confusion, plague my dreams.

All too soon I'm jostled awake, my head pounding. Through bleary eyes, I can just about make out Amanda's silhouette through the barely-there light. The thick silence surrounding her tells me no one else is awake.

"What?" I grumble.

"Get up," she hisses.

"No chance." I huff and roll over, pulling my cover over my head, hoping she gets the point.

She doesn't. A light chill hits my body and I groan, missing the warmth and comfort of my cocoon.

I roll back over, struggling to keep the bite from my voice when I say, "Amanda, I've barely had any sleep. What is so urgent it can't wait a couple more hours?"

"We're going to a drug store," she replies bluntly.

"What? Now?" I sit up, rubbing sleep from my eyes.

"Yes, now. Unless you want to explain to everyone else where we're going and why?"

I might not be able to see her, but we've spent enough time together this summer, I know if I could, she'd be standing with her hands planted firmly on her hips and her lips pursed. She has a point. I could lie and make up some kind of excuse, but the people on this bus are more perceptive than they let on.

"Fine." I throw my legs over the side of the bed and grab some clothes from my bag, then tiptoe to the bathroom to get dressed.

I'm about to leave when I catch a glimpse of myself in the mirror. Pasty skin, limp hair and circles under my eyes that make it look like I've gone a few rounds in a boxing ring stare back at me. God, I look awful. Taking a deep breath, I pinch at my cheeks in an attempt to add some color. It does nothing.

Stop stalling, just get it over and done with, I tell myself.

Admitting defeat, I follow Amanda off the bus and out of the festival to a waiting cab. She's thought of everything. Like, literally everything. When the cab sways along the

English country roads and nausea starts to kick in, she hands over a pack of saltines and a bottle of sparkling water without a word.

Right now, she knows me better than I know myself.

We sit in silence the entire way to the city, and I watch in a daze as the scenery whizzes past in the early morning light. If you asked me a couple of months ago how I thought the summer was going to end, waking up and sneaking away before the rest of the group woke to go in search of pregnancy tests with a person I not so long ago despised, would not have been the answer I'd have given.

Yet here we are.

I'm now locked in a toilet stall stinking of pee in Leeds City Centre, waiting for Amanda, my temporary arch-nemesis turned emotional crutch, to return. My spidey senses are screaming at me that change is on the horizon and not the kind you embrace with open arms excitedly. No, it's the kind of change that makes your gut churn and your fight or flight kick in. It's the kind that has you running for the hills like a zombie apocalypse is hot on your heels. I feel like I'm stuck in that scene at the end of *Titanic*. I'm Rose on that huge chunk of wood, bobbing in the freezing water, praying the inevitable isn't about to happen. That my life isn't about to end.

Standing, I bounce on the spot, trying to get my head around the fact that I'm relying heavily on the person who, in the past couple of months, has caused me so much animosity. I try not to get too agitated wondering what's taking her so long. After all, she's doing the one thing I couldn't bring myself to. Something so simple yet so final.

Outside the store, she recognized the fear in my eyes and took over. I wish she hadn't. I wish we could have jumped back in the cab and headed back to the festival, pretending none of this was happening. But this afternoon is the last set of S.C.A.R.A.B.'s European tour. I need to know the truth sooner rather than later so I can decide what to do for the best.

For all of us.

Amanda tucks her petite frame and oversized platinum blonde hair into the cubicle beside me and states, "I got one of every kind."

My eyes almost bug out of my head when I see the plastic bag she's holding, bulging at the seams. I'm pretty certain it only takes one test to get the answer we need, yet it looks like she bought out the store.

Taking in my bewildered expression, she shrugs. "I grabbed extras. I don't want to have to go back in if any come back unclear. Plus, if *Juno* is anything to go by, you're going to need more than one to convince you of the answer."

She's likening my scenario to *Juno*. I want the ground to swallow me up.

"Whatever," I reply far too grumpily considering all she's trying to do is help. "Can we get this over and done with? I'm about to pee my pants."

She hands over the first box she grabs from the bag.

I frown at the packaging, taking in the garish pink and blue colors. "Is this the most reliable one?"

She raises a perfectly shaped eyebrow. "Seriously, Abby? It's a pregnancy test, not rocket science. The answer is yes or no. How about you pee on it, and we question its validity afterward?"

"Coming from the person who practically bought out the whole store …" I grumble. "You could be nicer. Something life-changing is about to happen here."

"It might also not be, but we will never find out if you don't drop your pants and pee on the damn stick." She huffs.

The beauty of being stuck in this scenario with her is that any bitchiness I show, she can throw back tenfold. She's a pain in my ass but it's a pain I need right now. I watch as she shoves the boxes into her oversized tote bag, then begins tearing apart the plastic one before crouching down and spreading it out, being careful not to let her skin make contact with the ground.

"Erm, what are you doing?" I ask, a hint of amusement in my voice that feels alien.

She glances up at me with a shake of her head. "You could catch something off this floor." She wrinkles her nose. "You could have picked somewhere a little more hygienic."

"I was going for discreet. Somewhere no one would ever think to find us."

This time both perfect brows shoot up, so high I'm surprised they don't leave her head. "And who exactly are you expecting to find us? The firing squads?"

I narrow my eyes. "What does it matter whether the floor is clean?"

She raises a finger in the air. "Firstly, standards, Abby. Which, with you talking like you are right now, I'm wondering if Jake still has any."

My eyes become slits.

She plasters a sweet smile on her face, saying brightly like she hasn't just openly insulted me, "Plus, we need to know whether it's *you* who's pregnant, not anyone else."

I roll my eyes at how dramatic she's being, watching as she stacks the boxes carefully on the plastic now covering the floor. Admitting defeat, I open the box in my hands, pulling out one of the two tests inside, then rip open the foil.

Stick in hand, I freeze, waiting for her to leave the cubicle, or at least turn around. She does neither.

"What?" she barks, getting fed up with how long I'm taking. After how long she took in the drugstore, I could tell her she's not quite the queen of speed herself.

"Some privacy would be nice …"

We might be getting closer, but we're not *that* close.

Her cheeks flush ever so slightly. "Oh, yeah. Sorry." Before leaving, she suggests, "How about we open a few for you to do in one go? You know … so we can be certain."

"Yeah, maybe you're right," I say, trying and failing to give her a small smile.

We spend the next few minutes opening boxes, laying the tests out on the plastic, ready to begin the peeing conveyor belt. Each has similar images emblazoned on the front: a woman holding a test. The ecstatic expression on their faces is a stark contrast to how I'm feeling. They look like it's the best thing to ever happen to them whereas I feel like it's the worst.

"I'll be out here if you need any help," says Amanda, unlocking the cubicle door, ready to slip out.

I blame my raging hormones for the fact I mutter under my breath, "I'm peeing on a stick. I think I'll be able to manage."

She shakes her head vigorously and the light from overhead catches on her hair, making it sparkle. "Again, with the bitchy attitude. Next time you can receive your life-changing news alone."

Choosing to ignore her, I quickly shut the door when she's gone and drop my pants. Perched on the seat, I lean forward and grab a couple of tests, uncap them, then sit and wait. The silence is deafening.

A few minutes pass before Amanda asks through the door, "Why aren't you peeing already?"

"I think I have stage fright," I say with a groan.

"Please tell me you're joking?" she hisses.

"I wish. Nothing is happening. It won't come out."

She pauses for a second, then says, "Do you want me to come back in? You know, for moral support?"

"Please," I reply sheepishly. This is possibly one of the most humiliating moments of my life.

I don't even bother to pull up my pants when I stand and unlock the door. What's the point? My dignity is about to go out the window anyway. Amanda doesn't seem phased by my appearance, or when I sit back down with the grace of a baby elephant.

Saving me a job, she picks a few tests up from the floor and holds one out. "Pee."

I don't know why her being with me helps, but the issue is quickly resolved, and the faint trickle of urine reaches both of our ears.

"Don't waste it all! Use the sticks!" she demands when she realizes I'm not even holding a test.

After a quick panic, I hold each one she passes over under the flow, praying I'm doing it right. I feel under more pressure now than during my driving exam. Each time I pass one back, Amanda places the cap back on and lays it flat on the white plastic facing upward, just like the instructions told us to.

"What now?" I ask, wiping, then finally pulling up my pants.

"We wait. Most of the tests say it can take up to three minutes." All the time she's speaking, she stares me directly in the eyes. I know she's being extra careful not to look down without my permission and I'm thankful she's here with me, helping me to hold it together. "I'm guessing it's been over a minute already. Do you want me to look? Are you ready?"

I stare back blankly, my heart hammering in my chest. Maybe she's wrong, maybe we both are. Maybe we've been blowing everything out of proportion. We've been on a European music tour for almost two months, drinking more alcohol than can be considered healthy, surviving on a diet of junk food, while temporarily living and traveling on a bus. There's been enough emotional angst to upset anyone's system. My symptoms could be purely down to stress.

I nod, holding her gaze. "Do it."

Her eyes move down, and I wipe my palms against my jeans, waiting for her to give something away. Anything.

The only telltale sign I get is the sharp breath she takes in, before stammering, "A—Abby, look down."

Slowly, I lower my chin. My eyes take in the tests laid out on the plastic bag. That's the moment my world crumbles.

I don't need to crouch down to read them.

This is a new version of *Titanic*. One where Rose is the one to fall into the freezing depths of the ocean, taking Jack with her, anchoring them both at the bottom.

On each stick a positive result glares, tying me to Jake Ross permanently.

"Are you feeling okay?"

I glance up in a daze, my brain barely able to register Amanda standing in front of me. When I don't answer her brows pull together.

"Abby?"

In a bid to bring myself back to Earth, I shake my head. Unfortunately, when I land everything comes crashing down around me.

I'm pregnant.

What am I going to do?

Shit, shit, shitty shit, shit.

Swallowing hard, I manage a weak smile and reply, "I've felt better."

Amanda is sitting opposite me at the small table situated in the window of the coffee shop we decided to come to. We both agreed a little time was needed to process the news before being thrown back into the craziness of the tour one last time. I glance out the window and become lost in my thoughts again. The scraping of a cup moving across the wooden table draws my attention back to her. I frown when the smell of peppermint hits me.

"No caffeine," she explains.

I look longingly at her steaming cup of energy. "What do you mean no caffeine?"

"Everyone knows pregnant women can't drink caffeine, or alcohol, or eat Sushi. Sorry."

Wonderful. Besides my friends and family, caffeine is one of the constant joys in my life. When no one else is around, my trusty friend is there to warm me from the inside out, always helping to make things seem better. What little progress Amanda and I made toward a friendship, swirls down the drain with any hope I had for a cup of coffee.

"I think it's safe to say this summer has ended as badly as it started," I say with a sigh. Reluctantly, I pick up the tea and dip the tip of my tongue into the murky liquid. It tastes as bad as it looks and I wrinkle my nose in disgust, placing it back on the table.

I go to grab Amanda's coffee. "Just a small sip, please."

"No chance. No babies will be harmed on my watch," she replies, swatting my hand away.

"I think you're being a little dramatic. Besides, I don't even know what I'm going to do yet."

This time Amanda is the one to frown. "What do you mean?"

I look back out the window and drop my voice, "You know what I mean."

Her eyes widen, the understanding of what I'm hinting at clear. "Don't rush into a decision, not yet. At least wait until you speak to Jake."

"You think I should tell him?"

The shock on her face is replaced with disbelief. "Do not tell me you're thinking about keeping this from him. Abby, you have to tell him. It's *his* baby."

I wish I liked peppermint tea. If I did, I'd have a way of putting off this conversation. "If I tell him, it will ruin everything. Look how far the band has come this summer. It will all have been for nothing."

"But it's *his* decision to make. You can't do this alone." Amanda reaches across the table, grasps my hand, squeezing it so hard I'm not sure if it's me she's trying to reassure or herself. "He's a good guy—not just good, one of best. You're talking to the one other person in the world who knows. Give him a chance; please don't keep it from him."

I nod, knowing deep down she's right. Forgetting morals, in around nine months I'm going to be as discreet as a bus. There will be no hiding the truth.

"Okay," I agree, albeit reluctantly. "But I'm doing it in my own time and on my own terms."

She lets go of my hand and I watch enviously when she picks up her coffee, letting out a sigh of pleasure as she drinks. I want to grab it out of her hands and down the whole thing in one go, especially when the aroma of caramel hits me. I've never needed a caffeine hit like I do now, especially after the past couple of nights. My body is exhausted, but the day has barely begun.

When she's all but drained the cup dry, Amanda says, "We should get back. Are you ready?"

No! I want to scream. I'll never be ready to go back and see Jake, knowing the shit show that is about to unfold.

I've spent so long running from my problems, I've forgotten how to face them head-on. There's no running from this though.

It's time to face the music.

Chapter Two

Abby

A couple of hours before S.C.A.R.A.B.'s final set of the tour, I do a quick kit check, making sure I have everything I need in my bag.

"Are you feeling better?" asks Zach, walking up behind me.

I startle and turn around. "Excuse me?"

"I said are you feeling better?"

His voice is friendly, but there's something in his eyes telling me there's a deeper meaning to his question. Nausea creeps in that isn't baby-related.

"I'm feeling fine," I stammer, mentally cursing myself for sounding anything but. "Why'd you ask?"

"I heard you being sick in the bathroom the night before last. I just wanted to check you were okay, that's all."

My stomach drops.

"Stomach flu," I explain, praying to God he buys it.

"Must be a nasty case you picked up for it to keep coming back like it has," he replies. "Weird that no one else has picked it up."

He knows. I know he knows, and he knows that I know he knows.

"The worst." I smile sweetly, feigning ignorance. "I need to get over to the stage and get set up." I do one final check of my bag then pull the zipper closed, trying to ignore Zach hovering at my side.

"What about Jake?" he asks, not getting the hint.

I sigh and my hand lingers on the zipper, toying with it nervously. "What about him?"

"He's hurting, Abby," there's pain in his voice. Clearly, it's hurting him that his best friend isn't doing so well.

"Then now he knows how it feels," I snap.

I throw my bag over my shoulder and start to walk away down the bus, hating that this is how I'm leaving things with him after we've become friendly over the summer. But I'm exhausted and emotionally strung out. I can't cope with him pushing questions on me like he is, even though I know he only has mine and Jake's best interests at heart.

His voice comes out so low I could almost convince myself I don't hear him, "You have to tell Jake."

I stop dead in my tracks. "I don't know what you're talking about." I focus my attention on the doors at the front, trying to calm my racing heart. The walls are closing in and I can't breathe.

I have to get off this bus.

I don't say anything else, and I don't look back. I'm terrified that if I do, I'll see the expression on Zach's face, the one that will tell me he knows the truth and my secret isn't quite as secret as I thought.

I stumble down the steps and once outside, walk around the bus to the back, needing a few minutes to get my thoughts together before I head to the stage for the set. I sag against it as the strength leaves my body. Sliding to the ground, I'm too numb to notice the metal scorching my skin. I press at my temples and rub, trying to ease the headache that's formed while my mind races, trying to make sense of everything. All I want is to climb into bed, sleep for a very long time and wake up not pregnant. I've found myself walking along a path I never would have pre-empted, terrified I'm going to walk the rest of the way alone. Leaning forward, I place my head between my knees, sucking in the warm, humid air.

I'm pregnant.

Fuck.

How am I supposed to tell Jake? This will ruin everything.

Managing to get my breathing under control, I sit up straight and bang the base of my palm against my forehead, hoping it might give me some answers. It doesn't.

Stupid, stupid Abby. That's what everyone will say. This is so humiliating. My parents will be so disappointed and that's without the added complication of Jake and my dad's working relationship.

Fuck.

A sob builds in my chest and I'm about to let the floodgates open when Sam's and Ryan's laughter floats through the air from the front of the bus. I peep around the corner from where I'm sitting and find Ryan surrounded by a cloud of smoke, a joint in his hand. He raises the glowing tip and takes a long drag.

"Want some?" I hear him croak before he exhales.

The smell of weed drifts in my direction. It takes everything in me not to vomit.

"No, man," replies Sam, a goofy grin covering his face. "Gotta keep the voice in good shape. The ladies won't love me otherwise."

Ryan lifts the joint to his mouth again, inhales, then blows more smoke into the air. "Your loss. This shit's good."

Yawn. I hate eavesdropping and this conversation isn't even worth listening to. I'm about to stand and walk straight past them when Ryan makes a comment that leaves me frozen on the grass.

"Definitely needed after all that crap with Jake."

Sam lets out a long huff. "Yeah, it's pretty heavy. He'll come out the other side."

I shouldn't keep listening. But I can't stop myself; I need to know what they're talking about.

"You really think he will?" Ryan pauses, taking another drag of his joint. The expression on his face is one I've never seen before. For the first time, he looks serious and concerned. "No wonder he doesn't ever want kids."

"Yeah, I wouldn't either if I were him," agrees Sam.

They carry on speaking but I don't hear anything else they say, the ringing in my ears drowns out their voices.

He doesn't want kids.

Dread creeps in. Telling Jake that I'm pregnant was going to be a huge hurdle, throwing a massive roadblock in his career path. I already knew it had the potential to ruin everything he and the band had worked for. But now, knowing this, I don't think I can do it. I know deep down Jake would stand by me and the baby.

Even if he didn't want to.

By telling him the truth, I'd be tying him to the one thing he doesn't want. I'd be doing the thing he always told me not to let anyone do. I'd be taking away his control over his own life. Holding him back from living the way he wants and eventually, he'd end up resenting me for it.

No relationship could ever survive that.

I thought I knew what my heart truly breaking felt like, after all, Jake broke it not once, but twice, but the pain I experienced those times were just the warmup. The ache I feel in my chest now is unbearable. My mind is plagued with images of Jake and me together. Our first kiss. Watching him and the band practice when we were young, carefree. The way his eyes crinkle when he's genuinely happy. How his laugh, when he really laughs, comes out more like a deep rumble that makes his chest and the air around him vibrate. It's infectious. Then there are those deep brown, soulful eyes, unreadable yet at the same time full of emotion.

I want to fall apart, but I know once I start crying, I won't be able to stop, and I still have a job to do. I need to finish at least one part of the summer right.

Quietly, I walk away from the bus, in the opposite direction of what I'd originally planned, avoiding Sam and Ryan. It's a longer route to the stage where S.C.A.R.A.B. is performing but I need the extra time to get my shit together. I clutch my bag for dear life. The same bag that has a positive pregnancy test hidden at the bottom. A reminder that I'm not stuck in a nightmare. This is real.

Backstage, I'm greeted by Sooz with eyes so wide they look like they're about to pop, her hair sticking out in all directions. "Where have you been?" she screeches.

"I couldn't find one of my lenses," I lie.

Sophie and Zoe are standing in the distance. Their gazes burn my skin, but I avoid eye contact. They know me better than anyone and if they see my face, they'll know something is up. All it will take is one push for my walls to come tumbling down, and they can't.

Not here. Not now. Not yet.

I need to get through this set, *then* I can fall apart.

"Do you know where Jake is?" asks Sooz, panic in her voice.

I look up and find her eyes. "He's not here?"

She shakes her head. "No one's been able to find him, and he isn't answering his phone."

Dammit. This is my fault. He's avoiding me like I've been avoiding him.

"He'll turn up," I say, trying to sound confident. "I'm going to get set up."

Before anyone can say anything else, I dart away and head to the frontstage area. I fill my time setting up my camera with the right lens and adjust the settings so they're appropriate for the lighting. S.C.A.R.A.B. is performing on the main stage and it's huge. My stomach swirls with anticipation and the sound of the crowd behind me, chanting the band's name, makes it hard to concentrate. I don't think any of us quite realized what Sooz meant when she said this would be their biggest performance yet.

Despite how I'm feeling, the corners of my lips tug up in a small smile.

They've made it.

As the stage crew completes their final checks, the noise amplifies. The mood is intoxicating and for a little while, I forget everything. For one last time, I allow myself to be drawn in and lost in the tour. It's bittersweet. There will be no more performances after this. There will be no more Abby and Jake. Maybe there never was. Maybe all along we've been fighting for something that was never meant to be because it feels like the odds are never in our favor.

Relief floods my veins when a guitar strums from the side wing, out of view from where I'm standing, but telling me what I need to know. Jake turned up. In the same moment, my phone vibrates in my pocket. I quickly pull it out to check who it is, finding Dan's name flashing on the screen. I bite my lip and hit reject.

The band steps out onto the stage. To the outside world, they might appear like they've casually thrown something on, each dressed according to their personal style, but I know how much work has gone on behind the scenes. They're wearing the best, kitted out for sponsors. Amanda and her team have done an amazing job, making it look effortless.

A deafening roar of approval hits me from behind when Sam's voice sounds through the speakers, filling the late afternoon sky. Ryan hammers the drums with a beat that sets my pulse racing. I'm so lost in everything happening around me I almost forget I have a job to do. When I remember, I raise my camera and capture as many images as I can. I don't need to look up to know Jake is watching me. The hair on my arms standing on end as I walk back and forth is a dead giveaway.

During the last song of the set, I turn around to capture the crowd's expressions, and that's when I make my decision. The look of euphoria on every single person's face standing in front of me as they become lost in the music makes me realize I can't do it.

I can't let Jake walk away from all of this and into a life he never wanted because of a mistake.

I won't let him.

He won't walk away if he doesn't know.

Turning back, I lower my camera for the last few seconds of the song and stare up at Jake. My eyes burn knowing this is the end. It's our final goodbye. His eyes hold mine, reading me like a book. He continues strumming his guitar, but his entire body tenses. There's nothing he can do to stop me from leaving, especially when the crowd goes berserk, chanting for one more song, to which Sam all too willingly agrees.

I don't need any more images. I've done my job.

There's still one thing left to do, so as I turn, I pull out my phone, sending a message to Dan.

Not once do I look back as I walk away because if I see Jake's expression while he watches me leave, my resolve will crumble.

While S.C.A.R.A.B. finishes the last part of the set, I run back to the bus and grab all of my things quickly before anyone gets back and questions what I'm doing. I shift my weight from side to side, gazing vacantly into the crowds, a vice-like grip on the handle of my suitcase.

This wasn't how the summer was meant to end and now Dan's late.

Standing among the festival crew tents, away from the prying eyes of the world, I check the messages from him, confirming the time we agreed to meet. Over the summer, I liked to think it was fate that we met when we did. For poor Dan, it was just bad luck.

I wouldn't blame him if he didn't show at all. I made a promise that Jake and I were history, only to have him stand on stage and witness the complete opposite when Jake crashed his lips against mine in a kiss that took my breath away. A kiss that served as a reminder that as long as Jake and I are around each other, we will never be done. Dan was a bystander in our messy past and present, probably wishing he'd never bumped into me that night in Barcelona.

I shuffle again and look around, trying to pick him out in the crowds. How long do I wait? The last-minute flight I booked back to Cape Town is in a few hours and I'm cutting it close.

"Abby …"

My whole body relaxes when Dan's soft British accent reaches my ears, but when I look up, for the first time since we met, his familiar face is expressionless.

I clear my throat. "Dan, hi."

"You wanted to meet?" He shoves his hands into his black denim pants, sounding almost bored. I'd be bored with my drama too if I were him. His eyes move down to my suitcase, and he frowns.

"Erm … yeah. So, S.C.A.R.A.B.'s tour just ended, which means I'll be going back to Cape Town. I wanted to see you one last time … to … you know … say goodbye." I grimace. Even to my own ears I sound pathetic.

He folds his arms, and his distressed orange T-shirt pulls tight across his chest. "Goodbye."

I tense at his ice-cold voice. I can't say a thing because his response is what I deserve. "Are you going to talk to me properly or should I leave?" I snap, exhaustion getting the better of me.

"Unbelievable," he mutters, his blue eyes narrowing.

"Sorry?" I scoff.

It would appear Dan and I are finally showing our true colors. It's official. The summer romance is over. He looks around expectantly. I wonder if he thinks Jake will jump out from somewhere. I don't blame him because there's a part of me expecting him to do the same.

"I said *unbelievable*. I saw the two of you."

I look away, knowing he's referring to Jake kissing me, but he doesn't know the full story and I'm not sure how to explain. I can't tell him the truth—that I'm pregnant. I'm barely able to admit it to myself let alone anyone else.

"You don't understand," I murmur.

He tugs a hand through his hair and his voice grows louder, "Then explain it to me, Abby. I'm not a mind reader. I won't know what's going on unless you tell me."

My eyes dart to the ground and I shift my feet. "I can't right now …"

He throws his hands in the air.

In the short time we've known each other, I've never seen him like this. He's usually so calm and collected. But this is what I do, I fuck things up, piss people off and bring out the worst in them. At least that's what it feels like.

"Well, that's great," he says through gritted teeth. "You know what? I thought there was something about you, that you were different. I thought to myself, this girl could be the real deal. I was wrong."

The ache in my chest that started earlier becomes more painful. "Dan, I'm sorry. I don't know what else to say."

What he does next, I never would have expected from him. He laughs in my face. I'm not sure which is worse, this or his scathing words.

"What a load of crap, Abby. I've put myself out there with you more than once. I knew I should have walked away the night Jake put on that ridiculous show. I never get involved when there's drama following someone around and *this* is why."

"I'm sorry."

"I know. You've said that already."

His tone sends a shiver down my spine for all the wrong reasons.

He looks up to the sky as if he's searching for something. When he looks back down, his expression softens but is full of sadness. "I'm not sure where we go from here."

"Neither am I," I admit. "I wish I could explain, but I can't."

"Then I can't fight for you. Not when I don't know what it is I'm fighting for."

"Please don't hate me. It will all make sense when I *can* tell you what's really going on," the words are almost pleading. I know what I'm asking is unfair because neither of us knows when that will be.

He laughs again but this time it's bitter, resigned. "But you don't know when that will be, so what's the point? I'm not going to wait around. I deserve better than how you've treated me. Yesterday was humiliating. I bet Jake felt great knowing he had his hands on you while I was watching," he practically spits the last part out.

I step forward and reach to grab his hand, hoping the physical connection might spark some kind of reminder in him of what we had this summer. "Don't be like this … it isn't you."

It stings when he steps back, moving his hand out of reach.

"You don't know me, Abby, not really. So how would you know what I'm like? Maybe I've been putting on a show, you know like you've been doing with me. You made me think I could trust you when really, you've been jumping from one guy to the other while you decide which one you prefer. There's a name for girls like th—"

"Stop!" I snap, cutting him off.

He's letting his anger get the better of him and it's not totally unjustified, but I'm not the only guilty player in all this. Both Jake and Dan knew I was uncertain about pursuing anything, but they went there anyway. They both pushed and this is where we've ended up.

"Had you been watching properly the other day—rather than seeing what you wanted to—you would have seen me push Jake away. I could have carried on, but I didn't. I like you, Dan, but not when you're acting like this."

His face reddens. "Like you're one to talk."

"I can't talk to you when you're being like this," I say, shaking my head.

"Whatever." He shrugs.

My stomach sinks. I thought I'd be sad to say goodbye to the tour, but I can't wait to get on a plane and get back to Cape Town, forgetting that the past few months ever happened. "I'm leaving before one of us says something we'll regret. I really am sorry. I wish things could have ended differently." I sigh, accepting that all we're doing is talking ourselves around in circles. If we keep going one of us will eventually say something that can't be taken back.

All I get in return is silence.

In one last ditched attempt to at least part ways amicably, I look up into Dan's piercing blue eyes, praying the ice in them will thaw. I get nothing, not even a blink.

Having finally had enough, he storms away. He doesn't even say bye.

I'm not sure how long I remain standing, staring at the spot where he was. I wait until the anger and sadness subside a little, then take a few deep breaths, ready to say goodbye to everyone and every part of this summer.

All I want to do is forget.

I'm almost at the festival exit when I hear Sooz calling after me.

"Abby, wait!"

I want to keep walking, but I can't. Sooz isn't just one of my best friends, she's my boss and has every right to know where I'm going. I stop, waiting for her to catch up.

"Where are you going?" she asks, standing in front of me.

"Back to Cape Town," I reply.

"But there's still one more night?" She's looking at me like I'm acting crazy, because to anyone who doesn't know what's going on, I am.

"I don't want to be here anymore, Sooz. I never should have come. This whole summer has been a mess and I just want to go home."

Her lips form a tight line. "Did something happen with Dan or Jake?"

Music filters over from the festival in the background, all the different stages creating a weird mash-up. I could almost be nostalgic for the summer, but everything is too raw. The smell of hot dogs wafts under my nose and my stomach heaves, a telltale sign if ever I needed one, that it's time to leave.

"*Everything* happened with Dan and Jake," I answer cryptically. "Don't worry about work, I got everything we need."

Her brows draw into a deep frown. "I'm not worried about work, Abby. I'm worried about you."

"Don't be. I'm fine, at least I will be." I start to back away, my suitcase bouncing along the uneven grass, making my exit less than graceful.

Her eyes widen when she realizes I'm being serious. "You can't just leave without saying goodbye to everyone!"

"I'm not, you can tell them for me," I reply sadly, the reality of what I'm doing sitting heavy. "I'll see you at home, Sooz. Enjoy your last night."

Before she can convince me otherwise, I slip into the cab, doing what I do best: running.

Jake

Our last set of the tour *should* have been one of the best moments of my life.

Together we defied the odds when everything was against us. I know for Sam, Zach, and Ryan it was everything. Performing on the main stage at Leeds Festival is a big deal by anyone's standards, let alone us, the underdogs.

But it wasn't the best moment of my life, not even close.

The crowds chanting our name, singing our lyrics, thousands of people swaying to the music we put our hearts and souls into, meant nothing. All I could focus on was Abby. I didn't dare take my eyes off her, not for a second, scared that if I did, she would disappear.

It was a relief when we got to the final song and I still had her in my sight. But then Sam had to appease the crowds and agree to a god damn encore. She was there, in my grasp, then I had to watch her slip through my fingers. Again.

Ironically, the shortest of our songs felt like the longest we've ever performed. I couldn't get off the stage quick enough, throwing my guitar—my baby—into the hands of a stranger, charging through the backstage area, ignoring everyone and everything. All I wanted was to get to Abby, but it was pointless. Even though I was desperate I never stood a chance of finding her among the hundreds of thousands of people.

The sun is dipping behind the skyline when I get back to the tour bus, physically and emotionally exhausted. I expect to find everyone waiting but I'm greeted with silence. The bus is empty apart from Sooz, working on her laptop at one of the small tables.

"You missed ten interviews with some of the biggest magazines and radio channels in the country," she says without looking up from the screen.

"I was looking for Abby."

"I know where you were. I'm not an idiot. You screwed up today, big time."

"I don't care," I reply, clenching my jaw. And that's the truth. I couldn't care less about any of this without her by my side. I was an idiot for letting her go two years ago and I refuse to do it again. "Where is she?"

"She's gone, Jake." She sighs.

All the oxygen is sucked from my lungs. "What do you mean she's gone?"

"She caught an early flight back to Cape Town."

I start walking to the back of the bus. When I get there I start shoving my things into a bag.

"What are you doing?" asks Sooz.

"I'm going after her," I grunt, frantically looking around to see if I've missed anything vital.

"Don't."

I turn, frowning. "What do you mean don't? If I remember right, earlier in the summer you were the one telling me to put everything on the line for someone if I loved them. You told me Abby was worth every risk and every mountain I'd have to climb. I'm trying to climb, Sooz. Why are you stepping in my way?"

Her voice softens, "There's something wrong; I'm not sure what. Believe me, if it was the right time to chase after her, I'd be backing you all the way. But something isn't right."

She's almost repeating the conversation I had with Dan the night before last. The fact there might be something wrong with Abby isn't putting me off wanting to find her, it's merely adding fuel to the fire because when someone you love is hurting, you hurt with them. I need to know what's wrong.

Sooz can read me better than I thought, because she says, "Please trust me on this one. I've gotten to know Abby well over the past couple of years. We live together."

This is news to my ears. I knew their relationship was closer than the standard working relationship, but I didn't realize it was *this* close.

"I know Abby just like you do, and I know when not to push. If you go after her now, all she'll do is run further."

"I can't fight if I'm not with her, Sooz."

"But choosing to fight the battle at the wrong time is as bad as not fighting at all. Please, trust me." She looks at me earnestly.

But I'm too rattled by the news that Abby just up and left to hear the sense in her words. "I'm so sick of this. One minute people are telling me to fight, the next they're saying not to. I don't know what to do anymore. All I want is to be with her."

"And I know she wants to be with you. I promise I will update you on how she is and when the time is right. I promise, Jake."

I stare, taking in her expression. I've never seen her like this. I know she's genuinely concerned about Abby, which is why, even though every part of me wants to jump on a plane to Cape Town, I back down. But I won't wait on the sidelines forever. I'm done giving Abby up for everything else in my life. It should always have been the other way around and I'm an idiot for taking this long to realize it.

"I brought her here this summer for a reason," I throw over my shoulder before walking off the bus to find the rest of the group. "I want to be with her, and I know she wants to be with me. Whatever's wrong isn't going to change that."

Chapter Three
Abby

It's been two weeks since I hopped on a flight back to Cape Town faster than a speeding bullet. Some would say I have a knack for it. Not surprising since I've done it enough times.

I was able to run from some of my problems, Jake-shaped ones to be exact, but the pregnancy ones are kind of hard to avoid. Each day the nausea gets worse and harder to conceal, especially from Sooz. We're already one heated discussion down about the rising water charges for our apartment.

My answer: that we have a hidden leak somewhere.

The real answer: I'm taking extra-long 'showers' to cover the sound of me puking my guts up before we leave for work in the morning.

I'm sitting at my desk, googling how long morning sickness is expected to last when an extra-strong wave hits and I bolt to the restroom. Ten minutes pass before I'm able to even contemplate lifting my head from the toilet bowl. God, this is awful. What happened to pregnancy being beautiful?

Accepting that I need to get back to work before I get in trouble for slacking off, I clamber up from the floor, wait a second for the dizziness to pass, then fling open the cubicle door. I freeze when I find Sooz, standing with her hands on her hips.

"Explain. Now," she says with narrowed eyes.

My brain works at a million miles an hour trying to come up with a lie, but I'm exhausted and come up with nothing. I'm tired of hiding the truth and I've never felt so alone. The need to confide in someone has become unbearable.

I take a deep breath, then, for the first time, say out loud, "I'm pregnant."

Sooz stands, mouth hanging open, her perfectly lined eyes like saucers.

"Are you going to say something?" I ask when a couple of minutes have passed without her saying a word.

"What. The. Fuck."

"Yeah, tell me about it," I mutter. I gently push past her and walk to the sink, lean over and splash cold water on my face.

"Are you okay?" she asks, standing in the same place, her mouth opening and closing repeatedly.

"I've been better."

She frowns. "Do you want to talk about it?"

I glance over my shoulder, taking in our surroundings. There's no way I'm having another angsty conversation in a restroom. I spend enough time in them as it is.

"Can we do it at home? I promise I won't avoid you. It's just—I don't want to talk about it in here. If anyone overhears then half the office will know before the day's out."

The people we work with are constantly on the lookout, waiting for someone else to screw up and make them feel better about themselves. I'd outdo everyone in the building with this little nugget; they'd be feeling fantastic for months. Almost another seven if I've got my calculations right.

"It's fine, we can talk later." Schooling her expression, she steps forward and places a hand on my arm. "You don't look great. Why don't you go home and get some rest?"

She doesn't need to ask twice. I nod eagerly and my shoulders sag in relief. It looks like there are some perks to someone knowing after all. The past couple of weeks hiding this and powering through, acting like I'm fine, have been brutal. All I've wanted to do is hide away and my prayers are finally being answered.

"Are you sure it's okay—me going home?" I ask before we step out of the restroom.

Sooz nods. "Positive. As your boss, I'm telling you to go home. No one will question me, they daren't."

I smile weakly. "Thanks, Sooz."

"Just promise me you will try and eat something before you go to bed. You look like you've lost weight."

"Yeah. Who knew being pregnant could be a great diet tool?"

She lets out a laugh that's as flat as a pancake. We don't say anything else, and I don't waste any time grabbing my things from my desk. The moment I get inside our apartment, I head straight to bed, despite telling Sooz I would eat. Nausea is creeping in, and I know if I eat anything right now I'll only see it again within the hour.

I instantly relax when I climb onto the cloud that is my mattress, loving the feel of the crisp, cool sheets against my skin. I used to be one of those people who would toss and turn for hours before drifting off. Not anymore. Pregnancy nipped that problem in the bud. As soon as I close my eyes, sleep steals me away from the world. And for the first time all day, I feel content.

"Abby," says a distant voice.

It creeps into my subconscious, bringing me out of a crazy dream where Jake and Dan are standing in front of me demanding I choose one of them.

"Abby, wake up," says the voice, more sternly this time.

I stir, realizing the voice is actually real and unfortunately so was the scenario in my dream, only in real life I didn't pick either of them. "What time is it?" I ask groggily, my body not wanting to wake. I could sleep for an eternity, and it still wouldn't be enough.

"After seven," Sooz replies, softly.

When I finally manage to open my eyes, I find her perched on the side of my bed, long blonde waves of hair flowing around her shoulders in the way she allows them to only in the confines of our home. She claims her girl-next-door looks stop people from taking her seriously, so the outside world only ever gets to see her beautiful locks scraped back in whatever way the latest magazines define to be office chic. She's one of the sweetest people I know, but she's a badass in the PR business and no one dares cross her.

"It can't be that late?" My eyes skirt around the room, the last of the light filtering through the window creating a dull orange glow. It would appear I've slept the entire day without stirring once.

"Did you eat?"

I shake my head guiltily. "I was exhausted and feeling sick. I wouldn't have kept it down anyway."

Sooz nods. Under normal circumstances, she would be cross with me for not taking care of myself. But I can tell from the way she's biting her lip that for once, she's found herself in a situation she's unsure how to navigate. She's not the only one.

"Do you think you could manage something now?"

I nod at the same time my stomach growls loudly. "Well, that's embarrassing."

Sooz chuckles and gestures with her head for me to follow. "Come on, I'll see what I can scrape together, and then we can talk."

"Give me five," I reply, stretching. When she narrows her eyes, I laugh. "Sheesh, I need the bathroom, woman! I promise I will come through in a few minutes."

"Fine." She bustles into the kitchen, a woman on a mission.

As promised, five minutes later, I amble into our open-plan kitchen and dining area and sit down at the table. Sooz walks over with a plate full of plain crackers and cheese and a large glass of water. She places the plate carefully on the table in front of me then slides into the seat next to mine.

"For the first time, our empty fridge works in your favor," she says light-heartedly.

"This is perfect. You wouldn't believe how good a cracker tastes when you're pregnant," I admit, not missing the way her whole body tenses at the P-word.

She knows better than to try and get information out of me when I'm starving. Hangry Abby doesn't communicate well with anyone. Instead, she sits patiently while I work my way through the crackers at an agonizingly slow pace.

When I'm done, I lean back and push the plate away. Sooz frowns at the handful of crackers still left.

"If I eat any more, I'll start being sick again," I explain. "Trust me, I've eaten enough for now."

She sighs then quietly says, "What happened?"

A shrill laugh escapes me and I probably sound as crazy as I look. "Do I need to go through the birds and the bees with you?"

"Being pregnant doesn't mean you can be a bitch, Abs," she snaps.

"Sorry," I mutter. Guilt hits me like a freight train. All she's done today is try to look after me, and she's right, I'm acting like a class-A bitch. "I've not got my head around it myself."

"I mean, I know you and Jake hooked up, but I thought you were on birth control?"

"I am … was. It happened the night in the Czech Republic when we were all wasted. Turns out our parents were right. You can act too carefree and there are consequences to your actions. Especially when you puke up your birth control pill the next day and are too hungover to realize."

Staring down at the table, my eyes brim with tears for the first time since leaving Leeds. I've not let myself cry, not let myself feel anything. I've wallowed in numbness because feeling numb doesn't hurt, it's just nothing. Talking about all of this again with Sooz makes it feel painfully real. It's humiliating.

"What are you going to do?"

I don't answer, too focused on keeping my shit together. It's wasted effort because my shoulders shake as I try to stifle a sob.

"Oh, Abby."

Before I know what's happening, she has her arms wrapped tightly around me. That's all it takes for the floodgates to open, and weeks of pent-up emotions pour out. All the while Sooz sits with her arms wrapped around me, a reminder that I'm not alone in all of this; I have her. I could have a lot more people around me if I let them, but I'm not ready yet.

"I feel like I'm drowning, Sooz. I don't know what to do." I sniffle.

"Does anyone else know?"

"Amanda."

She pulls away and looks at me in surprise.

Lifting the hem of my oversized shirt, I wipe my face, attempting to get myself together before I elaborate. "She figured it all out before I did."

"So that's why the two of you kept disappearing. Zoe was convinced you were going to replace her."

I roll my eyes. "Of course, she was."

"Speaking of … have you spoken to her or Sophie yet? They keep ringing me to ask how you are and why you won't answer their calls."

I shake my head. "I can't face talking to anyone."

Sooz grabs my hand and stares me in the eyes. "They're your oldest and best friends, Abs. They will support you through this."

I know what she's saying is right, but I'm so embarrassed. I can't handle the thought of telling anyone. It's bad enough

Sooz and Amanda know, and potentially Zach. "I'll speak to them when I'm ready," I say firmly.

"What about Jake? And Dan?"

"What about them? They both hate me. I'll never see Dan again that's for sure, and Jake, well, I just don't know."

Sooz looks shocked. "He's the father; you have to tell him."

I frown. "Do I though?"

"You can't actually be considering keeping this from him?"

Avoiding answering her question, I pick at one of the crackers left on the plate and crumble it absentmindedly. It's easy for her to sit there and be all judgmental when she doesn't know the truth.

"Abby," Sooz says sternly, forcing me to look up. "You *have* to tell him. You can't do this alone."

"I will tell him when I'm ready." I sniff.

"Why would you consider keeping it from him? What good would it do?"

"What good would telling him do? This is a mistake, Sooz. A colossal fucking mistake, and right when the band is about to make it big. Everything they've worked for would have been for nothing."

She sits and contemplates what I've said. "There's more. There's something you're not telling me."

She's right, but I'm not about to admit that. I can't tell anyone what I overheard Sam and Ryan talking about—that Jake doesn't want children. It's not for me to tell and talking about it makes my new reality seem even harsher. Saying it out loud is admitting it's true and accepting that when I tell Jake I'm pregnant he will be less than happy with the news.

I refuse to trap him into something like this. I can't.

"There's nothing more," I lie. "Promise."

"Well, we need to get you booked in with an OB/GYN so they can check everything is okay. Then you can decide what to do for the best. How does that sound?"

"Okay," I say, my voice faltering.

This is it, shit's about to get real.

Sooz stands and grabs the plate from in front of me before I can destroy any more of the crackers. "You should get some more rest. You look like crap. I'll sort the appointment for you in the morning and then we can take it from there."

"Thanks, Sooz."

"It's what friends are for. You'd have a few more rallying around you if you'd just pick up your phone and call them."

She walks away and places the plate by the sink, before heading off to her room. Needing something to take my mind off the events of the day, I walk to the dishes and start stacking them in the dishwasher. It doesn't help though. Nothing helps stop my mind from going into overdrive.

All I can think about is that I'm pregnant and I don't have a clue what to do.

Sooz might have been sympathetic about my not-so-little pregnancy predicament, but what she wasn't sympathetic about, was my slacking in the work department. There was one area she was very concerned about: the tour photos. Not so much the photos as a whole, they were good, better than good, they were some of my best. However, you can't have official band photos when the collection is missing one key person. The lead guitar player.

"Abby, there are no photos with Jake. Not one. Fix it or both of our jobs will be on the line."

Sitting at my desk, I'm trying to do just that. It's not that I don't have the photos, I have hundreds. That's the problem. How am I supposed to sit for days editing all these photos of him? Just thinking about him is enough to make my lip quiver. Suck it up, West, I tell myself. Taking a deep breath, my finger hovers over the mouse. I lower it and click the file open with all the images of Jake.

His face fills the screen and my stomach twists in a tight knot. It's one from the band's final set and must have been one of the last images I took before leaving. He looks withdrawn, staring directly at the camera, jaw tight. There's no sparkle in his eyes like there was with the other members of the band. It should have been one of the best days of his life. Judging by the expression on his face, it was one of the worst. That's without him knowing about the baby.

Fingers snap in front of my face, startling me from staring vacantly at the screen. "Earth to Abby."

"Sorry, I zoned out there for a while," I say in a daze.

"A while?" scoffs Sooz. "You've been zoned out for weeks. It's shocking when you're actually with it."

I huff. "Do you blame me? I've had a few things on my mind."

Her eyes move to the screen and her brows draw together. She looks back at me and says, "I get it, trust me. I honestly don't know how you're holding it together, but you can't keep going on like you have. It's not healthy. Anyway, we need to get going before we're late."

"Late?"

Sooz rolls her eyes. "For the scan. Come on, Abby. I told you it was today. There's even a reminder on your screen." She points at the large box in the corner that must have flashed up while I was staring at the image of Jake without me realizing it.

The word *scan* reads clear as day and I struggle to swallow. The pregnancy doesn't feel any more real than when the two bold lines appeared on the tests.

"You're right. We should get going," I say, quickly closing the image of Jake on my screen and standing. I pause and look down at my desk, forgetting what I need to do next.

"Here," says Sooz, handing over my brown satchel bag. "Everything you need is in there. I checked. You'll also need this, and you need to drink it. *Now*."

My stomach churns at the sight of the large bottle of water in her hands. A sip is usually all it takes for the vom gates to open and the toilet to become my best friend. My eyes widen. "All of it?"

She nods. "All of it." She steps in closer and gently pushes me to the side.

I watch my friend take the reins yet again, shutting down my desktop and making sure everything is left organized how I like it. Drawing in a shaky breath, I tell myself it's time to pull my head out of the gutter.

This is it. There's no more hiding from the truth.

Chapter Four

Abby

Everywhere I turn there are little pairs of eyes watching me. Judging. I shuffle in my seat like I have been doing continuously for the past twenty minutes.

"What's wrong with you?" asks Sooz under her breath.

"They're staring at me," I whisper.

She glances around the room, bewildered. Her eyes take in the dozen or so women, each at different stages of their pregnancy. None of them are looking in our direction, too busy twiddling with their hands and hair or rubbing their bumps affectionately.

"Who?"

"*Them.*" My eyes bulge and I nod with my head toward the walls.

Sooz's eyes look at the same place I am, and she snorts. Every woman in the room turns and stares, their expressions curious. "Abby," she chuckles. "They're posters."

"They're definitely looking at me," I huff, folding my arms across my chest. "And why do there have to be so many?"

"We're in a maternity waiting room. It's kind of expected there will be images of babies."

Ignoring her comment, I look around. A woman with flaming red hair catches my eye and smiles. I wonder if she's felt the way I do right now at any point during her pregnancy. Lost.

"You good?" asks Sooz.

My chin quivers. "I just want to get this over and done with."

The sickness combined with exhaustion is relentless. Each morning when I look at myself in the mirror, I barely recognize my reflection. I don't want to be here. I just want to go home, crawl into bed and pretend like this isn't happening.

Sooz squeezes my hand. "It shouldn't be much longer."

"Hopefully." I try to smile at her, but it feels more alien with each day that passes. Instead, I grimace.

On cue, a small woman in scrubs walks in and all the women in the room, including myself, look up. "Abby? Abby West?"

I hold my hand up in the air.

"She wants you to follow her," Sooz murmurs.

"Right," I grumble, my cheeks on fire.

We stand and I follow the sonographer, my feet like lead. She walks into a large room and more posters of babies glare at me from the walls. It's the bed that stops me in my tracks, causing Sooz to crash into me from behind, almost knocking me off my feet.

She steadies me with her hands then steps around so she's in front, her face full of concern. "Abby, are you okay?"

I start to back out of the room, shaking my head. "I don't know if I can do this."

Her eyes hold mine. "You already are doing this. Remember, it's just another small step. I'm right here with you and everything is going to be fine."

I shake my head, this time more vigorously. "I'm not ready."

"I don't mean to sound blunt, but you don't have a choice. What's important now is checking that everything is okay and you're both healthy."

"Right!" I squeak, the word *both* making my heart race.

She places a hand on my shoulder and rubs her thumb back and forth. "We will deal with everything else after. You're not alone in this, I promise."

The sonographer clears her throat. "Is everything all right, Miss West?"

"Just some last-minute nerves," I reply, looking at the ground.

She nods and gestures to the bed. "In your own time."

I take a deep breath and make my way over, then perch on the edge. Sooz takes the seat beside me. Her face is a picture of calm, but her knee tells another story. I watch it bounce out of the corner of my eye.

The sonographer says, "Right, Abby. The midwife who's been handling your care mentioned you were unsure how far along you might be, so we're going to be doing a transvaginal ultrasound today."

I start to choke and suck in sharp breaths, trying to get myself together. The only word I hear is related to my vagina.

"Abby?" Sooz looks at me confused.

I clear my throat awkwardly. "Transvaginal?"

Sooz rolls her eyes and the corners of the sonographer's mouth twitch ever so slightly. "Yes. Transvaginal."

"Erm, what does that mean?"

"It means I'm going to leave the room and give you some privacy. When you're ready I need you to remove your pants then jump up on the bed and get comfortable. Cover your lower body with the white paper sheet."

"I need to remove my pants?" I squeak. "In the movies, they do that thing with your stomach?"

The sonographer smiles again. "You're most likely too early for that to be an effective way to see anything."

"So, erm, I take my pants off, then what?" A cold sweat covers my brow, this is not how I was expecting things to go.

"I'll insert the transducer into your vagina to hopefully get a clear image."

"What's a transducer?" I ask although I'm pretty sure I don't want to know.

The sonographer gestures at a long object that looks like the more robotic form of a … "It's a dildo." I want the ground to swallow me up. How do women do this every day?

Sooz groans at my side. "Abby, it's not a dildo. Stop stalling."

"I'm about to spread my legs for a stranger, I can stall all I like."

"Medical professional, Abs," snaps Sooz, throwing the sonographer an apologetic glance. "They need to do this to check everything is okay."

The sonographer clears her throat. "I'll step outside the room for a moment. Let me know when you're ready."

The door clicks shut and I stare at Sooz like a deer caught in headlights. "Transducer? It sounds like something out of *Transformers*—the porn version."

"They call it 'the wand' sometimes if that makes you feel better?"

My mouth drops open. "Does this magic wand give you a happy ending too?"

"Abby!"

"Well!" I throw my hands up in the air. "And how do you know all this anyway?"

"I Googled it, of course."

"And you decided not to tell me why?"

Sooz smiles sweetly. "Because I knew if I did, it would have been impossible to get you here."

"Touché."

"Drop your pants, West. That's what got you into this mess and it won't be the last time you have to during this pregnancy."

"Thanks for that." There's no point arguing with her any longer. I need to do this. I need to know if everything is okay because until I do, I can't make any decisions about my future.

When I've not so gracefully climbed on the bed, pantless, Sooz walks to the door and pokes her head out to let the sonographer know I'm ready.

The sonographer gives me a few more details, her face a picture of professionalism. You wouldn't even know the past five minutes just happened. Wand in hand, she asks, "Are you ready?"

I don't know, I want to shout. I don't know if I'm ready to face up to why my world is about to be turned upside down. What's worse is doing it all without the one person who could help this all seem less terrifying. Jake. Without him here beside me, I feel completely broken like nothing makes sense.

"Abby," says Sooz softly. "She asked if you're ready."

"Erm, yeah," I stammer, letting out a shrill laugh that says I'm anything but. "Ready as I'll ever be. I bet you don't get many women this reluctant to see their baby?"

The Sonographer doesn't give me the look I expect, she simply says, "You'd be surprised. Now, I'm going to insert the transducer and try to get a clear image. Let me know if it gets too uncomfortable."

I swallow, bracing myself. "Okay."

The room is silent apart from the soft whir of the air-con and the computers. My eyes focus on the sonographers' face as she stares intently at the little screen in front of her. I thought things would happen more quickly and my mind jumps to the worst-case scenario. I think I might throw up.

I choke out, "Is everything okay?"

"Just give me a moment," she says, her brow furrowed.

I look at Sooz but she's frozen in place, her cheery expression from earlier gone.

"Ah! There we are." I watch as the glimmer of tension disappears from her face. "You drank a bit too much water."

I give Sooz *the* look which she ignores.

"Would you like to see your baby?"

I'm not sure if I do but it seems like what's expected, so I nod. She turns the screen toward me and presses a couple of buttons. Suddenly, the room is filled with a rapid whooshing noise.

"That's the baby's heartbeat you can hear," she confirms, before spending the next few minutes taking us through the scan.

I smile and nod when it seems like the right moment. Really all I see is a small blob with a pulse.

"Oh!" gasps Sooz. "It's amazing."

"I'm putting you at eight and a half weeks," confirms the Sonographer. "I assume you have your healthcare set up and you're taking a daily vitamin? It's important that you keep taking it. Would you like some images printed so you can take them home and show your loved ones?"

I don't reply. Besides Sooz, there isn't anyone to show.

Sooz replies for me, "She would love some."

The sonographer busies herself printing out the scans and filling in paperwork.

"How are you holding up?" Sooz asks quietly.

Once again, I don't reply, too consumed by my thoughts. I don't know whether to feel happy or sad. Excited or terrified. In love or completely overwhelmed, as I lay staring at the baby growing inside me. I can see it with my own two eyes. It's not just a couple of blue lines on a stick anymore. This is a life-changing moment, one I imagined years ago

would play out like a fairytale. But this isn't a fairytale, there's
no happy ending and I've never felt so alone in my life.

We make a pit stop for food on the way back from my
appointment and I devour everything in sight, having not
eaten all day. Shortly after getting back in the car, nausea
rears its ugly head and none of the three stops we make
before getting home are pretty.

"You said it's supposed to start getting better," I
complain, collapsing on the couch and burying my face in
the soft fabric.

"Let me look," says Sooz, pulling out her phone. She
hates not having answers, so Google has become her most
trusted ally in my pregnancy so far. She looks up from the
screen but avoids eye contact. "It says some people can be
sick all the way through their pregnancy …"

"Please tell me you're joking," I groan into the cushions.
I can't take much more. The term morning sickness is a lie.
All-day and all-night sickness is more fitting.

"Try not to worry. Some sites say it can clear up at any
point."

This brightens my spirits—there's still hope. I lift my
head and say, "Okay. I can cope with a few more weeks.
Baby steps—excuse the pun."

Sooz chuckles. "That's the first time I've heard you crack
a real joke in weeks, which is a good sign. How do you feel?"
Realizing her poor choice of words as she takes in my green
complexion, she rephrases, "What I mean is, we got to see it
in there. An actual baby growing inside you. Do you feel
better knowing everything is fine?"

I look down, dragging my toes back and forth through the fluffy gray carpet while I contemplate my answer. "Honestly, it still feels surreal. The only thing I can focus on is what to do about Jake."

"I can't imagine how hard it is," she sighs. "But at some point, you will have to tell him. He has a right to know, Abby. He's the father."

"I know."

My phone lights up on the coffee table and Zoe's name flashes on the screen. I hesitate then hit reject just like I have done every day since we returned from the tour. Like clockwork, I receive another incoming call, this time from Sophie.

They're together. I hit reject again.

"Is it them?" asks Sooz. She's been screening their never-ending calls, reassuring them I'm fine and will be in touch when I'm ready. "You have to speak to them eventually. What good will ignoring them do?"

I look away. "I'm not ready to talk to anyone. Not yet."

"Then when? What are you going to do, Abby?" as she speaks her voice gradually grows louder. "Turn up one day with a baby in your arms and yell surprise? I know this summer was an emotional rollercoaster, but you can't ignore what's happening. This baby is coming whether you like it or not, and there are still so many decisions you need to make."

"Do you think I don't know that?" I snap. "Do you think I don't lie awake at night wondering how I was stupid enough to get myself into this situation? Sooz, I feel like a fucking idiot, and I'm scared of what everyone's reaction will be when they find out."

Her eyes soften. "Abby, those people I met this summer, love you, flaws and all. I know that when you tell them, they won't care, they'll just want to support you. But they can't do that if you don't tell them."

I want to hear what she's saying, but right now I can't. Especially after the afternoon we've had. It's too overwhelming. "I'm exhausted. I'm going to lie down."

"Don't do this, Abby. Don't walk away. It won't help anything. Let's sit and try to figure out what you're going to do, together."

I stand up from the couch and shake my head. "I'm not ready, Sooz. I'll speak to you later."

I can't look at her when I leave. I don't want to see how disappointed she is. When I get to my room, I collapse face-down on my bed. I pray for sleep but it's pointless. It's been weeks since I've spoken to my mom and best friends. It's the longest we've gone without talking and they don't have a clue why. I know how I'm behaving is wrong, but the more time that passes, the more reluctant I become. I'm in my own vicious cycle and I don't know how to break free.

Rolling onto my back, I stare at the ceiling. Accepting that sleep isn't going to come I tiptoe to my desk, not wanting Sooz to hear me moving around and attempt round two of the conversation. I pull out the folder with my pregnancy notes from my bag and flick to the ones from today. The scan images have been carefully placed in their own little wallet to keep them safe.

Placing the folder quietly on my desk, I tiptoe to the bed and lay back with my head resting against the pillows. Once comfy, I bring one of the scans closer so I can see it properly.

There it is. My baby.

The result of years of back and forth between me and Jake. My hand creeps over my stomach and rubs in a gentle circular motion. When I notice what I'm doing I stop immediately and roll onto my side. The scan falls from my hand and floats to the ground. The tears I've been holding in all day start to fall.

Once they start there's no stopping them. I don't just cry for myself; I cry for my friends and parents who I've ignored unfairly. I cry over every argument I've had with Sooz. I cry over my broken heart, torn between two men; neither of which I deserve.

But mostly, I cry for my baby, who is going to enter the world potentially without a father because of the poor decisions I've made.

The next few days pass in a similar pattern, with me refusing to acknowledge what is happening. I know there's only so long I can keep this going because time is ticking away and there's nothing I can do to stop it.

It's Friday afternoon and I'm tying up the loose ends on some projects before the weekend. I'm so ready to close my laptop, head home, and crawl into bed with Netflix for comfort. When Sooz stalks into my office, stopping abruptly in front of my desk with her hands on her hips, it's clear that's not going to happen.

"We're going out tonight," she says.

"You can," I reply, without moving my eyes from the screen. "I'm exhausted. I'm just going home."

She tuts. "You're pregnant, not dying, so stop acting like it. I refuse to watch you wallow like this any longer. We're going out and we're having some fun."

"Sooz, I really don't know …" I look up briefly to find her mouth set in a firm line the way it does when she sets her mind to something. There's no way she's backing down.

"You haven't got a choice. I booked us a table so you can eat actual food, not just crackers. Oh, and we're going to a gig."

That catches my attention and I raise a brow. "A gig?"

"Yes, a gig. It's one of those things where you go and see musicians on stage and watch them play instruments and sing. Most people get enjoyment out of it. We may have to see with you though."

"I know what a gig is. What I meant to say is should I really be going to something like that when I'm—"

"Pregnant?" she says so loud she might as well stand in the middle of the office and declare it to our colleagues.

"Shhh," I hiss, looking over her shoulder to check that nobody heard.

She smirks. "Get over yourself, nobody cares. They're all too absorbed in their own drama. Seriously though, you are coming out tonight, and yes you can go when you're pregnant. It's not on the list of things to avoid. Eating shellfish, yes. Poachies, the jury's not quite out on that one yet. But I'm pretty certain having fun isn't frowned upon by the midwives."

"I just mean …"

She softens her tone, "I know what you mean, Abby. That you feel like your life is over, and is it acceptable to go to something like this? The answer is yes. Being pregnant won't be the end of your life if you don't allow it to be. Funnily enough, a lot of women think this is the most magical time of their lives."

She's thought of every possible reason I might have not to go and prepared her answers in advance, making sure I can't say no, no matter which way I twist it.

"Fine," I huff. "I'll come. But if I feel like crap or it's boring, I'm coming home."

Her blue eyes twinkle. "I promise, tonight will be anything but boring."

Chapter Five
Abby

I'm reluctant to admit it to Sooz, but this was just what I needed.

The rest of the afternoon went quickly knowing I had something to do after work. Sooz booked our favorite restaurant down by the harbor and it was the best food I've eaten since before S.C.A.R.A.B.'s European tour. I almost started dancing on the table when the food arrived and there was no sign of nausea. Sooz watched on in horror while I inhaled the selection of dishes she ordered, forgetting some were for her. I know secretly she was relieved to see me eating.

Rubbing my overfull stomach as we walk, I say, "Are you sure we can't go home and chill, watch a movie? You've managed to get me out of the apartment, let's end on a positive."

"No can do. We're booked up," she replies.

I stop abruptly. "What do you mean, *booked up*?"

She grabs my hand and drags me along behind her. "We have places to be and people to see. You're not getting out of it. You need to interact with people who aren't me, work colleagues, or your OB/GYN, so that's exactly what we're going to do. I don't associate with recluses, it's not my style."

I refrain from pointing out that sometimes she could be classed as one herself with the hours she works. "So, where are we going?"

"I told you, we're going to a gig to listen to music," she chirps.

She's up to something, I can feel it. I narrow my eyes at the back of her head while we power along. "Anyone I know?" I ask breathlessly.

She looks over her shoulder and smiles, refusing to give anything away. "You've probably heard of them and I'm certain you will like them. Come on, we're already late. I didn't account for you eating as much as you did."

Normally, I'd amble along, taking every part of the waterfront in. I don't think I'll ever get over how beautiful it is here. The sun hanging low in the sky and the chatter of people filling the warm air with Table Mountain in the background—it's breathtaking. Sooz has other ideas though and I scurry behind, trying to keep up as she increases her pace.

When we get to the venue, she flashes her phone to one of the bouncers and they let us in without any questions asked. I don't have a clue what she's up to, but if I learned anything over the summer, it's to listen to my gut. The same gut that's telling me something is about to happen. Something big.

The room we enter is dark and the large crowd mills around with drinks in their hands, waiting for the gig to start. The smell of stale beer hits me, and my feet stick to the floor as we move closer to the stage. We find a place to stand at the exact moment one of the overhead lights pans down on the stage, highlighting a sole figure. Only a silhouette is visible, but I'd know it anywhere.

"Sooz, please tell me that's not who I think it is," I snap in her ear.

She looks at me and grins. "It's exactly who you think it is. Abby, it's time to stop running."

Light floods the room and the opening song kicks in. The figure's voice reaches my ears and the hairs on my arms stand on end. I blink, trying to get my head around what's happening. My eyes trail up and settle on Dan White's face.

"Was this the plan all along?" I ask through gritted teeth.

"Yep." She doesn't bother to take her eyes off the stage.

"What the hell? Why are we here, Sooz? You of all people should know I wouldn't want to be here. You know how things were left between us."

I look at the stage and my eyes drink him in. His dark hair is styled to perfection and his blue eyes glow in the bright light. He's a lot leaner than Jake, his image more clean-cut. But there's something about him that's drawn me in since the moment we were in Barcelona.

The song kicks in and his voice sends chills running down my spine.

"The point is, you can't keep going on like this," says Sooz, finally turning and focusing her attention on me. "It's not healthy, for you or the baby. Oh, and he also got in touch."

My mouth drops open. "He got in touch with you?"

"Yes," she replies, turning back to Dan.

"Why?" I ask, bemused. "He had my number. Why wouldn't he just ring and get in touch with me himself?"

Sooz shrugs. "He thought you wouldn't answer after how you left things, so he didn't bother trying. He called the office and asked me to help get you here."

"He came all the way to Cape Town, for me?" I frown, staring up at him.

At no point does he look down, even though we're close enough to the stage that if he did, he would find me easily. He's purposefully avoiding my gaze which doesn't fit the grand gesture he seems to be making.

"Pretty special, huh?" Sooz winks.

"Head fuck more like. The last time we spoke he basically called me a slut and said we were done."

Sooz's expression flickers from lighthearted to annoyed. "Give him a break, Abby. He stood and watched you kiss your ex while he performed on stage in front of thousands of people. He had every right to feel and act the way he did but that's not the point. What matters is that he's here now."

"But I'm pregnant!" I say, exasperated.

Sooz throws her head back and laughs. "Christ! You're having a baby, it's not the end of the world. Dan is a nice guy. He strikes me as the type who might hear you out. Yes, it might take time, but you said there was something between you. Is it not worth putting yourself out there and seeing what he says? What have you got to lose?"

"I don't know if I can put myself through all of this again."

Dan's the first person I contemplated giving a chance after Jake. Even Michael Becket didn't give me butterflies like Dan did and we were together four years. I thought he was worth taking the risk and putting my heart on the line for, but then he spoke to me the way he did at the end of the tour. I know I hurt him but there's no excuse for his words. They cut deep.

Sooz looks me straight in the eyes and says, "You're stronger than you think you are. You need to stop running away from everything. I hate seeing you like this. Please speak with him. I honestly think this will be worth your time. Give him a chance to help and don't just close off at the first sign of trouble."

She knows me too well.

My voice falters when I reply, "O—okay."

She beams and grabs my hand, squeezing it just like the day we went for the scan.

Maybe she's right. Maybe good things can come from this if I allow it. We don't talk for the rest of the gig and unlike the last time I saw Dan on stage, he has my full attention the whole way through. His voice is mesmerizing, and I could listen to him forever, but all too soon the set comes to an end. My eyes remain focused on Dan, and I watch him beam at the crowd.

Over the screams of his diehard fans, he says, "Thank you and goodnight, Cape Town." He looks down, catches my eye for the first time, and gives a subtle nod.

A nod that confirms two things: he knew I was standing here all along and the night is far from over.

Before the audience starts to leave, Sooz and I make our way to the back of the room. One of the perks of working a few PR events here in the past is that we know our way around the building. We walk quickly along the deserted back corridors heading toward the backstage area. We give our names to a burly guy guarding the door and he speaks into his radio. It's confirmed straight away that we can go backstage. We trail along a couple more corridors and my heart hammers in my chest, so hard I start to feel sick.

I stop. "I'm scared," I admit.

Sooz turns back and smiles. "That's natural. You don't need to have *the* conversation here. Why don't you invite him back to our place?"

"You wouldn't mind?" I ask, surprised.

She raises an eyebrow. "Really, Abby? Do you even need to ask?"

I giggle, then take a deep breath. My feet unglue themselves from the floor and as we continue walking, I roll my shoulders back trying to ease some of the tension.

Where the band's stage crew has set up is a bustle of activity. I watch them all together, visibly buzzing and in sync as they dance around each other. It all feels so familiar, and memories of the summer come to the surface of my mind. My eyes start to burn. Why is this so hard? It was just one summer.

"Can I help you?" asks a young woman wearing a headset, the word *crew* written clearly in white across her black T-shirt.

Sensing the change in my mood, Sooz steps in. "Yes, we're here to see Dan White."

The woman looks at us skeptically. "Who may I tell him is here?" her tone is sharp.

I wonder how many crazy fans she has to fend off each night.

"Tell him Abby West is here," says Sooz picking at her nails.

"I'll be back in a second," says the young woman over her shoulder as she walks away. Barely two minutes pass before she's back, this time her expression warmer. "Follow me." She beckons for us to follow as she walks toward a door in the distance.

When we get closer, I see Dan's name written clearly on a small sign. Of course, he has his own private room. I shouldn't be surprised because he's a world-famous rock star, but to me, he's just the down-to-earth guy I met in an ice cream shop one night by chance.

The woman knocks on the door.

I hear Dan's muffled reply from the other side, "Come in."

Sooz gently pushes me forward.

"You're not coming in with me?" I squeak, spinning back around.

She laughs. "Hell no. This is your mess to deal with."

Talk about throwing someone in the deep end. "You lured me here under false pretenses," I say, narrowing my eyes.

She smiles. "You'll thank me later. I'll just be waiting over here." She points to a couch close by then walks over and gets comfy.

Traitor.

The woman from the stage crew opens the door to Dan's room and I smile at her politely before stepping inside on shaky legs. The door clicks shut behind me and I'm left alone. The room's empty. Weird. I definitely heard his voice.

I look around, taking everything in. There are clothes discarded over a chair, a coffee table filled with water bottles, and a hamper of snacks. An acoustic guitar rests against a red suede couch. This must be Dan's room. My eyes catch on a door to the side of the room, partially open, the faint sound of a shower running filters out and is just audible over the noise from backstage. Unsure what to do, I take a seat on the couch and wait, fidgeting with my hands. It's been weeks since we last saw each other and I have no idea what to expect.

The shower stops and my heart skips a beat. I sit on my hands—it's the only way to stop them moving.

When the door opens fully, any hope I had of coming across as calm and collected flies out the window. It's like a scene from a movie. Steam billows out and Dan steps into the room with just a towel slung low around his hips. Oh, dear Lord. My cheeks burn and I start to sweat. Combined with my fidgeting problem, I'm a mess. I'm not sure if it's the water rolling down his toned, tanned torso, or the pregnancy hormones raging through my body that has me wriggling in my seat. I'm used to the butterflies whenever I see him, but not *this*. When my eyes finally reach his face, his expression is smug. He's doing this on purpose.

"H—hi." I clear my throat and hold my head high. "Hi," I say more firmly.

"You look like crap," the insult sounds odd in his British accent.

I frown. "Erm, thanks?" I don't have a clue how else to reply, and the fact he's still standing in just a thin towel—which doesn't leave much to the imagination—isn't helping. "Can you please put some clothes on? I can't concentrate."

He throws his head back and laughs a genuine, deep laugh, holding nothing back. Hope flutters in my chest, maybe this won't be so bad after all.

"Sorry, clothes police. I forgot to take them in with me. Believe it or not, I don't have to strip naked to get what I want."

"I don't doubt that, but I don't think anyone could ever say no to you if you were standing looking like *that*." My eyes flare and I clap a hand over my mouth. "Fuck."

"There's the Abby I know." Unphased, he grabs a pile of clothes, then turns back toward the bathroom. "Give me a minute so I can put my clothes on per your request, madam." He walks away and closes the bathroom door quietly behind him.

A couple of minutes pass then he returns with a familiar smile on his face, looking more like the Dan I know.

"So …" I look around, trying to figure out what to say.

"So …" he says back, eyes twinkling. It's very clear he's enjoying watching me squirm.

When the silence starts to get awkward, I decide to bite the bullet. "What do you want from me, Dan? Why am I here?"

"You tell me," he responds.

I frown. "You're the one who had Sooz orchestrate this whole thing. What would I know? The last time we saw each other, you were busy acting like a dick, and I was pretty certain we'd never see each other again."

The warm smile on his face disappears. "I was hurt and angry."

"And you had every right to be, but you could have heard me out. It's made me question how well I know you."

"Not very, seeing as we only spent a couple of nights together, a few hours at most. It takes more than that to really get to know someone," he says coldly, taking me by surprise.

I'm starting to think I've been seeing things between us with rose-tinted glasses. Maybe he doesn't deserve the pedestal on which I originally placed him.

"There's a whole life behind me you don't know about, Abby. Remember, I'm only human and I make mistakes, just like you."

I can't help grimacing at what he's referring to. I've made so many mistakes, and he doesn't even know them all.

"I say the wrong things sometimes, make poor choices. I have a temper, especially when I watch the woman I'm falling for being kissed by another guy right in front of me and I can't do anything about it."

I close off and shrug. "I guess shit got real?"

He chuckles, ignoring my childish remark. "Something like that."

He shoves his hands in his pockets and looks around the room. "I'm not a hundred percent sure why I'm here, Abby. That's the truth. I've always said I don't know what I'm doing when it comes to you. It scares the crap out of me. What I do know, is that in the weeks we've been apart, I've missed you.

"I don't miss people. I've learned not to do it. Being on the road is easier when you don't get attached. But every day since I left Leeds, all I've been able to think about is how much I need to see you. So, I got in touch with Sooz. I had to." He grimaces. "I couldn't stop myself."

I feel his pain because the situation he's found himself in and everything he's feeling, I've been through myself. With Jake. I know what it feels like to not know what you're doing and have no control over your actions. When the heart decides what it wants, there's no stopping it.

"Oh," is all I manage. He needs to know everything, but I can't do it here. I don't feel comfortable. "Would you like to come back to my place?"

His eyebrows shoot up and he's never sounded more British than when he politely says, "As much as I'd love that, I'd like to take things slow. I hope you're not offended."

I laugh so hard my eyes begin to water. When I manage to catch my breath I reply, "I don't mean like that. We need to talk about a lot of things, but I don't want to do it here."

The faint blush that covers his cheeks is adorable and the butterflies in my stomach start to flutter.

"That's fine," he says. "I can organize a driver to take us?"

I nod. "That would be great."

He pulls out his cellphone and after a few seconds starts speaking, never taking his crystal blue eyes off me. I signal that I'm going to leave so I can let Sooz know the plan. When I step out of the room, I don't feel any less nervous than when I entered. What we need to talk about, he isn't going to like. But for now, all that matters is that he's here and he's willing to listen.

Chapter Six

Abby

I'm pretty sure every teenage girl's fantasy is to have a rock star in their kitchen. I'm certain it's every woman's. Never in my wildest dreams did I ever think it would actually happen one day.

Sooz and I are standing, side by side, in the doorway to our apartment, mouths hanging open. Oblivious to the effect he's having, Dan White walks around our open-plan living area in all his rocker glory.

He spots the fridge, looks over at us, and asks, "Do you have anything cold? Maybe of the alcoholic variety? I could do with the wind-down."

Sooz's eyes glaze over. "I think I've died and gone to heaven. Pinch me."

I follow her request and do just that.

"Ow! That hurt!"

I shrug. "You asked me to."

"I didn't mean literally," she says.

I tilt my head to the side and smile. "Oh, well."

"You've perked up all of a sudden. Does it have something to do with the rock star we have standing in our kitchen?" She wiggles her eyebrows and stares in Dan's direction.

"*He* is standing right here," says Dan.

"Sorry," Sooz and I say in unison.

"So ... that drink?" says Dan, looking at the fridge longingly.

"Right, yeah, sorry," I mumble. God, this is embarrassing. Again. I walk over and pull out a beer that's been in there since before S.C.A.R.A.B.'s tour.

I hand it over, and he asks, "You're not joining me?"

I freeze and Sooz yawns dramatically before saying, "I'm going to call it a night. It's been a long week and I'm sure you both want some privacy. I'll see you in the morning, Abs. It was nice to meet you again, Dan."

"Thanks for letting me come over," he answers, flashing her a toothy grin.

She visibly swoons before retreating to her bedroom. And then, we're, alone. My palms sweat just thinking about what I need to tell him.

Plastering on the biggest smile I can manage, I avoid the subject and say, "This is as extravagant as our apartment gets. I apologize. Your tour bus is more glamorous."

Dan doesn't look phased by his surroundings or lack thereof. "I'm assuming you don't know where I come from?"

I shake my head.

He continues, "I didn't have the best upbringing. So, don't worry, the fame and money don't bother me. Plus, this is hardly living in squalor."

I hold my hands up sheepishly. "You're right. Guilty of stereotyping."

"Remember what I said earlier, Abby. There's still a lot we don't know about each other. We've barely scratched the surface."

I look away and mutter, "That's an understatement." Deciding it's time to stop tiptoeing around and get down to the real reason we're here, I gesture to the couch. "How about we sit down?"

He lifts his arm and rubs the back of his neck. "That serious, huh?"

"Kind of," I reply.

"Well, then, best get to it." He sits down at one side of our far too small couch, and I sit at the other. Before I get a chance to start, he raises the beer bottle he's holding up to his mouth and takes a long swig. When he's done, he places it down on the coffee table then sits back. "Hit me with it."

I ponder for a moment, thinking back to what Amanda said on the tour, it's like ripping off a band-aid. That's the approach I need to take with this—no bumbling about. I just need to get it out in the open.

While waiting for me to speak, Dan picks up his beer again and takes another drink at the same time I say, "I'm pregnant with Jake's baby." Okay, maybe that was a little blunt.

He starts choking and I watch in horror as he goes purple in the face. This was so not what I had in mind. When he finally stops coughing, he rubs a hand over his face and groans. "*That* was not what I was expecting."

I flinch. "I'm sorry. I didn't mean for it to come out like that."

His jaw ticks. "How far along are you?"

"Around nine weeks." I hold my breath, waiting for him to join the dots.

He stands and paces the room. Raising his arms in the air, he places both hands on top of his head, making his biceps bulge. I watch as he walks back and forth until finally, he stops and looks down at me, still frozen awkwardly on the couch. "That would mean it happened on the tour. That night in Arras, I asked if things were history between the two of you and you told me they were. To be pregnant you have to have sex with someone, and that timeline makes it clear— you and Jake *weren't* history."

I draw in a shaky breath then explain, "It happened before we went on our date, and it was a mistake. Jake and I *were* done, on our date. I swear. You keep reminding me there's so much we don't know about each other. I didn't know how you would react knowing what had happened and I wanted to give us a chance, so I chose not to tell you. I'm so sorry."

His voice rises when he snaps back, "Don't turn my words around on me."

I glance in the direction of Sooz's bedroom, wondering if she can hear. "I don't know what else to say, Dan. This is me being totally honest with you and putting everything on the line."

He hesitates then asks, "Was it just the one time?"

I know he doesn't want the real answer, who would? But if we stand any chance of moving past this, there can't be any more lies. I look down at my hands. "No."

"When?"

"In Benicassim."

He folds his arms across his chest and narrows his eyes. "Let me get this straight? We had our date, during which you lied to me about things between you and Jake being history, and *then* you went back and screwed him *again*?"

I look up, struggling to see him through the tears in my eyes. "I've made a lot of mistakes this summer, I know I have. But I can't change things. It's done. All I can do is try and move forward and do what's best for me and the baby."

He nods but stays silent and my heart races, having finally told someone else the truth. I didn't expect Dan's reaction to be positive, but I also hoped it wouldn't be this negative.

"Thank you for being honest and telling me, but I need time to take everything in."

I watch in dismay as he walks toward the door.

"You're leaving?" I splutter.

He turns back and shakes his head sadly, refusing to look me in the eye. "I can't be around you right now. I was falling for you, Abby. But *this* is too much. I don't know where we go from here. The last thing I want is to say something I will regret, so instead, I'm going to leave."

"Will I see you again?"

He gives a half-hearted shrug. "Maybe. I don't know." Then as quickly as he came back into my life, he walks right back out.

My life feels like one car crash after another. I can see the threat in the distance, but I don't know how to avoid the collision.

Sleep takes a long time to come. My brain is like a hamster on a wheel, going over the night on repeat. When I feel myself finally beginning to drift off, my phone starts vibrating. I try to ignore it but whoever's calling is persistent. When it rings for the fourth time, I give up and roll over. Picking it up from my nightstand, I squint at the screen, trying to make out the name on the caller ID. It's Dan.

My voice is groggy when I answer, "Hello?"

"I'm outside."

"Outside where?" I ask, rubbing my eyes.

"Your apartment."

I blink as his words register. What the hell is he doing here? "I thought you said you needed time?"

"Yes, well, I've been for a walk and now I'm back. I'd rather have this conversation face to face, so are you going to let me in or not?"

"Erm … yeah?"

Hanging up, I quickly grab the first thing that comes to hand —an oversized T-shirt—so I'm not standing in just my underwear. I tiptoe through the apartment, not wanting to wake up Sooz, then quietly open the front door and beckon for him to come in. He follows me back to my room, closing the door behind him.

The soft glow of the bedside lamp highlights the features that drew me to him when we first met. High cheekbones, a stubble-lined jaw, and brown hair, which is unusually messed up. I have the urge to walk over and touch his face, to check he's really here, but something stops me. I need to know why. "You're here," I say quietly.

"I am."

I don't miss the way his eyes trail down my body, settling where my T-shirt cuts off mid-thigh. I should have gone for more clothes.

He looks away and stares intently at a spot on the wall. Finally, he breaks the silence and speaks again, "I'm sorry for how I acted earlier. Christ, I feel like all I do is apologize to you."

"Dan, you're not the one who needs to apologize, it's me."

"I pride myself on being a nice guy, Abby. I hear people out no matter what. I haven't done that with you. I care about you more than I'm willing to admit. I hate that I can't tell you how I'm feeling, because I'm scared you'll pull the rug from under me."

Waves of guilt wash over me. I hate how I've treated this kind and considerate guy.

He walks over, places a hand under my chin, and lifts it so that I stare him directly in the eyes. "Please don't cry," he says softly.

My voice wobbles as I say, "I never meant for any of this to happen."

"You're human; we all make mistakes. It's part of what makes life interesting and it's what will make you a stronger person in the end."

His words help to ease the tightness in my chest. He knows everything about me and Jake, apart from how I feel. He's already walked out the door once tonight, so I figure I haven't got anything to lose by being completely honest. "Each time I feel like I'm about to move on with my life and start something new, Jake turns up and ruins it. He's like a damn yo-yo, and now, I'll never get to move on from him."

"He might be in the background, but you can still live your life how *you* want to."

"I get what you're saying, but Jake and I together always ends in disaster. This is evidence," I say, gesturing to my stomach.

His jaw tightens and he says through gritted teeth, "A baby isn't a disaster, it's a blessing."

"Is that the poetic musician in you talking?"

"No, it's the guy who one day hopes to have a family of his own. I might have fame and money but it's not the end goal. It's just a bonus."

He's saying the words most women would kill to hear. Hell, they're the words *I* long to hear. Unfortunately, it's the wrong guy saying them to me. I want it to be Jake, but it never will be because he doesn't want kids.

"Where do we go from here?"

"I'm not sure." He walks to my bed and before sitting down. Politely, he asks, "Do you mind?"

I shake my head.

He sits, then leans forward and rests his elbows on his knees, looking as exhausted as I feel. When he eventually gazes up at me, he looks defeated. "I don't know where we stand or what the future holds for us. But what I do know, is that no matter how hard I try to walk away, I can't. How about we press pause? Get to know each other properly. The last thing you need is to jump into a relationship with someone, but it doesn't mean we can't be friends."

I don't know if he's trying to convince me or himself. His mouth says one thing, his face another. He clenches his hands as if he's stopping himself from reaching out to touch me. I know because I'm doing the same. He might not light the same fire in me that Jake does, but there's still something between us, which I can't deny.

"You're right. For now, this is for the best."

He takes a deep breath. "I wanted to run something by you."

"Go on …"

"I fly back to England the day after tomorrow. Come with me."

"Excuse me?"

"Come with me," he repeats slowly, leaving a long gap between each word.

"Why?" I groan when I realize how abrupt I sound. Not cool, Abby. "What I meant to say, was why do you want me to come with you?"

"You clearly need a break. You look knackered and Sooz told me how you've been. I think a change of scenery might be good for you."

I raise a brow at what he's suggesting.

He holds his hands up with a mischievous glint in his blue eyes which suddenly seem brighter. "I promise, no funny business. I meant what I said. This is one friend reaching out to another, recognizing they need some time out. Space can help things seem clearer sometimes. Consider it a break from reality."

I get what he's saying, but I can't walk away from my job at the drop of a hat. "As much as I'd love to say yes, I can't just leave. I have responsibilities, deadlines at work …"

He ignores my reply. "Sleep on it and speak with Sooz in the morning. *Then* give me an answer."

"Okay? I don't think my answer will change though."

He shrugs. "If it doesn't that's fine. We can meet for coffee before I go. No big deal."

"Right," I reply, totally bemused because what he's asking *is* a big deal.

"Try not to overthink it. Get some sleep and call me in the morning." He leans in and places a swift kiss on my forehead, and I try to ignore the butterflies that take flight in my stomach again.

"Should I call you a cab?" Realizing my mistake, I backtrack. "Of course, you don't need a cab, you have a driver."

"Yeah, I do." He stares a few seconds longer than a friend should, then starts walking backward toward my bedroom door. "I'm going before I try to do something I shouldn't."

Overcome with tiredness, I look at my clock and see it's three AM. Dan leaves my room quietly and I smile to myself when I hear the front door to our apartment shut. Laying back on my bed, I mull over the night and Dan's crazy suggestion. Like I can just uproot my life without a care in the world. I'm pregnant and have a job I need now more than ever. I can't just hop on a plane and follow a rock star to England. Can I?

"He asked you to do what?" screeches Sooz.

We're standing in the kitchen, sporting our finest Saturday morning lounge wear, our hair scraped back in messy buns. We mean business.

"He asked me to go back to England with him," I reply.

She opens and closes her mouth a couple of times. "When?"

"Tomorrow."

She jumps up and down on the spot. "Shut the front door! You have to go!"

I pause. Her response wasn't what I was expecting. I envisioned her telling me that if I went I would be acting irresponsible and making yet another huge mistake. I don't know how to process this. "What do you mean I have to go?"

"You heard me. Go. Have fun!" I've never seen her look so eager. She's visibly buzzing, and it almost has me feeling excited myself.

Reality quickly creeps back in and spoils my fun though. "But what about work?"

Sooz stares at me like I've grown an extra head. "What about it?"

"Aren't there policies for how much notice you have to give? I can't just up and leave."

I watch as she picks up the tray of eggs she pulled out of the fridge earlier. Now the excitement is over, she goes back to making breakfast. Priorities and all that.

She cracks a couple into a frying pan. "As your boss, I'm telling you that you can and you will, or I'm taking your place."

I shake my head and laugh.

"Abby, the lead singer of Six Seconds to Barcelona just asked you to get on a plane with him and stay at his home. There is no freakin' way you are turning this down."

"I have responsibilities, Sooz," I remind her.

"Behave. I've told you before, being pregnant isn't a life sentence. If anything, your pregnancy is a reason to go, because once that little bundle is out, *then* life will change."

I sigh. "Maybe you're right."

"I am right."

She moves me out of the way so she can grab the salt, sprinkling less than normal onto the eggs, "because I'm pregnant." Apparently, I can't have salt, but I can uproot my life and follow a rock star around the world.

"What about work?"

"What about it?" she says. "I know your schedule, so I know you don't have much going on at the moment. I'm also the one who authorizes your vacation time and I'm telling you that you can go, so go."

I ponder what she's saying. "Just like that?"

"Not everything has to be as complicated as you make it out to be. And I don't mean to be harsh, but you've been on a downer since we got back and it's affecting your work. You can see it in the images. Go, have fun, then come back a new and inspired woman. You need this break. You've been working too hard, and you've been in a funk for weeks."

She has a way with words, *not*.

"I guess," I say hesitantly. I wish I could see it like she does, as just a little vacation, but there's something telling me it will end up being so much more.

She starts plating the eggs. "I'm right like I always tell you. Do it, or it will be another thing you regret."

Thinking about how complicated things between Dan and I already are, I ask, "But what if he wants more?"

"Did he say he wanted more last night?"

"He probably would have, had I not informed him I was pregnant with my ex's child. He said we should just be friends."

"He doesn't strike me as the type to mess around. If he said just friends, I'm assuming he means it. Give the guy a chance, and if you feel uncomfortable, come home."

"Simple."

"Yes, simple. Go, Abby. Have fun and stop overthinking it. For once in your life just *be*."

I finally back down. "Okay."

Her eyes sparkle and she stands a little straighter. "Okay as in okay you're going?"

"Yes, I'm going."

"Oh. My. God! Let me get your cell before you can change your mind."

She races out of the kitchen and grabs my phone off the coffee table, then walks back toward me with it held out in her palm on speaker phone. The caller ID reads *Dan*. I need to change my pin.

"What are you doing?!" I shriek.

"Helping," she replies not very helpfully. She winks.

Dan's voice echoes around the room, "Abby? Hello?"

I mouth *I hate you*, in her direction.

She blows a kiss back before throwing my phone into my hands. I fumble with it before switching it off speaker and raising it to my ear.

Dan says again, "Abby, are you there? Is everything okay?"

The grogginess in his voice lets me know we've woken him up, not surprising after how late he left, or should I say early.

"I'm here. I actually rang to say …" I pause, not quite sure if I can follow through with all of this. Talking with Sooz about it is one thing, doing it is another. My stomach somersaults at the thought of packing my bags and carting my ass off to England.

"To say …" he echoes, urging me to continue.

I take the leap before I have a chance to overthink it any more than I already have. "I made up my mind. I'm in. I'm coming to England with you."

I hear him chuckle down the line. "Took you long enough. Now, I'm going back to sleep. Someone had me up all night."

He hangs up and I'm left wondering what on earth I've agreed to.

Chapter Seven

Abby

Holy shit are the two words that spring to mind as I stare at Dan White's house. My feet are glued to the spot at the bottom of the steps leading up to his detached Georgian home. It even has its own driveway and trees!

"Abby?" Dan, looks down at me, perfectly framed by the elegant door surround.

My mouth opens and closes in response.

"Come on, let's get inside."

I take one last look at the red bricks and huge windows and shake my head. When I agreed to come with Dan to London I didn't realize I was signing up for this lifestyle. He always appears so down to earth and everything about him is understated. But there's nothing understated about living in Kensington.

When we step inside my struggle to speak doesn't improve.

"Are you sure everything's okay?" asks Dan, stubbing his toe against the gleaming hardwood floor.

They're perfectly polished and reflect the bright white walls. Everything is just so … bright. And white. Like does he even live here?

"I can't believe you live *here*," I finally manage to say. I don't know where to look. It's possibly the most beautiful house I've ever been in and we're only standing in the entryway.

"You like it?" asks Dan, leaning casually against the door frame to the living area with his hands tucked in the pockets of his fitted black jeans. He looks every bit the rock star in his worn leather jacket. Seeing him here like this is a stark contrast to the guy I first met in Barcelona.

"Erm," I purse my lips. "Mind if I make an observation?"

"Shoot," he replies with one brow raised.

"It's very … white. I think I need to wear my sunshades."

His shoulders start to shake with laughter.

"What?"

"And that is why I love having you around, friend. You don't give a shit about all of this." He looks around at his surroundings, the expression on his face makes him seem detached from it all. "It's refreshing."

"I'll take that as a compliment." I grin.

"I had nothing to do with the white."

"Interior designer?"

He nods.

"It's very clean."

He holds his hands up. "Again, nothing to do with me. I'm not here much."

"So, what now?"

He shrugs. "You're the guest, you tell me. What would you like to do?"

"I don't mean to be a party pooper, but I'm tired." I gesture down at my non-existent bump. "Pregnancy problems."

"Okay, get some rest. I have some things I need to sort with the band. I could run to the shop for supplies if you don't mind being here alone?"

"Do you not have people for that?" I smirk, surprised he would do such an everyday task himself when he lives in a small palace.

The happy expression disappears from his face, and I scold myself for lumping him into a stereotype again. "I try to keep my feet on the ground as best I can," he explains. "I only use those things when they're really needed."

My cheeks start to burn. "I'm sorry, I didn't mean anything by it. This is all new and a bit surreal. It was one thing being with you at the festivals, but seeing you in real life, I'm not sure what to expect."

He smiles. "How about you think of me as a normal guy? That would be a start."

He moves away from the door frame then grabs my shoulders unexpectedly, steering me to a sweeping staircase. Even his stairs are grand with the intricately detailed spindles and the elegant floor runner.

Continuing the conversation as we walk up to the next floor, I say, "That would be easy if you weren't famous."

"Come on, I'm not the first celebrity you've hung out with."

"Dan, S.C.A.R.A.B. doesn't count. I practically grew up with them."

"Fine. It's something we'll have to work on." He stops outside a door, opens it swiftly, and gestures for me to go in.

"This is *my* room?" I can't hide the surprise in my voice. It's huge. Homelier than what I've seen so far, but massive.

He laughs at my reaction. "I'm hardly going to have you sleeping on the couch, Abby."

I spin around in the center of the room, taking in the almost floor-to-ceiling bay windows and super king-size bed. The bed linen alone looks like it costs more than my month's rent. "I know, this is just a lot."

"I invited you here, remember? In case you hadn't noticed, this house is big enough for a football team. Take the room and enjoy it."

I shuffle over to the bed and sit down. I close my eyes and a sigh escapes. After the plane journey, it feels like heaven. When I open them, Dan is staring at me, and my breath catches in my throat.

"Is everything okay?"

He blinks, then stands tall. "Sorry. It's nice, seeing you here, in my home," his voice lowers. "I better get going."

"Right, I'll get some rest," I reply awkwardly.

He nods and starts to walk out of the room. When he reaches the door he says, "I'll wake you in a few hours. We can decide what you want to do then."

"Great," I say.

"Great," he says.

Like I said, awkward.

We smile at each other, and I start to wonder whether coming here was such a good idea. I'm struggling to keep my cool.

"I'll see you in a bit. By the way, I'm glad you came. More than glad."

Dan leaves and I lay back on the bed, feeling like I'm floating. But all the comfort in the world can't stop me from over-analyzing everything. Right before sleep takes over, I come to the conclusion that we're playing with fire and sooner or later, one of us is going to get burnt.

Hours later, I think I'm still dreaming when a faint voice and melody reach my ears. I slowly come round, trying to get my bearings, taking in the now dark room. Throwing back the chenille blanket that wasn't there when I fell asleep, I leave my room in search of Dan.

Once downstairs, I pause, standing just back from the door to the living area, and watch as Dan strums an acoustic guitar. He's playing a softer melody of the closing song he performed at the concert a couple of days ago. I don't have my camera to hand, so I settle for taking a snapshot in my mind. An image of a guy, vulnerable, putting his heart on the line for a girl who hasn't given him a single reason to trust her. He says we're just friends, but there's something in his eyes that tells me for him it might never be the case.

I could stand and watch all night, but my stomach has other ideas, and growls loudly, echoing off the walls.

He stops playing and grins when he sees me standing by the door. "Enjoy the show?"

I nod and walk into the room. "I could get used to private performances."

"I'll remember that when I want something from you," he winks, and those traitorous butterflies start again.

Trying to ignore them, I ask, "What time is it?"

"Getting on for nine. You left your phone down here and you were out cold when I came back. I didn't want to wake you."

"I feel a lot better," I sigh.

"Speaking of phones, yours has been ringing on and off for the past few hours. I may have seen the screen a couple of times. It was Zoe, and Sophie, and your mum." He picks it up from the large oak coffee table and hands it over to me, frowning when I shove it straight into the back pocket of my jeans.

"Are you not going to see what they want? It could be something important. They might want to check on you, check everything with the baby is okay."

I look vacantly out of the living room window. "They won't be checking because they don't know."

"What do you mean they don't know?" He tilts his head to the side and when a rogue piece of dark brown hair falls across his brow, he sweeps it out of the way.

"I haven't told anyone. The only people who know are you and Sooz. Oh, and Amanda, who you met on the tour."

His voice softens, "Why haven't you told anyone, Abby?"

I swallow, struggling to say the words out loud, "The more people who know the more real it feels."

"I hate to burst your bubble, but it is real and there's nothing you can do about it."

I narrow my eyes. "Thanks for pointing out the obvious."

He lets out a deep sigh and rubs a hand across his jaw. "Sooz mentioned there was an issue, but she wouldn't say what. You need to tell people. Especially your family and friends. You can't do this alone."

"I'll do it when the time's right. It's my decision." I huff, then flinch at my snappy tone, knowing I sound like a brat.

The thing about Dan is that he is a nice guy, one of the nicest I've met, but he's also not willing to put up with my crap. It's not surprising he challenges me where most would give up.

"And when will the time be right? When the baby's born? Abby, they're your best friends. You can't just shut them out."

"Dan, it's my life and my baby."

"Want to know what I think?"

"Not really," I mutter.

Choosing to ignore me he says, "I think you're running. But what are you running from? What are you afraid of?"

I purse my lips and we stare at each other, neither backing down. The silence surrounding us becomes oppressive. He's got me, but I refuse to tell him the truth. I refuse to tell him that one of the reasons I run is out of fear of losing my heart to Jake and the other, is the fear that somewhere among all the chaos and pain, I've actually lost myself.

Instead of the truth, I say dejected, "Please don't lecture me, I've had enough from Sooz."

He holds his hands up. "Fine, but this conversation isn't over."

With expert timing, my stomach growls again and I blush. "Is there anything I can grab to eat?"

"I got some bits, but I wasn't sure what you liked or if there was anything you'd gone off. I read that can happen. Maybe we could order in?"

A smile tugs at my lips knowing he's been reading up on pregnancy information. Trying not to focus on the tidbit he unknowingly revealed I say, "Sounds great. Order whatever you'd normally get. I'm sure I'll love it."

"I thought pizza would be a safe bet?"

"Perfect." I smile, then continue, "I'm going to head back up and unpack if that's all right?"

He nods and I walk out of the room. As I leave, I hear Dan say quietly, "Remember, Abby. You might feel alone in all this, but only you can change that."

The following days are quiet, and I don't know what to do with myself. I've barely seen Dan, who's been working hard with his band on their new album. Already I'm regretting my decision to come to London because now I don't even have work to use as a distraction. Instead, I'm alone in Dan's huge home with only my mind for company and we're proving not to be the best of friends.

It's a Thursday and I've braved a trip out on my own, navigating the streets of London with my trusty friend Google Maps. I've managed to find my way out of Kensington and into Chelsea when I wander past a quaint coffee shop. There's something about it that draws me in. It's not until I'm inside and at the front of the line, ready to order, I realize it's almost an exact replica of the one I visited with Jake the first time I returned to Brooklyn. Just the sight of the mismatched furniture makes my gut tug and not in that sexy, angst-fueled way you read about in books. This is more the heart broken, world-feels-like-it's-ended kind of gut tug. The kind that makes you feel like you can't breathe, and that the world doesn't make sense.

"What can I get you?" asks the server from behind the counter, startling me from my thoughts.

"Sorry. I'll have a Caramel Cinnamon Latte with an extra shot," I say, repeating the same order Jake reeled off perfectly after we'd been apart for years.

Seriously, Abby, stop. Not everything in life has a direct link back to Jake, I tell myself. If I keep going on the way I am I'm going to drive myself crazy.

The server calls over her shoulder to the barista at the coffee machine, "One Caramel Cinnamon Latte with an extra shot."

Hearing my order, I flinch when I realize the mistake I've made. "Erm, I'm really sorry."

The server looks at me with a roll of her eyes and the guy standing behind me lets out a huff of air.

"Can you make it decaf, please?"

"Make it decaf," she shouts over her shoulder.

When I hand over some money, she doesn't even smile. Apparently, customer service isn't a priority here.

When I finally have my drink, I settle in one of the pinstripe armchairs situated next to the floor-to-ceiling window that covers the front of the shop. It takes everything in me not to close my eyes and drift off when my body sinks into the cushions. I opt for taking a sip of my drink, grimacing as the taste of decaf coats my tongue. This is one area of pregnancy I won't ever get used to, and the lack of caffeine in my system is making me grumpier than normal. Admitting defeat, I set the cup down on the small table in front of the chairs, deciding that people watching will be more fun than pretending the drink I ordered tastes nice.

All I see are babies, everywhere. It's like the moms of Chelsea all decided to go for a walk with their little bundles of joy at the exact same time so they could parade them in front of me. With people watching off the cards, I glance around the shop and find a stand filled with magazines. I grab a couple of fashion ones, thinking to myself that Zoe would be proud, then get settled back in my seat.

All of ten minutes have passed when I start to get restless. I don't know what I thought would happen coming here. I don't know if I thought deep down that I might have some sort of epiphany over what to do and how to move forward. I was wrong. All I've managed to achieve is next-level boredom and guilt over the fact I'm hiding away from the people who love me when I should be leaning on them for support.

I can't forget the total confusion over why Dan invited me here in the first place when I've barely seen him. I get that this trip was about me resting and clearing my head away from my daily hustle back in Cape Town, but I thought we'd at least interact more than just the first day we arrived at his home. I literally haven't seen him, and now the shoe is on the other foot, and I'm being avoided without any explanation, I know how crap it feels and why he acted the way he did at the end of the summer tour.

Taking the bull by the horns, I pull my phone out of my bag and send Dan a message informing him that I'm ordering takeout and to be home around seven.

He responds, *Will do*. It's as simple as that.

I go back to reading one of the magazines and when I pick my coffee back up and take another sip, even that doesn't taste as bad now that my mood is lighter and my head feels clearer.

Back home, I take a nap in preparation. I'm hardly going to be good company if I fall asleep midway through the food.

Typically, I sleep through my alarm and end up having to scrape myself together so I look somewhat presentable. I look better than I have in weeks, even with the little effort I make. The black skinny jeans and fitted white vest along with a long gray cardigan have me looking casual and cute. Even if I only just manage to fasten the button on my pants.

I'd found Dan's takeout menu stash in one of the drawers in the kitchen the day after I arrived, and settle on ordering Chinese, despite the pizza pull being strong. Three times in a week is pushing it and being pregnant isn't an acceptable excuse. The food arrives on time, and I lay it all out on the coffee table in the living area, so we can sit and watch something on TV while we eat. The perfect remedy for potential awkward silences.

My hand trembles when I unload more of the food from the bag. I feel like a teenager again, full of nerves. Friends, Abby, nothing more, I remind the ever-increasing hormones racing around my body before they get any funny ideas.

"It smells good in here."

I startle and almost drop the tray of Chow Mein I'm holding in shock. "Jeez! Be thankful I'm not further along, you could send a girl into early labor sneaking up like that," I exclaim.

When I look around, my eyes take in Dan lounging lazily against the doorframe, his brown hair mussed and his face full of sleep.

"I didn't know you were home," I croak. "I was about to message. I wasn't sure if you would come."

He lets out a deep laugh that fills the room and my cheeks start to feel warm. "Where else would I go? It's my house, Abby."

Standing tall, he stretches his arms above his head and his T-shirt creeps up, revealing a set of toned abs I didn't know were there. I let out a small groan to which Dan narrows his eyes.

Trying to detract the attention away from my not-so-sexy, involuntary pregnancy noises, I say, "You know what I mean."

"I fell asleep when I got home from practice, sorry. Luckily, I set an alarm."

"Same." I smile then look away.

Why is this so awkward? It's not supposed to be like this. Things between Dan and I have always felt natural. When I look back, he's staring intently. As quick as it appeared, the moment passes, and Dan shakes his head as if he's telling himself to get it together.

"So, what did you order?" he asks looking over my shoulder.

"Chinese. I hope that's okay. I figured you can't go wrong with it … but maybe you can? I could always ring and order something else if you don't like what I got. I'm sure it wouldn't take long to ar—"

"Chinese is perfect." He takes a few large strides across the room and suddenly he's right in front of me, his body so close I can feel the heat radiating off him. Leaning down, he whispers into my ear, "Abby, you need to chill."

I'm left feeling everything I shouldn't, my body buzzing and feeling more alive than it has in weeks. This is not what I had in mind for the evening. It was supposed to be a casual meal between friends.

Dan steps around me and begins tucking into the food. With a full plate he sits down on the couch, and I wring my hands awkwardly. "Sorry, I'm nervous."

"Same." I blink, watching as he shovels food into his mouth like he's anything but nervous.

Noticing my silence, he looks up and gives me a slow, sexy smile. "You don't need to be nervous. We're just friends, remember?"

Just like that my temperature plummets with the ice-cold bucket of water he's poured over me. I swallow hard. "Right, let's eat then." Inwardly I curse. He's already started eating.

When I've chosen a couple of dishes, Dan looks up from his plate which is piled high, and frowns at the small amount on mine. "Not hungry?"

"I've lost my appetite. Pregnancy perks," I lie.

He doesn't need to know my lack of appetite is because of the riot of emotions that have been coursing through me since the moment he stepped in the room. I can't decide which was worse, not seeing him all week and being consumed by thoughts of Jake, or seeing him and being torn between thoughts of them both.

When we've finished eating, he switches on the television and we settle into a series on Netflix, which quickly has us both hooked. We're a couple of hours in when I start to shuffle uncomfortably in my seat.

Admitting defeat, I say, "I can't do this anymore."

Dan shifts his body so he's facing me, his face full of concern. "What's wrong?"

"This is so awkward, but I'm really uncomfortable. Do you mind?" I ask, pointing at the button of my pants.

His whole body starts to shake with laughter and eventually he manages to choke out, "Of course I don't mind."

I pop open my button, sighing with relief as my stomach expands.

Dan says, "Although I wish you were opening your pants for another reason."

My head snaps up and my eyes meet his wide blue ones. The atmosphere feels heavy, and I don't know what to do as understanding hits me. I suddenly understand why I haven't seen him this week. He's been avoiding me like I initially thought, and it's for this very reason. We might say we're just friends, however, the chemistry between us says we're anything but.

His eyes fall to my stomach and quietly he says, "We could make this work."

"Dan …"

The muscle in his jaw ticks. "I shouldn't have said that."

"You did though."

He groans and rubs a hand over his face. "This is so messed up."

"I'm sorry. I wish things were different," I say honestly because I do.

In another time or place, in a world where I wasn't pregnant, maybe we could have found our way onto the same path. But that's a dream and this is reality, one I'm quickly learning doesn't always work in my favor.

"But they're not," he says sadly.

"I won't apologize for this baby, Dan." I surprise even myself with my words. "I've reached a point where a small part of me is starting to accept what's happening and I refuse to go backward."

"I'm not asking you to."

"Then what do you want from me? You can't say something like that and then expect me to just forget."

"I don't want you to forget, Abby. I want you to look at me and say it's me you want."

This sounds scarily like the conversation I had with Jake and bile rises in my throat.

"I don't care that you're pregnant."

"Dan." I sigh. "We barely know each other. We've hardly spent any time together, especially not in real life. We had a couple of dates in the festival world. Don't get me wrong they were amazing, and I was ready to see where things would go, but that's still all it was.

"You said to me once, there's so much we don't know about each other. Even if the summer hadn't ended like it did, eventually we would have had to leave the fairytale behind, and real-life would have got in the way."

His expression changes and he stares at me, eyes full of fire. "You want to know what it's like being with me in the real world? It's like this."

Before I have a chance to register his words, he closes the gap between us and presses his lips firmly against mine. It's been so long that I'd forgotten what it felt like, tried to convince myself we weren't as good together as we are.

He doesn't go all in like Jake does. He waits for me to decide what it is I really want, whether I want the kiss to be anything more. Truthfully, I'm not sure what I want, but as his mouth moves slowly over mine, the butterflies in my stomach take flight. I shut down the part of my brain screaming that it should be Jake kissing me because it can't be. I need to leave the past behind.

Dan's lips are soft, almost hesitant, and the way his fingertips skim lightly over the skin on my arms tells me he's holding back. I pull away and stare him in the eye, my focus unwavering, challenging him to give me more. His throat bobs and his gaze drops to my mouth when I lick my lips. This time when he leans in and kisses me again, he's all in. His hands grip my waist firmly and his tongue sweeps against mine. I'm not sure how long we sit, lost in each other. Eventually, Dan pulls away, the strain on his face telling me he wants to do the complete opposite, but we both know it's for the best.

Dan chuckles when I try and fail to hide a yawn. "I'm sorry," I struggle to say as another yawn fights its way out.

He smiles and pecks a quick kiss against my lips. "Go to bed, it's fine."

I smile in relief that I don't have to try and fight the tiredness. We make our way slowly upstairs, leaving the takeout mess until the morning. When I reach my room and step inside, I turn back to close the door, but Dan's hand reaches up and his palm lays flat against it, stopping me.

His voice has a wistful tone when he says, "Promise me one thing. If you want me, be with me. But if you don't, please, don't go behind my back with *him* again."

I stand on my tiptoes and place a soft kiss on his cheek, then whisper, "Goodnight."

I don't promise. That's the reason I'm glad we didn't take things further tonight and don't know if we ever will. It's a promise I don't know if I'd be able to keep because when it comes to me and Jake, there's always a possibility.

There's always an 'us,' no matter how hard I try to convince myself otherwise.

Chapter Eight

Abby

What was meant to be a short vacation to gather my thoughts, turned into a three-week trip and counting. Each time I go to book a return flight to Cape Town, I back out, right when I'm about to hit *confirm*. I'd like to believe it's because I'm simply enjoying a well-needed rest, but deep down I know part of me won't do it because I've gotten used to having Dan in my life and the little routine we've settled into over the past couple of weeks.

When I told Sooz my plans to stay in London for longer, although disappointed, she replied "Do what you have to." Between us, we decided it was best for me to officially take a leave of absence, while I figure things out. She had some more of my things shipped to Dan's home to tide me over while I made up my mind. Thankfully, I have a good working contract and a nice nest egg of savings built up over the years to keep me afloat.

The part I keep neglecting on my little hiatus from life: the fact I'm pregnant and still need to keep up with my medical care.

I'm sitting in the kitchen when Dan strides in and confirms I have an appointment at The Portland Hospital for my twelve-week check. I almost gag on my honey hoops, spluttering that I can't afford it. He shakes his head, mutters something about money not being an issue, and that is that.

We arrive and are sitting in the waiting room when I begin to understand why Dan chose here. Not because he wanted to flash his money around, but because he wanted to be with me, and this was the only place where he could. The place houses celebrities and signs NDAs without batting an eyelash. If the press saw us anywhere else and caught wind of my 'situation,' it would be carnage and that's the last thing either of us needs.

Wriggling in my seat, I decide enough is enough and pop the button on my jeans. Glancing around the waiting room, I pray the other women haven't noticed. It's embarrassing enough. I don't exactly fit in, wearing too-small jeans and an old shirt. The greaseball hair and makeup-free face are a bonus. It's not surprising that Dan hasn't tried to lay a hand on me since the night we kissed. I wouldn't want to go near me either.

"Stop jiggling," Dan whispers. "You're drawing attention to us."

"I can't help it," I hiss back. "I need to use the restroom."

"Tough shit, mumma bear," he grins. "You'll have to hold it. Are you excited to see the baby?"

"That's one way of putting it," I grumble.

He takes in my expression and doesn't push the subject further.

Déjà vu hits me when a voice calls out, "Abby West."

Standing up at the same time, Dan and I leave the waiting area and move into a more welcoming room than the one used back in Cape Town. Apart from the odd piece of medical equipment, you wouldn't know we were in a hospital. It looks like the same interior designer that decked out Dan's home worked their magic here.

"I'm sure you remember the process, but I can talk you through it again if you'd like me to," says the sonographer. My eyes widen, remembering my first scan. There's no way the "wand" is coming near me with Dan in the room. Nada. Nope. Not happening. "Is everything okay, Ms. West?"

I bite down on my lip. I lean forward and, hoping Dan can't hear, say quietly, "Do you use that thing?"

The sonographer looks at me bemused and drops her voice. "Thing?"

I raise a hand so Dan can't see and mouth, *The wand.'*

"This is an abdominal ultrasound, Ms. West," she says with a chuckle.

I collapse back on the bed relieved, forgetting there are people with me, and exclaim, "Thank fuck for that." Instantly realizing my mistake, I clap a hand over my mouth. "Sorry."

Dan smiles behind his fist and the sonographer smiles, ignoring my little slip.

"I need you to lift your shirt around your ribs and relax. I'm going to be pressing down firmly and I apologize, the gel is cold. Dad, are you staying for the full scan?"

The way Dan's cheeks redden wouldn't be noticeable to those who don't know him. "Actually, I'm not the dad, just a close friend."

"That's fine," says the sonographer, brushing over it professionally. "Will you be staying?"

Dan looks to me for an answer.

"Yes, he will," I reply without thinking.

Dan's shoulders sag in relief and he smiles at me as he sits down on a chair beside the bed. I freeze when he grabs hold of my hand but try not to give anything away with my expression. There's something about this situation that doesn't feel right. When my stomach is covered in gel, I feel the pressure of the probe being moved around.

Almost straight away the sonographer says, "There we are!" I let out a sharp breath. "The heartbeat is nice and strong, but you have a little wriggler on your hands. I need to take some measurements. I can talk you through them at the end if you'd like?"

I shake my head no. "Just tell me if there's anything wrong."

"Okay, Abby. Try and stay as relaxed as you can."

I lay and watch, listening to the quiet hum of the computer, trying to avoid my thoughts. Dan sits and doesn't say a word, watching the screen and the baby move around in awe. I blink rapidly as my eyes begin to water. I can't cry, not here. My heart aches, watching the amazement on Dan's face. It should be Jake beside me, but he wouldn't want to be here even if he knew, I remind myself.

I have feelings for Dan, I'd have to be an idiot not to. He's an amazing and thoughtful guy who's proven more than once why he's a solid choice. But my heart wants Jake. It always has and it feels like it always will. I miss him, it hurts, and no matter how hard I try, I don't know how to make it stop.

Something's happened, I'm just not sure what. Story of my life.

The day after Dan and I kissed, things took a U-turn. Things between us changed and not for the better. After the scan, I could have left the country and Dan would have been none the wiser. There's been no communication between us, and I don't have a clue why.

I'm standing in the kitchen with a cup of herbal tea when Dan walks in.

I smile and acting as casually as I can say, "Hey," it comes out more like a squeak and I cringe.

"Hey," replies Dan, then goes about his business, doing what has become the norm, ignoring me.

We can't keep going on like this and I need to know where we stand and if he still wants me to be here. "Dan … Do you still want me here?"

I expect to see his now usual moody expression when he looks over, but what I find makes me want to stalk across the room and pull him into my arms. The pain written all over his face is unbearable.

He exhales then sits on one of the central island stools before placing his head in his hands. When he looks up, his eyes lack their usual sparkle. "Of course, I still want you here, Abby. Like I'd want you to be anywhere else. That's the problem."

"I don't understand. What happened this week? It feels like everything between us has changed and I don't have a clue why."

"I thought I could do this whole *just friends* thing, but then we kissed, and it reminded me that I don't want to. I want to help you. I want to be there for you, for both of you. Being at the scan with you made me realize how much."

It starts to make sense why he's been giving me the cold shoulder since we left the hospital. I know what he's doing because I do the same with Jake. I close off. I stare at him blankly. I don't have a clue what to do or say.

There's a part of me that wants to throw caution to the wind and give this thing between us a chance. But that would be unfair to Jake. We're forever tied together, he just doesn't know it yet. There will always be a part of him with me and I don't know how to live my life with someone else. I don't know if I want to.

"What if we tried for more?" asks Dan hopefully. "What if for once you gave yourself a shot at happiness, without Jake being the one deciding when and how."

My heart screams for the one that got away, but my head tells me that maybe, just maybe, with a little bit of time and perseverance, I could begin to feel about Dan the way he does about me. Maybe if I try harder, eventually I will forget about Jake. But what if I don't?

"I don't know what to say," I answer honestly. "The baby could change how I feel about *everything*." Dan looks crestfallen, but I hold a hand up, signaling that I have more to say. "I'm not saying no. I'm asking for time, so I can decide what is best for all of us. I understand if you can't."

I know what I'm asking is a lot on top of everything he's already given me, but I refuse to make a promise I can't keep. I refuse to dive into a relationship when my whole life is up in the air, affecting my judgment. I refuse to make the same mistakes over and over. It's time to take a breather and do what feels right for me and this baby. For now, we're all that matters.

He looks at me confused. "It's not a yes but it's not a no?"

"It's a *let's wait and see.*"

Then, Dan does what I needed Jake to do back in the summer. He proves why logically he's the better choice. "Okay."

He gives me time.

A week passes in a blur without me realizing and I don't know how much longer I can stay here hiding away. I'm fourteen weeks pregnant and real life is coming to find me. I can feel it.

There is one thing I can't hide from: I can no longer fit in my pants. Apparently, I've hit *that* part of my pregnancy. The part where your body parts start to expand and there isn't a thing you can do about it.

My daily routine of lounging around the house and watching reruns of *The Vampire Diaries* is interrupted, when Dan arrives home early from his practice with the band, to find me sprawled on his couch, sans pants. Rose from *Titanic*'s got nothing on me.

When he demands I get dressed because we have somewhere important to be, I try not to show how heartbroken I am that my time with Stefan and Damon has been cut short.

I had my reservations about walking the streets of London with my pants open (button problems), but it ends up being a pleasant afternoon. We start with some sightseeing before we find ourselves ambling along the streets of Chelsea, with Dan kitted out in his usual disguise of a ball cap and sunglasses. So original. I feel like a walking cliché with him by my side. All we need is to get *papped* and I'd be in my own real-life version of *Notting Hill.*

I'm spending too much time watching Netflix.

"Where are you taking me?" I ask when I'm no clearer what was so important.

"Somewhere I think you will appreciate," Dan answers cryptically.

I wiggle my eyebrows. "Does it involve food?"

Now the nausea is starting to pass, from the moment I open my eyes it's one of the only things I think about. Well, that and Jake. I can't quite decide whether my food consumption is due to pregnancy cravings or comfort eating my way through a broken heart.

"That bit comes later, but I think you will like where I'm taking you, eventually."

I frown. "Eventually?"

"You might have to get your head around my reasoning."

I stop in my tracks. "So, you want me to trust you?"

He shrugs and keeps on walking, calling over his shoulder, "I was hoping that you already did …"

I shuffle quickly to catch up with him and when the gap between us is closed, I shove him playfully and say, "I'm getting there."

Eventually, we stop outside a store, large by Chelsea's standards, which is known for its expensive boutiques. I cringe when I see the giant baby logo emblazoned across the store window.

"Baby stuff, really?" This is not my idea of fun.

"I didn't bring you to buy stuff for the baby, but we can if you'd like?" His optimistic look quickly disappears when I shake my head. "I actually brought you here for you."

"Me?"

"I told Sooz about the jean situation, and she suggested maybe you'd want to start thinking about maternity wear." He rubs at his jaw waiting for my reaction.

I should be suspicious that he's been speaking with Sooz behind my back, but that isn't what gets me riled up. "Basically, you think I'm getting fat?"

He holds his hands up. "I was only trying to help, Abby. You're not fat, you're growing a human. This"—he gestures to the store—"is kind of unavoidable."

I tug my oversized coat around my middle.

"I'm cocking this up, aren't I?"

"Royally, I think is what you Brits would say." As much as I dislike this, I know he's right. I need to stop bitching and accept that it's something I have to do. "Thank you for bringing me."

He lets out a sigh of relief. "You're not mad?"

"Embarrassed a little. Mad? No. How could I be when you're only trying to help? I can barely get my lounge pants up. I think the saying is, I've popped." I air quote the last part.

"Do you want me to come in with you?" His mouth says one thing, but his face says another, as he looks at the store with an expression, I'm most likely wearing myself. Fear.

"I'm good. This is something I'd rather do on my own."

"In that case, I'm off to the pub for a pint to celebrate you not killing me in broad daylight."

I roll my eyes, wishing I could join in the fun. "Any excuse. Have one for me. In fact, have ten."

"A third of the way there. It won't be long!" He goes to high-five me, but I leave him hanging.

The end isn't something to joke about. The whole pushing thing makes my skin crawl.

"Don't remind me," I say, shuddering.

"I'll leave you to it then."

I watch his retreating form disappear around the corner further up the road before I give the store my attention once more. Staring at the window, all I can see is pink and blue. Accepting that I'm not going to get anywhere by standing outside on the sidewalk, I take a deep breath and step inside. At first, I'm overwhelmed. There are teeny, tiny baby things everywhere I turn. I'm ready for running back out when a store assistant approaches me, asking if she can help.

"I can't fit in my pants," is all I manage to say, to which she chuckles. There's a kindness in her eyes that tells me her laughter isn't at my expense and I'm not the first person to walk in here feeling like a duck out of water.

Over an hour later, I walk back out with bags of things I never thought I'd need. The bra front was an issue, and when the sizing was explained, images of udders flashed through my mind. The jeans, however, are heaven. I love them *so* much I bought four. I also put a pair on and skipped out of the store to go meet Dan.

"You look a lot better than you did earlier," Dan beams when I find him sitting in a quiet corner of the pub nursing his drink.

"I can breathe again, need I say more?" I laugh, shrugging my coat off then sliding into the seat across the table from him with my back to the room.

He pulls an odd face then grins when he looks down at my new pants. "They look comfier."

He's being overly enthusiastic, and his knee bounces so hard that his pint all but sloshes over the sides of the glass each time it hits the underside of the table. Trying to ignore how odd he's acting, I broach something that's been plaguing my mind.

"So, I was thinking it's time I get in touch with the girls, and my mom."

Dan's voice takes on a pitch he doesn't even reach in his songs when he replies, "Yeah, that's a good idea."

I frown and nod. "They need to know, it's not fair I've left it this long."

A throat clears behind me, and I watch Dan's eyebrows shoot up, his gaze flickering over my shoulder.

"What exactly do we need to know, Abby?"

My stomach feels like it plummets to the core of the Earth.

When I spin around, my eyes settle on my mom, Zoe, and Sophie, all standing, their facial expressions ranging from anger to confusion. I stand awkwardly, ready to explain. There's no need though because their gazes drop to the tiny bump I'm now sporting which does the job for me.

It's official, my not-so-little secret, isn't a secret anymore.

Chapter Nine

Abby

I've had some awkward moments in my life, it comes with the territory of having Zoe and Sophie as best friends. However, riding in Dan's town car back to Kensington, with the three of the most important women in my life staring daggers at me, has been something else entirely. Each time I go to open my mouth to say something and break the awkward silence, I come up empty because there's nothing to say. I've ignored them for months and deserve the anger directed at me. Of course, the journey takes longer than normal, just in case it wasn't torture enough.

Finally, the vehicle stops. The driver opens the door and I jump out quickly, sucking in the crisp fall air, trying to get myself together. The others climb out slowly and look up at Dan's home, their faces filled with awe.

It's Dan who says, "Don't stand out in the cold." He runs up the steps and unlocks the front door, then holds it open with a tight smile, waiting for us all to follow him inside.

Nobody moves until I work up the courage to say something. "Come on. I'm not having this conversation outside for the world to hear."

It's not unusual to see paps skulking outside the gates at all times of the day and night, hoping to get a picture of Dan. It's one of the reasons we've been extra careful about going out together. My mom tsks and shakes her head pushing past me. Sophie and Zoe follow closely behind, their expressions blank. It's official, I've shocked the unshockable.

The animosity passes for a few short minutes when they all hum their approval at how stunning Dan's home is. When they're done taking in the entryway, he leads them to the left into the living area which sets them off again. I don't get it, but I never have. The fame and money side of things has never bothered me. I'm here for Dan, not for his perfectly styled home with its polished wood flooring and Italian leather couches. When I look around, all I see is white.

Away from the outside world, Sophie and Zoe seem more relaxed and settle on one of the couches situated underneath the large bay window. The soft glow of the lamps as evening creeps in makes the atmosphere feel warmer than it is.

I settle down on another of the couches, no clue what to do or say.

"Tea anyone?" asks Dan, a fake smile plastered across his face.

Zoe giggles. "Christ, Dan, we're not British. I think a vat of Vodka would be more appropriate."

I smile and when Zoe's eyes meet mine, her expression turns cold. Okay then, that joke wasn't for my benefit.

"I can't tell if you're being serious or not," replies Dan.

"She's being very serious," says Sophie. "Ignore her."

"Please don't." Sophie turns and stares daggers at her. "What?" She scoffs.

"Do you not think requesting Vodka is a bit inappropriate?" snaps Sophie.

Zoe looks completely baffled. "Why would Vodka ever be inappropriate?"

"Erm … because, you know …" Sophie cocks her head in my direction with a grimace.

"Because I'm pregnant," I say loudly, addressing the elephant in the room.

"Pregnant!" shrieks my mom, her head raised to the ceiling as she paces back and forth.

Dan remains standing in the doorway to the living area, looking like he wishes he was anywhere but here. With the spectacle that is unfolding, if he goes, I'll be joining him.

My mom finally stops pacing and looks at me confused. "You're pregnant?"

"I am," I say boldly, mentally high-fiving myself for not cowering into a ball.

She blinks once, then twice. "How?"

I laugh awkwardly. "Mom, you're the sex columnist. I don't think I need to explain *how*."

The confusion on her face disappears, replaced by disappointment. "Now is not the time to be giving me attitude, Abby."

I look down at my lap. Being scorned in front of my friends like a child is humiliating yet fitting after how I've handled the situation. The embarrassment doesn't end there, it only gets worse when she turns her attention away from me to Dan, still standing in the doorway.

"Are you the father?" she spits, not caring one bit about his fame.

My hands fly up to cover my face and I groan.

"Unfortunately, not," replies Dan with a forlorn look.

My mom looks between the two of us. "I don't understand. If you're not the father, then why are you here? Abby?" She turns her attention solely back to me.

After taking a deep breath, I say, "Dan got in touch with Sooz, and visited me in Cape Town. When he found out I was pregnant and wasn't coping well he suggested I come here for some space. I stayed longer than I thought I would."

"Evidently," Mom replies.

Ignoring her comment, I turn to my two best friends, watching them digest the information.

"Wait. Sooz knows as well?" asks my mom when the penny drops.

I nod, flinching when I say, "And Amanda."

Zoe and Sophie sit silently, meanwhile, my mom throws her arms up in the air. "Who else knows?"

"That's it," I reply. "Actually, I think Zach might have suspected something."

My Mom stands with her mouth hanging open. I can see the cogs turning in her mind while she puts everything together. "Let me get this straight. Four people knew you were pregnant … *Four*. Before I did?" the last part she chokes out and the torn expression on her face is heartbreaking.

The Shitty Daughter of the Year Award goes to Abby West.

I never meant to hurt her by keeping it a secret. I never meant to hurt anyone. I just wasn't ready to deal with it all. I still don't know if I am. I don't say any of that out loud. What I do say is, "I'm sorry, Mom."

"Did you know when you came back to Brooklyn during the tour?"

"No. It was as much a surprise to me as it is to you."

"Well, you've had plenty of time to get your head around it," she snaps.

I gasp in shock at how she's speaking to me. "Why are you being like this?"

It's a stupid question because I know why.

"Because you're pregnant, Abby," she says. "And I'm only just finding out now and you're over three months in! No one has heard from you and it's only thanks to Dan and Sooz that we even know you're alive."

I look up at Dan. "You've been speaking with them? Why didn't you tell me?"

"They needed to know you were okay," he replies, his face blank.

"That wasn't your decision to make," I bite back.

He starts walking backward. "And that's my cue to leave. *This* is nothing to do with me. I'll be upstairs." He leaves without another word.

He's right, I know he is. They all are. I should have told them. But how do you tell your best friends and parents that you've royally fucked up? That you dated two guys at the same time, then wound up pregnant by an ex, who is still very much an ex.

My gaze flickers between Sophie and Zoe. "Are you going to say anything?"

It's Sophie who speaks first, "Who's the father?"

"Yes, who is the father, Abby?" my mom chips in.

Zoe throws her head back laughing at the two of them. "Like you even need to ask. It's obvious."

Sophie gasps when she realizes.

"Do not tell me it's Jake Ross," my mom says, loudly.

If I thought she was pissed before, she's livid now.

"Fine, I won't," I reply. This couldn't have gone any worse if I'd tried.

"How could you let this happen, Abby? How could you be so irresponsible?" she says exasperated.

I roll my eyes. "Mom, really? I'm twenty-six. I'm not a child. It was an accident. One that happens to a lot of people.'

"You're saying it like you bumped your car!" she exclaims. "You're *pregnant*. I thought you were on birth control?"

"Mom, please, stop! I get that you're upset, but I haven't exactly been sitting around loving life. Not telling you all was the hardest thing I've ever done, but I was humiliated, and I didn't want to admit what was going on, even to myself." My heart's hammering in my chest when I finish.

Sophie asks softly, "How do you feel now?"

My shoulders slump in defeat and I admit out loud for the first time, "Not great."

I'm flooded with relief as the words fall from my lips. It feels so wrong to say, but nothing about this situation is right. Now they know, I can finally voice how I'm really feeling to the people I know will never judge me, even if they are pissed.

"What about Dan?" asks Zoe.

"He was upset when he found out the truth," I say. "Nothing's going on between us."

She looks at me confused. "Then why are you here? Are you even going back to Cape Town? What about work?"

I sink back into the couch feeling exhausted with the number of questions they're throwing at me. "I don't know what I'm going to do, about anything," I admit.

"I know you're tired," says Sophie, "but I have to ask. Does Jake know?"

I shake my head no and they all look oddly happy.

"So, he didn't just leave you to deal with all this on your own, he just doesn't know?" asks Zoe, explaining their odd reaction.

I nod.

"When are you going to tell him?" Zoe continues.

"I don't know if I am."

My mom frowns, Sophie sucks in a sharp breath and Zoe shakes her head in despair.

"I could make this work around my photography." I gesture at my small bump, trying to explain. "But Jake couldn't. How could he fit the demands of a baby around the band? I can't do this to him. Not when they're so close to making it big."

"But it's his child!" exclaims Sophie.

"So what? I tell him and he loses sight of the finish line because of one silly mistake we made together," the lie rolls off my tongue far too easily, but I can't tell them the real reason I don't want to tell him. I won't do that to Jake.

Sophie stares, her eyes glistening. "A baby isn't a mistake, Abby."

I wonder how many more times I'm going to be told that before I accept it. "Soph, this is my baby. Whether you agree or not, it's up to me whether I tell Jake. Now, I'm asking you to please respect the decision I've made." I widen my eyes at her, pleading. She can't tell Jake. If she does it will ruin everything.

They all look away, but the fact they don't argue, tells me what I need to know. They will keep my secret, for now. My decision is final, and no matter the outcome, for me and Jake, the timing isn't right.

It never is.

This day has felt longer than the day I found out I was pregnant and believe me that was loooong. In the end, we all agreed to disagree on what to do for the best.

I'm about to turn in for the night when my phone lights up and I smile to myself when I pick it up to answer. I collapse back on the bed with it raised to my ear. "To what do I owe the pleasure?"

"Long time no speak. I thought I'd check-in and see how you're holding up."

"The girls put you up to this, didn't they."

"I don't have a clue what you're talking about."

Even though we're an ocean apart I can tell Amanda's lying. "Yes. You do."

"Can a friend not call to ask how a friend is doing anymore?"

I pause. "Is that what we are now? Friends?"

"I think so. I'm not sure. But as a potential friend, I'm calling to tell you that what you're doing is wrong."

I picture vividly in my mind the glare she'd be giving me if she were here. I take a deep breath and brace myself for what I'm about to ask. "Did you know?"

"Yes," she answers without missing a beat.

"How?"

"It was a conversation we'd already had."

I try to ignore the flicker of irritation, as her words remind me that on some level, she knows Jake as well as I do. After all, they were in a relationship longer than we were. "Right."

"I think things would be different with you. Everything is different for him with you. *He's* different with you."

"Why didn't you tell me?" I feel a little put out that she would know something so important, yet still encourage me to tell him, knowing what it would do to us. Could it be that she actually doesn't have my best interests at heart?

"Because of this 'woe me' shit you've got going on."

I sit upright on the bed and my grip tightens on the phone. "Excuse me?"

"You heard me, Abby. Woe me."

"Amanda!" The hand at my side that isn't holding the phone tingles and I dig my nails into my palm. I'm not one hundred percent sure what she's getting at, but I can tell from the bite in her tone it's bad.

"Sorry, Abby. The truth hurts sometimes."

"Why are you being such a bitch? I thought we were past this?" And genuinely I did. At the end of the summer when she helped me, it felt like we moved on from the past and any issues we had to do with Jake. Apparently not.

"We are. And yes, we're friends, but sometimes friends kick other friends up the ass when it's needed. As I'm thousands of miles away, this is the only way I can kick you."

"By woeing me?"

"I don't need to woe you; you're doing a fantastic job of it yourself."

"What exactly does it mean?"

"It means that you have poor little old me syndrome."

"Amanda," I snap, beginning to lose my temper. I bring my phone away from my ear and my thumb hovers over the red button on the screen. I fight the urge to hang up on her.

Her pitchy voice echoes around the room, "The reason you're about to hang up on me is that you know what I'm saying is true."

I place the phone back beside my ear. "I hate you right now."

"Good. It's what you needed to hear. You're feeling sorry for yourself because things aren't working out perfectly in your life. Newsflash: Life isn't perfect. When shit gets real, we prove who we really are."

"And who do you think I am?"

"Do you really want me to answer that?"

I grit my teeth. "Can it get any worse?"

Laughter floats down the line. "Everything is always about you and how you feel. Yes, you're pregnant. Yes, you fucked up. Yes, it's a big fat mess. But did you ever wonder when you were wallowing in your bed day after day how this would affect everyone else in your life? And I'm not just talking about Jake."

My eyes burn with the realization that in all of this I've perhaps been more than a little bit selfish and not considered everyone else's feelings. Of course, it's Amanda who's pulled me up on my shit again. I gulp and say, "No, I didn't. Not really."

"When Jake broke up with me, I was heartbroken. I actually hated you. I genuinely believed one day we would get married, but then you came back to Brooklyn that summer and fucked everything up."

"I'm sorry."

I can hear her hair swaying down the line as she shakes her head. "Not good enough. I accepted what happened and told myself he loved you and the two of you were meant to be. But who you're being right now isn't worthy of Jake and everything he has to offer. So, yeah. We might have this newfound friendship, but that doesn't stop me from being pissed that my broken heart might have been for nothing because you're too busy being scared and feeling sorry for yourself to tell Jake the truth."

"Amanda …"

She stops me before I can say anything else. "Don't say you're sorry again. I don't want to hear it. Actions speak louder than words, Abby. It's time for you to grow up and deal with your problems instead of running away. I'm going now, I need a drink."

The line goes dead and my lip quivers, knowing that every single word she said is true.

Chapter Ten

Abby

Last night was a disaster of epic proportions. I knew things wouldn't go well when I finally told the girls and my mom the truth, but I didn't quite expect things to unfold as they did. The conversation with Amanda finished things off perfectly and now I'm questioning everything.

It's still early when there's a knock on my bedroom door. Shuffling to sit up with my back against the headboard, I call out, "Come in," just loud enough that whoever is on the other side can hear.

The door opens slowly revealing Sophie and Zoe on the other side. They walk straight over to my bed and both perch on the edge.

"Do you hate me?" I ask, unable to look either of them in the eyes.

Zoe sighs and replies, "We could never hate you, Abs. You've fucked off on a plane for much less before. We're just …"

"Hurt," finishes Sophie. "Why did you think you couldn't tell us?"

I look up and find their expressions are as downcast as my mood. "I was humiliated," I admit.

"We know *how* it happened," says Zoe, "but what *actually* happened?"

"I threw up my birth control in Kralove and didn't realize," I explain, picking at a loose piece of thread on the cuff of my shirt. "I'm such an idiot."

"Now that sounds like something *I* would do," says Zoe with a smirk.

Hearing the humor in her voice makes me smile so hard my face hurts. "I'm sorry I didn't tell you," I say, "and I'm sorry I ignored you for so long. It was wrong of me. I should have known you'd only want to help. I'm the queen of bad decisions at the minute. I'm working on it."

"At the minute?" says Zoe jokingly. "We've all made bad decisions in the past. Maybe not quuuiiite this grand. I never thought you'd be the one to take the crown I have to say. However, you're forgiven. Christ, you've put up with enough of our crap over the years. Just promise us one thing."

"Yeah?" I ask, my voice much brighter than when the conversation began.

"Don't shut us out like that again," she replies.

"We're your best friends." Sophie nods. "Mistakes and all. There's nothing you can't tell us. I was going to say that we've done worse. However, Zoe's right, this one comes up top."

I start laughing, really laughing for the first time since I left them behind in Leeds, and just like that, with my best friends by my side, everything doesn't feel as overwhelming.

I never should have shut them out and it's a mistake I won't be making again.

There's another knock at the door and my stomach flips. There are only two people it can be, and I have a strong suspicion which one it is.

"Come in," I call out again.

My mom opens the door and steps inside my room, still in her nightwear. The dark circles under her eyes tell me she slept as well as I did.

"We'll leave you both," says Sophie. She stands to leave, and Zoe follows.

When they're gone my mom walks over and perches where they were just seconds ago.

"Hi," she says.

"Hi," I reply, trying to hold her gaze, but failing when all I see in her eyes is disappointment. Instead, I focus my attention on the window. My eyes are extra sensitive and swollen after a mini-breakdown following my call with Amanda and the stark sunlight makes the room painfully bright.

"Look at me, Abby," she says sternly.

My eyes find hers and we sit looking at each other, neither knowing what to say.

Deciding I created this whole mess, so I need to fix it, I take a deep breath before I begin. "I don't want to say, I'm sorry. It's all I seem to do at the moment. But I am."

"I know you are, and I am too."

"You've got nothing to be sorry for. This was all me."

"No, you needed support last night and how I reacted wasn't right. It only reinforced the reasons why you didn't tell any of us in the first place. I was just shocked that you didn't feel like you could come to me, and I put my own feelings before yours without considering why you might have done what you did. Even parents make mistakes. Something you will learn." The smile she gives me doesn't reach her eyes.

"I feel like all I do is mess up."

"That's life, Abby. Nobody is perfect."

"This is taking it to the next level."

She leans forward and squeezes my arm. "I'm not going to lie, you're right. This is bigger than some mistakes and has a bigger impact on your life, but it's nothing we can't work through together. Your father and I, and your friends, we have your back. Always. Mistakes not only make us human, but they make us better and stronger when we learn from them."

My eyes burn, and I look away, struggling to keep hold of my emotions. "I feel like I'm drowning. I don't know what I want anymore."

"Tell me what happened."

"I think you know what happened, Mom. We don't need to have the whole birds and the bees talk again."

"I mean after. How did you get to this point?"

"I couldn't tell him. Jake. It was the end of the tour and I tried," I lie, not wanting to tell her the truth. "Every part of me wanted to, but then all I could think about was that the band was about to make it big. It's taken years for them to get to this point and if I'd told him, and he walked away from his dreams to support me and the baby, it wouldn't have just ruined things for him, but for the whole band."

"You're not teenagers anymore. Things don't always have to be so black and white. You could find a middle ground."

I shake my head. She's making this so much harder. "We couldn't."

Mom lifts her hand and grasps hold of my chin, then gently turns my head so I can't avoid her gaze. "There's more to this, Abby. Please, let me in."

Deciding there's no point in fighting, that she will keep pushing until she gets the truth, I say, "He doesn't want kids."

She looks at me confused. "He told you that?"

"I overheard Sam and Ryan talking."

"Maybe they were wrong?"

"Amanda confirmed it."

"Hmm."

We sit in silence while she ponders what I've told her.

"I understand that Amanda might be a reliable source, however, what Jake felt and told her, might not be the same when it comes to you. There could be much more to the story."

"He also tried to tell me the truth about what happened back in high school, and I wouldn't let him."

A line forms between her brows when she frowns. "But all along this is what you said you needed from him, closure."

My pulse starts to race with frustration. There's a part of me that wishes the first summer I returned to Brooklyn never happened. There's a part that wishes our paths had never crossed then everything would be much simpler. "What if he told me the truth and I still felt the same? What if it wasn't enough? What if after all these years of wondering *what if* and thinking the truth would fix things, it didn't? Where would we go from there? And with a child tying us together, one he possibly doesn't want."

"Relationships take work. You know that. Look at you and Michael Becket, you managed to make a relationship with one of the biggest assholes in the NFL last four years. If you can do that, Jake will be a piece of cake."

I let out a small laugh at the reminder of my giant, football-playing ex. "Michael wasn't that bad. There was more to him than meets the eye."

She purses her lips. "I'll have to trust your judgment on that one. But what about Jake? What have you got to lose really? Him not wanting kids could be a misunderstanding and the baby affecting his career is his choice to make, not yours. There's more to this. What's really going on in your head? You love him, I know you do, so why aren't you fighting for him when he's finally fighting for you?"

I don't answer straight away. I can't because I'm too consumed by the memories flooding my mind. The time we spent together in high school where he became my world. Our first kiss, *my* first kiss. When he told me he loved me, only to backtrack a few days later and act like he couldn't give a damn.

"Abby, say what you *really* feel. For once!"

"Because I don't trust him! He broke me, Mom. You were there, you saw it all. I thought I'd never be happy again. How can I trust he won't do it again? Give me everything, tell me what I want to hear, and then leave me behind? Leave the both of us behind."

"You either have to take the risk," she says gently, reaching up and wiping tears from my cheeks, "or move on with your life."

"I don't know what I'd be moving on to ..." A sob escapes and the walls I've built over the years come crashing down.

The hardest thing to accept when Jake walked away all those years ago, wasn't the heartache, it was the fact he took a part of me with him. He was the one who brought me out of my shell. He taught me how to live. He taught me how to be Abby, not the shy girl who tried to please everyone. He made me feel invincible. He made me believe I could be whoever I wanted to be. When he left, I didn't know how to do that anymore. I didn't know who I wanted to be without him in my life. I still don't know if I do.

"What about Dan?" I sniffle.

"Abby,"—she smiles—"only you know which man you want to give your heart to."

I don't say out loud that there was never a choice to be made. Instead, I shift my body and climb across the bed, lay on my side, and place my head in her lap. She holds me like she did on the front steps of our home when Jake first left. The similarities of the moment aren't missed, and my shoulders shake when the emotions I've been holding back bubble to the surface again.

"It hurts, Mom. It still hurts."

"Shhh, baby, I know," she says, stroking my hair.

Unlike eight years ago, my heart doesn't shatter into a thousand pieces. There's nothing left to break, the damage has already been done.

When I feel like I can catch my breath, I say, "I want to come home, Mom. For good."

Mom left my room not long after our heart-to-heart. Since then, I've been sitting, trying to decide what to tackle first. The thought of speaking to Dan is daunting, so I go for the easier choice and grab my phone from the nightstand to call Sooz.

"Hey, baby momma," she answers after a couple of rings.

"I prefer to be called by my name," I reply, laughing.

"And I prefer to call you baby momma."

If I could see her, she'd probably be winking to try and wind me up.

"Is everything okay?"

"Ermmm."

The brightness disappears from her voice, "That doesn't sound good."

I hate that I'm about to let her down, not just as a roommate but as a work colleague too. "I've made the decision to move back to Brooklyn to have the baby. Permanently."

"Okay."

I wince and when her words—or should I say word, singular—registers, I say, "That's it? Okay?"

"Would you like me to shout at you? Would that be better?" the amusement is back in her voice, and I know she's only kidding, but her reaction stings a little.

Remembering Amanda's 'woe me' comment last night, I pull on my big girl pants and say, "Ignore me, I'm being an idiot."

"I'm going to miss you, Abby, but this was kind of inevitable."

"It was?"

She laughs and I pull the phone away, rubbing at my ear.

"Abby, everything you need is in Brooklyn. Your family, lifelong friends. *Jake*. The moment I found out you were pregnant I knew this was coming, it was just a case of you coming to terms with it and deciding it was the right thing for you. *That's* why I'm okay with all this because if you're telling me about it, it means it's what you want and as one of your best friends, that's all that matters."

"Thanks, Sooz. I don't know what I'd do without you."

"You'd probably still be hiding here in your room." She chuckles. "Want me to have a look at couriers to get your stuff shipped to your parents?"

I hadn't even thought about all the things I'd left behind. "No, you've done enough, I'll sort it."

"Abby, you have enough going on. Let me help. I want to. Plus, I'm here. It makes sense that I'm the one to organize it."

There's no point arguing with her. When Sooz makes her mind up on something, that's it. "Okay, as long as you're sure. When will I get to see you again?"

"I'll be over the first chance I get, and I'll definitely be there when it's time for the baby to arrive. Anyway, I need to get back to work, but remember, you're not alone. We're all rooting for you, and I know when you do decide to tell Jake it won't be as bad as you think."

I smile, to myself when I hang up, but it doesn't stick. My face drops knowing I've said one goodbye and now I have to say another.

Chapter Eleven

Abby

I'm about to utter what are potentially some of the most hated words in the world.

For hours I've been hidden away in my room, trying to work up the courage to talk to Dan and let him know my decision, one I've no doubt he will be disappointed with. Seeing the time on my phone and knowing he'll be meeting with the band soon, I tell myself it's now or never. Mom and the girls want to book flights back to Brooklyn and I can't put it off any longer.

Letting out a huff of anxiety-filled air, I walk down the hall and knock on the door, three down from my own, before I can change my mind.

"Yeah?" Dan shouts, his voice muffled through the thick wood.

Struggling to swallow over the lump in my throat, I open the door and step inside his room. Unlike the rest of the house, which feels like I'm taking part in an episode of *MTV Cribs*, Dan's room is just that, Dan's room. It's so at odds with the rest of the house you could be convinced you were somewhere else. Band posters cover the walls, along with a couple of shelves filled with various music awards which Six Seconds to Barcelona have won over the years. Band T-shirts strewn haphazardly across the floor finish off the teenage boy image he's got going on—the only difference is the smell. Rather than being a sweatbox—the kind that would have my super sensitive pregnancy nose running for the bathroom—I'm hit with the scent of wood and sage.

"We need to talk."

Dan stares at me from the bed where he's sitting with pieces of paper scattered all around him. He sets down the notepad and pen he's holding, then clambers over the mess to the edge, patting the bed beside him.

I shake my head, preferring to stand. My heart knows what it wants deep down, but when I'm close to him, my body has other ideas.

"Want to know a secret?" Dan says, smiling at me weakly.

I nod.

"I hate those four words. Nothing good ever comes from them."

You're not the only one, I think to myself. I clear my throat. "You know I care about you, right?" I try to keep my focus unwavering, attempting with my eyes to show him how much I do. "I will never forget how you've helped me ..."

"You're leaving, aren't you?"

"I have to go back to Brooklyn, it's the right thing to do." Realizing the error in my words, I correct my mistake. "It's what I want."

Dan looks down at his hands. "Can I ask you something?"

"Anything."

"Actually …" He looks up and his blue eyes bore into mine.

Those traitorous butterflies start to flutter in my stomach and my heart starts to race. I don't think I'll ever not be able to react to him when he looks at me like he does. Like the world starts and ends with me.

"I have two questions. One, I don't have a right to ask, but if you tell me, I promise I won't tell a soul."

"O—okay," I stammer.

"Why didn't you just tell Jake you were pregnant? If he loves you like he claims he does, why isn't he the one beside you, helping to hold you together through all this? Why did you tell me and not him?"

I frown, not quite sure how to answer. Instead, I walk over and perch beside him on the bed despite my better judgment. Staring at the carpet, I struggle to decide whether telling Dan the truth is betraying Jake in some way. I come to the conclusion that it's not exactly a secret. Sam and Ryan were talking about it openly where anyone could hear, and Amanda already knew. "Jake doesn't want children, that's why I didn't tell him."

I can feel Dan staring at me while I keep my eyes focused on the floor. The seconds before he answers tick by painfully slow.

"Oh."

"Yeah, oh." I laugh. It's the kind of laugh that says this situation is anything but funny.

"How do you know?"

"I overheard Sam and Ryan talking about it on the tour, right after I found out I was pregnant."

"So, he hasn't told you directly?"

"No, not directly. But Sam and Ryan know him better than most. They have since we were teenagers. If he told anyone, it would be them. And Amanda, his ex-girlfriend, confirmed it."

"Abby, I still don't get why you wouldn't tell him? People change how they feel about things."

I expected Dan would be the one jumping for joy at the news, but I should have known better. He's a good guy and will fight for what's right, even if it means he's the one that misses out.

"Jake deserves to know the truth."

"I'm scared of telling him. I'm scared if I do, he will give up the band and then further down the line resent me for ruining his future."

"The only person he would resent if what you're saying is the truth is himself. You're not to blame for this, Abby. It was a mistake made by both of you. Tell him. You can't do this alone."

"That's why I'm going back to Brooklyn, so I can. Well, not just that. It's time. I've spent years running, all to avoid *him*. Crazy, huh?"

Dan shifts on the bed, twisting his body so he faces me properly. "Not crazy at all. When you love someone you do stupid things sometimes. I have one more question."

I nod, signaling for him to carry on.

"If it weren't for the baby, would I have stood a chance?"

I go to turn away, but Dan grasps my chin, slowly moving his face closer to mine.

"Answer the question, Abby."

"I can't," I reply quietly, "it's not fair to anyone if I do."

He leans in, closing the little gap. I can feel his warm breath on my skin right before he presses his lips to mine. I freeze. All I can hear is the pounding of my heart, or maybe it's Dan's, I'm not quite sure. When he moves his lips slowly, I feel nothing compared to what I feel when Jake kisses me. It's not Dan I want. I know that now.

I press my hands against his chest and push him back gently. "There was never a choice to make. It will always be Jake." I'm about to apologize for what feels like the millionth time, but I stop myself.

"Thank you, for being honest with me," Dan says, and I know he means it. If he's upset by my answer, he hides it well.

Pushing a loose strand of dark hair away from his forehead, I reply, "No, thank *you*. I should go start packing, my mom's booking the flights for tomorrow. She managed to find some seats." I stand and walk toward the door.

I'm halfway through it when Dan calls out, "Can we still be friends? I mean it this time, no funny stuff."

For the first time, I believe him and reply, "I'd love that."

Most of my adult life-changing moments have started in an airport. What can I say, I love a bit of aviation, so why should this one be any different?

I knew there was something missing when I began my departure from London earlier. Everything was slotting into place too easily.

It was missing a bang.

If only I knew how bang-worthy it was going to be.

Dan's private car pulls up outside the departure zone for Heathrow airport and I sit frozen in place. Every single person in the vehicle (apart from the driver) continuously throws nervous glances my way, no doubt wondering if I'm going to follow this through.

"Let's do this," I say, feeling like I'm about to take on the world.

"That's my girl!" hollers Zoe.

Placing my hand on the door handle, I hold my head high, wishing I felt as confident as I'm making out to the others. I begin to pull on the handle and lean my weight ever so slightly against the door to open it. At the same time, the driver attempts to open the door from the other side.

The result: me tumbling out of the vehicle, with Dan diving after me, saving me from any kind of impact with the ground.

"Shit, Abby, are you okay?" he asks, struggling to right us both.

"Gwufar," I mumble into his chest, trying to regain my balance.

Wrapping his arms around my waist, Dan manages to get me standing on my own two feet.

I look up at him, smiling warmly. "Thanks."

Of course, that's the moment we get *papped*. It couldn't have been one of the other times we've been out and about walking the streets of London. It had to be when we were standing in a compromising position. Stars fill my vision. Scrap that, it's the flashes of cameras, coming at us from all angles, closing in and backing us up against the vehicle.

"Dan, who's the girl?"

"Mrs. White, give us a twirl."

"When's the wedding, Dan?"

"Aren't you Jake Ross' ex?"

Now I know why Dan has always worn the ball cap and sunshades, which today of all days he hasn't. Because without them he's prey. Media prey.

I've never really witnessed the extent of his fame. Now it's clear he's shielded me from it. There's a reason why, in the weeks I've stayed in London, we've rarely been out. Especially not together. If we had, *this* is what would have happened. We've let our guard down at the wrong time, in the place where the paparazzi is known to be most rife.

Dan quickly ushers me back into the vehicle as the crowds press inward. When the door slams shut, it's like we've been vacuum sealed away from the rest of the world. The noise and the chaos suddenly disappear.

"Oh my God!" exclaims Sophie. "How are we going to get out of here?"

"I'll call my security team," replies Dan, whipping out his phone, as if having his own personal bodyguards on call is totally normal. It might be in his world, but not in mine. "Are you okay?" he asks after hanging up, turning to me with his brows drawn together.

"I don't know," I reply.

Genuinely, I don't. What does something like this mean? I've never been part of a media fallout before and have no idea what to expect. *I* know the position Dan and I were caught in was innocent and meant nothing. But if those pictures are leaked, I have no idea what to expect.

Thank God it's fall, and I wore a big-ass coat that covers my stomach, otherwise, we'd really have a scandal on our hands. I'd be known to the world as the rockstar's baby momma, but little would they know they had the wrong rockstar.

It takes about fifteen minutes for Dan's security team to arrive. His phone lights up, alerting him they're here and then there's a rhythmic knock on the glass which is our signal to leave.

Dan turns to me for a second time to say goodbye. "I'm going to miss having you around, Abby."

"I'm going to miss being around. But you'll be coming in a few months for the awards ceremony, right?"

He nods his confirmation to both.

I look at the girls and my mom, mentally preparing myself for going back out into the chaos. "Are you all ready?"

They nod, looking anything but. Unfortunately, there's only one way to get to our flight and that's through the vultures. I tug Dan into a quick hug and then he raps his knuckles against the window, mimicking the rhythmic knock the security team used when they arrived. It's the signal they need that we're ready to leave.

We all suck in a sharp breath when the door to the vehicle opens. The noise, which was loud before, has increased tenfold, like the size of the crowd.

"Holy cow," mutters Zoe as we scramble out and the *paps* press in, desperate to get whatever photos they can.

The crowd is big, but the security team is huge, not just in quantity. I mean who's so famous they need more than ten bodyguards? Dan White, that's who. No, they're huge in size, too. Each guy is easily over six feet tall, and a couple don't seem too far off being as wide. They form a wall around us, forcing the swarms of people back as we enter the airport. I thought things would get easier once inside, but I was wrong. The *paps* calling out Dan's name draw more attention to us and high-pitched shrieking from gaggles of fans make the noise unbearable.

One of the security guards glances over his shoulder and says loudly, "We've had approval to take you straight through airport security. They can't follow you in there."

None of us respond, too overwhelmed. All we're capable of doing is placing one foot in front of the other until eventually the noise starts to die down and everything becomes calm. The wall of giants opens, then forms a line behind, blocking us from the view of the crowds behind. Without saying a word, we each move through airport security and the security escort us in the direction of our flight.

"Mr. White has arranged for you to get on the plane early. He didn't want to chance you being hounded again," explains the same guy.

None of us question it, all relieved to be away from the carnage that is Dan White's reality.

"That was crazy," says Sophie, settling into her seat and letting out a sigh of relief. "Are you okay, Abby?"

"I'm just looking forward to getting home," I answer, settling back into my seat.

And for the first time, I really am.

When we land at JFK, nausea hits, and I barely make it off the plane. I tell my mom and the girls that it's delayed travel sickness. It's not though. It's the nerves kicking in at the thought of having to tell my dad that his baby is carrying her own baby.

After parting ways with Sophie and Zoe outside the airport my mom and I spend most of the journey home in silence, neither of us knowing what to say. The cab pulls up alongside the sidewalk and I hop out while my mom pays. I walk around the back of the vehicle and pop open the trunk to get our bags.

"Don't be ridiculous," says my mom, coming up beside me and moving me out of the way.

"I'm perfectly capable of carrying my own bag, Mom," I huff. Being molly-coddled by her and the girls over the past few days has been more tiring than being pregnant.

"You shouldn't be lifting heavy things."

"You know that's a lie, right? There are women who do CrossFit and lift objects heavier than me at like nine months pregnant."

"I don't care about *them*. I care about *you*. Now stop using this as a reason to avoid going in and talking to your father."

Busted.

Looking up at the brownstone building, I sigh. It's now or never.

Making my way up the front steps, I notice Mom isn't following and turn to find her messing with a tag on the bags, making it appear like she's busy. I could pick her up on it because I know what she's doing, but I decide not to. I need to have this conversation with my dad alone.

I step inside and my eyes burn as familiar smells of my childhood, overwhelm my senses. Everything is the same as it's always been. Everything, that is, except me.

"Dad?" I call out.

"In the kitchen," he calls back.

I find him sitting with his arms resting against the table, his eyes focused on the worn pine. He doesn't look up to acknowledge me. It's in that moment, staring at the frown lines on his forehead and the tight set of his mouth, that I realize there's nothing to tell.

He already knows.

"I'm sorry, Dad."

When he doesn't reply, I ask, "Are you mad?"

Finally, he looks up. His eyes glisten in the soft light. "I'm not mad that you're pregnant, Abby. I'm disappointed that you didn't think you could come to us. That you hid this from us all."

My voice cracks, "I was embarrassed."

The sound of Dad's chair scraping against the floor as he stands fills the room. He takes three long strides and then I'm engulfed in his arms. His warmth helps my muscles to relax and erases anxiety I didn't know was there.

"You have nothing to be embarrassed about."

"I screwed up, Dad."

"You didn't screw up. You've just taken a new path."

"What about the band? I've messed everything up for Jake *and* you."

He chuckles. "It's my job to worry about *you*. You're *my* baby, not the other way around. Don't worry about the band, they will be fine."

"I need to tell him."

I know now it was never a question of if I would tell him, but when. I just hope he can forgive me for taking so long when he finds out, regardless of whether he wants this baby or not.

"Of course, you do."

"What if he doesn't want anything to do with us?" I ask, being careful not to reveal the truth.

"It will be a shock, but he's a good man, all things considered. He will make a good dad. He will *want* to be a good dad."

I pull away. "All things considered?"

"Sorry, baby," he says, stepping back and walking over to the kettle. He turns it on then spins around to face me again. "That part of the story isn't for me to tell."

I purse my lips and bite back a remark. The reason I'm in the dark is that it was my choice. He wanted to tell me, and I wouldn't let him.

"I know I only just got home, but if you don't mind, I think I'm going to see if I can meet with Jake now so I can tell him. There's no point in waiting."

Dad's gaze snaps up from the cups, a teaspoon filled with coffee granules hovering in mid-air. "Erm, you can't."

I frown, confused. "What do you mean I can't?"

"Because," he starts to explain, setting the coffee-filled spoon into the cup. "S.C.A.R.A.B. flew to Asia yesterday morning to start their first tour there. He will be gone for the next two months."

If I wasn't concerned already about how our lives would fit together with a baby, this news has made everything crystal clear. Jake and I are on two completely different paths in life and I don't know how we'll ever make things work.

Chapter Twelve
Jake

Everything about the tour in Asia felt wrong, from the moment John West invited us into his office four weeks ago, sitting behind his huge exec desk and confirming that the sales figures made it look a promising place to hit next.

A new market, a fresh start. That's exactly what he said, staring me directly in the eye, saying without saying, that he knew what a disaster the summer had been for me and his daughter. I didn't want to sign the contracts, there was something in my gut, twisting away, telling me it wasn't the right time, not with how I was feeling. But then I saw the excitement on the guys' faces, watched Sam bounce up and down like an Energizer Bunny, and any resilience in me was pushed to the side.

This isn't just about me, it's about them. We're a team. That's what I tried to convince myself, standing on stage, performing in front of thousands of fans in

Tokyo earlier tonight, and failing … epically. The summer with Abby plagued my mind with every strum of my guitar, throwing me off. Not even the frantic screams from the crowd could help keep my focus and I hit bum notes left, right, and center. The last time I performed as badly as I did tonight was in the weeks following my and Abby's break up back in high school. We stepped off the stage to a lack luster applause and the guys couldn't look me in the eye, pissed that I would do this to us at such a pivotal point. I didn't join them for drinks afterward. I had nothing to celebrate.

A few hours later, I'm back at the hotel, sprawled across one of the twin beds in mine and Zach's room, staring upwards, watching the neon lights of the city strobe different colors across the ceiling in the darkness. When the door to our room opens, light floods in as Zach steps inside. I don't even bother looking over and saying hi, too consumed by the pity party I've got going on.

"Seriously? This is what we're doing now?" he says, flicking on the lights.

"I messed up," I mutter.

"That's putting it nicely, but anyway, I didn't come back to talk about that. There's something you need to see."

I sit up, waiting to hear what's so important he'd come back from blowing off steam with Sam and Ryan. "Okay …"

The door opens again and Sam and Ryan both step in, their faces as concerned as Zach's.

"Have you shown him yet?" asks Sam, running a hand through his hair, causing it to stick out more than usual.

"Well considering you saw me walk in the hotel room about a minute ago, what do you think?" snaps Zach.

I frown. It's not like him to lose his temper. It's then that my eyes zero in on the glossy magazines in his grip, hanging at his side.

"What are they?" I ask, nodding at what he's holding.

The guys look between themselves, shifting awkwardly, and I watch Ryan's eye twitch.

"Zach," I say sternly, "hand over the magazines."

"Just remember," he says, stepping closer to the bed, bringing them up to his chest, grip firm so I'm unable to see what's on the front. "We don't know the context."

"Screw the context; show me what's on the front."

He drops them to the bed and the pile slides, scattering across the white sheets. Each cover reveals a full spread image of Abby, standing in Dan White's arms, his shirt fisted in her hands as she stares up at him intensely, and he looks down at her in the same way.

Fuck.

All I can hear is the pounding of my heart and the guys' voices are muffled in the background. I should listen to what they're saying but I'm transfixed on the images sprawled out in front of me.

What the hell?

Why is she with him?

I need to know what the headlines say, but I'm not going to find any answers in the magazines unless I become magically fluent in Japanese in the next few seconds. Ignoring everything and everyone around me, I grab my phone from the nightstand and open Google, typing in the name, Dan White. A second that feels more like an eternity passes by as I wait for the search to load and then I'm greeted with hundreds of results, all related to *them*.

How did I miss this?

Of course, I missed it because I never look. I learned early on, to avoid the gossip columns at all costs. It's like going down the rabbit hole when you enter the media world. It's made of a huge web of lies, expertly spun to bring in the biggest dime.

I know this, I do, but it doesn't stop the stab of jealousy hitting me when I read the headlines. They all read similarly, informing the world that Abby is Dan's new girlfriend, questioning whether he could have finally met "the one." The headline that has me throwing down my phone, jumping off the bed, and searching for my bag though: *Meet the new Mrs. White.*

Barging past the guys with such force Ryan almost falls to the ground, I grab whatever belongings I can find and shove them into my hold-all.

"Erm, are we going somewhere?" asks Sam, one brow raised. "Last time I checked we had another show here tomorrow night."

"I'm not doing the tour," I answer absentmindedly, my eyes darting around the room, searching for my wallet.

"Say what now?" Ryan's mouth drops open and he stares at me like I've lost my mind.

Maybe I have.

All I know is I need to find Abby and find out exactly what's going on. I know I can't trust the media, but the irrational part of my brain is jumping to all kinds of conclusions. She said she couldn't choose either of us, yet there she is in his arms, staring at him like he's her always. Maybe she said it as an easy way out, so as not to hurt my feelings.

She wouldn't just be hurting them. She'd be decimating them like I did hers once.

If I were to trust the pictures, I'd have my answer, and it would be easy to fly off the handle, go back to that dark place where I've been the past couple of years. This summer taught me something though. The feelings I have for her aren't just some unrequited high school crush, which is why I need to hear the truth from *her*.

Finding my wallet on the floor by the dresser, I walk over, pick it up and shove it in the pocket of my pants. "I'm going to find her and find out exactly what's going on."

"But the tour …" says Sam, joining Ryan in the gormless club, standing with his mouth open.

I groan in frustration. Which bit of this don't they get? "I can't do the tour right now. If I do, every set will be like tonight was. A fuck up. I've walked away from Abby twice, partly because of *this*," I say, gesturing around the room that was supposed to be us living the dream when actually it's just a fancy room filled with fancy things that have no meaning. "I don't want this life, not if there's a chance it's what's pushing her away. One day when all of this is gone, I'll have nothing, when I could have had everything."

"And what if the pictures are true?" asks Zach quietly.

Leaning over, I zip up my bag, then stand tall and shrug the strap over my shoulder. I walk over to the small armchair situated underneath the window, where my guitar is resting, and pick it up. I take one last glance out over Tokyo, the sky as bright at night from the neon lights as in the day, then turn back to the guys. "If they're true then I'm sorry I walked away from this for nothing. But this tour needs each of us to give it everything we have, and I can't do that when my heart isn't in it."

"Let's get us some flights booked then," says Sam, grinning like a fool.

"Us?" I ask, confused, having anticipated a completely different reaction, one of the negative variety.

He smirks. "You didn't think you were going alone, did you? We're a band. A team. One thing though …"

"Shoot," I say.

"How exactly do you plan on finding Abby? She's not exactly known for staying in one place for long."

I grab my phone off the bed and scroll through my contacts. When I find the one I'm searching for, I raise it to my ear not bothering to check what the time difference is. Sam, Zach, and Ryan all stare, waiting to see who I'm calling.

"John, we need to talk …" I say, reaching out to the one person I know will be able to help.

I had this whole grand gesture planned. I pictured in my head, that with the band behind me, we'd race through the airport, jump on a flight home, and within a few hours I'd be back in Brooklyn with Abby falling into my arms, declaring her undying love for me. Almost forty-eight hours later and we're finally touching down in JFK. My eyes feel like sandpaper and the sensible thing to do would be to go home and get some rest first. Unfortunately, when it comes to Abby West, I'm known for being anything but sensible.

It seemed like a good idea at the time, hopping on a flight, throwing my dreams away on the assumption that all the articles were a lie. The further into the flight we got, the more my stomach began to churn and what we were doing started to feel like a bad idea, just like John West told me it was. I could be forgiven for not listening to him, even if it was *his* daughter we were talking about. He's like a yo-yo. One day he says walk away, the next he says fight. We came full circle when I called him in Tokyo and, just like Sooz did at the end of the summer, he told me to give Abby time, not to throw the tour away.

The strain in his voice told me what I needed to hear: there was more to the story than he was letting on. *"We'll be on the next flight out of Tokyo,"* is how I ended the call, hanging up abruptly.

We grab our bags from the luggage carousel and attempt to race out of the airport, struggling through the thick crowds. When we do eventually get to the cab station, the line's long. Unnecessarily long. I stand bouncing my weight between my feet, constantly poking my head out to check whether we're getting any closer to the front, which we aren't.

"Do you think we can pull the fame card?" I huff.

"No," says Sam, folding his arms across his chest. "I refuse to let you be that douchey. Seriously, man, you're acting like a toddler about to pee their pants, get it together and wait. It's six AM. Abby won't even be up."

I roll my eyes and stand still, accepting there will be no racing or running in this plan. I'll get to Abby when the universe decides it's time. Finally, we get to the front of the line. I'm ready for falling to my knees and thanking God when I catch Sam shaking his head no. I'm being over the top and dramatic, even by my standards, but what I'm about to do, feels monumental.

I'll be the first one to admit I messed up this summer in a very big way. It only took a few weeks of moping for the truth to hit me, understanding that what I did, dragging Abby on the tour, was the worst move I could have made. Of course, she was going to be pissed and fight me every chance she got. I forced her hand and made her come to me when it should have been the other way around. There's nothing romantic about making someone be by your side; they have to want it too.

What I did was immature and selfish. What I should have done was drop everything, like I'm doing now, proving that nothing else matters but her. It's time to stop telling her how much I love her. I need to show her.

I squeeze into the back of the bright yellow cab, Sam and Zach following behind. Ryan always takes the front. We only had to experience his motion sickness once for it never to be an issue again.

I've lost count of how many times we've done this journey from the airport, coming back from a tour. All those times in the past, we were all exhausted in the best kind of way. Now, you could cut the tension with a knife. This is the first time we've walked away from a gig of any kind, and we've just walked away from twenty-nine of them in one go. Even my grandpa and what he thought was his iron-fist hold on my life couldn't stop me from missing a performance.

Fuck, I hope I've made the right choice.

I struggle to swallow over the lump in my throat when the cab takes the exit off the highway. After a painfully slow journey to this point, time speeds up as we move through the just awakening streets of Brooklyn, a blur through the window. We pull up outside Abby's home and my heart aches when I stare at the same steps where I never should have broken her heart. If I hadn't, maybe we'd still be together.

"Leave the meter rolling," I tell the driver, clambering out.

I know Abby and I know that no matter how romantic the gesture, she's going to put up a fight, just to prove a point. She's not the same timid girl I met back in high school. She's a woman and a feisty one at that.

I make it to the top of the steps and turn back to the cab one last time, before knocking on the door. Sam and Zach have their heads hanging out of the back passenger window and Ryan is leaning over the driver, forgetting that personal space is a thing.

They all give me a thumbs up—the signal I need to turn and rap my knuckles against the long rectangle of glass. I wait a minute and there's no response. Reaching up with my hands, I cup them around my eyes and move in closer, finding darkness inside. Like Sam predicted, they're not awake yet.

It's anti-climactic, but I refuse to let it deter me. I have two choices: sit on the steps and wait, knock until somebody wakes up and lets me in. It's the sleep deprivation that makes the decision for me, and I stand, hammering my fist against the door continuously until the hall lights turn on and Mrs. West opens the door hesitantly.

"Jake?" she says, voice thick with sleep.

Rubbing at the back of my head awkwardly, suddenly feeling unsure of myself, I ask, "Is Abby home?"

"It's not even eight AM, Jake. Where exactly would she be? It's early and she needs her rest. I think you should leave. I'll tell her you stopped by, and *she* can let you know when *she* would like to see you," her words are polite yet calculated, her tone cold.

I know she's not my biggest fan and her reaction is nothing more than I deserve.

"Mom?" My pulse quickens and my throat runs dry at the sound of her voice. "Is something wrong?"

Mrs. West shakes her head at me, a signal to stay quiet, then replies over her shoulder, "Just a delivery. Go back to bed."

No way. I've not slept in over forty-eight hours. My grand gesture won't be quite so grand if I walk away now. "Abby!" I shout, cringing at how desperate I sound.

Her mom rolls her eyes and opens the door wider, muttering under her breath, "Looks like we're doing this now."

"Jake?" Abby says, her voice getting closer.

Finally, she comes into sight. Every muscle in my body tenses and my jaw goes slack. It's the first time I've seen her in nightwear, and I hope it won't be the last. I watch as she pads barefoot along the hardwood floor, each step bringing her closer. I'm mesmerized by the cherry color painted on her toenails, there's something fascinating about the way the gloss catches the light. I never thought of myself as a foot guy, but when it comes to Abby, I'm an anything guy. My eyes trail over smooth skin, drinking in every inch of her lean legs on show thanks to her shorter than short shorts which settle around her petite bump perfectly. They're almost, but not quite, as blue as her eyes.

My dick twitches in my pants, ignoring something in the back of my mind trying to push forward. If Mrs. West wasn't standing, acting as a barrier, my grand gesture would be much grander.

Before I even realize it, she's right in front of me, her eyes drawing me in more than they ever have before. I knew she'd be hesitant at seeing me standing on her doorstep unexpectedly like this, but I wasn't expecting the pained expression that makes me start to panic.

"Jake, what are you doing here?" she asks with an edge to her voice I'm not familiar with. It's like she's scared to see me as she rubs her stomach gently.

My eyes move back down slowly, watching her caress the petite bump my eyes conveniently skimmed over when I first saw her. All I can do is stare and my breath catches. At first, my mind is blank, and I don't know what to say. All I can do is stare.

When Abby says, "Jake?" again, my brain kicks into gear and I back away, almost falling down the steps.

Regaining my balance, I turn and back away, ignoring the shouts of Abby and the band, not wanting to face any of them, feeling totally numb.

Now I know why Abby and Dan were staring at each other the way they were in those images. They aren't just together. She's having his goddamn child! Everything suddenly makes sense. Why she was so distant during the last couple of days of the tour. Why she wouldn't hear me out. She told me she couldn't choose because her decision had already been made.

I thought I stood a chance and I thought I could fight for us, but I never pre-empted Abby being pregnant with Dan White's baby.

There is no us anymore, there isn't an always.

There's only *them*. All three of *them*.

Chapter Thirteen

Abby

Yesterday was a disaster and that's putting it nicely.

Startled awake by a round of persistently loud banging, the last thing I expected to find when I padded downstairs was Jake. He was meant to be in Asia with the band, so what the hell was he doing standing outside my parents' front door? Panic set in when I heard his voice, and I froze on the bottom step, while my mom guarded the door. I could easily have turned back because she gave me an out when she shouted over her shoulder that it was just a delivery, but I quickly came to my senses. If I'd turned and walked back up the stairs I'd have been doing the same thing I've always done. I'd have been running away from my problems rather than facing them.

The whole point of me returning to Brooklyn is to tell Jake about the baby. Unfortunately, it didn't happen quite how I pictured it in my mind. There was no telling, just showing. When his dark eyes moved over my body, at first, they missed the blatantly obvious sign. I didn't have to wait though. His face went pale as he put the pieces together, and all he could do was stare.

When the shock subsided, his reaction was everything I feared it would be. He backed away, eyes wide with terror, and stumbled down the steps like I had the plague, confirming what I already knew. He doesn't want children.

I've never felt pain like I felt in my chest when I watched Jake storm off along the block. Only when he disappeared out of sight did I focus my attention on the cab, sitting in the middle of the road, engine still running, with the other three members of S.C.A.R.A.B. staring at the bump beneath my pajama top. I'm not sure if the chill that ran down my spine was because of the crisp winter air hitting my exposed skin or the cold look Sam gave me from the back of the cab. A look he's never given me in all the years we've been friends, despite the fuck ups I've made.

Nobody said a word, apart from Ryan, who muttered something to the cab driver, who then hit the gas with such force the wheels spun as they took off, leaving me standing with my mom close behind.

So that was mine and Jake's grand reunion. Honestly, you couldn't make this shit up. It's been more than twenty-four hours and I've not heard anything from him since. He's ignoring me and the seven texts I sent asking if we could talk. Sophie and Zoe haven't left my side since I called them. After a brief update, lots of gasping, and an unacceptable amount of cussing, we settled into watching re-runs of *Pretty Little Liars*. How fitting.

We're over halfway through who knows what episode when there's an odd sensation low down in my stomach. I shift, trying to get more comfortable and the mattress moves with me, disturbing the girls. When I'm settled, I feel it again, a flutter. I frown and move once more.

Zoe gives me the side-eye, her bare face looking thoroughly annoyed. "Do you need to go pee or something? You're ruining the best part."

I shake my head, but when it happens for a third time, I feel a small jab as well. I jump off the bed. Well, crawl slowly—the days of me jumping anywhere are long gone.

"What's wrong?" asks Sophie. Her serious expression is at odds with the carefree way her golden hair's piled up in the messiest of buns, the sloth wearing a baseball cap on my "sloth life" T-shirt staring at me.

"I think I just felt the baby move!"

Zoe bounces up and down with excitement and then weirdly starts twerking.

"Gross," says Sophie, catching an eyeful thanks to Zoe's hotpants. "I did not need to see that, and those moves are inappropriate. We're grown-ups now."

"You can be as grown up as you like." Zoe smirks, giving another twerk before jumping off the bed. "I'm still having fun." She throws her platinum waves—this week streaked with hot pink because apparently that's what's in fashion—over her shoulder, and moves toward me. "Do you think I can feel?"

"I don't think so. It's the first time it's happened," I explain. "You should be able to feel it in a few more weeks when the movements get stronger."

Sophie stares at my stomach lovingly, then stands and walks over, pulling us into a group hug. "I can't believe you're having a baby."

"I know," I reply, my throat clogged with emotion. This is what I needed all along, my family and friends beside me. When we pull apart, I find their eyes glistening with tears, just like my own. For the first time since finding out I was pregnant, they're happy ones.

"Are you okay?" asks Sophie when I frown, taking everything in.

"More than okay. It's just strange. I feel different … lighter. Being home, facing up to everything—it's helping. Is it weird to say I feel at peace even though Jake finding out went badly?"

"Not at all," replies Sophie. She shakes her head vigorously and a few strands of hair fall from her messy bun. She blows them away and continues, "This back and forth between you and Jake has been going on for years. I know this isn't what you planned, but I think this will be a good thing, for the both of you."

"That's if you can find him," mutters Zoe, picking at her nail varnish, making it perfectly clear how pissed she is after his performance yesterday morning. "I can't believe he ran off. Who does that when they find out they're about to become a dad? Did he say *anything*?"

"Nothing. He was too shocked. But before we go all anti-Jake, please remember I did the same. The running thing," I explain when Sophie and Zoe look confused. I can't hold Jake's reaction against him because I reacted the same. I'm over halfway through the pregnancy and only just accepting it. Unfortunately, with how things have panned out, time isn't on our side.

Glancing at my desk clock, I find it's only late afternoon. There's not much of a time difference between New York and London, but what little there is, mixed with being pregnant, has me exhausted and ready for climbing into bed. But I need to find Jake. Sending a few texts telling him we need to talk isn't pushing the boat out, and I know if he doesn't want to speak to me he will avoid me at all costs. The saying "It takes one to know one" has never been truer. We're as stubborn as each other.

I walk over to my dresser and open one of the drawers, pulling out an old, larger vest. I whip my pajama top over my head and replace it with the vest, then do the same with my pajama bottoms, swapping them for a pair of black maternity jeans. "Hmmm," I say when I look down, finding the vest isn't as big as I thought. The material pulls against my bump, stretching the vintage band logo on the front so much so it looks distorted. "A trip to the store may be in order."

I look down and rub my bump, surprised when a huge surge of love rushes through every part of my body. The baby moves again, much stronger this time, but I don't tell Zoe or Sophie. I keep the moment between the two of us because it's the moment I know for sure that everything will be okay.

"Where are you going?" asks Sophie, watching as I walk to my desk and grab my satchel from the back of the chair.

"I'm going to find Jake. All we ever do is walk away from each other and leave things unsaid. This is one thing we can't walk away from. This baby is happening, and we need to talk about it, whether he likes it or not."

"Go get 'em tiger!" hollers Zoe, when I throw my bag over my shoulder, leaving them behind in my room with my head held high.

I opt for a cab to Jake's home which he still shares with the band. I shuffle rather than race up the front steps, which are almost a replica of the ones at my parents' home. When I get to the top, I hammer my fist against the front door. It's the only movement I can do dramatically with a human on board, so I decide to roll with it. Waiting a few minutes, I shift my weight from one foot to the other. I don't knock again. The dark entryway makes it clear there's no one home. I pull my cellphone out of my bag, find Sam's name in my contact list, and hit call.

"Yes?" answers Sam abruptly after a few rings.

"Hello to you too," I say sweetly. "Is Jake around?"

"He's around."

"Sam, don't mess with me. Where's Jake?"

A huff floats down the line. "He doesn't want to see you. Do you blame him?"

His response stings, but I ignore it. "I need to talk to him."

"It's a bit late for that, don't you think? Do us all a favor, Abby. Ride off into the sunset with Dan and let Jake move on."

Before the line goes dead, I hear the clink of glasses and rock music in the background, and a voice I'm almost certain is Shaun's. They're at Riff's, where else would they be?

Let Jake move on my ass, I think to myself as I walk down the front steps, ready to hail another cab. *He* is the one that dragged *me* on *his* European tour, which then led to this predicament. A detail Sam seems to have forgotten.

Twenty minutes later I'm outside Riff's unsure what I'm about to find. I don't wait around, afraid if I do, my newfound confidence will disappear. It's busy considering it's mid-week, not that it matters in Brooklyn. It also doesn't matter that the workday isn't over. The type of crowd Riff's attracts goes to the beat of their own drum, doing what they want when they want. Like getting wasted in the afternoon, which is how I find Jake.

From where I'm standing, to the side of the entrance, I know it's him. He's just about sitting on one of the bar stools, his upper body slumped against the bar, his head resting on the arm covered with a tattoo sleeve of a piece of music. The rest of the band are seated beside him, looking like they've had a few drinks themselves. I watch as Shaun walks over to them behind the bar and his body starts to shake at something Ryan says. When he calms down, he tugs the towel from his shoulder and starts wiping the top of the bar, stopping when he looks up and his eyes find mine. His brows draw together. The band, barre Jake, notice and turn in their seats. Their faces all drop when they see me, making it blatantly obvious I'm not wanted here.

I take a deep breath and throw my shoulders back, quickly walking to where they're sitting, or slumping in Jake's case. Four sets of eyes focus on the bump peeking out of my open jacket. I keep my attention focused on Jake.

"So, this is a thing now," I say, observing the mess in front of me. "You're just going to let him get wasted like this?"

"What do you expect, Abby?" slurs Sam, confirming my suspicion, along with his ruffled blond hair and beer-stained shirt, that they're also drunk.

"I'm not doing this here, Sam," I reply through tight lips. "I need to talk to Jake."

He smirks, eyes ice-cold, and gestures at his almost unconscious best friend. "Go ahead, talk away, he won't remember much."

"Why did you let him get like this?"

"*We* didn't let him do anything. He's a grown man and makes his own decisions. Before you start critiquing our actions as his friends, remember we're here with him. We can't stop him doing shit, but we can stay by his side and make sure he's safe, which is what we're doing."

I contemplate my answer before diving in, understanding what Sam is saying but also acknowledging how bad Jake being like this in public will be for their reputation. All it takes is one person to snap a picture and it end up on *TMZ* for them to become the laughingstock of the music industry. "Please," I plead, staring each member of S.C.A.R.A.B. directly in the eye. "Take him home."

"Fine," snaps Sam and they slide off their stools to leave.

Ryan and Zach manage to maneuver Jake so he's resting one arm around each of their shoulders. His feet refuse to work, so they end up dragging him, head lolling, toward the exit, with Sam following closely behind. I don't go with them because they probably wouldn't let me in their home anyway. All that matters is Jake being out of the public eye.

When his dark hair disappears from view, I let out a huff of air, then with a short struggle against gravity, manage to lift myself up and sit on one of the now-empty bar stools. Expecting Shaun's reaction to be the same as the other guys', I'm surprised when he walks over and rests his arms against the bar, directly in front of where I'm sitting.

I raise a brow. "Coming in for round two?"

He grins. "Nah, I know you feel shit enough."

"That's an understatement," I say under my breath.

"Drink?"

"I'm good."

His eyes sparkle mischievously to which I narrow mine.

"You're enjoying this, aren't you?"

I watch him turn and start stacking empty glasses into a tray, ready to wash. "I love a bit of Abby and Jake drama. It's the best form of entertainment," he says over his shoulder.

"I could say the same about you and Zoe."

He stops mid-turn and the glass in his hand hovers in the air. I can't see his face, but I know if I could, his brows would be drawn together, and his lips set in a tight line.

"While we're on the subject of communication, have you spoken to her?"

He spins around and there's a smile on his face that doesn't quite reach his eyes. "Why ask a question you already know the answer to?"

"Shaun …"

"Abs …"

"You can't ignore each other forever."

Pointing at himself he says, "Pot." Then he points at me. "Kettle." Then points at the glossy bar. "Black."

I hold my hands up and laugh. "Fine. But she cares about you, you know that right."

"What's there to care about? *It meant nothing*," he says, referring to the night in Benicassim when they hooked up.

Admitting defeat, I opt for changing the subject. "If you were me, how would you handle this?"

He shrugs. "They have a meeting at the label tomorrow at nine thirty."

I smile, knowing what he's suggesting. "Thanks, Shaun."

"Yeah, yeah. Go home and rest. You and that bump are ruining my vibe."

I roll my eyes playfully and take it as my cue to leave.

A few hours later, I'm tossing and turning, losing the battle for space in my bed thanks to the huge pregnancy pillow my mom had delivered while I was out. Apparently, in the coming months, we will become best friends. I'm yet to be convinced. It's bigger than I am.

I feel another flutter in my stomach and smile. My plan for the morning is simple. I'm literally going to stand outside the label and wait for Jake to come out. It's probably not the best idea I've ever had, but neither was having unprotected sex and puking up my birth control.

Chapter Fourteen

Jake

A blinding white light floods the room, stirring me from an alcohol-induced coma. I can barely lift my head from the pillow, which wreaks of vomit. My stomach turns at the smell, and I groan. It's been a long time since I've woken up feeling like this. Prying my eyes open just about, I squint, finding Zach opening the final set of blinds making the room brighter and my head pound even harder.

"Rise and shine, sunshine," he sings, the pitch ringing in my ears.

"Can you not talk so loud," I grumble, moving my head and pressing my face into another pillow that doesn't smell as bad, trying to block out the light.

"You need to get up," he says. "We have a meeting at the label in just over an hour."

I raise my head, trying to gauge from his expression whether he's messing around. "Since when?"

"Since you thought it would be a good idea to walk away from the tour. We told you about it three times but clearly, you were too wasted to remember." He walks over to my chest of drawers, pulls out some fresh clothing for me to change into and sets them down neatly in a pile at the end of the bed.

"I wasn't that bad," I lie, knowing I was bad, really bad. Like don't remember the past forty-eight hours bad.

"Do you remember seeing Abby?"

I grimace when the image of her standing in front of me with her gorgeous bump on show flashes through my mind. "How could I forget," I say bitterly, looking away.

"I'm not talking about outside her house. I'm talking about last night in Riff's."

My head snaps back, following as he moves over to my desk beneath the window. "Abby was in Riff's?"

He nods. "She was, and she was less than impressed with the little show you put on. Scrap that—there was no show, you were passed out against the bar."

I groan again, feeling like a total ass. I was supposed to have moved past all of this, but how else are you supposed to process finding out the woman you love is pregnant with another guy's baby other than with the help of a bottle of liquor? "What did she say?" I ask, not really wanting to know the answer.

"Not much. She made us bring you home and that was it."

"Okay …"

Zach grabs the towel hanging over the back of my desk chair and throws it in my direction, wrinkling his nose when he clocks the puke bucket beside my bed. Before he leaves, he says firmly, "Get a shower and get yourself together. This meeting is important, and I won't let you fuck it up."

My bedroom door clicks shut and I fall back on the bed, allowing myself a couple more minutes of wallowing before acknowledging he's right. A hot shower and a fresh set of clothes later and I'm feeling human, ready to face whatever John West has to say, which I know isn't going to be good.

"Which part of *stay where you are*, did you not understand?" snaps John, sitting at the head of the record labels conference table, fists clenched, staring daggers at each of us.

He's more pissed than I pre-empted. Luckily, despite the perimeter of the meeting room being floor to ceiling glass, it's soundproof, blocking his raised voice from the unusual amount of people passing by, making it blatantly obvious they're attempting to eavesdrop.

"The stay bit?" I joke, then bite my tongue, wishing I hadn't when eyes resembling Abby's so much it's uncanny threaten to pop out of his head. "Sorry," I mutter.

"Sorry doesn't cut it, Jake. What were you thinking?"

I'm about to reply when he holds his hand up, stopping me.

He looks at the rest of the band. "Can you leave us?" It's not really a question.

Without needing to be asked twice, they nod and scurry out of the room without so much as a backward glance. Traitors.

When the door shuts, sealing us off from the world, he stares me in the eye, and I start to sweat. Amenable John West is gone. In his place is the record exec, proving why he runs the show because when he wants to be, he's pretty fucking terrifying.

"Continue."

"I wasn't thinking," I answer.

"Yes. That was clear when you walked away from a tour that cost millions to set up. Would you like to know how many tickets were sold? How many fans you walked away from like you couldn't give a damn?"

I stare at the table, not wanting to see his face when I reply, "I do give a damn, but I give a damn about Abby more."

He barks out a laugh. "Funny. It seemed quite the opposite when you dragged us all out of bed only to run off at the first sign of trouble. Trouble being my daughter's pregnancy."

I flinch at the word, which doesn't go unnoticed. John's face turns almost purple.

"You were there?"

"It's my home, Jake. Where the hell do you think I would be?"

I shrug.

"Look, your relationship or whatever you want to call it, has never been an issue before. However, it's starting to look like we have a conflict of interests and I'm not sure where we go from here."

My stomach drops and I'm hit with a wave of nausea that has nothing to do with my hangover, at the realization that I've messed things up, not just for myself, but for the band. Coming back like we did, putting everything on the line was all for nothing because she's with Dan, she's having his baby. "You told me to fight for her," I say quietly, trying to explain my reasoning.

"Yes, well, things change."

"Again?" I snap, frustrated at how often he changes his mind when it comes to me and his daughter.

He frowns. "I don't think I need to explain to you *what* has changed. You can figure that one out for yourself. Anyway, the purpose of this meeting was to inform the band that we did some damage control and told the first few tour dates one of you fell ill and need to fully recover before any more shows could go ahead."

I'd know this if I hadn't been so wasted I was unable to check my phone and see what was happening in the media following our departure. "What about the rest of the dates?"

"You have two weeks to get your shit together and then you will be on a plane to Hong Kong for the next leg of the tour. Do this for the band, Jake," he says when I grimace. "This is their dream too.

"And don't worry. You'll be back for the baby. We'll reschedule Japan for another time. Use this next couple of weeks wisely and don't mess up again. There won't be any coming back from it if you do. Now, I have another meeting, so you can see yourself out."

I watch as he stands, straightening his ash-colored tie, before gathering some papers from the table and stalking out of the room without another word. At first, I don't move, trying to process everything that's been said, but my brain keeps coming back to one detail.

You'll be back for the baby.

What the hell is that supposed to mean? Does he expect me to be there celebrating with Dan? Holding his hand through the whole thing when it should have been me? I stand up and leave the meeting room, thinking to myself I'd happily go back to Asia today if it meant being as far away from this mess as possible.

Abby

I've been standing outside the building where my dad's record label is located for over an hour, freezing my ass off. Note to self: buy a coat that fits because New York winter does not care whether you're pregnant or not. I arrived early, just in case the meeting ended sooner than anticipated, not wanting to risk missing Jake.

It's been an eventful hour, filled mainly with people watching in Times Square. Spiderman has asked four times if I need saving; I've taken at least seven group photos and watched one proposal. If I weren't so cold and anxious, I might be close to enjoying myself. Only in New York.

Finally, I see the band moving through the reception area and take a deep breath, preparing myself for what's to come. They're each wearing a pair of shades despite it being overcast—a poor attempt at disguising themselves. You can spot them a mile off, and even through the lightly tinted glass, I can tell Jake looks peaky. Good, it serves him right for getting so drunk.

I wait until they step outside the building before making my presence known.

"Jake!" I call out.

He freezes mid-step, mouth parting in shock. If it weren't for the fact his eyes are covered, I know I'd find them zeroed in on my bump. He shakes his head and stalks off along the sidewalk, submerging himself into the throngs of crowds, moving deeper into the chaos of Times Square.

"Yeah, *see you later, Sam*," Sam shouts after him, then turns and says to me before I follow. "Good luck with that."

I don't reply, there isn't a chance because Jake's head, bobbing above the crowds of tourists, is already becoming less visible.

"Jake!" I shout, scurrying after him, darting through the bodies, and proving surprisingly agile considering my center of gravity is out of whack. "Jake, please stop. I can't keep up!"

He stops in his tracks, quickly turning around. Misjudging how fast I'm moving; I stumble trying to stop myself from crashing into him.

"Shit!" he hisses, lunging forward and catching me in his arms before I hit the ground.

A small group of people passing by throw us concerned glances and when I manage to right myself and stand tall, I give them a reassuring smile, acknowledging that I'm fine.

"Abby, what the hell are you doing?"

"What does it look like?" I snap.

My cheeks begin to warm, my body becoming hyperaware of Jake's arms still firmly wrapped around me. My skin burns where his hands touch my lower back, the multiple layers I'm wearing may as well not be there. We're standing so close his warm breath tickles my skin and now I'm feeling disorientated for completely different reasons, barely remembering why I'm here.

When he lets go of my waist and takes a step back, one of his hands skims lightly against my bump and I hear him inhale sharply.

"I need to talk to you," I say breathlessly, struggling to recover from the moment.

It's like a switch is flicked and he stands taller, backing away. "I have nothing to say to you. Just go back to Dan, Abby."

"Dan?" I step forward, refusing to allow him to put distance between us. If I have to chase him, I will—albeit slowly.

"Sorry, do we refer to him as baby daddy now?" he sneers with venom in his voice.

I shiver and everything goes silent. I don't hear the sound of people hurrying past chatting on their cellphones nor do I hear the laughter and shouting of tourists or the beating drum of a street performer close by. The noise from the yellow cabs, creeping by, hammering their horns as they struggle to fight against the mid-morning traffic, might as well be a jumbo jet passing through, because I don't hear any of it.

All I hear are the words *baby daddy*, running on repeat through my mind. The pieces start to slot together and it all makes sense. When I come crashing back down to reality, the noise startles me and I realize Jake has walked off, leaving me behind … again.

"Jake!" I shout, chasing after him.

Thankfully, a gaggle of young girls see through his 'disguise' and start shrieking, demanding to take a photo with him. Of course, he can't deny his fans. I step in, my face plastered with a sickly-sweet smile, and offer to help. The girl attempting to take the photo nods eagerly and joins her friends, all standing uncomfortably close to Jake. I struggle to bite back my laughter when a hand belonging to one of the little deviants darts out and slips inside his open jacket, attempting to stroke his abs. These girls are crazy! They must be like thirteen? I don't ever remember being so forward.

"Glasses off, *Jakey*," I tease as he bats the hand away.

The girls all start squealing for him to do it. When he does, they cheer even louder, and I smile at the faint blush creeping up his neck. It serves him right for running off on me like he did.

About fifty photos later, the girls let poor Jake go and I step forward.

"Jake, we need to talk, *please*." At this point, I'm all but ready for getting down on my knees and begging.

"Talk to her, dude," says my Spiderman friend, who decided to join in the photo fun.

Without his glasses on, I can see how torn Jake is. He shakes his head and says, "Fine, not here though. I can barely hear myself think. Follow me."

He walks off and I almost lose him in the crowds. I can just about see him when he glances back over his shoulder, frowning when he doesn't find me. I throw my hand up in the air and wave to catch his attention before I'm lost in the hustle and bustle. The next thing I know, his hand is wrapped around mine and he tugs me so I'm following close behind. A jolt of electricity that could light every billboard in Times Square shoots from where his skin touches mine and my whole body hums. I've never felt more alive, and all from a simple touch.

We walk for around five minutes, getting as far away from Times Square as possible. Even when the crowds have subsided and Jake has slowed his pace so I'm able to follow easily, he keeps hold of my hand. My pulse races and all I can think is how good it feels to be walking along like we are doing, hand in hand, like a couple. I smile to myself as we amble. Jake no longer seems to be in a hurry, but I daren't look at him, scared of ruining the moment. I ruin it for myself when I glance down and my bump catches my eye, reminding me why I'm here and of the conversation we're about to have.

I snap my hand away abruptly and Jake looks at me confused. All I want is to take it back and pretend everything is fine, but nothing is, because I'm about to turn his world upside down. I opt for messing with the zipper on my coat as an easy out. He doesn't look convinced but doesn't pull me up on it which I'm thankful for.

"I thought we could go to Central Park," he says, breaking the uncomfortable silence we've found ourselves in. "Do you mind if we make a stop first? I need sustenance."

I don't need to ask why. I witnessed the answer firsthand last night and can only imagine how bad he was when the guys got him home and how ropey he must feel. All I do is nod. A couple of minutes later we're standing outside the same coffee shop we came to when I first returned to Brooklyn, the place that set off a chain of events which led us to this point.

"I'll wait outside," I say when Jake goes to push the door open. It's freezing, but the thought of going inside and being reminded of the past makes my stomach twist in a painful knot.

"Do you want anything?"

"Just a coffee please."

"Usual?"

I nod again and he starts to walk inside, but then I remember the minor detail of me being pregnant and that my usual caffeine fix is a no-go. "Wait."

He doesn't hear me, already halfway through the door.

Rushing forward, I grab his arm and he twists back. Suddenly we're chest to chest. Well, face to chest thanks to him being so tall. I raise my chin, and everything slips away. Every insecurity and every worry over the future disappears. When Jake looks at me like he is, huge brown eyes holding mine, telling me what I need to hear with unsaid words, I forget why the two of us can't be together.

A throat clears behind us, breaking me from his trance and my cheeks set on fire. We move to the side so we're no longer blocking the door and the person behind us slips inside, muttering to themselves. Jake closes the gap between us and raises a hand, brushing a loose strand of hair away from my face. Tingles follow the path his fingers make when they trail lightly against my skin, and I shudder.

He leans in and under his breath, murmurs, "Abs …"

That's when the baby decides to move stronger and more vigorously than ever before.

"Oh!"

"Oh?"

"Sorry,"—I cringe—"the baby moved."

Just like that, the moment disappears. I don't know if it's a good or a bad thing.

Jake steps away, rubbing the back of his neck, giving me a weak smile. "Did you want something else?"

"Decaf," I squeak. When he raises an eyebrow, I tell myself to get it together. "No caffeine." I point at my small bump, or should I say *our* bump, which he has yet to find out is *ours*, trying to make the point hit home.

"Ahhh," he replies in understanding. "So, same just decaf?"

"Please." Thankfully he leaves before things can get more awkward.

A few minutes later, he walks out, a cardboard cup in each hand, both billowing steam into the cold air.

I take the cup from his outstretched hand and say, "Thanks," then we walk toward Central Park.

The silence that before was a little uncomfortable has turned awkward as fuck. I dread to think how awkward it will be once he knows the truth. It takes everything in me not to blurt it out and get it over and done with, but there are too many people around.

Once inside the park, we keep walking. It could almost be pleasant, the break from the franticness of the city, the last of the fall leaves crunching underfoot, but we've already clocked up a hefty distance, and my body aches in an unfamiliar way. I'm not used to feeling so unfit and it throws me, emphasizing one of the not-so-glamorous parts of being pregnant.

The other not so beautiful part, the decaf, which I choke down. It tastes as bad on this side of the pond.

Jake looks at me out of the corner of his eye, catching my grimace. "That good?"

"Worse," I reply, fighting to hide my smile. Now, away from the tourist traps, would be the opportunity to tell him everything. It's peaceful and the depths of the park act as a shield from the rest of the world.

Jake takes the decision out of my hands, taking a sip of his own drink before breaking the ice. "You wanted to talk?"

"Erm, yeah," I reply, discarding my almost full cup when we pass a trashcan.

"So?"

"So …" I say, blushing. God, I have no idea how to start this. "The baby …"

"I don't need to hear the ins and outs of it all," he says with a bite to his tone.

Our slow and steady pace increases, and I scurry, trying to keep up.

"You've got it all wrong," I call, as the gap between us increases. "Jake, Dan isn't the father."

He stops walking and turns, eyes wide with disbelief. "You were screwing someone else as well?"

I stare, blinking a few times, unable to comprehend what he's suggesting. "I'm sorry … what?"

"Were you sleeping with someone else besides me and Dan?" he asks accusingly.

I feel like I've been sucker-punched. Clenching my hands at my sides, I snap, "You have got to be kidding me? How many times are you going to suggest that I'm a slut? It's getting *really* old, Jake."

I storm off and this time it's his turn to chase after me.

"Abby, wait!"

A couple of joggers passing by throw a look in our direction.

"No!" I shout over my shoulder, surprising myself at how quickly I'm able to move.

"Abby, please!" Jake dives forward and grabs my hand, causing electric bolts to shoot through my body.

"Contrary to what you believe," I spit, "I'm not a whore. Dan isn't the father, because the only person I had sex with this summer was you. I won't leave you to figure it all out, because you keep getting it wrong. I'll just put it bluntly." I jab a finger into his chest and he winces. "*You* are the father, Jake. No one else. *You.*"

Jake's face pales and his mouth drops open, then closes. No words come out.

When I storm off, he doesn't follow.

I never expected him to.

Chapter Fifteen
Jake

I'm going to be a dad.
A dad.
I'm. Going. To. Be. A. Dad.
Daddy.
Dada.

It doesn't matter which way I say it or phrase it, it sounds as alien to me now, six hours later, as it did this morning when Abby told me.

"Earth to, Jake," says Sam, snapping his fingers in front of my face.

"Sorry," I mumble, strumming a couple of bum notes. I haven't got a clue what song I'm meant to be playing.

"Come on, what Abby said can't have been that bad." He punches me playfully in the arm before walking over to the mic.

It's funny, this rehearsal room, the same run-down hole we've used since high school, has always been the place where I've come to figure things out. Over the years it's been my saving grace, my hideout from a world I hated being a part of, but not anymore. There's no hiding from this.

Ryan counts us down from the back, smashing his sticks together above the drums, while Sam takes a deep breath then opens his mouth wide, ready to sing the song we're rehearsing.

He never gets a chance to start because I say out loud, "I'm the father."

This time it's Zach's turn to hit a bum note on bass and his head snaps up. "Sorry, what?"

Sam throws his head back and laughs. "Good one. Now stop messing around; we have to get this right before Hong Kong."

He faces the mic, ready to start the song again, but I jump in before he can begin. "I'm not messing around. That's what Abby had to tell me. Dan isn't the father, the baby isn't his. It's mine."

"Ohhh," sings Sam into the mic, the sound reverberating around the room.

There's a minute of awkward silence before Zach mutters, "I knew there was something wrong."

I focus my attention on him. "What do you mean you knew?"

"One of the last nights on the tour I heard her puking in the bathroom, it was pretty late. Then I heard her and Amanda talking but it was muffled so I couldn't make anything out. When they kept disappearing, I started to put it all together. I tried to ask her about it, but she wouldn't talk to me, and then she left."

I'm staring at the worn carpet, mulling over the fact Amanda knew and didn't tell me when Ryan says, "Well, shit. I thought you didn't want kids?"

I frown, remembering the offhand comment I made to one of the foreign magazines we did an interview with a couple of years ago. The words slipped out of my mouth, and I couldn't take them back. Thankfully, the article was run in Danish—a language I know for a fact Abby wouldn't be able to translate.

"I don't. I mean …" I pause and the guys' stare at me expectantly. "I don't know. I always thought I didn't, but this is Abby. Everything's different with her. Why wouldn't she tell me?" This is the part that's confused me the most. That she kept it a secret.

"Where are you going?" asks Sam, when I shrug my guitar strap over my head, unplug the wire linked to the speakers and pack it away.

"I'm going to find her."

No one tries to stop me or pull me up on the fact I'm walking out of a practice we desperately need. They know there's no point, because without answers, I'm useless, and there's only one person I can get them from.

Abby

Following my grand reveal in Central Park, I went to the only two people I knew would be able to help make me feel better: Zoe and Sophie. We spent the day binging on junk food and watching Netflix—the only things I seem to have done since returning to Brooklyn.

It's early evening when I decide to go home. After the crap I've put my mom through recently, I promised myself I'd be on my best behavior. When I step through the front door, I find her pacing back and forth in the entryway, noticing she's dressed overly formally for finishing a day at the office. I cringe, remembering she mentioned that she and Dad were going to some event tonight, she'll be annoyed I've made them late. Then I remember I'm twenty-six years old and my curfew is self-imposed. They could have left if they wanted to.

I shrug off my coat and hang it up, before saying, "You look nice." The silk dress she's wearing is classically beautiful and the emerald color compliments the copper highlights, similar to my own, in her perfectly curled hair. "You didn't have to wait for me to come home. I would have been fine."

She looks over her shoulder then steps in closer and whispers, "You have a visitor."

Even though I know the answer, I still ask, "Would that be a Jake-sized visitor?"

She nods and I swallow hard. I haven't emotionally prepared myself. I thought he'd need at least two or three days to process. Apparently not.

"He's in the kitchen. We have to go; we're already late. Will you be okay?" she keeps her voice low so it doesn't carry through the house, and I sense her hesitation.

I know she wants to stay and stand by my side to protect me. I almost say yes. Almost. But then I remember this is my mess, and in the not-so-distant future I'm going to have my own child to look after, which means I need to grow up and deal with my own problems. "I'll be fine," I reply, my voice cracking, a dead giveaway of how uncertain I'm feeling.

She places a hand on my shoulder and squeezes. "If you need anything, call me and I will come home."

"I won't need anything, but thanks, Mom. For everything."

When she smiles there's a sheen in her eyes. "John! Hurry up!" she barks, flinging open the front door causing cold air to spill inside.

My dad walks down the stairs. I avoid asking why he isn't sitting with Jake talking business. The way his mouth is set in a tight line, tells me not to pry.

"Have a great night," I say, watching as they make their way down the front steps to the black town car which must have been driving around the block, waiting for them to call.

The click of the door closing echoes around the now almost empty house. Almost empty apart from Jake and me, something my body becomes all too aware of. With each small step I take toward the kitchen, my pulse elevates. When I'm standing just outside it there's a strong possibility I might pass out.

"Are you going to come and talk to me or hover by the door all night?" there's a playful edge to his voice.

Suddenly the conversation we're about to have doesn't feel as daunting. I step through the door and find Jake sitting at the table with his arms resting on the top, hands clasped. He doesn't look up straight away and I use the opportunity to take in his appearance. The black T-shirt he's wearing pulls taut across his upper body, every muscle is wound tight. I can tell by the way his brows are drawn together that he's stressed. Overgrown stubble covers his jaw, which tenses each time he grinds his teeth. The dark circles under his eyes make it obvious that my return to Brooklyn hasn't exactly been a happy occasion for him. Seeing him look so defeated, knowing it's my fault, sits heavy in my stomach.

"You can sit down, you know. I won't bite." He looks up through his thick lashes and his irises look almost black.

"I was going to grab a drink," I lie. I actually have an uncomfortably full bladder and more fluids are the last thing I need, however, I'm not about to tell him that. Procrastination is my best friend right now. "Want something?"

He shakes his head and watches intently while I busy myself in the kitchen. I wonder how long I can make the process of pouring a drink last. The glass shakes in my hand when I walk over to the table, sloshing water over the sides and onto the floor.

"Dammit," I mutter, setting the glass down on the table and turning to grab a cloth.

Jakes' hand closes firmly around my arm, and I jump as a bolt of electricity shoots through me from his touch.

"Stop avoiding me, Abby."

"I'm just goi—"

He shakes his head and I find myself mesmerized by the way his dark hair sways with the movement. I've never seen it this long and the way it curls and shines in the light makes me want to run my hands through it.

I tell myself to snap out of it at the same time Jake says, "It's water, it will dry. Sit."

So, we're really doing this. We're finally going to talk about the baby. I don't know where to begin or what to say; how to explain my reasoning. It all seemed perfectly logical at the time but now, with Jake sitting beside me waiting for an explanation, it all feels insignificant.

"So, I'm pregnant." Talk about stating the obvious, Abby.

"We've already covered that part." He smirks.

"The baby's yours."

The smirk disappears. "You weren't joking?"

"Seriously, Jake? You think I would joke about something like that?"

"I don't know what to think anymore, Abby, because I'm struggling to get my head around why you would keep something like this a secret. Why didn't you just tell me?" at the last part, his voice softens. He reaches across the table and grasps my hand in his.

This is not the reaction I prepared for. I thought telling him would make everything change between us. I expected there to be lots of shouting about how I'd ruined his life and that he hated me. But he's staring at me the way he always has. He hasn't run in the opposite direction, and I don't know what to think. I struggle to come up with an answer, so he lets go of my hand, raises one of his, and grasps my chin. He lifts it so I'm staring him directly in the eye.

"Talk to me," he urges. "No more secrets. Tell me what happened, please."

"I didn't tell you because I know you don't want children," I croak, then pull his hand away. I can't think straight when he's touching me.

He grimaces and leans back in his seat, confirming what I already know. "How do you know that?"

"I overheard Sam and Ryan talking at the end of the tour. I'd just found out I was pregnant."

"Okay …"

"I didn't know what to do, Jake. I was already in shock. You were at the end of an amazing tour, and you were all so excited about what was going to happen next. The thought of telling you already terrified me. Then when I heard Sam and Ryan talking and they said what they did, I couldn't. I was afraid of ruining your life with something you never wanted.

"The whole summer was a mistake. I walked away, to give myself chance to figure things out. I was going to tell you, I promise, but I had to do it in my own time." I stop and take a breath. The room is deathly silent apart from the odd drip from the tap. "I'm sorry for how badly I handled things and how you found out. It wasn't right." I raise a hand and rub my small bump protectively. "But I won't apologize for this baby. It's taken me a long time to get to where I'm happy and ready to be a mom. I'm doing this with or without you by my side."

A few painfully silent minutes pass. Accepting there's no point in prolonging the awkwardness, I open my mouth to say something along the lines of we should call it a night when Jake clears his throat.

"What you heard was right. Sam and Ryan were telling the truth. I *didn't* want kids."

"Right," I stammer, trying to ignore the pain in my chest. "Well, I guess that's it then."

I reach to grab my glass before standing but stop when Jake carries on speaking, "You missed a minor detail, Abs. *Didn't*. Past tense. They were referring to an answer I gave in an interview with a Danish magazine a few years ago."

"Okay?"

"If you'd let me tell you the truth when I told you I was ready, this might have made a bit more sense. But you didn't."

My defenses kick in causing me to bite back. "And I asked you for time, which you didn't give me."

"And you wouldn't listen," he snaps. "If you'd told me what was going on rather than running away we could have figured things out together."

We sit glaring at each other. I don't reply straight away, knowing if I do, we'll do the same as always. Go around in circles and never move forward.

"Jake, we've both made mistakes, but we have to let go of the past if we're going to figure this out. If that's what you want? I need to know what you want. Please."

He looks away then his eyes flicker back to mine. "Can I tell you the truth now?"

"The truth about what?" We've been doing this back and forth for so long, I've forgotten why it started.

"Why I ended things between us in high school."

Oh. That truth. Fuck. One of my biggest fears is simmering just below the surface, waiting. What if when he tells me it changes nothing? We can't keep doing this, dancing around our secrets, always wondering what if. We have a chance to lay all our cards out and decide how we really feel. Even if what we decide is painful and messy.

"Fine." I sigh, resigned.

"Could I have a beer?" He gives me a small smile, looking nervous. Jake never gets nervous.

"Yeah, give me a second." I stand and walk to the refrigerator, needing a break from the tension. I stand with my head stuck inside, making out like they're hard to find when really they're right in front of my face.

"They're on the third shelf down, right at the front."

I look to the side, finding an already empty bottle on the worktop.

"Your mom told me to help myself when I was waiting earlier."

Dammit. I grab a bottle and shut the door, then amble to the utensil drawer for a bottle opener.

"Abs," says Jake.

I look over to where he's sitting and find him waving the bottle opener in the air.

Admitting defeat, I walk back to the table and sit down with a huff. "Okay, let's do this."

Jake raises a brow and I cringe. Next time I need to go for sounding less preppy. Whatever expression is on my face it draws a deep laugh from him. The sound makes every part of my body tingle and the baby flutters. Instinctively I rub my stomach again and Jake's eyes zero in on the movement. The tension in the room increases as I wait.

He rolls his head from side to side, cricks his neck then says, "I lied when we broke up and I told you my feelings had changed. I was forced to end things."

My eyes widen. "Forced?"

"By my grandpa."

"I don't understand." I never met the guy but from the few snippets of information Jake gave me, I came to the conclusion that wasn't a bad thing. Still, I can't believe he would have something to do with us breaking up.

Jake pops the cap off the top of his beer, leans back in his chair, and takes a long drink. "He threatened to report me for rape of a minor."

My mouth drops open. "Who?"

His expression turns grim. "You."

My mouth opens and closes as I try to make sense of what he's saying. "I'm sorry, what? But how? We never … Not back then."

"We know that, but it didn't matter. My grandpa was an asshole. He could say whatever he wanted and people would go along with it. Anything to keep the peace." He takes another long drink of his beer.

"Your mom walked in on us. She knew what happened. She would have told people the truth."

Pain crosses his face, fleeting, but I catch it. "My mom was as bad as him. She did whatever he told her to."

I don't know what to say. I never thought that all the times he'd avoiding telling me the truth it was something as dark as this. "Anyone who knew you wouldn't have believed them. I would have told people the truth."

His eyes lack their usual fire when they find mine. "It wouldn't have mattered, Abby. Even if people didn't believe him, he would have scared them into saying they did."

"But you were his grandson …"

His grip around the beer bottle tightens and his knuckles turn white. "He didn't give a shit about me. All they wanted was for me to keep up appearances for the family name. Unfortunately, you didn't fit the bill. I couldn't drag you into that world, not when I didn't want to be there myself."

"I—I—what the hell?" I keep replaying everything he's told me, but it doesn't help. What he's saying is surreal.

His jaw ticks and he picks at the label on the bottle. "Pretty fucked up, huh."

The breakup makes sense now. Why it was so random. Why it felt like I watched a person I didn't know walk away from our relationship. The feeling I was missing something was right because I was. "You could have told me," I say quietly.

"No, I couldn't."

His response stings and for a moment I wonder if he felt that way because he thought he couldn't trust me. "Why?"

"Because you would have tried to make me stay. I couldn't take that risk, for either of us. You might not like what I have to say next, but as much as I wanted us to work, I also wanted my music. It was the only thing I had in my life besides you."

"We could have hidden it like you did your music."

He shakes his head. "I would have gone to jail if he found out, Abs. He was ruthless when he didn't get his way and it wouldn't have just been me he punished; he would have found a way to make you suffer too. I couldn't do that to you, I wasn't prepared to call his bluff."

"I wouldn't have cared. All I wanted was you."

He grabs one of my hands. "Abby, I know it's hard to see my logic right now. I know you think I walked away because of a hurdle we could have avoided, but we couldn't. When I left, I was trying to give us a chance in the future. I believed if we were meant to be, we would find our way back to each other. It was the hardest thing I've ever had to do, especially when I saw you move on with your life."

"Why didn't you tell me the summer I came back to Brooklyn?"

"My grandpa passed away and I was just getting to grips with the fact my life was mine again. I was trying to figure out what I wanted and then you fell at my feet literally and everything I thought I'd figured out changed."

"And the tour?"

"Honestly?"

I nod.

"At first I wanted to mess with you."

I grit my teeth.

"Hear me out," he says when he reads my expression. "Everything changed the moment I saw you again. It became clear that whatever I thought was my reason for wanting you there, wasn't. I just wanted to see you, Abs. Watching you walk away almost broke me and I missed you every fucking day. Those two years without you felt longer than the six before."

"Now you know how it feels," I huff, then backtrack. "Sorry, I'm trying to get my head around all of this. I still don't understand why you don't want children."

"My grandpa told me once that we're a product of our upbringing and we become the people who raise us. I was scared I was going to become him. The thought of putting a child through the shit I had to deal with felt wrong, so I got it into my head that I just wouldn't have them. I answered the magazine's question without thinking it through."

"It wasn't just a flippant comment to a magazine, Jake. Amanda knew as well …"

"Amanda?"

"She told me it was true, so you must have said as much to her."

He groans. "I did because she wasn't the one for me. I couldn't see that life with her. When you came back that summer, things changed."

My breath catches in my throat when he reaches up and rubs his thumb gently against my skin. He leans in close so there's hardly any space between us and I struggle to focus on what we're talking about.

"I can see everything with you, Abs. I want that future."

"What does that mean?" I reply, leaning away, needing space to breathe, terrified of the answer.

"It means I want this baby. Am I pissed you didn't tell me? Yeah. But we're both guilty of keeping secrets when we should have talked and figured things out together. I want to move forward from all this. I want to be there for the baby. If you want me there that is.”

My lip quivers and I bite down, not wanting to give away how overwhelmed I am. “I don’t know where we go from here. I just … I don’t know.” I didn’t prepare myself for this. The walls I’ve built around my heart over the years are strong. The thought of taking them down and trusting him after everything we’ve been through is more terrifying than the thought of raising this baby alone. At least doing it alone, I only have myself to rely on and the only expectations I have are the ones I set myself.

It’s clear Jake can sense my reluctance when he says, “It’s been a long day. We can do this slow. There’re no set rules. We can figure out what works for us and do it our way.”

“Okay,” I reply. My instinct is to run and hide, but instead, I offer him a chance to prove this is what he wants. “I have a scan booked in a couple of days. I missed one when I moved back from London and I’ve only just managed to get my medical care here set up. Would you like to come?”

His eyes light up. “Seriously?”

“Yeah,” I say, grinning at his reaction. “I’m sorry you missed the others and I’d love for you to be there. If you want to that is?”

“I’d like that.” He drains the rest of his beer then pushes his chair back, the screech of it moving against the floor signaling the end of the conversation. “I should get going, it’s late.”

“Okay.”

We both stand and I follow closely behind as he walks to the front door.

“I’ll message you with the details of the appointment tomorrow.”

He shrugs on his jacket and our gazes clash. He takes a deep breath and I prepare myself for what he's about to say or do. I'm stumped when he replies, "That would be great. I'll see you later."

A sinking feeling hits me when I watch him step out into the night. Everything has changed and I can't decide if it's for better or worse. We discussed the past, we discussed the baby, but at no point did we discuss what everything means for us.

After all that's happened, I don't even know if there is an us anymore.

Chapter Sixteen

Abby

I'm a giant ball of anxiety. My scan is tomorrow and as promised, I sent Jake the details of the appointment and he agreed to be there. Not an ounce of small talk, just: *See you there.*

I still have the whole of today and tomorrow to get through. Time is passing painfully slow and my nerves are getting the better of me. I grab my cellphone off my desk to call the one person I know will help make things seem clearer.

Sooz answers on the fifth ring, "Let me guess. He knows and his reaction wasn't as bad as you thought it would be."

"And you came to that conclusion how?" I grin even though she can't see me.

"My superpower is knowing all."

I roll my eyes.

"Stop rolling your eyes."

Maybe she really does have hidden powers.

"Are you there?" she asks when I don't say anything.

"I don't know, you tell me …"

"Har har, very funny."

"I know I am. I might even venture into comedy."

"Sorry, Abs, I hate to be the one to tell you but you're too uptight for that."

"Coming from the workaholic." I scoff.

"Hey," she says, her voice turning serious, "I actually wanted to speak to you about something so it's perfect that you called. It's going a bit off-topic, and I know you had something you wanted to talk about which is why you rang, but can I run this by you first?"

"Shoot." I flop back on my bed, playing with a strand of hair absentmindedly. My body sags into the mattress and every achy muscle relaxes. I passed the halfway mark in pregnancy and it's like the baby went "Right, let's grow." Every day my stomach gets bigger. It's fascinating yet terrifying at the same time, watching my body change like it's doing. And the tiredness, now that's something else entirely.

Sooz clears her throat and I'm hit with something I never expected. "Okay, so, I've booked my flight to come and see you. However, I may have booked it for a couple of months earlier than we planned and I may have made it a one-way ticket."

I blink and frown at the ceiling. "I'm sorry, what?"

"Remember how we always spoke about jumping ship. I did it; I jumped."

"What about your job?"

"Duh, I handed in my notice."

"Wait," I say, trying to put the pieces together. "Let me get this straight. You've handed in your notice and you're coming here. To Brooklyn?"

"Permanently," she confirms.

I try to sit up quickly but gravity has other ideas. It's more slow motion, accompanied by a grunt. "What are you going to do when you get here? How are you going to find a place to live?"

I should have known better than to think she wouldn't have such minor details figured out. This is Sooz, she has *everything* figured out.

"Well, there's this little thing called technology that allows you to do virtual tours of apartments. I found one I liked, and it was an absolute steal, so I signed the contract. It's three bedrooms and there's plenty of space for all the crap babies come with."

I grin to myself so hard my face hurts. "Three bedrooms and baby crap. Anyone would think you were suggesting we live together."

"That's exactly what I'm suggesting."

"And work?"

"We start our own PR company like we said we wanted to."

My grin turns to a frown. She's taking a huge risk and about to uproot her life yet she's rattling things off like it's as simple as hopping on a bus. "We need more than two people to handle all that stuff."

"That's why we have five," the smirk in her voice is clear down the line.

I can tell she's loving dragging this out, knowing something I don't. "And those five are?"

"Me, you, Amanda, Sophie, and Zoe."

My mouth drops open so far I'm surprised my jaw doesn't hit the floor. "How long have you been plotting this?"

"Since I found out you were pregnant. Actually, since the summer when I saw how well we all worked together on the tour. I had the idea and when you told me you were pregnant; I knew a lot of things would change. So, I started plotting, speaking with the other girls, and hey-ho, a foolproof plan was born."

I knew something was off with her. She took everything in her stride. The few times I called, extending my trip in London and then when I told her I was moving back to Brooklyn, she sounded like she couldn't have cared less. Now I know it's because she had this in the pipeline all along. She didn't care that I wasn't returning to Cape Town because she wasn't going to be there either.

I hum down the line, not quite convinced by what I'm hearing. I mean, it makes sense, in some warped kind of way, but there are so many loose ends, especially where Zoe and Sophie are concerned. So, I say as much. "Where do Sophie and Zoe fit into all of this?"

"Well, with Zoe's social media profile, we have access to a huge market. Think of us being a one-stop shop. PR execs, check. Photographer, check. Make-up and hair artist, check."

"And Sophie?"

"Sophie's spent so long in college she's qualified to cover any job she wants."

I start laughing uncontrollably and the baby swirls around, joining in the fun. It's only when I stop a couple of minutes later, I realize I haven't laughed or felt as content as I do in a long time. A really long time. The future, although not what I imagined it be, and not following the easiest of paths, looks the brightest it ever has. I finally feel like everything is coming together. Well, everything apart from me and Jake.

"Okay," I say breathlessly, recovering from my spurt of laughter. "You've convinced me, but we're going to have our work cut out. Starting from scratch is going to be hard."

"And that's where you're wrong."

"You really do have all the answers today, don't you? Go on …"

I picture her in my mind, pacing what is now our old apartment in Cape Town, itching to put the final piece of the puzzle in place.

"Two of the biggest rock bands in the world have agreed to use our services."

The smile is wiped right off my face. "Sooz, no."

"Yes, Abby," she says, determined. "We're professionals and we can do this. I have a plan to recruit more bodies once we start getting more business, so you wouldn't even have to work with them. I know you want to say no, but you can't. Opportunities like this don't come along very often; we'd be stupid not to take them on as clients."

I let out a long exhale, but I don't say no. She fights well. It's why she's the best.

Shoving down any negative feelings I have about working with Dan and Jake, I all but squeal, "We're really doing this?"

Sooz takes the squealing reigns and I hold the phone away from my ear, protecting it from the high-pitched shrieking that fills the room.

When she calms down, she says, "So, you need to meet up with Amanda in a few days to scope out office space. That way we can get contracts signed and things set up ready for when I arrive."

I nod, bemused.

"Can you do tomorrow?"

"No can do," I reply.

"Big plans?"

"I have a scan and Jake's coming with me."

She gasps. "Okay business talk can wait. Tell me everything."

I spend the next five minutes going over everything that's happened between me and Jake since I returned to Brooklyn.

"Wow. I mean … wow. This is a good thing, right?" she sounds as unconvinced as I am.

"It's a good thing as far as the baby is concerned but as far as things for me and Jake, I don't have a clue."

"What do you want to happen?"

The high from earlier evaporates and I'm left feeling flat, not knowing what I want to do with this area of my life. It could all be so simple, we could ride off into the sunset together, play happy families. But what happens when shit gets real? When Jake's on tour for weeks on end. Hell, the last time we were together for an extended period of time was in high school. We've both changed since then. We know we love each other, there's no questioning that, but can we work as a couple? There's a big difference.

"I think," I say, swallowing over the lump in my throat that's suddenly appeared, "I want us to stay friends." The baby gives a huge kick and I take it as a sign that my decision is the right one.

"Your friend list is increasing rapidly," she jokes, referring to me and Dan.

"I'd rather have Jake in my life as a friend than risk not having him in my life at all. So much is about to change, adding a relationship to the mix wouldn't be right, it would be too much pressure and we'd never work."

"Abby," says Sooz gently down the line. "You don't need to explain to me, you don't need to explain to anyone. Do what feels right and it will all work out in the end."

"You sound so certain."

"I'm not at all, but life is about making choices and when you do, they have to be the ones you want, not anyone else."

We carry on chatting for a while, keeping the conversation light. When it's time to end the call, I say, "I can't wait for you to be here."

"Me too," replies Sooz. "It's been a long time coming."

We hang up and I feel a million times lighter. Life feels like it's moving forward, but there's one thing still not sitting right with me.

Sam.

In all the time I've known him, never has he been as cold toward me as he was last night. We've been through a ton of shit together and he's always given me the benefit of the doubt, but this time, I feel like some groveling might be in order. I don't bother putting my phone down. Knowing what I need to do, I find him in my contacts and hit call before I have a chance to second guess myself. It rings for a while then diverts to voicemail. I don't leave a message because I know he won't listen to it. Instead, I hang up and hit call again.

I repeat the process four times before he barks down the line, "What?"

"Hi, Sammy."

"What do you want, Abby?"

"To talk to you," I reply sweetly.

"You rang, you talked, job done."

Before he can hang up, I quickly say, "If our friendship has ever meant anything, you won't hang up right now."

There's silence and then he sighs. "Pulling the friendship card, low blow."

"Not low blow, Sam. You won't hear me out. You haven't even heard my side of the story."

"I don't need to. It's the same old shit it always is. You fucked up, Abs."

Abs. It's not *Abby bear* but it's better than plain old Abby and even though what he's saying hurts, there's a glimmer of hope. "Meet me somewhere so we can talk. Please." If he were here with me, I'd be down on my knees begging.

"Fine. Meet me in an hour at Riff's."

"Riff's? Seriously? I don't think this is the kind of conversation we should have where everyone we know can hear."

"When you fucked off without saying goodbye, pregnant with my best friend's child, you gave up the right to make that choice. This is the only chance you get. I'll see you there."

The line goes quiet before I can say anything else and when I look at my screen, I see he's hung up. Not so gracefully, I stand and walk to my mirror then stare at myself. Teary eyes gleam back at me. I allow a few to fall, telling myself for today they'll be the last. Sam's reaction is far from unjust, but what's important now, like with so many of the mistakes I've made recently, is how we move on.

"Chili cheese fries, really?" I wrinkle my nose at the plate of spicy grease across the table.

Sam stares at me, his icy blue eyes cold for reasons other than their color. "If you're going to start critiquing my food choices feel free to leave."

We've been in Riff's for over half an hour and that's the longest sentence he's said to me.

"I'm not critiquing your food choice … it's just …" I hate how quiet I sound but being in public with him acting like he is, isn't fun.

He cups his right ear with his hand and leans forward. "Speak up, Abby, I can't hear you."

I scowl and a string of names too inappropriate to be spoken in public run through my mind. Gritting my teeth, I try to keep my cool. "Sam, I'm pregnant."

"Yeah, I know, and you left it what si—"

"Sam!" I snap. "Stop. I get it, you're pissed with me. I'm pissed with me. I've spent most of this pregnancy hating myself for how I handled things. But part of being pregnant is a heightened sense of smell." I lean across the table and throw the plate of fries a look of disdain. "Unless you want me to puke everywhere, I suggest you get rid of the chili cheese fries."

He glances down at the fries and then back up at me. My words must give what is most likely the green tinge to my skin a new meaning because he stammers, "I'll be right back."

I watch as he grabs the fries and speeds off, discarding the plate at the bar with Shaun who looks over, concern written all over his face. I give him a reassuring nod, but he doesn't take his eyes off Sam who slides back into the booth where we're seated.

"Sammy, I know you're upset, and you have every right to be, but will you please hear me out?"

"Fine." He crosses his arms tightly over his chest and scowls like a toddler.

I refrain from rolling my eyes; the last thing this situation needs is him on the defensive more than he is already. "Why are you so mad at me?"

He tilts his head to the side.

I decide to rephrase, "Maybe what I should ask is which are you most mad at me for?"

"Keeping this from Jake. He might be acting all mature but I'm not him and I'm not afraid to say that what you did was wrong. I expected more from you."

"I know. I'm sorry."

"Are you going to get that shit tattooed somewhere?"

"Sam …"

"Abby …"

We stare at each other. Neither wanting to back down.

"I heard you and Ryan talking at the end of the tour." If he wants the truth, I'll give him all of it, even the bits he won't like.

"Talking about what?" he asks before I get a chance to continue.

"About Jake not wanting kids."

This time it's Sam's turn to look green. "You heard that?"

"Yep. Around four, five if we're pushing it, hours after finding out I was pregnant, and my world was about to be turned upside down. I guess I could be forgiven for not being in the right frame of mind to act rationally."

For so much of my pregnancy, I've felt guilty about how I handled things. The more I say everything out loud, I realize that although my actions were wrong, they weren't unjustified. They were merely an abnormal reaction to an abnormal situation.

Ice age Sam disappears along with his cold demeanor. He drags a hand through his dark-blond hair the way he always does when he's stressed and looks at me sadly. "Abs, if I'd known you were there …"

"You wouldn't have said anything. I know, I get it. There are so many things that could be different if we'd all known the truth. A bit like me knowing about Jake's grandfather."

"You know?"

I nod. "Jake told me last night."

"Oh …"

"Yeah." I chuckle. "Oh."

The noise from the rest of the bar amplifies, the laughter and clinking of glasses sound like they're from another reality. In my peripheral vision, I catch a gaggle of groupies standing and gazing in our direction, pointing at Sam and whispering. If they come any closer, this conversation is over. The last thing Jake and I need is our dirty laundry making front-page news again.

"Erm, right." Sam cracks his knuckles then knocks them against the table. He's one big ball of nervous energy. "So … *you know.*"

"Sam, are you going to spend the whole time repeating yourself?"

"Yes. No. I don't know. Wow. *You know.*"

"Sammy," I groan.

"Do you feel differently now …"

"*I know?*" I reply, wiggling my eyebrows. "Honestly. It hasn't sunk in yet. I never expected what he told me."

Sam's expression turns serious, something that never happens; he's the life and soul of the party. "I get it. It's a lot to take in. His grandpa was such a prick."

"Understatement of the century."

"It would appear we agree on something for the first time since you came back."

"Sam." I sigh. "I've never not agreed with you. I know I handled things badly. I know I fucked up more than usual and that this is different than before. I get that. Why do you think I'm fighting so hard? I want to make this right, not just with me and Jake. With all of you. I need to. It's not just about me anymore."

His eyes trail down to my small bump, hidden beneath my black tank and oversized purple plaid shirt which hangs open slightly. "You're going to be a mom."

"And you're going to be a godparent. I mean if you want to that is …" He jumps up, cursing when his thighs connect hard with the table causing my extra-large glass of water to wobble dangerously. "I mean, I have to run it by Jake."

"No, you don't," he grins. "I accept."

I giggle and make a mental note to tell Jake before I forget. "So, does this mean I'm forgiven?"

I expect him to give me some kind of speech and that to be it. What I don't expect is him to shuffle out of the booth and sit beside me. He tugs me into his side and engulfs me in a hug I've needed since the moment I found out I was pregnant.

"God, I missed you, Abby bear," he murmurs into my hair and my shoulders start to shake. He pulls back looking alarmed. "*That* made you cry?"

I grab one of the napkins and wipe my nose before the situation can become any more embarrassing. "Hormones."

Sam grimaces. "How many hormonal months to go?"

I shrug and sniffle. "Four. I think?"

"You think?"

"I have a scan tomorrow. They will confirm everything then. Another perk of pregnancy: being forgetful AF."

"Do you need someone to go with you?"

I shake my head. "Jake's coming."

Sam looks surprised but when he sees my frown he smiles. "That's great. Really. This will take time, for both of you, but I think you guys can do this. I know you can make things work after everything you've been through."

My pulse quickens knowing what he's suggesting, and unease sweeps through me. "Sam … I don't know if I want to be with Jake right now."

"I don't follow."

"I think I want us to be friends. Just friends."

"But, Abs—"

I hold my hand up before he can say anything that might make me question my own judgment. "Sammy. I *need* us to be friends. What he told me yesterday has changed everything and I don't know what I think or feel anymore. I need to get my shit together first. If I don't, it will be a disaster."

I wait for him to fight back and tell me I'm wrong, but he doesn't.

"I get it."

"Really?"

He nods then asks, "Want to know what I think?"

I hesitate. "Even if I say no you're going to tell me anyway."

"I think you and Jake were always meant to be together; the timing is just a little off."

"Like eight years off?"

He laughs. "Eight years out of a lifetime is nothing."

"I'll try to keep that in mind."

"Abs, it's true. When you and Jake are meant to be together the pieces will slot together and you'll wonder what the problem was."

"You've changed your tune."

Sam laughs. "I was pissed that's all. I'm rooting for the two of you. If there's a guaranteed always in this world it's the two of you."

I smile up at him. "Are we cool?"

He smiles back. "As long as you don't break my best friend's heart again."

I keep my expression neutral, trying not to give away how his words make me feel. I might have broken Jake's heart once, but mine breaks each day when I wake and Jake isn't by my side. I love him and my heart wants him more than anything. But sometimes life isn't about what the heart wants, and this pregnancy has opened my eyes to that.

What if Sam's wrong? What if it was never about our timing? What if all along we were never meant to be together?

Chapter Seventeen

Jake

As promised, Abby messaged with the time and place to meet for the scan.

I spent an hour staring at my phone, trying to come up with a reply. I was still sitting at the center island in the kitchen when Ryan walked in and asked what I was doing and why my face looked weird. He probably wasn't the best person to go to for advice, but the other guys were out, and I was desperate.

The *see you there*, he recommended, fell flat because I haven't heard from Abby since.

"How are you feeling?" asks Zach, walking into the entryway as I'm shrugging on my jacket, ready to leave.

"Fucking terrified," I admit.

"This is just routine though? Right? Abby's had all the important scans and appointments already."

I raise a brow.

He continues babbling, "I mean, I'm just guessing, judging by how far along she looked when we saw her at Riff's ..." Stopping himself, he grabs a handful of chips from the bag he's holding and shoves them in his mouth.

"Have you been googling baby stuff?" Normally, I'd laugh but I'm too fucking nervous to do anything.

Half-chewed chips fall from his mouth and back into the bag when he goes to answer. I make a mental note not to have any leftovers.

He finishes chewing and swallows before attempting to answer again. "It's called being supportive."

"I know. Thanks," I reply, failing to smile.

"I'm sure everything will be fine. Did you sleep? You look like crap."

"No, I couldn't. I don't know what I'm doing." I groan.

"Well, duh." He laughs. "That's kind of expected. You just found out Abby is having a baby and that it's yours. I'd say feeling out of your depth is a normal reaction."

"I know, but I feel like I should be doing more. Helping her in some way. I don't know where to begin or how to ask what she needs. You should have seen her the other night. She was a closed book. I haven't got a clue what she's thinking."

"Don't do anything yet. Just be there for her. She's spent half of her pregnancy thinking you didn't want kids and that she was going to be a single parent. This will be an adjustment for her too. Just showing up today will be enough. Use it as a chance to prove to her that you want this and you're not going anywhere."

He's right, I know he is, and his words are exactly what I needed to hear. I stand taller and straighten out my jacket, then rub my palms against my pants, letting out a ragged breath. "Okay, I can do this. Thanks, Zach," I say on an exhale, feeling some of the anxiety leave my body.

We fist bump then I pick up my keys and shades from the side table ready to go.

I'm at the door and about to open it when Zach calls over, "Before you go, don't forget we're not just a band, we're brothers, as Ry likes to put it. You're not alone in this either. Whatever the two of you decide to do to make this work, the band will support you."

"Thanks," I say quietly and leave before he can see how overwhelmed I am by his words.

Thirty minutes later I'm standing outside the building where our appointment is scheduled, waiting for Abby to arrive. Get it together, I tell myself as I lean back against the wall and look up, inhaling the crisp air. It does nothing, I feel like I'm about to pass out.

"Are you okay?"

My head snaps down and there she is standing right in front of me, eyes bluer than the clear November sky, cheeks glowing pink from the cold, framed by her dark, wavy hair. She isn't wearing a scrap of make-up, but she doesn't need to, she looks perfect without it. I always thought she couldn't get any more beautiful, but I was wrong. Seeing her in front of me, bump poking out through the gap in her coat, knowing it's our child she's carrying, has my heart hammering in my chest. Nothing could ever compare to how I feel about her and even though everything is a huge mess and we're both pissed at each other for a multitude of things, it doesn't matter. Since the day I ended our relationship, I've always felt like there was something missing in my life.

There was.

Her.

"Jake?" she says, breaking me from my thoughts.

"Sorry," I stammer. "I'm fine. Just nervous." Pushing away from the wall, I stand straight, towering over her. "Should we go in?"

She nods and I walk behind, letting her take the lead.

It feels like we've only just got settled in the waiting area when Abby's name is called, and we follow the nurse into a large room. While Abby gets settled on the bed and her OB/GYN rattles off information, I glance around, taking everything in. Posters full of information stare at me from the walls, making everything feel even more real and stars begin to creep into my vision.

"You can sit down," says Abby quietly, grasping my hand and squeezing.

I sit, sheepishly, but when I catch Abby's eye, all the feelings of embarrassment disappear. I remind myself she's been here twice already, feeling how I'm feeling. Embarrassment is replaced by guilt when I realize she's had to process all of this alone.

She didn't have to be, I remind myself.

The next few minutes are a blur and I struggle to hear the OB/GYN reeling off information over the ringing in my ears.

Abby's soft voice cuts through everything, "Jake, look at the screen."

My eyes move slowly from hers to the screen and everything stops.

I'll never forget the moment I watch our baby moving inside her for the first time. It's the moment I know, no matter what it takes, no matter how long I have to wait, that nothing else in life matters apart from this.

"Do either of you have any questions?" asks the OB/GYN with a warm smile.

"I'm fine," replies Abby.

I'm incapable of doing anything other than shaking my head. It must be a normal reaction because she doesn't seem phased and focuses her attention back on Abby, scheduling her next check-up. I go to log the date in the calendar on my cell when I remember I'm supposed to be on the other side of the world, touring Asia until almost the end of Abby's pregnancy. A minor issue we have yet to talk about.

"Are you ready to go?" asks Abby.

"Yeah, sure," I answer, still in a daze. I didn't even notice her getting up from the bed or putting her coat back on.

"Is everything okay?"

When did we get in the elevator? "Everything's fine."

"Jake …" Having none of it, she steps closer and if I was in a daze before, it's nothing compared to now, having her standing almost pressed up against my chest with her hand on my arm. My head swims when her perfume hits my nose, the same one she wore in high school that lingered on my sheets for days after I had her in my bed.

Something takes over and I can't stop myself from leaning down, closing what little gap's left between us. Her lips part and she tilts her chin, giving me the signal I need that she wants whatever is happening too. Like with everything in our relationship, the timing isn't right and the elevator pings, causing Abby to jump back just when the doors start to slide open.

"So, what now?" I ask, rubbing the back of my neck.

Her eyes follow my hand, and a smile tugs at her lips. "We could go somewhere and talk?"

"Let's go back to mine," I suggest.

We might have Ryan to deal with but it's better than the wrath of John West. I've managed to move from being one of his most promising artists to the top of his shit list in a relatively short space of time. For now, I think it's best we keep our distance, especially when it comes to things involving his daughter.

A split second is all it takes for everything to go wrong. When we step outside the revolving doors to the building, we're suddenly swarmed by paparazzi.

"Shit," I mutter when they start pressing forward, their faces replaced with cameras and flashes.

I don't know where to look or how to get us out of this and Abby looks worse than I feel. Unknowingly, she does the worst possible thing she can, raising a hand to her bump protectively. That's all it takes to spark the fire and shouts fill the air. Everything is frantic and I'm barely able to make out what they're saying, until one guy rushes forward, shoving his camera in my face.

"I thought the daddy was White. What's going on, Jake?" he says, beaming like we're best friends.

The others see it as their window, and more step in close, too close. This isn't good. With each second that passes, more paps join the crowd. I've never seen anything like it and when I look down at Abby I notice she's gone pale and clammy and her eyes are glazed over. She's slipping away from me, going to that same dark place she's been before, after the night she was drugged.

We have to get away and there's only one way out: through the crowd.

I wrap an arm around her shoulders, tucking her into my side, shielding her as best I can. Pushing forward with my other shoulder, I force our way out. We've almost broken through to the other side and I'm ready for making a dash to the cab rank close by when another pap darts forward. It all happens in slow motion. I feel like I'm a million miles away, watching in the split second it takes him to grab at Abby's coat, forcing it open and taking a prime shot of her bump.

"Back off!" I roar, knowing I shouldn't, but not caring when a cracking sound reaches my ears. It takes me a second to realize it's my fist making contact with the asshole's jaw.

I don't get a chance to enjoy it because I see Abby out of the corner of my eye, slipping away into the darkness. Instinctively I dive forward, my sole focus to stop her from falling to the ground.

Abby

Sprawled across Jake's bed, I watch as he paces back and forth.

"Are you sure you're, okay?"

I roll my eyes. "For the last time, I'm fine. You, however, are not." I sit up and point at his hand covered with a bag of frozen peas.

His nostrils flare and his face reddens. "There was nothing fine about what just happened." The bed shifts when he sits down next to me. "I'm so sorry."

"We don't know who they were there for, Jake. You have nothing to be sorry about. It was probably linked to the photos with Dan when I was leaving London."

Choosing to ignore what I'm referring to, because we haven't even touched on the subject of Dan yet, he says, "This can't keep happening."

"Excuse me?" I scoff. "What exactly do you think is happening?"

He stares and my stomach flips. Even after all the crap that just happened, he still manages to draw this kind of reaction from me.

"You blacked out, Abby."

"I don't know what you're talking about …"

"Yes, you do."

"You're overreacting." I focus my attention down on my bump.

"Abs …" He moves in closer, tilting his head so I'm forced to look him in the eye.

"Jake …"

"You can't pretend this isn't happening. I'm guessing there have been other times besides what happened on the tour and today."

Avoiding his gaze, my eyes shift to the window, knowing he's right. There have been multiple occasions, never quite as bad as the two Jake is referring to, but close calls. Particularly on nights out when some guys like to get too handsy. When the black dots start to creep in, it's my signal to get away quickly. But these two instances have proven that when the situation is out of my control worse can happen. But it can't because there's more than just me to worry about. My reaction today didn't just put me at risk, it put the baby at risk too.

"Abby, look at me."

Slowly I turn my head so I'm facing him, instantly wishing I hadn't. The way his eyes swirl with emotion makes me want to crumble and right now I'd happily agree to anything he asked. I always thought Jake was a closed book, but that's not the case. Every page has been there, open, waiting for me to devour everything he's willing to give and more. What I thought was him being unreadable was the opposite. When he looks at me there are so many emotions it's impossible to pinpoint just one.

His stormy eyes flicker down to my lips, and I shake my head, attempting to break the trance he's pulled me under. The baby kicks at the same time. "Oh," I squeak.

"Was that the baby moving?"

"Yeah." I place my hand over where I felt the baby move. It moves again, but this time I don't just feel the swirling sensation in my stomach. There's a slight pulse against my skin and my eyes widen in shock.

Jake watches me intently and when he sees the change in my facial expression, he frowns. "Is everything okay?"

"I think I just felt it move with my hand. Oh my God, I've never felt that before." A goofy grin takes over my face.

He rubs the back of his neck and his voice falters when he asks, "Can I feel?"

I nod eagerly. "Of course."

I replace my hand with his. He clears his throat looking uncertain. "Is this right?"

"Perfect." As an afterthought, I add, "You might want to press a little harder." He looks concerned so I reassure him, "Don't worry, you won't hurt us."

Us. Referring to myself as two people still feels weird.

"Okay."

We sit and wait, but nothing happens, and I start to panic. He's going to think I made the whole thing up as a ruse to get his hands on me. I'm about to give up when the baby gives one of the biggest kicks yet.

Jake's hand flies away and I'll never forget the look on his face. If I could take a picture, it would be one for the baby book. "What the fuck was that?"

I laugh so hard I'm at risk of peeing my pants. "That was the baby moving."

"Seriously?"

"Seriously." I gasp.

His brows furrow, forming a deep line down the middle. "Does it hurt?"

"Not now. But apparently, when the baby gets bigger it can get uncomfortable."

"Amazing." He stares at my stomach in awe, then smiles timidly, glancing up at me through thick lashes. "Do you mind if I feel again? I'll try not to freak out this time."

My mouth goes dry, and I struggle to reply, so I smile weakly and nod. Seeing him like this is too much. A surge of emotions hit me. This is the dream, the perfect moment. At least it should be. "Jake …" I whisper.

"I hate it when you say my name like that."

"Why?"

"Because it never means anything good."

I don't deny it because he's right.

"We n—" He presses a finger gently against my lips.

My eyes close when his finger is replaced with his lips. For a fraction of a second, he doesn't move and I wonder if he will or whether this is it.

A swift kiss.

A simple goodbye.

I should have known better. Jake never likes to keep things simple between us.

At first, he moves his mouth slowly against mine, but the kiss quickly turns deeper. He teases my tongue and my body shudders. The hand on my bump snakes around my waist. When it finds my lower back, it flattens, pulling me in.

There's no room to think or breathe. All I want is him to climb over and make me forget why we can't be together.

But that's the reason we're in this mess, and it's that fleeting thought which brings reality crashing down.

"Jake," I try to say, but it turns to a sigh when he peppers kisses along my jaw, trailing his lips to the crook of my neck.

I plant my hand firmly against his chest and push him back.

"What's wrong?" he asks, hooded eyes focused on my lips, making his intentions perfectly clear.

"This," I say, gesturing between us, "is wrong. We can't do this."

His eyes move away from my lips, and he looks confused. "Why?"

"You're kidding, right?"

He stares at me blankly.

A snort escapes as I laugh in disbelief at how oblivious he's being. "Jake, we're about to have a baby together."

He leans back. "And? Most people who have babies together tend to be in a relationship ..."

"Which we haven't been in since high school. We don't even know if we work together as a couple without a baby, let alone with one."

He scowls. "You're actually doing this ... walking away from us, again."

I shake my head. "There is no us, Jake, and if we jump into a relationship together right when our worlds are about to be turned upside down there never will be an us."

"This baby could be the making of us ..."

"Yes," I agree. "It could be the making of us as *individuals*. S.C.A.R.A.B. is about to make it big. You can't walk away, and I believe that even more now that I know the truth. This is your chance to prove to yourself that you're better than the life your mom and grandpa had planned for you."

Jake leans over, cupping my jaw with his hands. He's so close all I can focus on is the feeling of his warm breath against my lips, already sensitive from his kisses. Every part of my body aches to throw caution to the wind. But for the first time in my life, my head is the one running the show, not my heart that knows only one thing: him. I refuse to keep doing the same dance we always have because if we do, it won't be the making of us, it will be the end.

"There's more to this than just the baby. You still don't forgive me for ending things back in high school, do you?"

I can barely see him through the tears. Then I do what I've never done. I tell him exactly how he made me feel all those years ago because it was more than just a broken heart, "For a while, I couldn't breathe without you. I forgot how to exist on my own. Every decision I've made in my adult life so far has been made with you at the forefront of my mind. I don't know who I am or what I want without you."

His grip tightens and he tries to lean forward. I know he's trying to silence me with his kisses, but I turn my head to the side, refusing to let him.

"We can do this together. Let me help you figure it out."

"No."

He must hear the resolve in my voice because he pulls away putting some much-needed distance between us. "Why?"

"Jake, if we're together I'll shape myself into what I think you want rather than who I want to be."

His eyes glisten. Everything about us is bittersweet. We're at the start of something huge but we both know we're saying goodbye to the past, not knowing if there's a future for us.

"I just want you."

"But what if the me you want isn't who I really am? What if we tie ourselves together and we were never meant to be?"

I know to Jake and everyone else it all seems easy. They think we should be together. But it would never work when I feel the way I do. How can I give someone every part of myself when I don't even know what those parts are? Before I can trust someone and let them love me I need to learn how to love myself and trust my own judgment.

"I want to be in this baby's life. I want to be in *your* life," he says earnestly.

"And you will be. But you also need to chase your dreams. I do too. But not together."

"I don't get it. Abby, I want this … *us*. I want *you*. The baby hasn't changed how I feel."

"But it could. Jake, we've not been on a date since high school and the most time we've spent together was on a tour bus, which was because you made it impossible for me not to be there. The strains of a baby … the pressures of our career … as well as somehow trying to make a relationship work—it would tear us apart."

"So, what do you suggest we do?" he snaps.

I swallow before answering. "I'd like us to be friends."

"Friends?" He laughs bitterly. "Abby, we will never just be friends."

"Please, Jake. This is what I want." I stare, pleading with my eyes, trying to convey how much I need this.

Eventually, he sighs and rubs a hand over his stubble-lined jaw. "Fine. Friends."

I blink, not quite believing he's backed down so easily. "Thank you," I reply before he can change his mind. I climb off the bed and explain, "I should get home. I'm exhausted."

I grab my bag from the floor and make exceptionally quick work of putting on my shoes.

Jake never takes his eyes off me and I'm almost at the door when he stands abruptly and starts to follow. The silence when we leave the room and make our way down the stairs is unbearable.

What's more awkward … being welcomed by the other members of S.C.A.R.A.B. when we're almost at the bottom.

Ryan bounces over eagerly. "Looking good, Abby. So, I've been reading up on some stuff, you know to be supportive and all that crap …"

"Just ask her." Sam snickers, a mischievous glint in his eye that tells me I'm not going to like what comes out of Ryan's mouth next.

"Is it true that your 'V' goes from like this size," he says, eyes peeping through the small circle his fingers make, "to this size."

I wince when his hands motion a much larger circle, and he mimics trying to push his head through.

"Seriously," snaps Jake, smacking him around the head. "I told you to pack that shit in this morning."

Sam and Ryan stand, snickering while Zach fails to fight a smile.

Going for the old, if you can't beat 'em, join 'em, mentality, I gesture with my finger for Ryan to come in closer.

When he's near, I say quietly, "Want to know a secret?"

He nods eagerly.

"Apparently, you crap yourself too. You can come watch if you'd like?"

He stands back looking appalled, and I mentally high-five myself. I doubt there will be any more birth-related questions coming my way.

Jake grabs my hand and pulls me carefully behind him to the front door. "Can you leave us alone for a few minutes?" he throws over his shoulder to the guys.

All he gets in return are huffs and mumbles as they disappear, leaving us alone, standing in awkward silence.

"We have to go back on tour next week," says Jake, scuffing his toe against the floor. "Will I see you before I go?"

I shrug. "Not unless the group is together. I think it's best if we have some space."

Jake frowns and at first says nothing. I'm taken by surprise when he steps forward once, then twice, then a third time. I'm pressed against the front door with nowhere to escape.

"Want to know what I think?" I don't say yes but he continues, "I think what you said before was crap."

"Ja—" I go to argue, but he carries on, refusing to let me say another word.

"I think you're scared. Abs, life's about taking risks, and sometimes no matter how much we want them to, things don't work out. Is it not worth taking the risk, if the alternative meant not knowing how good something could be?"

"I already took the risk, Jake, and you walked away."

He tilts his head in amusement. "You mean like you did to me … twice."

"And did you come after me? Did you fight for me?" I hiss. "If you care as much about me as you say you do, you wouldn't have let me go."

A frown crosses his face, fleeting, and his lips part as if he's about to say something but stops himself.

"Exactly what I thought. And before you even think about bringing this summer up, don't. *That* was not fighting for me. There was nothing romantic about the temper tantrum you threw."

His hands press against the door as he cages me in with his arms. He says quietly into my ear, "I'll play along, for now. But I'm not just going to be in this baby's life. I'm going to be in your life too, and it won't be just as friends. I'll give you the space you need, but I'm not going anywhere, Abs. I want you and I know you want me. Even if I have to wait a year, or ten. It will be worth every second because when we're together nothing else compares. Nothing else matters because it always has and always will be you."

Chapter Eighteen

Abby

It took a large security team to get me from A to B. A being the band's place and B being my parents' home. What should have been at most a ten-minute drive, took over an hour, with one detour after another as we tried to get rid of the paps following.

Finally, when I say goodbye and open the front door, tiredness takes over. Every part of my body aches. My brain is frazzled. Rationality has gone out the window. And my heart hurts like hell.

I'm bustled into my mom's arms as soon as I step inside, enveloped in a much-needed hug.

"What a day you've had," she hums into my hair.

I pull back. "How do you know about my day?"

Not giving anything away, she says, "Your dad is waiting in the kitchen."

A sinking feeling hits my stomach that has nothing to do with the baby moving. "Erm, why?"

"Just come with me," she sighs, walking away, expecting me to follow.

I don't at first. Instead, I wrack my brain, trying to figure out what could be going on. The exhaustion I felt just moments ago is replaced with anxiety and my heart pounds. My fight or flight response tells me something isn't right and to be prepared for the worst.

When I enter the kitchen-dining area, I find my mom and dad sitting at the table, their expressions grim.

"What's wrong?" I ask, pausing at the door.

"Sit down, Abby," says my dad, nodding at the seat directly across the table.

I swallow hard and walk over, sitting down hesitantly. There have only been a handful of times in my life where we've sat and had a serious conversation at the dinner table like we are doing. None of them have ever been positive.

"Seriously, what's wrong?" I ask again when neither of them says a word.

My dad doesn't look me in the eye, simply slides his phone across the table, the screen already open with something on it he wants me to see. Spinning it around as I pull it closer, my eyes fall on an image of me and Jake from this morning.

The headline: *Jake Ross in Love Triangle With Dan White.*

Fuck.

Trailing one finger over the screen, I move through the article, my eyes skimming the words, not needing to read it in depth. The word *bike* jumps out multiple times and stings. If people were unsure whether to believe the article, the selection of images of me with both Jake and Dan seals the deal. When I've had enough, I tap the back arrow, bringing up the Google search my dad ran. My eyes are greeted with headlines, all saying similar things and referring to the apparent love triangle I'm in.

But they're wrong. For there to be a love triangle I'd have to be torn between the two. Really, there's only ever been one person I wanted.

A laugh escapes, small at first, turning hysterical. "I'm sorry," I say when I'm able to speak.

I look up and find my dad shaking his head, his mouth set in a grim line. "You have nothing to be sorry for. This is all part of being in the public eye for Jake and Dan. Unfortunately, you're collateral. The paps love things like this, even more so now S.C.A.R.A.B. is moving up the charts. They're direct competition with Six Seconds to Barcelona, so for the media, it's the perfect setup to create drama and good headlines."

"What do I do?" I ask, feeling completely out of my depth.

"I'll do what I can on my end with the label, but really, it's a simple case of lying low and weathering the storm. You're going to have to be careful over the next couple of months, no missteps because they'll be watching you like a hawk. Jake's tour couldn't come at a better time because it means there's no chance of you being photographed together to stir things up."

"Okay. I have a few people that might be able to help diffuse things."

Dad smiles. "That's a good idea, it will help. Don't worry though. This will disappear as soon as there's another scandal, which in the celebrity world is probably happening right this second. Tomorrow you'll be old news."

I smile back weakly. "I'm really tired, it's been a long day. I'm gonna head up to bed if that's okay?"

They both nod and I leave on shaky legs. I pull my phone out as soon as I'm in my room, bringing up Amanda's number and hitting call. Business first, breakdown later.

Even though it's late, she picks up after a couple of rings. "What took you so long?" I can hear the amusement in her voice. When I don't answer she says, "So, you've officially become a celebrity. Front page news …"

"For all the wrong reasons," I mutter.

"Hey, don't beat yourself up. Some people pay good money to have shit like this made up. You did it unknowingly, you're a natural."

"Hardy har," I reply, unable to fight back a giggle.

"What would you like me to do?"

"Do you have a magic wand you can wave that will make it all go away?"

"Sadly not."

Dammit.

"No magic wand, but luckily for you I'm fabulous at my job. It might take a few days, but I'll see what I can do."

"Thanks, Amanda."

"Any time" she says with a yawn.

I glance at my clock and am shocked by how late it is. A thought springs to mind. "I actually need something else from you."

"Shoot."

"Do you think you could get me Michael Becket's number?"

"Becket, like *the* Becket? Sex tape Becket? Your ex?"

"Yes," I wince. "*That* Becket."

I don't know the ins and outs of what happened after we broke up because he blocked my number, but shortly after, he was part of a media scandal that shook the NFL. If anyone knows what I'm going through right now, it's him. But that's not the reason I need to speak with him. The nights when we were together were long. Lying awake, listening to things he unknowingly revealed, secrets about his past he would never speak about in the light of day. A bit of snooping throughout the time we were together painted a bigger picture, one that tells me he's someone I can speak to and can help with the whole blacking out issue. It might not be the conventional way of dealing with things, but I'm not a conventional person and even though our relationship didn't work out, I still trust him more than I trust most people.

Amanda doesn't ask any other questions. "I'll get it to you tomorrow."

"Thanks, Amanda. For everything."

"Actually, I want to say sorry."

"Erm, for what?"

"I shouldn't have said what I did when you were in London. I've been feeling a bit lost myself and I shouldn't have taken it out on you. My *bitchterior* took over."

I snort. "*Bitchterior*?"

"Yes. Sometimes I forget I don't need to be her outside of work. I'm sorry."

"I'm sorry too. I never meant to get in between you and Jake the summer I came back. I—"

"Don't say it."

"How did you know what I was going to say?"

"I know you better than you think, and I know you were going to say something along the lines that you wouldn't have come back if you'd known how things were going to go. Abby, we can't change the past and I'm a firm believer everything happens for a reason.

"I spent a long time resenting you when, actually, I should have been thanking you. You helped show the cracks in my relationship with Jake before it was too late. He told me about you when we first met and I ignored the warning signs and went all in any way knowing he'd never feel about me the way he did about you. You're it for him. You always will be. Now that's all I have to say, so get some rest," her voice changes as if she hasn't dumped a load of information on me that will once again change the dynamics of our newfound friendship. "Apparently, we have office spaces to look at in the next few days."

"Sooz?" I chuckle.

"Her *bitchterior* is worse than mine."

"It's why she's the best."

Amanda jumps in and corrects me, "*One* of the best."

I roll my eyes.

A few minutes later we say goodbye. Only when the line goes dead, and I drop my phone on my nightstand, do I allow my mind to run through the day and feel all the emotions that come with it. But it's not just the emotions of the day that hit me. It's the past six months. Hell, the past eight years.

Every single moment Jake and I have been together and apart. The good and the bad. I'm tired beyond belief but still can't sleep as my mind mulls over everything. Even after reflecting for hours, I still feel lost, wondering where we go from here, if anywhere.

Jake

"Take a seat, Jake," says John West, gesturing at the empty one across from his own.

Slowly I sit down at his huge-ass desk, in his huge-ass office which overlooks Times Square, wondering what he could possibly have left to say to me. Most likely another ass riding for how I treated his daughter.

"I owe you an apology."

That wasn't what I was expecting. "For what?" I ask bluntly.

"For prying in your relationship with Abby."

I lean back in my chair and cross my arms, waiting for him to expand.

"You're not going to make this easy for me are you, Son?" He laughs.

I shake my head no, still saying nothing, trying to ignore the fact he called me son, something he hasn't done since before the news of Abby's pregnancy. I always hoped one day he'd be calling me it for real.

"I shouldn't have spoken to you the way I did, and I shouldn't have let your relationship with my daughter affect our professional relationship. It was wrong and I made a mistake. I'm sorry for sending mixed messages and getting involved in things I shouldn't have," he reels the words off like a rehearsed speech, words that have a woman's touch, a woman who is most likely Mrs. West. "I never should have interfered. I should have let you follow her and let the two of you figure it out yourselves."

"Why did you, then?"

He doesn't reply straight away. After mulling over my question, he replies, "Please remember the woman you love. I love more. Unconditionally. You might understand this a little more now you're going to be a father yourself, but if you don't now, you will as soon as that baby is in your arms.

"Abby is my daughter. Besides my wife, she's my reason for living. All this," he says, motioning around his swanky office, "means nothing without them. But I know you know that already."

I tilt my head to the side, intrigued. "And how do you know that?"

"Because instead of chasing your dreams and continuing the tour in Tokyo, you gave it all up and chased my daughter, regardless of the consequences. The record exec in me wants to tell you what a huge mistake you made. But the father in me is proud to have someone like you fighting for my daughter after everything you've been through."

"It's made no difference," I say bitterly. "She doesn't want us to be together."

"She's afraid."

"I know."

"Have you told her that I told you not to follow when she left?"

"No," I reply, staring through the glass at the flashing billboards behind him.

"Why not? If you did, she'd probably change her mind."

"For two reasons. The first: I want Abby to believe she can trust me because I'm still here fighting for her, regardless of the mistakes we've made. She needs to learn that just because something doesn't work out perfectly to begin, doesn't mean it can't work out in the end."

He nods, admiration in his eyes. "And the second reason?"

"I don't want to throw you under the bus. I know Abby and I know she'll be pissed."

He lets out a hearty laugh. "It won't be the first time I've pissed off my daughter and it won't be the last. Leave her to me."

"Yeah, I get that. But I respect you both enough not to get in the way. I also believe that what we have is strong enough for it not to matter."

"So, what are you going to do?"

"Wait. Until the time's right."

He frowns. "And what if there's never a right time?"

"Then I'll have to make sure there is."

Chapter Nineteen
Abby 4 Months Later

My due date is impending and I'm waddling around with a beach ball attached to my middle. My breasts have made the transition to becoming fully functional milk machines, leaking at the most inconvenient times.

Some of the changes in the last three months have been good, like spreading my wings and finding an apartment with Sooz. The work changes are pending. Turns out starting up a company like Sooz had in mind is a bit more complicated than when I began freelancing with photography. If anyone can get it all off the ground though, it's Sooz and Amanda. The plan is to have everything in place ready for when I'm able to start working again.

The baby could come at any time, a direct quote from my OB/GYN that had me squeezing my legs together at the thought of what's to come. The whole birth thing wasn't the only problem. A mix-up with the dates meant S.C.A.R.A.B. only just wrapped up their tour of Asia a couple of days ago. With the time difference and their crazy schedule, all communication with Jake has been in messages and emails.

If I thought a grand reunion was in the cards, I was very much wrong. As soon as they touch down in JFK tomorrow, they'll be hot-footing it to the VMA's, because whilst on tour, their career wasn't just launched, it was catapulted into something none of us ever could have predicted. The result … S.C.A.R.A.B. was nominated for Artist of the Year, along with Six Seconds to Barcelona. The media has been eating it up. For weeks there have been articles running, predicting a bust-up between Jake and Dan.

"How is there still so much left on the list?" moans Zoe, scanning over what we have left to buy.

Who knew something so small required more stuff than a full-sized human?

"I don't know. Just let me know when you have everything," I say, leaning back in one of the baby store's huge, squashy armchairs. We could find the stuff cheaper elsewhere, but I've purposely made us come to this store multiple times because the seating is amazing. When you're full-term, these things matter.

Zoe hits me around the head with said list and says, "No way. You're not getting out of this. It's *your* baby."

I look at her and smile sweetly. "But you keep referring to it as *ours*. I need to rest. Being heavily pregnant is hard you know."

"I do know because you tell me every chance you get."

"Whatever," I grumble.

"Are you ready for Jake getting back?" she asks changing the subject.

My stomach flutters. "About as ready as I am to push this baby out …"

"So not at all," she replies, spinning around quickly and avoiding the hacky look I throw her way.

"When does Dan land?"

"Anytime now." I smile to myself.

With the way his schedule has worked out, I haven't seen him since I left London, which hasn't necessarily been a bad thing. I'm praying the space will have been what we needed and help us navigate a friendship after our short-lived romance. I'm trying not to think about what it will mean if we can't. In the short time I've known him, he's immersed himself into my life in a way that means I can't imagine not having him there. Unfortunately, my gut is telling me that no matter how hard we try to make it work, at some point, we will have to part ways. We're prolonging the inevitable but at least we have the distraction of the awards ceremony and the baby coming soon. Not that I'm avoiding things …

We smash through the list of baby items in record time, well, Zoe does. When we're finished, we head home, multiple bags in hand, so I can take my obligatory afternoon nap. I wake late afternoon and walk into the kitchen of mine and Sooz's new apartment, finding Zoe standing with a steaming cup of coffee. I stare jealously as she takes a drink, scrolling through her phone with her other hand, most likely checking her social media feeds.

At first, I can't put my finger on what I'm thinking and feeling, but as I sit, nursing my herbal tea, subtly observing her, I realize there's something different. She's still my sometimes-clueless best friend, lacking a filter, but she seems … flat.

"Zo, can I ask you something?"

Not looking up from her cell, she says, "If it's about Shaun, no."

"How did you know I was going to ask about him?"

She looks up. "Because you used that ridiculously sweet voice you do when you're prying."

I huff and she laughs.

"Seriously, I'm not talking about him."

"How ironic. You jump down my throat, the first opportunity you get, claiming I have avoidance issues, yet here you are doing the same thing."

"Shaun and I are different. It was just one night." She looks back at her cell, refusing to engage in any eye contact.

It's a dead giveaway that she cares about him more than she's willing to let on. Zoe rarely cowers away from her feelings and rarely gets embarrassed, no matter what situation she finds herself in, but Benicassim was different. Even though she refuses to speak about it, I know, deep down, it was more than just a one-night stand. The fact she chased him after she declared it meant nothing and he heard proves it. If it were any other guy, she would have shrugged her shoulders and let them walk away. If only she'd speak about what happened when she caught up with him.

"He cares about you. A lot. Couldn't you give him an explanation as to why you said the things you did?"

This time she looks up at me when she answers and her eyes are hard. "How can I when there isn't one to give?"

I'm wasting my time, but I give it one last attempt. "He could be good for you, but he won't wait around forever."

As expected it falls on death ears. "There's nothing for him to wait around for."

The pain in her eyes only someone who knows her better than she knows herself can see, tells me I'm not the only one whose heart has been damaged. Maybe I recognize it more than anyone else because when I look at her, I see the person I used to be.

I see the Abby who returned to Brooklyn almost three years ago, avoiding her feelings at all costs, making countless mistakes at the expense of her heart. And that was a very sad place to be.

"Mom ... please can you explain why there are five bottles of olive oil in the bathroom?"

She doesn't look up from the magazine she's reading. "Perineal massage."

"Excuse me?" I scoff.

Zoe looks over and smirks, while Sophie and Sooz look as horrified as I feel. Amanda snorts from where she's sitting in one of the armchairs in our living room, typing on her laptop, frantically going over last-minute details for the awards ceremony tonight. This is her last big event before she goes rogue with us.

"Massage," continues my mom. "For your perineum. It's part of your va—"

I hold my hand up to stop her before she goes any further. "I know what it is, Mom. Why do I need to massage it?"

Her glasses are perched on the end of her nose and she looks up at me over the rim of them. "Did you not listen in your birthing classes?"

"Erm ..."

Zoe throws her head back and laughs. "Do you even know your daughter? She's going into this shit blind."

I narrow my eyes at her. "Helpful … *not*."

My mom ignores us both. "As I was saying. It's a massage to … how can I put this nicely … keep things intact?"

I close my eyes and take a deep breath. "Honestly, Mom, we're days away from me giving birth, I think I'm past that point."

She shrugs. "Better late than never. This dry spell you're going through isn't going to last forever. You need to think about when you jump back in the sack."

Ground, please swallow me up. "Mom! I'm not one of your projects and can you please keep your voice down. Dan is in the house and does not need to hear these things."

"You'd be surprised by what men like. I'm covering it in the latest article. Most like things a bit kinky in the bedroom, so whatever you don't use now, you can save for a later date. You'd be surprised what you can use it for." The way she's talking you'd think we were discussing how to prep dinner.

My mouth drops open while Amanda and Zoe start howling with laughter.

"I did not need to hear that. And believe me, Dan will not find *those* kinds of details about my vagina kinky."

The room goes deathly silent, and every set of eyes look over my shoulder.

I close my own. "Dan's behind me, isn't he?"

"He is."

My ears are greeted with a husky British voice, one that would have millions of women all over the planet dropping to their knees and doing whatever he asked in a second. When I turn around and find him standing in just a towel, his skin glistening with small beads of water from the shower and his usually styled hair falling tousled and wet across his forehead, for a fleeting second, I question why I haven't done the same.

"I don't mean to be nosey, but why are there loads of bottles of olive oil in your bathroom?" A mischievous glint appears in his eyes as he watches me squirm with embarrassment.

"Wouldn't you like to know," says Zoe, wagging her finger.

"Baby stuff!" I jump in before the conversation can escalate further and move back onto the topic of my vagina. "Can you put some clothes on?"

"Please don't," calls Amanda from behind, smirking over the top of her laptop screen.

"Ever," agrees Sophie.

"Sorry, Abs. I've changed my mind, I'm moving to London," beams Sooz, unable to look away from Dan's half-naked torso.

My mom trails her eyes over his body, critiquing him. "Dan, have you ever considered modeling? You'd be great fo—"

"Mom!" I interrupt before she can say what I think she's going to. I turn back to Dan and mouth *sorry*.

He laughs, deeply. It's the kind of laugh that makes every muscle in his body flex and the girls stare at him wide-eyed. I usher him out of the room, putting an end to the spectacle once and for all. He carries on laughing and I can hear the girls grumbling about how I'm spoiling their fun.

"I actually came down because I can't find my bag. It was in my room when I went for a shower …"

I look over my shoulder in the doorway, looking at each of my friends with suspicion, all of whom are looking anywhere but at me.

"I'm sorry," I groan. "My friends are …"

"Unique." He winks. "I'll go back up. If you could find my bag that would be great. I need to meet the band so we can go through hair and makeup before the awards."

I nod and walk back into the room, placing my hands firmly on my hips. "Seriously? Where is it?"

"A little birdy told me they saw it in your room," says Sophie absentmindedly, messing with the TV remote.

"You guys are something else," I mutter.

"A thank you for the show would be nice!" hoots Sooz.

The sound of them cackling follows me up the stairs.

It doesn't take long to find Dan's bag, tucked away underneath the bed in my childhood room. I shake my head in despair at the lengths my friends will go to. Knowing Dan doesn't have much time, I quickly leave, bag in hand, and rap my knuckles against the door of the guest room where he's stayed overnight in my parents' home.

We wanted to spend some time together after months of barely any contact and with my due date just around the corner, this seemed like the best solution. A hotel room was a no-go unless we wanted to stir up headlines again about me being the "rock and roll bike," which one magazine kindly referred to me as the last time I made it into the gossip columns. Mine and Sooz's new place was out of the question being that there are only two beds and it would have been awkward to figure out. So, here we are.

When I asked my parents if it was okay, my dad all but jumped for joy at the news. He's been trying to poach Six Seconds to Barcelona for years, and if the boring conversation they had at the dinner table last night is anything to go by, it won't be long until he gets his way.

The bedroom door opens, and I'm greeted with the sight of Dan, still half-naked. I expect to feel something, anything, but there's nothing. Not even the slight stirring of butterflies which used to take flight whenever I saw him.

He looks at me, his expression warm and when I hand over his bag, he chuckles. "Thanks. I'll get ready and have to head straight off."

"Are you nervous?"

He shakes his head. "Nah. If it's meant to be it will be. I'll see you later when we get back?"

"I'll be here waiting … with the gang." I cringe.

He grins. "Who needs VIP? Best after-party ever."

He closes the door and I shuffle away, suddenly feeling out of sorts. Everyone is so excited about tonight, but all I feel is dread. To me, there is absolutely nothing exciting about an old love interest and a … well, who knows what, love interest, going head-to-head for one of the biggest awards in the music industry. The night has the potential to end with fireworks, and not the good kind.

Jake

"I can't believe we're about to do this," says Sam, coming up beside me in the dining area of our shared home.

Stylists bustle around, packing away their gear. I never knew a group of guys would require so much make-up. You'd think we were preparing for an episode of *America's Next Top Model* with the amount of crap we've had caked on our faces. It's my least favorite part of all this and I know I'm not alone. It's tedious but apparently necessary.

Picking up my beer, I ignore the glasses of champagne provided by the PR team, and down the remainder of my bottle in one. "It's crazy, isn't it?"

The three bottles I've plowed through while getting ready have done nothing to calm the nerves churning in my stomach. The efforts of the make-up team are going to be wasted shortly because I'm sweating like a pig. When we signed with the label, none of us considered we might be nominated for awards one day and the whole thing is surreal. If we win this award, it will change things. Our lives, our careers, will never be the same. My stomach churns again. This, along with Abby and the baby—which could come at any time—is a lot. I'm struggling to figure out which I should be focusing on more.

Abby might have told me to go on the tour and I might have agreed, but I've spent every spare moment thinking about her and the baby. We said we would make it work, but how can we? Each time I picked up the phone to get in contact with her, someone walked over and plucked it out of my hand because there was something more important to do. Is this what it will always be like?

I haven't seen her since the night she said "let's just be friends" and truthfully, I'm more nervous about seeing her again than I am about the possibility of having to set foot on stage and receive an award in front of millions of people, or even worse, lose an award in front of millions of people.

One of the assistants managing our schedule steps forward, clears their throat, and says, "The limo's waiting outside."

Sam and I look at each other and nod. It's time. Bile rises in my throat as we step out into the night. I keep reminding myself that the odds of us winning are minimal, there's no chance we will win. It doesn't make any difference, it's still as daunting. We're going to be sitting alongside some of the biggest names in music. People who were our inspiration when we were young, who we dreamed of one day becoming are now our direct competition.

Once we're all inside, the limo pulls away and we make our way into Manhattan. The guys are buzzing, and their chatter fills the vehicle, reminding me of one of the first times we got to ride in one and we thought we'd made it big. If only we knew then how far we'd come. That was child's play compared to how things are now. And the moment when I should be reveling in it all, celebrating how far we've come, all I can think about is Abby. It feels wrong she's not here, by my side.

We each peer out when the vehicle crawls alongside Madison Square Gardens, the huge, curved building glowing in the night. Even through the tinted windows of the limo, I can see the glass twinkling, reflecting the lights of New York.

Everyone takes a deep breath when the limo comes to a stop and even Ryan the calmest of us looks nervous. Camera flashes are visible and the sound of the fans screaming is audible. In here we're in our own bubble and we all sit in silence, reflecting for a moment before being hit with the chaos.

"No matter what happens tonight," says Sam seriously, "even if we don't win, we've made it. I'm proud to be here with you all."

We each nod and lean forward, bumping fists in the same way we always have. There's no time to say anything more, as the door is flung open, and the breath is sucked from each of us when the noise hits like a sledgehammer.

"Holy fuck," says Zach, throat bobbing as he gulps.

Amanda comes into sight, dressed to the nines, platinum blonde hair tumbling over her shoulder. She sticks her head through the door. "You're holding up the line, you need to move."

We all sit blinking.

"Now!"

We look to each other, plastering on our best smiles before climbing out to be greeted by fans as we're ushered along the red carpet. That's the easy bit, smiling and waving. It's when we get to the end and see the paps surrounding the official photo area that my stomach drops. I remind myself of the words Amanda used to say when she coached us for our first event, "step, smile, repeat."

It sounds simple, but actually, it's terrifying, not that we'd ever let it show. The limelight isn't all it's cracked up to be. The images you see in the media. Fake. The media make it all look so cool and glamourous. It's not. The paps are like vultures, demanding our attention and screaming for us to look in their direction, some taunting us to get a reaction, anything that will make their image stand out from the rest.

We've almost finished when things get crazy, and the paps go even wilder. Their attention, and cameras, jump back and forth between us and something off to the side. My gut tells me not to look, but I can't stop myself, too intrigued by what all the fuss is about.

That's when my eyes lock with Dan White, standing with his eyes narrowed in my direction.

"Don't react," hisses Zach under his breath.

"Jake, we're holding up the line again," says Sam quietly, bringing my attention back around to what we need to do.

We're greeted with a round of boos from the paps, disappointed by the lack of drama when we simply turn and walk out of the photo area without a word.

"Thank fuck that's over," mutters Sam as we carry on walking.

"Yeah," I agree, "nice coincidence having them right behind us."

We all look at each other knowing it was anything but. We've just witnessed firsthand how ruthless the celeb world can be. Somebody purposefully set it up to get a reaction that would qualify for front-page news. Unfortunately, for whoever was responsible, they failed.

We're ushered inside and a waiter greets us each with a tall glass of champagne. I hate the stuff but after that little drama, I pick up two. Zach frowns and takes one from my hand. So much for numbing the pain.

"Here they are," beams John West, striding over. "Come with me, I have some people who want to meet you."

We spend the next half an hour being overly polite with what feels like every big name in the music business. Another side to this world that people don't get to see, the *'schmoozing'* as we refer to it. It's always long and boring, but necessary. Finally, John West saves us from our misery, declaring it's time to find our seats.

The whole venue has been transformed, looking like it has done each year when we've sat and watched it live on television. The only difference, we're here in person, shit suddenly feels real. Rows of seats are lined up, like they usually are for concerts, steadily filling with hundreds of celebrities and influential figures from the music industry. Then in front of the huge stage is a large pit filled with fans, screaming, and waving their phones high up in the air, either trying to capture an image of their favorite artist or taking a selfie with their friends.

We find our seats, thankfully with John beside us, talking us through everything, making sure we don't mess up. The awards ceremony begins and it's painfully slow. For the first time, I don't care about all the other awards, I'm too nervous. All I care about is the one we've been nominated for.

A random celebrity walks on stage, sashaying over to the podium on heels so high I wonder how she manages to stay upright and a skintight dress that leaves nothing to the imagination. When the crowd settles, she clears her throat, and everything goes as silent as it can for a space with thousands of people contained in it.

"Has everyone had a good night?" she asks, playing the crowd perfectly.

The roar of approval that follows has her throwing her hair back and laughing, revealing a set of perfectly white teeth that glow brighter than the stage lights. When the noise starts to settle, she clears her throat once more, ready to dive into presenting the award.

"It's time for the final award, Artist of the Year. Let me tell you, this year, has been crazy. For the first time, we had ourselves a tie, can you believe it?"

A round of whispering sweeps through the crowds, everyone discussing in hushed voices who the two artists could be. My stomach starts twisting and turning, wanting her to get it over and done with.

"Luckily, we have each artist that's shortlisted submit a song, just in case. The submissions go to a judging panel to cast the final vote."

I frown, vaguely remembering John explaining this a while back and us picking one of our biggest hits so far. It seemed trivial at the time, and I'd found out about the baby a couple of weeks before, so it was all a blur.

I swallow nervously and Sam's leg bounces so high beside me, I'm surprised he hasn't taken off out of his seat.

"So … the two bands who drew, were Six Seconds to Barcelona." My stomach sinks and I hold my breath. "And … S.C.A.R.A.B."

My mouth drops open. Holy cow. I look to the side briefly and find each of the guys sitting with theirs open too, frozen in shock.

John West leans forward with his hands clasped on his knees, staring intently at the stage, murmuring to himself, "Come on."

I can feel the tension around me. The world knows this is a big deal, but only each band truly knows the significance of this moment. Dammit, why couldn't it have been someone else? This is only going to make our loss harder to deal with, knowing how close we were, and then losing to *him*.

The presenter picks up a golden envelope from the podium and the trophy glints in the light. I shake my head and look down at my lap.

Finally, she continues, "So, the panel cast their votes based on the song each band offered."

I look up briefly, catching the presenter opening the envelope and pulling out a slip of paper. My heart pounds so hard I'm at risk of breaking a rib.

"And the winner is …"

Chapter Twenty

Abby

I wake up early evening feeling as awful as I did during my first trimester. My body is achy and restless, and to top it off I feel flushed.

"You don't look too great," says Sooz, when I walk into the living area, where the girls have set up, ready to watch the awards live on television.

My mom walks over and holds the back of her hand against my forehead, frowning. "She's right, you look a bit peaky and you're burning up."

I shake them both off, ignoring the twinging in my stomach as I do a quick mental log of everything, I've eaten in the past twenty-four hours, trying to figure out if any of it could be the culprit. Coming up with nothing, I decide collapsing on the couch is my best bet. The less movement the better.

Sophie and Zoe walk in with a tray of snacks and drinks, setting them down on the huge antique coffee table situated in the middle of the room.

"Sheesh, Abs, you look like crap," says Zoe. "You should go take a nap."

"I've already had one," I reply through gritted teeth, rubbing at my stomach as it twinges and the baby gives a huge kick, right underneath my rib cage. I'm so over this pregnancy.

"Put on the TV; the awards are about to start!" squeals Sophie, detracting the attention away from me.

Everyone gives me a side-on glance when I shift in my seat struggling to get comfortable.

"Are you sure you're, okay?" asks Sooz. I nod and gesture at the television, not wanting to miss a moment.

It's a big night for S.C.A.R.A.B. and Six Seconds to Barcelona. Initially, I was disappointed when I decided I was too uncomfortable to go, wanting to be there in person to support them both. The way I'm feeling right now, I've realized it was the right decision.

When the screen lights up and we're greeted with live footage from outside Madison Square Gardens, my disheveled appearance and feelings of discomfort are quickly forgotten and we all sit, discussing the vast array of outfits that fill the screen. The awards are great but for us, the red carpet is always the best bit, and the VMA's never fail to please.

I almost bite my tongue off when S.C.A.R.A.B. step onto the red carpet. It's surreal seeing them on the screen. If they're nervous, you can't tell. They move along like the pros they are, giving the paps just the right amount of attention and looking gorgeous in their expensively tailored suits. I've been eager to see what they would be wearing, especially after Amanda revealed her idea to have each member wear a suit in the color that most suited their personality. Zoe jumped right on board and began pulling up sample colors on the Internet excitedly. In the end, it was decided Jake would wear red, Sam turquoise, Zach yellow, and Ryan orange. The girls spent hours finding the perfect shade of each color and the result is fantastic.

Although not classed as official business, this was the first project they worked on as a team and seeing the band stand out from all the other celebrities, their outfits screaming edgy and cool, only shows the potential of what's to come with our future projects. Sooz's idea to throw all our talents together in one pot was genius.

What wasn't genius, whoever had the idea to have Six Seconds to Barcelona walk the red carpet straight after S.C.A.R.A.B. Somehow, I don't think it was a coincidence. We each hold our breath, watching for Jake's reaction when he clocks them to the side. All he does is shake his head and carry on walking, much to the disappointment of the paps and the relief of the band.

My stomach twinges again and I shift uncomfortably. Mom narrows her eyes in my direction then comes over with a large glass of water.

"Do you need to see a doctor?" she asks, giving me another once over.

"I'm fine, Mom." When she doesn't look convinced, I say, "Please. I'm just anxious for the awards."

She huffs and walks back over to her seat. The whole way through the ceremony she watches me like a hawk, and as the twinges get more uncomfortable I wonder if she's right. But then the presenter for the final award steps on the stage and I forget everything. It's time. She spends a while explaining that there's been a draw between two artists.

I barely hear any of it, too nervous. What I hear loud and clear: when she reels off S.C.A.R.A.B. and Six Seconds to Barcelona as the final two competitors.

"Oh," says Sophie.

"My," says Sooz.

"God," finishes my mom.

We all sit forward on the edge of our seats, and I rub at my bump as the baby shifts around, responding to my rising stress levels.

"Holy shit," groans Zoe, raising her hands to her face, peering through the small gaps in her slightly parted fingers. "I can't believe this is happening."

"Shh!" I hiss when the presenter starts to pull a piece of card out of a golden envelope.

The room is silent apart from the noise filtering through from the television. She clears her throat and says, "And the winner is …"

I think I'm going to be sick.

"S.C.A.R.A.B."

I gasp in shock. Then it hits me. They won. Jake won. They did it. Every sacrifice we made was worth it.

I shriek and jump up from my seat, bouncing in a way I didn't know was possible for a woman at full-term pregnancy. Water trickles down my legs and I stop moving.

"I know you're excited, Abs, but you didn't need to pee yourself," wheezes Zoe.

Sophie, Sooz, and my mom stare at the puddle at my feet.

"Zo, that's not pee," says Sophie. "Abs, your water has broken!"

"No, it hasn't," I squeak, refusing to look down and see the evidence.

"Yes," says Sooz.

"It has," finishes my mom, who then jumps to her feet and starts clapping her hands together. "It's baby time!"

The awards long forgotten, the girls start running around, gathering whatever they can get their hands on.

"Guys!" I shout, snapping them out of their sheer panic. "It's not time yet."

"But your water went …" says Zoe looking confused.

"Looks like I'm not the only one who didn't listen in birthing class." Zoe rolls her eyes and ignores my smug response. "It will be ages yet. Hell, it could even be tomorrow."

My voice sounds calm but inside I'm a mess. My brain is going haywire, in disbelief that this is it. I knew it was inevitable, but I went for the old pretend it wasn't going to happen approach which I'm quickly realizing wasn't the best idea. Especially when another twinge hits, this time longer and more intense, almost taking my breath away.

Apparently, what all the books say and what you learn in class, isn't always right. Most say it can be a long experience and there's no need to rush. That's not the case with this baby and having decided it's time to make its way into the world, there's nothing holding it back. I'm hit with one contraction after another, and only half an hour in, decide it's unbearable and that we need to get to the hospital, and quick. The franticness resumes as everyone bustles around me, grabbing whatever they can while my mom speaks on her phone while searching for her car keys.

Another contraction hits and it's a big one, I struggle to stay upright on the couch. When it passes, we manage to get outside and get me into the front seat of the car with the seat pushed back as far as it will go to give me room. I spend the whole time groaning as my mom races through the streets of

Brooklyn, the girls are all pasty white and unusually quiet in the back seat.

When we arrive, a nurse comes rushing out with a wheelchair. Everything is a blur as I ride the waves of pain that come with each contraction, steadily getting closer together. Panic rises and my chest pulls tight. I'm consumed by two thoughts.

The first: I'm not ready to do this.

The second: I can't do this without Jake, I need him here.

"Jake!" I cry out, leaning against the bed as a particularly strong contraction kicks in.

The birthing classes were wrong. They made a big deal about what a beautiful experience childbirth was. There's nothing beautiful about this. I'm ready for grabbing my bags and walking home.

"Shh," says my mom, brushing some hair away from my clammy forehead. "He's on his way."

A midwife walks into the room and says, "Abby West?"

I nod and grimace. When the pain subsides briefly, I'm able to clamber up onto the bed.

She smiles warmly. "My name's Karen and I'll be your midwife today." She's talking to me like we're on a goddamn tour bus, ready for taking in the sights of New York. "I need you to take off your pants please."

Zoe stares in alarm. "Why does she need to take her pants off?"

"How else do you think she's going to push the baby out? Do you think it just magically appears out of thin air?" My mom laughs.

Zoe looks a little green and doesn't say another word, just watches on in horror along with Sooz and Sophie, as I grip my mom's hand tight, struggling with the pain.

When she asks if she can get me anything, I say in a voice deeper than the core of the Earth, "Get me the fucking drugs."

She gives me the same look she gave our TV screen years ago when we watched The Exorcist together.

The midwife pops up from the end of the bed and says cheerily, "No can do, Abby! It's time for you to push this baby out."

"What about the drugs? The classes said there'd be drugs!" I all but plead, sweat beading on my forehead.

"Nope, no drugs, baby. It's time," says my mom.

I turn on her and narrow my eyes, unable to keep the venom from my voice. "What. Do. You. Mean. No. Drugs?"

She backs away and looks to the midwife for assistance. "Abby, unfortunately, we can't give you any pain relief. It wouldn't be effective because you're too far along. I need you to start pushing."

I shake my head and the five women in the room stare at me bewildered. "No. Not without Jake." I look away and start breathing deeply, fighting my body's urge to do as the midwife says.

I need him here.

I can't do this without him.

I won't.

Jake

"And the winner is … S.C.A.R.A.B.!"

There's activity all around but all I can do is sit in shock, with one image clear in my mind, Abby. The day I broke up with her back in high school, I left my heart in her hands, telling myself I'd fight like hell to get to the top, make the pain worth it. I needed to prove to myself that unlike what my grandpa used to say, my music wasn't a waste of time, I wasn't a low life because of it. I'm worthy of her. I know that now.

The roar that fills the arena hits me like a freight train when I come back to the present. The arena lights flood down, highlighting us to the world.

I blink. We did it. We actually fucking did it.

Glancing to both sides, I find the rest of the band doing the exact same as I am, sitting in shock. None of us imagined this would ever happen. We laughed when John West said we'd been shortlisted for the award. Never in our wildest dreams did we think we could win.

"Stand up!" yells John, struggling to make himself heard over all the noise. "Come on, you have to collect the award."

He doesn't leave us, knowing we don't have a clue what we're doing. We stand and shuffle along the row following his lead. I try to keep my attention focused on his back. Try and fail, because my eyes move sideways, taking in the hundreds of celebrities, people we've idolized over the years, applauding … for *us*.

We walk along the black, glossy stage with shaky legs, thousands of eyes following each step. I try not to think about the millions at home watching this all live on television, just like Abby. John leads us toward the podium where the presenter of the award is standing and clapping. She air kisses each of us and murmurs her congratulations.

My stomach flips when I realize I never even thought about a speech. Thankfully, Sam is an expert at talking shit and bluffing his way through things, so he steps forward and takes the mic, thanking the audience and all the fans for their support. While he waffles on, I get sidetracked thinking of Abby and what her reaction might have been. My eyes move across the crowds and connect with Dan White's. All he does is nod, but sometimes in life actions speak louder than words. The nod he gives is a white flag billowing in the air. The next thing I know we're being escorted off the stage, being led by some of the assistants to the VIP area backstage where the official after-party is taking place.

The room we step inside is almost as big as the arena itself, and for what feels like the millionth time tonight, I stand in shock. Aerial artists swing from the ceiling, floating back and forth through huge LED balls that hang at different heights, each glowing brightly and illuminating the room in a multitude of colors. A DJ set up in one corner fills the room with electro music—not our usual jam, but it fits the vibe. In the center, is one of the biggest bars I've ever seen, bright white and a hub of activity as bodies zone in, filling their glasses, ready to celebrate.

We don't step into the chaos at first, instead, we take a moment to ourselves, as a band, for the first time since exiting the limo. John West joins in when we form a huddle and begin jumping up and down, chanting that we did it.

John laughs and claps each of us on the back. "No one deserves this more than you guys," he says, the whole time staring in my direction.

He frowns when his cellphone starts to ring, pulling it from the inside pocket of his suit jacket. He glances at the screen, then silences it and goes to put it away but is stopped when it instantly starts ringing again. He raises a finger in the air and gestures for us to wait. He throws us an apologetic look when he steps away with his phone pressed to his ear.

"I think we could all use a drink," says Zach, nodding in the direction of the bar. "John will know where to find us."

"Let's do this," grins Ryan, rubbing his hands together, eyes gleaming with excitement.

We're about to start walking when a blonde head of hair I would recognize anywhere charges in our direction.

With a speed that seems superhuman, given the skyscraper heels she's wearing, Amanda closes the gap. She looks at me with wild eyes and pants, "Jake! I've been trying to find you. It's Abby."

In that same moment, John West hangs up and powers back over to us, his face taught. "The baby's on the way, we have to leave."

I stand, struggling to process the two life-changing moments that have been thrown at me within the space of ten minutes.

"Now!" he snaps.

I jump into action, and we all race behind Amanda, who expertly maneuvers her way through the throngs of celebrities, all trying to capture our attention and give us their congratulations. We ignore them all. I couldn't care if I'd just been named president, I have to get to Abby.

We're led out of the afterparty and along dimly lit back corridors, soon stopping outside a huge metal door, which Amanda knocks against rhythmically. The door swings open revealing two burly security guards standing side by side who nod down at us all. When they part, there's a limo, the engine running, ready to go. Wasting no time, we all pile in, Amanda included, and the vehicle screeches as it takes off along the back alley with speed.

Nobody speaks to me. They know not to.

All I'm able to do is watch the city fly by one second, crawl by the next. Each time the vehicle slows, and we hit traffic, I shift in my seat and my pulse elevates. I'm not ready for this. We've not seen each other since I left to tour Asia and the contact we have had over the few months I've been gone has been minimal. We were supposed to have more time. I had this whole plan to come home and for us to spend time together, so I could convince her we can do it, together. Now I'll never get a chance because this baby is coming whether we're ready or not.

After a particularly bad spell of traffic, we make good progress, soon pulling up outside the hospital. The limo barely comes to a stop as I fling open the door and dive out, stumbling forward toward the doors. Once inside I run to the reception, frantically asking for directions. I'm not sure how I digest all the information they spew at me, but I manage to make it finally to the area of the hospital where Abby should be.

"Abby West," I say, leaning against another reception desk, panting.

When I confirm who I am, the woman seated behind the desk smiles and walks into the main room. I follow her along a corridor where screams reach my ears. Panicking, I run past the nurse, toward the door where the noise is coming from. Seeing Abby's name written on the sign is all the confirmation I need, and I push through it, only to be greeted with gasps. Trust Abby to have a whole goddamn audience. You can barely move for all the bodies there are.

A short midwife steps forward and says sharply, "You can't be here!"

"Jake," whimpers Abby from the bed.

I don't see anything else, just her. It's like the moment we first met when I saw her from a distance in the park and knew instantly she was the one for me. Those feelings I had back then were tame compared to what I feel now.

"There are too many people in here. Some of you are going to have to leave," demands the midwife.

I turn and find the band, Amanda and John West standing, mouths hanging open as Abby cries out in agony, knees up, gown billowing around her waist, *everything* on display.

"Oh, for Christ's sake," exclaims Mrs. West. "It's not a sideshow. I'm sure you've all seen a vagina before. Now, like the midwife said, *out!*"

There's a flurry of activity and everyone that shouldn't be in the room leaves.

I'm about to turn and follow when Abby's mom grabs me by the arm and rolls her eyes. "Not you. You got her into this mess, you get to see it through to the end. Get by her side and act like a grown-up man for once in your life." The next part, she says quietly so only the two of us can hear. "She was refusing to push until you got here. You have to make her push; the baby is starting to show signs of distress."

The serious look in her eyes, along with Abby calling out my name, has me rushing over to the side of the bed.

"I can't do this," Abby murmurs into the crook of my neck when I lean forward, pulling her into me.

"You already are and you're doing amazing," I whisper into her hair. I pull back and take her pale, clammy face in my hands, staring straight into bright blue eyes. "Abby, I'm here and I promise I'm never leaving you again. Not you and not this baby. I love you both more than anything, now please, push."

At my words, a look of determination crosses her face, and the atmosphere in the room changes. The midwife rushes over with towels and her mom stands on the opposite side of the bed. The look she gives me, full of respect and understanding.

The midwife glances at the monitors and positions herself at the end of the bed. "Now, Abby, when I say, you need to push like you've never pushed before. We've waited too long, and the baby is starting to get tired, we have to get it out."

Abby nods and grips both mine and her mom's hands in each of her own. A contraction starts and the monitors begin bleeping. Concern flashes across the midwife's face, it's fleeting, but it's there. "Push!" she urges.

I watch desperately as Abby tucks her chin down against her chest, clenches her jaw, and does as the midwife instructs.

"Good," says the midwife, looking relieved that Abby is finally doing what she needs to. "Another one is going to come quick. Same again. A couple more pushes like that and you will have your baby in your arms."

I lean down and whisper into her ear, "You can do this."

She pulls back, her face full of anger and grunts, "You did this to me. I hate you right now."

I smirk, something I'll no doubt hear about later but couldn't care less if it gets the desired effect.

"Good." the midwife nods in my direction that it's time again. "Now push."

A roar I didn't know was humanely possible travels up her throat, ending in a sob.

"I can see the head! Again, Abby, straight into it, push!"

That's the moment our lives change. I watch as Abby with every ounce of strength she has inside her, pushes, and I've never been more in awe of someone in my whole life.

"The heads out. Same again," says the midwife.

Abby's mom takes the reins this time. "Come on baby, one last push."

The next few seconds are a blur. I feel like I'm out of my own body, floating above, watching as everything unfolds. Abby gives another huge push, and the midwife cries out in relief.

"She's out!"

There's a brief pause and everything is silent. I hold my breath, only able to hear the ringing in my ears, and watch as Abby sags in exhaustion against the bed. It feels like an eternity passes then a wail fills the room. I watch as the midwife holds the baby, then brings it forward, bundling it against Abby's chest.

Not *it*. *She*. Our daughter.

"Congratulations, Mom and Dad."

I can't do anything, too transfixed by the image in front of me. Abby with our baby in her arms. Something I never thought in my wildest dreams could have happened, yet here we are.

"I'll leave the three of you alone," says Abby's mom, cheeks wet with tears of joy. Before leaving she leans in and presses a kiss on Abby's forehead and gently strokes the baby's head. "You were wonderful, darling. I'll go and tell the others the good news."

The room may as well be empty as the midwife busies herself in the background filling out paperwork. If I could, I'd bottle the moment up, or never leave the bliss that settles around us. For now, nothing else matters but the three of us.

"We did it," gasps Abby, looking up at me, eyes wide with disbelief.

"No, *you* did it. You were incredible."

"Dad, you can cut the chord in a few minutes. Do you know what you'd like to call her?" asks the midwife and we both glance over. "It's fine if you don't, it's just for paperwork."

Without missing a beat, Abby responds, "Clara."

I suck in a sharp breath and the emotions that were burning in my eyes spill over. "You're sure?"

"It was never meant to be anything else," she replies, placing a kiss on Clara's head.

Before she knows what's happening, I reach down and gently lift her chin, closing the gap between us, placing my lips on hers, in the softest kiss we've ever had. It's so small and brief you could almost be convinced it never happened, but it's the kiss that in our whole history means the most. It's a promise for the future.

"Thank you," I say against her lips before pulling away.

If ever I needed a sign to reconfirm what I knew all along, that despite everything that's gone against us, Abby will always be the one for me, this is it. The moment when she promised me a future that was a far cry from my past and named our little girl after the woman who raised me and taught me that despite the flawed relationship with my grandpa and my mom, there was love out there.

She named her after the only person who ever really cared for me, my grandmother.

Later when Abby is sleeping, and I have Clara in my arms, I make a promise to my little girl, that one day in the future, when the time is right, I'll make sure we're a family and I'll be there for the both of them and love them unconditionally.

Always.

Chapter Twenty-One
Abby 3 Years Later

It doesn't matter how much time passes; this moment never gets any easier. There's a small tug at my hand and I look down, smiling at Clara. Her eyes are wide with excitement, her dark hair wild and curly, just like Jake's when it grows too long.

"Dad—dee!" she screeches, and my heart skips a beat.

The noise around us, the clicking of the cameras from the paps gathered behind Jake's security team, all disappears when my eyes find his as he walks confidently out of the arrivals area at JFK. Before I get a chance to stop her, Clara rushes forward and jumps into his arms.

A loud "Ooof" escapes him as she makes contact with his chest. If he's in pain, he doesn't show it. Instead, he lowers his guitar to the ground, gripping her firmly with his other arm. He grins and nuzzles his face into her hair. Like I do every time I see them together like this, I take a snapshot with my mind, packing it away into a box of happy memories. One of his security team walks over to them and grabs his guitar, while Jake strides over to me with Clara in his arms in the same way he does each time S.C.A.R.A.B. returns from a tour.

Becoming bored of our family reunion, the cameras start clicking and flashing when the rest of the band walk out. My shoulders sag with relief.

"Hi," I say with a smile.

"Hey." He flashes a toothy grin and butterflies swarm around my stomach. I ignore the itch in my hand to reach up push some of his hair out of his eyes.

"You need a haircut."

"It's my new image."

"Says who?"

"My stylist."

"I prefer it short. I like it when I can see your eyes." I bite down on my lip when it hits me what I've just said. Little things I keep saying.

Three years might have passed, but my feelings for Jake are stronger than ever. I thought my decision for us to just be friends would get easier, but each time Clara and I wait for him at the airport after another long stint away, my feelings come back tenfold.

Deep brown eyes hold mine and I start to panic at my fuck up. Before either of us has a chance to say anything else, Clara starts wriggling in his arms. "We should get going," he says.

His voice is rough in the way it only is when he's just woken up, and when I really take him in, I see the dark circles under his eyes. "You're exhausted, you don't need to do this tonight, you've just got back."

The "this" I'm referring to is his and Clara's reunion sleepover they have whenever he returns home from touring. Despite many an argument, he always wins, refusing to leave it even a few hours before spending time with her. It makes my heart swell painfully every damn time when I watch them walk through the airport together hand in hand.

Ignoring my comment, he crouches down and tickles Clara under the chin. "Mint or chocolate?"

"Choclaaaaaa!" she squeals.

They walk off and I trail behind, letting them share the moment together, wondering how it would be possible to feel for anyone how I feel about Jake.

I drop my keys on the side table an hour later when I step inside my and Sooz's apartment. "It's just me," I call out.

Sooz wanders out in a vest and super short shorts, her long blonde locks flowing around her shoulders. "Fuck me, it's hot."

"Sooz …"

She wafts her makeshift fan in front of her face and lets out a puff of air as she tries to blow a piece of hair out of her eyes. "Chill, Clara isn't here."

"Yeah, but the last time I let you off the hook you were cussing around her for weeks. Do I need to remind you what her first word was?"

She turns around with a "hmmmph."

"I preferred it when you were the angelic South African," I joke, following her into the kitchen. "Brooklyn has tainted you."

She pours us each a glass of wine then hands me one. She raises hers to her lips and replies, "Brooklyn made me."

We share a knowing glance, knowing she's right. Sooz moving to Brooklyn was the start of a new chapter for all of us. "No more cussing."

"Coming from Queen Potty Mouth."

"What does that even mean?" I laugh, the large sip of wine flooding my veins and making me feel a little lightheaded in the heat.

"I can't be bothered to explain. Anyway, how was Jake?"

I make slow work of taking another long drink of my wine. "Good."

"That's it? Just good?"

I roll my eyes. "What do you want me to say, Sooz? We were together less than an hour and the whole time he was focused on Clara. We're just friends."

"You have a human together; you will never just be friends."

She purses her lips and gazes at me in amusement. "You're blushing. You don't even believe it yourself. Little tip, Abs, if you're going to lie, you have to convince yourself of it first before anyone else will believe you."

"Fine," I snap. "There are still feelings there for him. What exactly am I supposed to do? Years have passed a—"

My phone pings and lights up on the kitchen counter. Pausing the conversation, I pick it up. A face-splitting grin takes over. "And I have a date!"

"What the hell? With who?" says Sooz, taking my glass and filling it to the brim.

We walk over to the couch and sit. "That guy I met while I was out running the other day. The one who asked for my number."

"You can't go on a date with a stranger."

I shake my head at how irrational she's being. "Sooz, everyone dates strangers. It's the whole point of dating. You don't know the person, so you get to know them."

"Hmmm." She grabs her own phone and starts ignoring me.

"Sooz. Stop. I know you want me and Jake to make things work, but it's not going to happen. Please, can you be happy for me?"

She lets out a sigh and sets her phone down. "I think you're making a mistake, but it's your life, Abs. Do whatever feels right."

I hold my head high. "This feels right. He seems like a nice guy."

"What's his name?"

"Chad."

She snorts into her wine glass and coughs at the same time she says, "Preppy."

"Sooz!"

She holds her wine glass up, laughter in her eyes. "Fine. No more. Let's do a toast. To Chad."

"To Chad." I grin.

We spend the rest of the night discussing my up-and-coming date. The first one I've had since S.C.A.R.A.B.'s debut tour in Europe with Dan. The whole time we avoid the elephant in the room. How the hell I'm going to tell Jake.

Trying to navigate through the morning rush of New York is an impossible task. I curse to myself when it feels like the record label is getting further away rather than closer. It was a wasted effort styling my hair for the day as it's now sticking to the back of my neck uncomfortably. My frizz factor is probably off the charts.

Eventually, the label comes into view, and I let out a sigh of relief, shrug my kit bag further up my shoulder and increase my speed, needing the journey to be over sooner rather than later. Thank God for air-con. The chill hits me when I step out of the early morning heat into the foyer, and I almost do a little jig on the spot.

One uncomfortably cramped elevator ride later and I step out onto the floor of my dad's label. I'm heading in the direction of his office when something catches my attention through the glass window of one of the conference rooms. I stop and look again, finding Jake and Clara seated at the room-length table. Clara bounces in the seat, her eyes full of excitement as Jake strums his guitar, a look in his eyes he saves for her alone.

The lump of muscle in my chest I've learned to ignore over the past few years aches. There's only one word that springs to mind that can describe how I feel when I watch him with her. Longing. I don't just hate that I've put us in the friends' zone, I despise it. Those words Jake murmured to me that night at his door were right. Us being friends is an impossibly painful task.

Jake and Clara are in their own bubble, totally unaware I'm there, watching the two of them together. It's rare I get to see them like this, so I seize the opportunity and pull my camera out of my bag, fumble as I try to remove the lens cap quickly, raise my camera and snap a picture on a slow shutter speed before they notice my presence. I manage to get a few images before Jake looks up. His expression changes when he sees me. Not unreadable. Not closed off. Too many emotions I don't want to admit to seeing because it makes me question every choice I've made about our relationship.

I give him a tight smile; one I don't feel in any part of my body and make a decision. I need to go on the date with Chad, like yesterday. Zoe's right, the best way to get over someone is to get under them. Jake waves for me to go in the room and seeing him do so, Clara turns around and grins when she sees me through the glass. Before I go in, I quickly pull out my phone, sending Chad a quick message asking if he's free tonight for a date.

I step inside the conference room and without the soundproof glass, Clara's squeals fill the room. I laugh when she charges over and grabs me by the legs then tries to clamber up my body. She'd definitely get a role in *Twilight*; her spider monkey abilities make her appear superhuman at times. When we've finished cuddling and she's told me every minor detail of her Clara-Daddy sleepover, most of which I don't understand, I lower her to the ground and smile at Jake. It's a false smile and he recognizes it for what it is instantly.

"What's wrong?" he says, face grim.

"Clara, baby. Want to go see Grandpa?"

She jumps up and down excitedly, and Jake stays where he is while I walk her to his office. He refrains from questioning why I need him to watch her. Thank God.

When I get back to the conference room, Jake looks up at me expectantly.

I slide into the seat next to him and take a deep breath. "I need to tell you something."

He groans and drags a hand over his face. "Hit me with it."

"I have a date," I mumble, staring at the table.

"Okay."

My eyes dart up to his. "That's it? Just okay?"

He throws me an infuriating smirk and his brown eyes sparkle. "What do you want me to do, Abs? Go all caveman on you and throw a chair across the room?"

"No," I snap, annoyed. "I just …"

"Wanted more of a reaction from me. I know."

"Jake I—"

"Abby. Stop. Go on your date. Have fun."

I sit and watch at a loss as he stands. I expect him to disappear out of the room without saying anything else.

Instead, he gets closer, leans down, and his cologne invades my senses, the scent I only recognize as him. He tucks my hair behind my ear. "Feel free to ring me when it's done and tell me what a disaster it was." His hand trails down from my hair and his fingers skim over my collar bone, my skin scorching beneath his touch. "Always us, Abs. *Always.*"

Without another word, he leaves the room and I'm left a pile of mush in my seat, praying he isn't right. If he is, then it means only one thing: He's officially ruined me for all men.

"So, Chase, tell me a bit more about yourself."

"Abby, my name is Chad."

I wrack my brain trying to figure out why he just said that then realize I've called him the wrong name. *Again.* This is a disaster. I briefly place my head in my hands. Dammit, Jake. He knew exactly what he was doing when he leaned down and said what he did. He got my heart pounding, pulse racing, my body tingling in a way only he knows how and it's all I've been able to think about for the entirety of the day. Including the duration of my date with Chip. I mean Chad.

I look across the table at the poor guy sitting, looking like he wishes he were anywhere but here with me. I don't blame him. The worst bit, he looks a bit like Jake in that he has dark hair and dark eyes. They're the only similarities, but I see them now for what they are. Belisha beacons. Warning lights flashing brighter than those of an emergency vehicle, signaling that what I'm trying to do is replace Jake with something similar. I'm such an idiot.

"Chad." I mentally high-five myself that I've finally got his name right. "I'm so sorry. I shouldn't have agreed to go on a date with you."

He nods. "There's someone else, I get it."

My shoulders slump and I feel relieved that he understands.

"We're splitting the cheque," he says, bringing our brief time together to an end.

Sooz creases over with laughter. When she's done, she sits up and wipes the tears from beneath her eyes. I refrain from telling her she's smudged her eyeliner across her face. It's what she gets for spending the best part of half an hour laughing at my self-imposed misfortune.

"You can say it now."

I shake my head. "Nope."

"Do it, Abby."

"No."

She grins. "You're going to say it eventually, why delay the inevitable?"

"Fine," I huff. "You were right."

"Poor, Chad," says Sophie from my laptop screen.

I almost don't hear her over Zoe, who has also spent the majority of the Zoom call howling with laughter.

"See this as a rite of passage," says Sooz.

I look at her questioningly. "How would a date disaster be a rite of passage?"

"You're one step closer to realizing that this idea you had for you and Jake to be friends is ridiculous."

I stare at Sooz then down at the screen where Sophie and Zoe now have serious expressions. "Do you both think that too?"

"Erm, duh," replies Zoe.

Sophie just nods yes.

I let out a long groan. "What am I going to do? I'm tired of fighting this. I thought it would get easier but it's just getting harder."

"Then stop fighting it and just let it be," says Sophie.

"What does that even mean?"

"It means stop overthinking every aspect of your life," says Zoe. "Roll with it and see what happens."

"What if it doesn't work?"

"And what if it does," says Sooz. "You'll never know unless you try."

Chapter Twenty-Two
Jake

The last thing I expected when I woke up this morning was to get a call from John West. He hasn't called me personally since right before the awards that took our career to the next level.

The elevator doors slide open, and I let out a huff of air, my eyes taking in the same sight they have for the past five years since he first began poaching the band. The label has become a second home. For all of us.

Stepping out into the reception area of the label, people buzz around, asking if there's anything they can help me with. Mandy who mans the phones winks and licks her lips. I offer her a tight smile in return, trying not to come across as rude, then make my way to John West's corner office and knock against the glass door. Pointless because he can see me clear as day.

Still on the phone, he looks up and gestures with his hand for me to step inside. Once settled at the chair opposite him, I focus on the view out the window, drinking in the sight of New York humming below, trying not to listen in on the remainder of his call.

Finally, he finishes and slides his phone on his desk. "Sorry about that."

"No problem," I reply.

"We officially signed Six Seconds to Barcelona yesterday," he says, getting straight to the nitty-gritty.

It's now clear why he wanted to see me in person. Despite the years that have passed and the fact neither of us has been romantically linked with Abby, things are still tense whenever Dan White and I are in close vicinity to each other. Something which is going to be more likely if we're signed on the same record label.

I clench my jaw. "Congratulations."

"Do I need to be concerned?" he frowns, seeing through my attempt at not caring.

I stare back out the window and the lie rolls off my tongue. "Not at all."

It's not a lie. I don't care about Dan White right now. All I can think about is the date Abby went on last night which I pray to God was a disaster.

"Good. That's all I wanted to say. I thought the way gossip goes, it would find its way around the party tonight and I wanted you to hear it from me."

"I appreciate you taking the time," I say politely.

"Jake ..."

"Yeah?"

"My granddaughter is my world."

"Okay?"

"And my daughter. Nothing makes me happier than seeing them happy."

I frown. "I don't think I'm following."

"I have a very happy granddaughter, who's lucky to have a wonderful Mother and a fantastic Father." His eyes gleam, full of admiration. It disappears when he starts to speak again. "It's unfortunate the same can't be said about my daughter. Being happy that is."

"She seems fine to me," I grumble, thinking back on how chirpy she was when she informed me of her date.

"Abby is an expert at hiding her feelings, you should know that better than anyone."

I frown. "I don't get where you're going with this."

"I stand by what I said last time. I made a mistake telling you not to go after my daughter. A big mistake. She's not happy. At all and I hate seeing my daughter unhappy. There's only one person I know can change that … you."

I stare him in the eye, looking for any sign of insincerity, but I find nothing. He's telling the truth. It's been three years since Clara entered the world and turned our lives upside down. Abby was right when she said it wasn't the right time for us to give our relationship a go. Even apart, the sleepless nights and chaos of dealing with a baby pushed us to our limits. If we'd been together like she predicted, it would have broken us. Especially when there was still so much left unsaid. So much lack of trust, on her side more than mine.

The two of us together at that point in time would have been a recipe for disaster and following S.C.A.R.A.B. winning Artist of the Year at the VMAs, our schedule went from wild, to unmanageable.

But Clara's not a baby anymore and I'm getting tired of avoiding my feelings for Abby. It's physically painful and the only solace is my music.

"She doesn't want anything to happen between us." To my own ears, I sound as defeated as I feel.

John leans back in his chair, his lips pulling up at the corners. "You and I both know my daughter is excellent at running away from things."

"What exactly are you suggesting?"

"That you do what I stopped you from doing the summer she came home. Fight for her and don't let her go."

Abby

"If you can raise your hands just a little, great. Now turn to the right, your right. Perfect don't move."

I mess with the command dial on my camera briefly, adjusting the settings to suit the light on set. When everything is as it needs to be I press the shutter release. The rhythmic click as I move around, capturing the model from different angles is all I can hear and I zone out from the world, focusing on only one thing. Capturing the perfect image.

A few hundred photos later and I think I finally have enough to work with, there has to be a decent one somewhere. It's been a long tiring day, but it's the good kind of exhaustion. It's the kind of exhaustion that when you climb into bed at the end of the day, you feel like you're doing something with your life, achieving what you were always set out to do.

It's taken a long time to get to this point. Sooz had this whole big plan set out. The idea was she would move to Brooklyn, we'd find an office, Sophie, Amanda, and Zoe would join us and we'd have a successful business within a few weeks. Like anything in life, it was never going to be that simple. Even for a control freak like Sooz. Everything that could go wrong did go wrong. Flooded offices, botched marketing, muck ups with new clients, and a photographer with a baby who screamed twenty-four hours a day, seven days a week, meaning no actual photos were taken, were just a few of the challenges we faced. Now, three years later, the temporary photographer that covered me while I struggled in the early days with Clara, is a permanent member of our team along with a few others. And our company—Next Level PR—now has a rep for being one of the best PR teams in New York. State, not just city.

"Are we ready to start wrapping things up?" asks Sooz, standing by my side, glancing down as I flick through the small preview screen to double-check we have enough to work with.

"Yeah, I've got what I need."

"I can't believe Allure magazine is letting us handle the launch of their new office in Florida," she squeals.

Zoe walks over with a smug look on her face. "At least Becket was good for something … his connections."

I roll my eyes and ignore her comment, refusing to get onto the subject of my ex and how much she dislikes him yet again. He did us a huge favor helping to set this up, along with the other things he's helped me with that no one else knows about. Like I said all along, the world doesn't know the real Michael Becket. Hell, after four years together I barely scratched the surface, but what I do know, is that deep down he's a good guy.

"I can't stay for clean-up, sorry," I say, pulling a face.

Zoe huffs. "I think I need to have a kid if it means getting out of all the shitty jobs."

"The way you ran scared out of the delivery room … I find it hard to believe that will ever happen." I wink and she goes to swat me.

Sophie calls from across the room, "Abs, it's after five. Jake's rang asking where you are."

"Crap," I mutter to myself. Like always, time was forgotten as soon as I had my camera in my hands and now, I'm late. "Queue grouchy Daddy Bear."

His grouchiness is going to be increased after the bombshell I dropped on him about my date. In hindsight maybe it would have been a better idea to have kept it to myself and inform him had it shown signs of developing into something. Poor, Chip. I mean, Chad.

The girls all chuckle, but before I leave, Sooz grabs me by the arm and says, "Don't forget, your ass is ours tomorrow."

"Like I could forget," I grimace.

"Welcome to the dark side, you only turn thirty once!"

I laugh and quickly throw my kit into the right bags, slinging them over my shoulders and shuffling outside. Inside was warm but nothing like outside. The transition from Spring to Summer hasn't been kind and the most recent heatwave we've been hit with has been relentless. Sweat covers my skin and I've barely moved.

Pulling out my phone from the pocket of my denim shorts, I decide walking and catching the subway is off the cards and opt for ordering an Uber. It's a luxury I try not to use. Between childcare costs, rent on mine and Sooz's apartment, and the relentless expenses of a new business,

I've learned to be stringent with money most days. Today isn't one of them though. Needs must and all that.

After half an hour and a lot of rush hour traffic, the uber pulls up outside our apartment building. It's a sad moment when I step outside and have to say goodbye to the air con, especially knowing the hot box that's awaiting. Three flights of stairs and a lot of huffing and puffing later, I'm back to where I started. A hot, sweaty mess.

"I'm home!" I shout, tossing my keys down on the side table like I always do and dropping my bags on the ground.

All I get in return is silence. It's never silent.

"Boo!" screams Clara and I shriek, very nearly but not quite, peeing my pants.

I look around but still can't see her. When a small giggle reaches my ears, traveling up from the ground, I bend over and find a pair of huge brown eyes glowing in the darkness from under the couch. She giggles again and I smile. I might be exhausted from the long days we've been clocking in recently, but nothing beats coming home to this.

I almost pee myself for the second time in a minute when I'm suddenly lifted from the ground and find myself being spun around in the air.

"Jake, put me down!" I scold, whacking him hard between the shoulder blades.

"Oooo ow, please don't hurt me," he chuckles, lowering me to the ground.

The deep vibrations of his laughter travel through me, as my body skims slowly against his and I feel every muscle tensing.

Suddenly the weather isn't to blame for the fact I'm overheating, it probably has something to do with his hands on my hips, burning through the thin material of my vest. I shouldn't look up, but I'm a glutton for punishment. I know what happens each time Jake and I find ourselves in awkward moments like this. First, my heart feels like it's about to burst out of my chest and nothing makes sense, then the moment breaks, and the following weeks are spent trying to get my head back on straight while he tours the world surrounded by groupies.

I look down and as predicted, the moment is gone as quick as it appeared. Jake frowns and watches as I walk to the kitchen, avoiding him at all costs.

"Clara, bathroom and get cleaned up ready for dinner," I say over my shoulder.

She toddles off and busies herself doing the opposite of what I asked. I pull out a few random things from the refrigerator, deciding she can have a snack meal, her favorite kind. I'm midway through chopping when a shiver runs down my spine. I turn my head and find Jake leaning against the worktop, arms folded across his chest. My eyes flicker down to his biceps, watching the muscles strain beneath his tattoo sleeves. I quickly look away and go back to preparing Clara's dinner, who I can hear in the background playing and singing to her dolls happily.

"Go on a date with me."

I'm so shocked at the words coming from his mouth I misjudge what I'm cutting and slice straight into my finger. "Ah," I hiss and dart over to the sink, running the cut under the cool water.

"Dammit. Sorry. Let me help," says Jake and begins opening and closing random cupboards, searching for the first aid kit.

"Top left," I inform him, and he slides past, the front of his body brushing against my back in the small space. Note to self: find a place with a bigger kitchen.

I watch out of the corner of my eye, trying not to make it obvious what I'm doing. What our apartment lacks in floor space, it makes up for in height, so the top left cupboard is pretty damn high. So high that when Jake stretches and extends his arms as far as he can to grab the first aid kit his gray T-shirt rises, revealing his taut stomach. What the hell is wrong with me? This was all so easy until it wasn't. I should have known better than to tell him about my date. It's like a switch has been flicked. It was supposed to be an opportunity to move on. All it's done is added fuel to the fire. Now, all I can think about is Jake.

First aid kit in hand, he steps in close to my side, so close I can feel the heat pouring off him and forget how to breathe. You'd think over the years my body would learn to have less of a reaction, would get used to being in proximity with him. It doesn't, everything just gets worse, every reaction heightened to the point it's become unbearable.

"Here," he says, grabbing a towel and wrapping it around my hand.

He turns slightly, giving me, some much-needed space and I gulp in what little air there is in the room, while he busies himself searching through the kit for the right-sized band-aid. When he finds the right one, he grins at me, waving it in the air.

"What are you doing?" I frown, trying to ignore the way my stomach keeps somersaulting.

"Helping," he replies, grabbing hold of my arm and tugging it toward him gently. When he pulls the towel off, I watch, mesmerized as he purposefully skims the rough tips of his fingers along the palm of my hand. The band-aid is firmly in place, but he doesn't let go of my hand. "Go on a date with me."

All day I'd mentally prepared myself for him to be pissed after how I handled things yesterday in the conference room. I don't know how to cope with how he's being. It's too familiar, too much. I want more.

"I think there's a word missing from that sentence."

He crouches down so his brown eyes are level with my blue ones. "Please, Abs."

I shake my head and snatch my hand back. "No."

He stands tall, the hopeful look disappears from his face. "That's it, no?"

Taking a step back, I busy myself with Clara's dinner once more. "Just friends, Jake. You seem to be forgetting."

"I haven't forgotten, I'm just choosing to ignore it. I've given you time, Abby. A lot of time. And that little game you decided to play wasn't funny. How did your date go? Is there going to be a second? Want me to take a guess?"

With every word, he moves in closer, and we find ourselves backed up against the wall. I duck around him and go back to Clara's dinner.

"You can give me all the time in the world, and it won't be enough. There isn't an us anymore." His shoulders shake as he struggles to hold in his laughter. "What's so funny?"

"You. That you believe what we have is over."

"Jake, seriously? Have you been reading Sooz's romance books or something since you got back? That alpha male crap isn't going to work. N-O spells no. Clara!" I shout, praying for once she will listen and provide a much-needed distraction so we can end the conversation.

Our little brown-haired ball of chaos comes barreling in and I let out a sigh of relief.

Admitting defeat, Jake leans down and scoops her up in a hug before leaving. He's almost at the door to the apartment when he shouts, "Have a nice birthday."

My stomach sinks, knowing it will be more than nice, it will be great, but it will be without the one person who matters more than Clara. Him.

Chapter Twenty-Three
Abby

Standing in front of the mirror in my childhood bedroom, I take in the sequined dress Zoe picked out. It sits just above the knee and falls softly around each shoulder, exposing just the right amount of skin with the love heart neckline. It's casual but dressy at the same time, and the mint green and pale blue of the leopard print pattern make my eyes appear even bluer. Thanks to Zoe's expert hand, my hair sits in perfectly tousled waves around my shoulders and my eyes pop with the help of the smokey liner and many layers of jet-black mascara she used.

The only no-go was the shoes. She kicked up an absolute stink when I refused to wear the heels she picked out, but there's no way I'm traipsing around whatever bars and clubs they have planned for the night with my feet aching. I want to have fun, which means no heels. I give the black converse on my feet a smug look then move away from my reflection.

"Abs, you look amazing," says Sophie.

"God, I'm good," says Zoe. "In the mood for being daring?"

I raise a brow. "Are we talking edgy daring or more along the lines of public indecency daring?" She widens her eyes and fakes being shocked. "Don't pretend you don't know what I'm talking about."

"Whatever, Mother," she huffs. "Now can I finish the look?"

She pulls out a deep plum lipstick and I freeze. It's not me at all, but when has she ever been wrong? I hate to admit it, but never. Which is why I nod yes when she says, "Can I?" Her expression turns serious while she concentrates on lining my lips then fills them in with the lipstick. Finishing with a little bit of gloss for the topcoat, she steps back and admires her work. "Perfect."

I turn slowly and look back in the mirror, smiling at what I see. "Thank you."

"What, no bitchy comment? What's wrong with you?"

"Well, I'm almost thirty you know." I chuckle. "I'm trying out the mature thing."

Zoe holds her hand up. "You have precisely"—she glances at her phone to check the time—"six hours and twenty-two minutes left of your twenties. Maturity doesn't kick in until midnight and even then, any actions of your twenties self, do not impact the following day. Them's the rules. It's your birthday, which means it's time to get wasted."

"And what will be your excuse for why we wind up carrying you home?" asks Sophie, fluffing her golden hair.

"I don't need an excuse." Zoe laughs. "I go to the beat of my own drum. Now, one final check before we leave."

We each stand in front of the full-length mirror checking our reflections. I'm not entirely sure what I'm looking for, but I go through the motions to keep her happy.

"I hate to break it to you, Zo," says Sooz, fanning herself. "This effort you've put in might be wasted because I'm already sweating my ass off."

"Meh. Soon we'll be too wasted to care. Let's do this, bitches!" sings Zoe, stalking out of my room and leaving Sooz, Sophie, and myself to follow behind.

"What are we even doing tonight?" I ask Sophie.

She answers vacantly, "Just some bars. The usual."

I narrow my eyes. "So why the extra effort?"

"Because it's your birthday and since having Clara, you *never* let your hair down." She flounces off and I'm left trailing behind with Sooz typing frantically on her phone.

"Mommy, pwincess," squeals Clara, watching me from the bottom of the stairs.

"Thank you, baby," I say when I get to the bottom, crouching down so she can run into my arms.

"Do not cry. You'll ruin your make-up," says Zoe sternly when she notices the sheen in my eyes.

"I think I should be more worried about you spilling drinks on me later." I wink.

She winks back. "Well, it is your thirtieth. I've been a good girl recently. I've been saving it for a special occasion."

"Touché."

"You look beautiful," says my dad, wandering over to take Clara off my hands. At first, she refuses to go, grumpy and exhausted with it being past her bedtime, but eventually, she gives in and climbs into his arms. He places a brief kiss on my head. "I'm going to take this little one up to bed. Make sure you save me some champagne."

"We have champagne?" I ask, focusing on the small, but very important detail he let slip.

"Er, of course we do. You only turn thirty once." Sooz chuckles, clapping her hands together.

Acknowledging that the girls are right and that it really has been a long time since I've let my hair down, both physically and metaphorically, I hoot, "Show me where it's at!"

My parents' open-plan kitchen-dining area has been decorated with balloons while we've been upstairs. The most important feature that captures my attention, the bottles of champagne set on ice ready, the flutes beside them glistening invitingly.

"Before we open them, I want a twirl," my mom says with a laugh when she catches me staring intently at the alcohol on offer. "I never get to see you dressed up like this and that dress is gorgeous. You did a good job, Zoe. Shame about the shoes though."

Sophie and Sooz nod their agreement while I spin around quickly, feeling awkward at being the center of attention. When I finish putting on my little show, I walk over toward the champagne and am about to grab a bottle, when a figure jumps up from behind, frightening the life out of me.

"Surprise!" screams Dan, laughing when I bend over hyperventilating.

"What the hell!" I gasp.

He walks around the center island and pulls me into his arms, avoiding the playful punch in the arm I try to throw his way. "You didn't think I'd miss your birthday, did you?"

"I thought you were on tour?" I ask when we pull apart.

"I am. Even rockstars get a break, especially for something important." He tugs me back in for another hug.

"You've come all this way for a night out?"

"Stop questioning and just enjoy it. Not everything has to be overanalyzed. Fancy that champagne now?"

I look over at the bottles skeptically. "Is anyone else going to jump out? I'd actually like to make it into my thirties."

"No more surprises, promise," says Sophie, wandering over. "You're too nosey for us to get anything else by you."

My mom begins popping the corks on the bottles and filling the glasses. When she's done and my dad has joined us after putting Clara to bed, we raise them high, and the room is filled with the sound of clinking glass. There's no doubt in my mind that this is as civilized as the night is going to get. The first sip is the best and I relish the feeling of the fizz as it travels down and settles in my stomach, soon creating a warm buzz that takes over my body and has me sighing with contentment.

I look around, surrounded by my closest friends and family, thinking to myself, what a difference a few years can make. Clara forced me to grow up and be more decisive, to speak out for the things I wanted or needed. Thanks to her, thirty looks different from what I imagined it would be and I feel optimistic the best is yet to come. My life is just beginning and with her by my side I know it's going to be a hell of a ride.

I could have spent the night standing in my parent's kitchen, drinking champagne, but eventually, Zoe shouts over the steadily increasing noise level that our cabs are waiting outside. We pile out into the sticky heat of the evening, ready to head to whatever destination, I don't know, but I'm sure it will be a good one.

"You said no surprises," I hiss into the darkness.

I hear snickers all around.

"Actually," says Zoe, "*you* said no surprises. We chose to ignore you."

Struggling to walk in a straight line, I sway thanks to the cocktails and shots from the previous couple of bars coursing through my veins.

"I hope it isn't a strip club. If it is, I'm going home."

There are more snickers and I hear a door opening while we carry on walking. Suddenly the hands guiding me lift from my arms, then there's nothing.

"Guys?" Still nothing.

This is so typical of Zoe and Sophie. I stand blindfolded not knowing what to do and feeling like an idiot. Getting fed up, I huff and lift the blindfold away from my eyes.

I almost fall over when the room erupts with a giant, "Surprise!"

Balloons fall from the ceiling, and I'm showered with multicolored confetti. It takes a while for my eyes to adjust, and when they do, I manage to take in my surroundings properly. We're standing in the middle of Riff's, which I barely recognize thanks to its transformation. Decorations hang from every surface, including the metal beams across the ceiling. The girls have gone overboard, but the venue is perfect, and I love it.

I glance at the bar which is filled with rows of cocktails and champagne. To the side of the bar, there's a huge table, filled with food, and my eyes are drawn to the giant cake in the center topped with a sparkling number thirty decoration. All the doors that lead to the large terrace are open, so the guests can spill out to the outdoor stage where a band has already started performing. A net of thousands of fairy lights creates a canopy overhead in the now darkening night sky. Everything feels magical.

The best bit is the people I'm surrounded by. I tear up when I spin in a circle, taking in the faces of all my guests. Zoe and Sophie have made sure not to miss anyone off the list, and there are even old friends from high school they both know I've kept in touch with over the years via social media. And in the middle of the room, their arms around each other, beaming at me proudly, are my parents.

I can't contain my squeals when my eyes settle on Shaun, Sam, Zach, and Ryan. I run over jumping into each of their arms excitedly. Things might have been awkward between us all during my pregnancy when everything was so confusing and messed up, but the moment Clara made her way into the world, everything changed. I'm not the only one who grew up.

When I'm finished being over-excited with the guys, I move around the room, trying to make time for every guest, a drink in my hand at all times. Even though I'm distracted playing my part of social butterfly, my eyes skit around, searching for Jake. I can't stop myself.

We're about an hour into the party when I decide I need a quick break from socializing. I make my way to the bar and spend a couple of minutes trying to decide which cocktail to have next. Who knows what number it is, I'm having too much fun to keep count. When I decide, I turn and lean my weight against the wood behind me, feeling a little drunk.

My eyes are focused on the outdoor area when Sam walks over.

"He's not over there." He smirks.

"Who?" I ask innocently, knowing exactly who he's referring to.

"Come on, I'm not the idiot everyone thinks I am." He pulls a face that says otherwise and has me not so gracefully snorting the bright orange cocktail I chose out of my nose.

"Zoe's going to kill me," I say, using the napkin he hands over to wipe my face, grimacing when I see streaks of her expertly applied foundation on the paper. When I've finished mopping up the mess, I admit, "I'm only trying to see him before he sees me. I need the upper hand."

He raises a brow. "Please tell me we're not back to playing games after all this time."

"We're not, I swear. I just …" I don't know why I'm looking out for Jake, or what I expect to happen when I see him.

"…want to play it cool?" Sam finishes.

"Something like that." I laugh.

"Well, if it puts your mind at ease, you won't find him anywhere."

Disappointment hits me and an "Oh," slips out before I can stop it.

Sam smirks at my reaction. "Chill. He messaged about ten minutes ago to say he was running late, which means you've got time to get yourself good and wasted, ready for when he does grace us with his presence."

Deciding we've focused on Jake enough, I ask, "How've you been?"

With work and Clara, I haven't had a chance to catch up with any of the guys, and whenever there has been a lull in my schedule, they've been away on tour.

"I'm fine," he smiles. "I got myself a girl."

I can't hide my surprise. "Really? Who?"

He points straight ahead to where Shaun is standing with two women. One has her arm looped through his and the other, a petite red head, has her body angled, not so subtly watching Sam and I talk.

"Somebody finally tamed the beast?"

"I wouldn't exactly say that." He chuckles. "She's nice though. Things are going well."

"She's made it longer than some."

He stands taller when the red head makes it blatantly obvious that she's unimpressed with how long he's been talking to me, staring daggers in our direction. "I better get back to me lady."

"I'll speak to you later." I give him a small wave and watch as he leaves.

There's no time for rest because the girls saunter over with a huge tray filled with shots and my eyes nearly pop out of my head. The last time we did shots like this, it resulted in Clara making her way into the world. Part of me wants to protest and say we shouldn't, but then I think what the hell. It's my birthday and it's been years since I've gotten wasted, letting my hair down one time won't hurt.

Zoe looks shocked when I grab two shots straight off the tray without any fuss and hold them up in the air for the others to follow suit.

"To thirty!" I shout.

We all down the shots in one go.

The hour that follows is a blur.

The party is in full swing, and I spend most of my time with the girls, outside, dancing to the music. After a while, drinking on an empty stomach becomes too much, and my stomach groans in protest. I make my way to the buffet table and pile a plate high with food. A hand snakes around my waist and I freeze for a second, then relax when I hear Dan's voice.

He places a swift kiss on my cheek. "Are you having a good night?"

I nod, then realizing I've barely seen him all evening, say, "Sorry. I haven't spent much time with you."

He shrugs. "It's your birthday, Abby. Don't apologize for having fun. It's enough watching you with that huge grin on your face."

I smile to myself. "It's been an amazing night."

"It's not over yet," he says, his eyes twinkling mischievously.

I narrow my own. "What are you up to?"

"Nothing," he sings.

"Why don't I believe you?"

"Because you're suspicious of everything?"

"Whatever." Knowing he's being playful, I give him the one-fingered salute and walk off in search of my parents, who I also haven't seen for a large chunk of the night.

Everything goes quiet when a voice clears over a mic. "Hello? Can everyone hear me?"

I look and find Dan standing in the middle of the room. I blush. He clears his throat again and I squirm when it dawns on me that he's about to start singing. Thankfully, it's not just him. The whole room joins in so loud my ears ring, while Sophie, Zoe, Sooz, and Amanda carry the giant cake toward me.

"Make a wish," says Amanda when the song ends.

I close my eyes, doing as she says, then begin the task of blowing out the huge number of candles. When I'm done, I feel lightheaded and in need of a drink. I spin around to go to the bar, slamming straight into a wall of solid muscle.

I don't fall back like I expect to. Instead, my eyes burn a slow path upward, drinking in the sight of Jake in a black tux. When I reach his face, my eyes are held by his, which sparkle in amusement when I stare longer than is acceptable for someone who wants to just be friends.

There's a magnet between us, a pull so strong even if I were to try I wouldn't be able to break away. I swallow and feel myself starting to sweat more than I already am in the oppressive heat.

Finally, I work up the courage to speak, "Hi."

His eyes search mine, looking for something, I'm not sure what. "Happy birthday, Abby." His breath caresses my skin.

"You're late," I croak.

His body shifts and for a fleeting moment, I fear he's going to kiss me. Instead, he leans down and says quietly, "Let me make it up to you. Let me take you on a date."

I frown. He's seriously doing *this* again, at my party, in front of everyone. I step back, putting some much-needed space between us. "I better get back to my other guests. Have a good night, and thanks for coming."

I turn and walk away quickly before we get tangled in the same messy dance we always do.

The girls are standing off to the side of the room and when I reach them, Sooz hands over a large drink with a knowing look. I smile back, the best I can and try to shake the moment away. I'm taking a large gulp of my drink when Dan throws an arm around my shoulders, tugging me in close to his side. I know what he's doing and I'm not in the mood for playing games.

I shrug him off with a small smile, look to the girls and say, "I could do with a trip to the restroom."

Sophie replies, "I'll come with you."

Once out of earshot, Sophie doesn't waste a second. "What the hell was that?"

"I haven't got a clue," I groan. "I really do need to pee."

I shuffle off and when I'm finished, walk over to the sinks. Sophie leans against one, waiting.

"Are you mad at Dan?" she asks, having picked up on the little show he put on for Jake.

"I'm too wasted to care," I admit.

"When does he leave?"

"In a few days," I confirm. "The band signed their contracts with my dads' label, so he'll be spending a lot of time there before he goes home."

"That's exciting for him."

I fake touching up my make-up as I change the subject. "So, Sam has a girlfriend …"

"I know. Weird, right." She completely misses what I'm hinting at, so I decide not to push it.

"And Shaun? I always thought he and Zoe would get together."

At this, she looks thoughtful then sighs. "Me too. I guess some things just aren't meant to be."

Like me and Jake, I think to myself sadly.

Taking a quick glance at my phone, I see that it's past ten pm and hours have flown by without me realizing it.

"Hey. There are officially less than two hours left of my twenties. Fancy going out with a bang?" I wiggle my brows at her, and she laughs.

"Do you even need to ask? Let's make sure your thirtieth is one birthday you won't forget."

Chapter Twenty-Four

Abby

There are some things in life that never change, even when you turn thirty. Waking up with my now part-time waster friends is one of them. But, for the first time in years, when I open my eyes, I may be hungover beyond belief, but I have no regrets. If only the same could be said for the others.

"Oh, sweet mother of God," groans Sooz into the pillow of her makeshift bed on the floor. "I don't know why I let you guys do this to me."

"Can you speak quieter? Scrap that. Just don't speak," moans Zoe from somewhere in the room.

I might be able to open my eyes, but I'm not quite ready to sit up and look around. We all lay for a while, wallowing in our own misery. One thing nobody tells you about turning thirty, the hangovers suck. The older you get the worse they get, and this one is next level.

"Where's Soph?" I murmur, realizing I've not heard her speak up yet.

"Who cares," grumbles Zoe.

"Really …" I scold, before managing to lean over and grab my cellphone from the nightstand, sending a quick message to her to check she's okay.

A few minutes later there's a knock at my door. I whimper at the thought of having to get up and choose to ignore it. The knock comes again and Sophie's voice filters through the solid wood. "Are one of you lazy bitches going to get up?"

Admitting defeat, I drag myself out of bed, treading carefully toward the door and being extra careful not to move abruptly and chance there being a trip to vom town.

It was worth the effort of getting up because when I open the door I find Sophie standing with a tray filled with coffee and pastries.

"Angel!" I exclaim, standing to the side so she can walk through. She places the tray on my old desk and then jumps onto Zoe.

"What the fuck?" she yelps from underneath her cover. "Are you trying to make me throw up?"

"Suck it up. It was your idea to do all those extra shots at the end of the night."

Zoe continues muttering but then stops and pokes her head out. "Is that coffee I smell?"

Sophie nods. "Feel free to say thank you."

"Why are you so chipper?"

Sophie looks smug. "Because unlike some, I've learned what my limits are as I've gotten older."

"Smart-ass."

Another thing turning thirty hasn't changed, their incessant bickering.

I sigh. "Pack it in. Both of you."

"Spoil sport." Zoe smiles, her mood lightening considerably when I hand her a steaming cup of strong coffee.

"Did I hear someone mention coffee?" asks Sooz, raising slowly up from the floor like the living dead.

"You did." I hand her a cup then settle down on my bed with my own. The first few sips are heaven. My body absorbs the caffeine, and I can feel myself gradually becoming more alert. "So, last night"—

"Oh God, what did we do?" asks Zoe, apprehensive.

—"was amazing!" I shriek and start giggling. "Seriously, thank you so much. I can't believe you all went to so much effort."

"You enjoyed it then?" Sophie smiles.

"No, I didn't enjoy it, I *loved* it," I reply. "Honestly, it was perfect."

"I'm just impressed you and Jake managed to be in a room together without any drama." Sooz snickers into her coffee.

"Well, there was something …" I reply.

"If you're referring to when it looked like he was about to strip you naked in the middle of the room, don't worry, we all saw it." Zoe laughs.

"There's nothing going on," I say taking another sip of coffee.

"Right," all three of them reply together.

"What?" I scoff, widening my eyes innocently.

"Seriously, Abby. If the room hadn't been full of people, I bet you'd have jumped him in a second."

I narrow my eyes at Zoe's comment. "It's not like that between us anymore." She rolls her eyes. "Why don't you believe me?"

"You can play dumb all you like. It will *always* be like that between the two of you."

"He asked me on a date."

Sophie squeals. "Like a date, date?"

"What other kind of dates are there?"

"So, what did you say?" asks Sooz eagerly.

"No."

All three of them groan.

"Twice."

"The two of you are painful sometimes, you know that right," says Zoe.

"Gee, thanks," I mutter.

"No, seriously. What the actual fuck, Abby. What more do you want from the guy?"

I go to speak but she holds her hand up in the air to stop me. There's fire in her eyes, the kind that tells me I'm in for a stern talking to.

She takes a deep breath then lets me have it. "Twelve years this has been going on. Twelve. Goddamn. Years. After everything that's happened and him finally giving you the truth, you still say no. This whole friend's thing is bullshit. You know it, we all know it.

"How long are you going to use Clara as an excuse? She's not a baby anymore, Abs. She's getting bigger and she will keep getting bigger. Soon she won't need to be the sole focus of your universe and what will you have left …

"Jake loves you and despite all the crap you've been through together, he's still fighting for you."

"Fighting?" I say in disbelief. "Sorry, I didn't realize throwing a huge temper tantrum and demanding his own way whenever it suited him was classed as fighting."

Sophie shakes her head. "There's still a lot you don't know, Abby. Zoe's right though, he has been fighting for you. All along …"

"Oh, great," I snap, the euphoria and happy vibes from what was a magical night long gone. "Here we go again. More secrets and things I don't know. Let me guess, nobody's going to tell me. I have to speak to Jake about it. We all know how that went the last time, don't we. So, let's figure out the timeline then. Shall we say another six years until I find out this round of secrets and everything will be fine? No, because there will always be something."

"Have you finished throwing your little hissy fit?" asks Sooz, amused.

"I don't know," I huff.

"I'll let that one slide. It is your birthday after all. But honestly, Abby. Right now, what have you go to lose?"

"My heart, again."

Sooz smiles, stands up, and sits down next to me, wrapping an arm around my shoulders. "You can't lose something you haven't got."

"Is that your way of calling me a heartless bitch?"

"No. It's my way of reminding you that you once told me you gave Jake your heart a long time ago, and you never quite got it back." She grabs my phone from the nightstand where I set it back down and passes it to me. "There's only one person who can help you to find it. *Him*."

Jake

Thirteen. That's how many bum notes Zach has hit in practice so far today and we're not even an hour in. We have a big performance in two days, and we can't afford to mess up, yet here we are, playing the worst we ever have.

Another bum note echoes off the walls of the rehearsal room. Make that fourteen.

"Sorry, my fault," he says sheepishly. "I don't think the shots were a good idea."

Ever the one to lighten the mood, Sam says, "Come on, give yourself a break. It was Abby's birthday and when was the last time we all had a day off? It's fine to mess up sometimes." He frowns in my direction. "At least he's messing up at practice, not on stage in front of thousands of fans."

I don't say a word because he's right. Out of all of us, I'm the one who's screwed up the most over the years. Feeling guilty, I look to Zach and say, "Sorry."

"It's fine. But can I say something without you all biting my head off?"

"Shoot," says Ryan in the background, spinning one of his drumsticks the way he does when he's bored.

"This song isn't working."

We all remain silent, knowing he's right. We have a show in two days. An unplugged performance live at The Angel Orensanz to release our new single and it's crap. No matter how hard we practice, it's just not fitting together. Luckily, we haven't gone through the recording process yet. This performance is meant to act as a teaser of what's to come and it could be our biggest release yet.

Apart from the fact it sucks.

Sam groans.

Ryan slams his sticks against the drums dramatically before saying, "So, what do we do now then?"

My phone bleeps from the other side of the room, then again straight away. As we're clearly not getting anywhere there's no point ignoring it, so I walk over and pick it up, frowning when I read two names I wasn't expecting.

Abby and John West.

I open Abby's text first. I always do no matter what.

When I read her message, I don't take it in until I read it for a second time.

Let's do this date thing. She's not known for being one with words.

Unsure of what to reply, I exit the message and open the one from her dad.

Record label, now. Alone. Again? Seriously?

Looking over to the guys who are standing gormlessly, I decide we're not going to make any progress in the next few hours. The best thing we can do is have a break before we decide what to do. Nobody knows, apart from the label, that the show is meant to be for the reveal of our new single. Worst case scenario we don't say anything and use our usual set.

I begin packing up my guitar and slide it over my shoulder before I explain, "I need to head out for a few hours."

"Everything okay?" asks Zach.

"John West." I sigh.

"Again?" says Ryan, echoing my thoughts.

"Yep."

"Christ, he loves you as much as Abby."

"Not funny," I call over my shoulder, walking toward the door. The more time I waste here, the less time we will have later to sort this mess out. "Won't be long. Get writing."

Thankfully, the rehearsal room we rent isn't too far from the label. It's not the smartest idea choosing to walk. Paps follow our every move, but it will take as much time to get through traffic in a cab as it will to walk, and frankly, I could do with the fresh air. When I get to the label I make my way through reception quickly, avoiding eye contact with everyone not wanting to be held up.

I'm walking in the direction of John West's office, where I feel like I spend more time than I do my own home.

He pokes his head out from one the meeting rooms and shouts, "In here, Jake."

Changing direction, I walk to the meeting room. I find him standing at the head of the meeting table looking awkward. Sitting in the chair next to him is Dan Fucking White.

I'm about to turn and walk straight back out, but Dan's voice stops me in my tracks. "I need to talk to you."

"Really?" I say to John.

He shrugs. "When you're as stubborn as you are, sometimes you've got to do these things."

"You do remember I'm an artist on your label, right?"

"Yes." He nods. "*My* label. But thanks to your relationship with *my* daughter, things between us aren't as clear-cut. Now, sit."

There's a part of me that wants to leave, but all I'd achieve in doing so is make myself appear like even more of a dick.

"What's this about?" I ask when my ass is planted in the seat across the table from Dan.

"Believe it or not this is business."

I turn my attention back to John, finding the same blue eyes as Abby's. "How so?"

"Like your relationship muddies the waters with us, it also muddies the waters between the two of you. I do not need a pissing match each time the two of you cross paths, so, I want you to sort it out. You don't leave until I'm sure you can be in a room together without the risk of punches being thrown." He starts walking toward the door.

"Where are you going?" I ask.

He laughs. "This is between the two of you. I'll be in my office. Mandy on reception will be keeping an eye on you both."

With that, he leaves us alone in what is possibly the most awkward silence I've ever witnessed. At first, I don't turn around, but when the door clicks shut, I realize I have no choice.

When I turn Dan's staring at me with his stupid hair styled in the stupid way it always is, pointing up through the air. I don't know what Abby saw in him.

"So." Dan smiles.

I don't smile back. "So."

"How're things? I heard you have a big show coming up, feeling ready?" his British accent makes him sound extra polite, and it annoys the hell out of me.

"Cut to the chase. What is this really about?"

Dan leans forward and clasps his hands on the table. "I wanted to talk to you about Abby."

"I don't," I reply, glancing out of the floor-to-ceiling glass wall.

The polite mask disappears, and he sneers, "I don't get what she sees in you. I never have."

My head snaps back. "Funny I was just thinking the same thing about you."

The awkward silence fills the room again and we stare at each other, both refusing to back down.

It's Dan who eventually shakes his head and rubs a hand over his face. "I didn't come here to argue with you."

"Then why am I here? By the way, I enjoyed the little performance you put on last night at the party. It's a shame Abby didn't enjoy having your hands all over her."

"Stop," he says firmly. "I know she doesn't want me. I've known that all along. That *little performance* was for you."

"I'm sorry, what?" I try to get my head around what he's saying, remembering how I arrived at the party late after Clara's sitter called when she couldn't get in touch with anyone else, informing me she'd woken and refused to settle.

I'd planned on being at the party from the very beginning so I could get as much time with Abby as possible, but like they tend to do a lot since having Clara, my plans changed. The last thing I wanted was the sitter calling Abby or her parents again and ruining her night, so I sorted it myself. When Clara was finally out for the night, I made it to the party only to find Dan serenading Abby, *again*.

"What are you doing, Jake?"

I frown. "I'm sitting here talking to you."

He rolls his eyes. "What are you doing with Abby?"

"That's none of your business."

"Actually, it is."

This guy is unbelievable. I push my chair back from the table, ready to stand up and leave when he continues. "There was never anything between us, I know that now. I saw the way she looked at you last night. She's never looked at me like that and most likely never will as long as you're around. So, it's time for you to make a choice."

"Enlighten me."

"You need to decide if you're going to fight for her. Because if you're not, move over and give someone else a chance, for Abby's sake. She deserves to be happy, but as long as you're there, hovering in the background, she'll never move on."

"Not that it's any of your business, but I already am fighting for her."

He laughs then mutters under his breath, "Not very hard."

"Excuse me?" I snap.

I thought John was being dramatic when he started talking about us throwing punches, but sitting with my fists clenched at my sides, I suddenly feel pretty damn close.

"I said, you're not fighting very hard."

"What do you know?"

"Quite a bit actually. I listened to all S.C.A.R.A.B.'s songs. I figured it out, Jake."

My pulse elevates. Nobody knows apart from the band.

"Tell her," he urges when I don't say anything. "It could change how she feels about everything."

"Why do you care?"

"Because contrary to what you believe, I'm actually a good guy and I want to see Abby happy. Even if you stepped to the side, nobody would ever compare to you. In her eyes, she'd be settling for second best, but she's scared. Prove to her that you've been fighting all along."

I ponder over what he's said, staring at the gleaming black meeting table. Then to the person I never expected to, I say out loud my biggest fear. "What if it's still not enough?"

I expect from the way I've treated him, some snide remark along the lines of it being nothing more than I deserve, but what I get is something more profound, because like Dan said, he really is a good guy.

"Then it's just not meant to be, but as long as you hold this card in your back pocket, you'll always wonder 'what if,' and life's too short for that shit."

My eyebrows shoot up at him cussing, because it sounds weird with his accent and doesn't suit the nice guy image he's got going. "And what if it works and then after all this, we don't end up working out?"

Dan leans back in his chair and exhales. "Well, because you're a prick I can see that happening. Then Abby will come running back to me and realize what a big mistake she's made."

We hold each other's gaze and when the corners of his mouth twitch he ends up grinning like a fool. I bark out a laugh so loud that a woman walking past the room startles and drops her things, despite the soundproof glass.

"Thanks. I think," I manage to say when I calm down.

He holds his hands up. "I'm doing this for Abby. So, what are you going to do?"

I pull my phone out from the pocket of my pants and open the message Abby sent earlier.

"I'm gonna try my way one last time. If that doesn't work, *then* I'll try your way."

Chapter Twenty-Five
Abby

Clara jumps up and down, squealing in excitement. Her eyes grow wider when she tilts her head back as far as it will go, gazing up in awe at some of the taller rides in Coney Island.

"Me please," she says, staring me down with her big brown eyes and I'm a goner. I would do anything for her anyway, but when she looks at me like she is doing now, I struggle to say no.

"Maybe," I reply, trying to pacify her as we're still waiting on Jake.

I should have known better than to arrive early, it's the worst thing you can do when you have a toddler and you're somewhere exciting. She doesn't buy my response, and her face scrunches up in anger, signaling that she's about to go nuclear, which in the blazing midday sun and stifling heat, will be even more disastrous.

I glance at the time on my phone and see we're only a few minutes past the time Jake and I agreed to meet. Trying to keep her entertained, I crouch down so I'm at eye level while she sits in her stroller and work my way through the handful of nursery rhymes I know, praying no one can hear.

"You have the voice of an angel," comes a voice from above, a voice I know better than I know my own.

Caught off guard, I wobble in my crouched position and fall straight on my ass. Cool, Abby.

"Mommy funny." Clara giggles, swapping her tantrum face for the angelic one she uses with Jake to get her way.

'Traitor,' I mouth, and she giggles again.

"Want a hand?"

Jake moves, so he's standing in front of me. My eyes trail up his body, from his Converse-covered feet, over his fitted black jeans and white T-shirt which reveals his tanned, tattoo-covered arms.

I swallow nervously and reply, "Sure."

When I grasp his hand, electricity shoots up my arm from where our skin touches, and he tugs me up from the ground. His strength catches me off guard and I fall into his chest, feeling every muscle tense through the thin cotton of my vest. His hands find my waist and I suck in a sharp breath when his fingertips skim underneath and trail along my skin.

He smirks, knowing exactly what he's doing, then turns and looks down at Clara lovingly. A frown crosses his face, and close to my ear, he murmurs, "This wasn't what I had in mind."

With expert timing, Clara screeches, "Daddy, out, now!"

He sighs and steps back. I'm left blushing furiously having been caught out.

"I couldn't get a sitter," I grumble.

He looks at me and mouths, *'no sitter my ass,'* then focuses his attention back on our grumpy toddler. I watch as he crouches down to unbuckle Clara from her stroller and my heart flutters the way it always does whenever I see them close like this.

"Shall we go find some rides?" Her squealing is all the answer he needs, and they walk away together, hand in hand, leaving me to maneuver the stroller.

It seemed like a good idea at the time, bringing her with me to avoid being alone with Jake, but now I'm a hot, frustrated mess, and regretting not giving a *real* date a shot.

We enter the amusement park and make our way to where the smaller rides are. When we get there, Clara points at a ride and I decide it's big enough for her to go on, so I make a decision.

"You take her on," I say, smiling at her tugging on Jake's arm.

"You're sure? It's her first time on one …"

"I'm sure. You miss out on things like this when you're working, so go, enjoy."

They run off to join the line and as they do, Jake looks back over his shoulder and grins. It's the kind of smile that can break your heart, I know, because it already has mine, over and over. I try to shake the thought away and wave for them to go and enjoy themselves.

It feels good watching them like this. We haven't done the happy family thing often, not unless the group has been involved. Not knowing the full dynamics of our relationship has made things awkward to navigate at times.

Jake makes sure never to take his eyes off Clara, checking she's safe when they climb on the ride, double-checking when he thinks I'm not watching. I try not to laugh out loud.

The next couple of hours fly by and Clara runs from one ride to another, dragging Jake with her the whole time. She forgets I'm even there and I stand back, letting them make these memories together. S.C.A.R.A.B. is due to release a new album in the following months and with that comes a world tour, which means less time for them to spend together.

"Hey, dinner!" I call to them, when I see what time, it is.

Nobody needs to witness the wrath that is Clara when she misses a meal. She's obviously hungry, because she runs over and climbs into her stroller without a fuss and Jake ambles behind, messing on his phone. I frown but chose not to make a comment, assuming it must be something to do with the band.

We walk to where the food stands are located and Jake says, "Tell me what we need and I'll get it. You grab a table."

I rattle off options for him to come back with and he nods, mentally logging the list, then disappears. We've found a table, got settled, and a little while passes. Clara starts to get restless. I'm about to pull out my phone and call to see if anything is wrong when I see Jake's head bobbing above the crowds in the distance. When he gets closer, I see he's not alone.

By his side, is Zoe.

"Tee Zoe!" shrieks Clara when she sees her and wriggles in her seat eagerly.

"Hey," I say, plastering on a fake smile. "What are you doing here."

She shrugs. "Jake messaged to say you couldn't get a sitter. You never called."

Busted.

My lips form a tight line and I say through gritted teeth, "I did. You must not have gotten my message."

Not picking up on the hint, she frowns and pulls out her phone, totally oblivious to how embarrassing this whole thing is getting. After tapping the screen a few times, she looks up and says, "There's no message."

"How weird." I cringe at the pitch of my voice. "Your phone must be broken?"

She shakes her head. "My phone is f—"

"Zo, seriously, it doesn't matter," I say narrowing my eyes and tilting my head not so subtly in Jake's direction.

Her eyes widen and she finally understands. "Ohhh yeah, my phone's totally broken."

Jake looks between the two of us and snorts. "Yeah, you two suck at lying."

"Jake!" I hiss, looking down at Clara.

He groans and turns to Zoe. "Everything she needs for now is on the stroller."

I'm about to jump in and explain her routine, which is pointless because Zoe has looked after her enough times to know everything already, but Jake holds up his hand to stop me.

He crouches down and says to Clara, "Would you like some ice cream and a sleepover at Grandma and Grandpa's?"

"Yeahhhh!" she squeals.

I roll my eyes. Like she would have answered otherwise when ice cream is involved.

Jake places a kiss on her head and strokes her hair, telling her to be a good girl for Auntie Zoe, then stands tall with a smug look on his face.

"Happy?" I say snarkily.

"Very."

"Go," says Zoe, ushering us away before Clara can get upset and ruin their plan. "Have fun, please."

Jake grabs my hand and pulls me away. Trying to ignore the heat traveling up my arm from his touch, I look back over my shoulder at Zoe and she makes a blow job motion with her mouth and winks. I shake my head and turn back, only to find Jake also looking over his shoulder at her.

I want the ground to swallow me up, especially when he says, "Now that would be a very fun date."

I feel like I'm about to combust. "You should be so lucky."

He doesn't miss a step, leaning in and nipping the exposed skin on my shoulder. "Very lucky."

My stomach flips. Who the hell is this? Then I remember, *this* is Jake.

Carefree Jake.

My Jake.

This is the Jake I fell in love with back in high school, who chased me relentlessly, not caring how uncomfortable he made me feel when he pushed me out of my comfort zone. He reveled in making me live life on the edge. He made me feel alive and take risks I never would have without him by my side. This is the Jake I knew before the world became mesmerized by the way his fingers expertly strummed the strings of his guitar, creating melodies that settled deep inside anyone who listened, taking a little piece of them with him when the final chords settled in the air.

This is the Jake I knew before everything went wrong.

"Where are we going?" I ask, laughing when pulls me along harder, quickening his pace.

He doesn't answer at first, just carries on walking, and I realize he's making sure we're out of Clara's sight.

Once we're a safe distance away, he stops and asks, "Which ride first?"

"Erm …" I look up at one of the old-school wooden rollercoasters and point. "That looks, okay?"

"Great." He spins back around and tugs me along again. I'm in line for the ride, with him standing behind me before I have a clue what's happening.

"What are we doing?" I ask, looking up at him over my shoulder.

He stares down, brown eyes smoldering and suddenly I don't care what we're doing.

"We're having the date I planned," he answers, "finally."

My gaze flickers to his mouth and my lips part. Heart racing, all I can think about is how much I want him to kiss me. It's been too long. Over three years too long. His face moves a little nearer and my eyes close of their own accord. I wait, but nothing happens. Awkwardly I open one eye, only to find him still staring down at me, amused.

"Considering you brought our daughter along, you're pretty eager …" Heat travels up my neck and I look away. When he speaks again, he closes the distance between us. The skin of his lips almost brush against my lobe. "It's our turn, Abs," he says huskily, and my heart goes from racing to hammering in my chest, wondering what he's referring to.

The ride attendant waves his hand in my face and I feel mortified, realizing it's our turn to get on.

Once strapped in, I shift in my seat so I'm facing him, unable to keep the bite from my voice. "You're doing this on purpose."

"What?"

"This," I huff, the ache between my legs putting me in a pissy mood.

I go to move so I'm facing straight ahead, ready for the ride to start, but Jake stops me. He grasps my face in his hands, trails the calloused pads of his thumbs against the soft skin of my jaw.

"You mean *this*?"

Before I get a chance to reply his mouth finds mine. I'd forgotten what it felt like. Forgotten the harshness of his kisses, the way his mouth moves at a pace that makes me forget where we are or who I am. My tongue moves, ready to sweep against his as the kiss becomes deeper when the ride suddenly jerks to life and the carriage rushes along the track, forcing us to break apart.

Jake lets out a hearty laugh and I know it's a moment I'll never forget. It's the perfect end to a perfect day, but it's not over yet. When the ride is finished and I feel slightly nauseous from the motion, he drags me off and we spend the next couple of hours moving between rides and game stalls, in our own perfect bubble.

It only becomes apparent how long we've been out when everything around us glows in the darkness. The vibrant colors and smells of carnival food, everything becomes more vivid. My eyes follow every move Jake makes, and each time he steps in closer and his body brushes against mine, goosebumps cover my skin.

"So," I say as we walk hand in hand toward the exit of the amusement park. "It's been a great date ..."

Jake glances at me out of the corner of his eye and replies, "Abs, we're no way near finished."

"What do you mean? It's late and you have a performance tomorrow night."

He doesn't answer as we walk through the exit and the crowds close in around us, struggling to move through the small space. Instead, he keeps his head down to avoid drawing any unnecessary attention. We've walked for a couple of minutes along the boardwalk, and the noise of the park is dulled by the sound of the water rolling against the sand when he pulls me into his arms and pushes my back up against the rail, every inch of his hard body presses against mine.

"Where are we going next if the night isn't over?" I ask, trying to ignore the flames coursing through me and the urge to circle my hips into his.

"Queens."

"Erm, random. Why?"

He places a finger under my chin and tilts my head back. "What do you see?"

I take in the sky, glowing from the lights of New York City. The only thing that stands out is the moon.

"A full moon," I reply slowly, and he pulls away, grasping my hand and we start walking again.

"You've learned well, young *Padawan*."

"Jake, *Star Wars* is my thing, not yours."

"Let's see if you manage to figure it out before we get there." He stops briefly and his eyes move over my body, focusing on my clothes. "What you're wearing will do."

"What do you mean, *will do*?" He's talking like I'm wearing pajamas in public or something equally ridiculous. I stay quiet, remembering that has actually happened.

He doesn't answer and I'm left wondering what he's up to. A thirty-minute Uber ride later I have my answer.

"Aren't we a little old for a Full Moon Festival?" I ask, frowning at the sight before me.

"You're only as old as you act, Abs."

"So, you're still adolescent?"

Jake grabs my face and I'm lost in a searing kiss, forgetting what we were even talking about when he bites down on my bottom lip.

"I'll remember that comment later." He smirks, backing into the crowds, wiggling his eyebrows.

I don't have a clue what's happened over the past few weeks to lead us to this point. But seeing Jake like this, happy, like the weight of the world has been lifted from his shoulders, I couldn't care less.

Tonight is a reminder of why we're worth fighting for.

When there's no drama, no hurdles, our love is the kind that songs are written about.

It's epic.

I chase after him, into the throngs of people all dressed in white and decorated in neon paint. I get what he meant now when he said what I was wearing would do. I'm in a grey Cami and black denim shorts, a stark contrast to the uniform every person surrounding me is wearing.

"Wait!" I shout.

Jake stops, looking at me questioningly when I approach a group of girls in their early twenties.

"Hi," I say sweetly, and they all smile. "I don't suppose you have any paint spare for me and my friend?" I gesture back at Jake, knowing the reaction I'll get.

The girls all begin screeching when they clock that underneath the shades he put on when we arrived, is Jake Ross, the lead guitar player for S.C.A.R.A.B.

A round of photos and signatures later, I have a selection of neon paint to work with.

This time it's Jake's turn to ask where we're going as I drag him toward the block of restrooms. Not caring who sees, I pull him behind me into one of the larger cubicles with its own washbasin and mirror. He locks the door behind us and tilts his head to one side.

Waving the paint in the air, I explain, "We can't do a Full Moon Festival without it."

"Work your magic." He winks, and I do.

A few minutes pass and a lot of concentration is used on my part.

"What do you think?" I ask.

"You drew a dick on my face," he says staring at his reflection in the mirror.

"Head."

"Sorry, what?"

"I drew it on your head," I explain. "Get it? Dick … head."

"Very funny. You've been spending too much time with Dan speaking like that."

"I thought so." I smirk back at him in the way he does that drives me mad, choosing to ignore the Dan comment.

"You know," he says, lowering his voice and stepping toward me. "It would be a shame."

"What would?"

His eyes skirt around the larger-than-average cubicle we're standing in. "To waste this opportunity."

My breath hitches, but refusing to let him see how affected I am, I ask confidently, "What did you have in mind?"

"Well," he replies, lowering his head and nipping at the sensitive spot on my neck, the one he knows makes me say yes to anything. "I've grown accustomed to fucking you in public places."

A searing heat surges through my veins, pooling between my legs and I squirm, remembering Jake making me come in the small dark room in Kralove, harder than I ever have before.

The reckless night that led to Clara, acts as a harsh reminder and makes me see sense.

"You shouldn't have." I laugh, trying to hide the panic in my voice. "It's not going to happen."

I shift my head to the side before his lips can find their target because if they do I'll forget why this is a bad idea.

"Avoid all you like, Abs, but you want this, I know you do."

I shake my head, struggling to reply. I've let my guard down too many times tonight and I know what happens when I let him in.

My world falls apart.

Every. Single. Time.

"You won't be getting a happy ending tonight, Jake. It's not even worth the effort."

What's not worth the effort, is even taking the time to say the words out loud. Even though my brain is screaming at me when I walk out of the restrooms leaving him behind, telling me to run as fast as I can before I can get hurt again, the large thumping organ in my chest has other ideas.

The heart wants what it wants, and every bit of mine, shattered parts, and all, wants Jake.

It always has and always will.

Chapter Twenty-Six
Jake

Not worth the effort my ass.

Quickly readjusting myself because I have one female already pissed at me and don't need the wrath of anymore, I chase after her.

"Abby, wait!" I shout, wishing for once she would wear heels and not Converse, so she'd slow down.

Her size doesn't work in her favor being that she's over half a foot shorter than I am. I close the gap between us before she can clear the restrooms. When I grasp her upper arm, she doesn't resist, telling me what I need to know. I was right. She wants this as much as I do.

"I shouldn't have pushed you back there. I'm sorry," I say, praying to God that for once, tonight will work in my favor, and we might actually break through some of the barriers she puts up when it comes to our relationship.

She looks up through thick, dark lashes, blue eyes sparkling in the moonlight, and it takes every ounce of strength I have inside me not to pull her back into my arms. The only thing stopping me is the knowledge that if I do, it's game over, because right now, she's on high alert, ready to bolt at any second.

"It's my fault," she says, shoulders sagging. "Jake, I don't know what I'm doing."

I take one step closer and pause, judging her reaction. When she remains still, I take another step, pause, then another. Her body's millimeters from mine, the soft hairs on her arms brush against my skin, and my pulse skyrockets.

Dammit, I love this woman. I want to tell her as much, but now, isn't the right time.

"Don't overthink it," I say for the second time in our relationship.

The deep house music from the festival pulses around us and she smiles, knowing the moment I'm referring to. "I don't have anything to swing."

"How about we dance instead?"

"I could do dancing," she replies, visibly relaxing.

"Actually …" She frowns and I quickly carry on. "Nothing bad. I was thinking a few drinks might be in order?"

"Jake …"

We both know what happens when alcohol is involved.

I shrug. "What's a couple of drinks between friends?"

"I thought this was a date?"

I groan. "You're giving me whiplash."

"Fine. A couple. That's all."

We're four beers down when we eventually head over to one of the main stages, a spare drink in hand. It's not the usual music we listen to and it's not our usual crowd, but I couldn't care less as long as Abby is by my side. Bodies press in and the heat around us soars. I'm about to pull Abby back against me when a wasted asshole crashes into her side and she stumbles. It's like déjà vu and I watch as a vacant look creeps into her eyes.

But as quick as it appears, it disappears. I go to step in when she rightens herself and says to the guy scathingly, "Watch it."

He mutters his apologies and walks off. No drama.

"So, you've become a badass?"

"Hardly," she laughs.

"Seriously though, you handled that well."

She frowns up and the strobe lights from the stage flicker, constantly changing the color of her skin. "Why do you sound surprised?"

"Abby …"

"Fine." she sighs in defeat. "I did what you asked. I got help."

"From who?"

"It's irrelevant. All that matters is that I'm good. More than good."

"Okay." With the mood broken, I ask, "Want to leave?"

She looks disappointed. "Sure."

We're standing outside the festival and the Uber I ordered pulls up alongside the sidewalk. We clamber in and I rattle off both of our addresses. The heat of the day has been relentless, but rather than cooling when night set in, the temperature has risen. The air in the back seat is stifling and Abby shifts uncomfortably.

I place a hand on her thigh and trail my fingers up and down. She stills and I continue, moving my fingertips back and forth along her damp skin. When I reach the frayed edge of her denim shorts, she sucks in a sharp breath, audible only to my ears above the whirring of the shitty air con.

Playing with a loose thread, I wait for her to tell me to stop. She doesn't. She also doesn't stop me when I slip my fingers underneath her shorts and continue moving them upward, or when I begin toying with the lace edge of her underwear.

"Make it one stop," I say to the driver, when I pull them to the side and stroke, feeling how wet she is, fighting back a groan.

It's the longest twenty minutes of my life.

I don't take things further in the uber because I know even though she wants it right now, in the morning it's something she'll regret. The moment we step through the door to my place, all bets are off. I pull her against me before she can change her mind, not caring that the front door hasn't clicked shut behind us and the world can see what we're doing. My lips are on hers in seconds and I lose my mind when our tongues tangle together.

"I'm sorry," she says breathlessly pulling back. "I need to use the restroom."

Looking up to the ceiling, I exhale through my nose, trying to get my shit together when she walks off in the direction of the downstairs bathroom. Instead of hanging around in the entryway, I close the front door, then walk through to the kitchen to get us both a drink.

Thankfully, Ryan has plenty of beers left in his supply, so the couple of bottles of white wine we have stored in the refrigerator haven't been touched. I've popped the cork and filled two glasses when she walks in, coppery brown hair sticking out in all directions.

"The fancy stuff, you're really pushing the boat out," she comments, picking up a glass.

She lifts it slowly, takes a sip, and lets out a small sigh that makes my dick throb. I've had enough and go to take the glass from her hands, but she shifts and holds it out of my reach. I cage her back against the countertop.

"What are you doing?" she asks, the words catching in her throat.

"What I should have done years ago," I reply and kiss her again, tasting the crispness of the wine on her tongue, knowing this time she won't be moving away.

She sets the glass down and I spread my palms wide, stroking them along the back of her thighs, before cupping her ass and lifting her up. She wraps her legs tightly around my waist and her hips roll against mine, the friction causing a soft moan to fall from her lips.

Her eyes widen in shock when I turn and drop her promptly on the kitchen table then begin tugging at her shorts. She lets out a yelp when I pull them down, leaving her in just her underwear and vest.

"Jake … the other guys …" she pants when I lean over her and start kissing her neck.

"… are staying at your place on the floor," I confirm, kissing lower.

I don't miss the frown in her voice when she says, "You had this all planned out …"

I lift my head, chin hovering just above the line of her underwear. "Are you complaining?" I stand and pull the hemline of her vest up, removing it so she's left perched on the table. My mouth waters at the sight of her in just a black lace thong and bra, legs spread wide.

She doesn't answer, distracted when I pull her underwear to the side and circle her clit with my thumb. "Abby." Adding pressure, I slide a finger inside her, and she moans again. Pulling it out slowly, I cover her body when I press her back down against the table, my mouth hovering above hers. I slide two fingers in, then out, circling my thumb at the same time. "Are you complaining?"

She shakes her head and I increase the pace of my fingers, making her writhe against my hand.

"Do you want me to stop?" I ask when I feel her clench around me.

"No," she breathes. Placing a hot kiss on her lips, I pull away, watching her face as my fingers continue circling and moving inside her at a relentless pace. Her back arches off the table and she shudders, crying out as she's hit with wave after wave of her orgasm.

I groan and kiss her swiftly, then lift her from the table. Her legs wrap around my waist involuntarily.

"Where are we going?" she murmurs.

I almost miss the bottom step when she bites down on my neck. It takes all my strength not to drop her and screw her against the stairs. This moment has been a long time coming though and I need to show her how much it means to me.

"My bedroom," I grunt, trying to stay focused.

"But I thought you'd enjoy fucking me against the table." I feel her grinning against my neck when my dick twitches at the thought.

I don't answer until we get to my room, and I throw her against the bed.

Shrugging down my pants and pulling off my shirt with a speed Usain Bolt would be proud of, I climb over her, sucking on the soft skin just below her ear. "It's been over three years; I want to take my time."

She tenses and I wrack my brain trying to figure out what I've said wrong.

"What do you mean? It's been over three years?"

"Abs," I huff, gesturing down at my boxers, tented with a painfully hard erection.

I go in to kiss her again, but she holds a hand up to my mouth, stopping me. "Answer the question, Jake."

"As I said, it's been over three years."

"Since we had sex, you mean?"

I shake my head. "Since I've had sex period."

Her mouth drops open and I use the opportunity to keep her silent with a slow, languid kiss. I think I'm in the clear when she presses her hands against my chest and pushes me back against the bed.

Stretching her body across mine, she whispers into my ear, "Want to know a secret?"

"Maybe once I've come inside you?" No luck. She shakes her head and moves so she's sitting directly on my dick, only the thin material of our underwear separating us. Admitting defeat, I reach up and play with her hair. "Enlighten me."

"Until I came on your kitchen table, it'd been three years for me too."

"Is that so?" I smirk, heart soaring at the knowledge the last time someone touched her, it was me. "Technically," I continue, "It's still been three years. Fingers don't count."

"Well," she says, reaching over and opening the drawer of my nightstand, pulling out a box of condoms. She grabs one from the box and I raise a brow when she whips my boxers down and rolls it on expertly. "You better change that."

I watch, mesmerized as she removes her thong and shrugs off her bra, then settles herself above my dick, lowering herself slowly. She rides me hard and I'm ashamed to admit I come too quick, something I rectify when I spend the rest of the night screwing her until she's exhausted.

When she passes out later, breathing softly against my chest, I understand that everything leading up to this moment mattered, even the bits that hurt us both. Because without all the crap that came before it, I never would have appreciated where we are right now.

I wouldn't know the significance of what's happening.

I wouldn't know with absolute certainty that *this*, is it.

Abby

Tracing my fingertips along the lines of the giant scarab beetle that covers Jake's upper body, I lean in and place a kiss on his chest. He looks down and smiles sleepily.

"Why a scarab beetle?" I ask. "I get that it's linked to the band's name, but why? What does it mean?"

He struggles to stifle a yawn before replying. "You really want to know this now? You're not too tired?"

I nod and urge him to continue.

"It symbolizes rebirth."

I prop myself up on one arm so I can see him better. "I don't understand."

His sigh tells me his answer is much deeper than I was expecting. "We changed the name of the band not long after my grandfather died. Around the same time, I got the tattoo. I saw his passing away as my fresh start and the band felt the same. It was as if without him in the way, we could finally pursue things properly and had nothing holding us back.”

My gut tugs, remembering how I brushed over something so significant when he finally told me the truth. “I owe you an apology.”

He raises a brow and trying to change the subject, says, “Is it because of that move you pulled earlier when you almost broke Jake Junior? I already told you it’s fine.”

I slap him hard against the chest. “I’m being serious.”

“So am I. Abs, it’s fine.”

“You told me the truth and I disregarded it like it was nothing.”

It’s something that’s plagued my mind in the years that followed, since the night when Jake told me the truth. It wasn’t my finest moment. He gave me everything I said I needed, and I was more concerned with what was happening with myself. But as time has passed by and I’ve replayed that night over in my head, I’ve come to learn that what he was saying was right. Even if he’d told me the truth in high school, it wouldn’t have mattered, there were too many things out of our control.

“We kind of had a lot going on. It’s understandable. Maybe I should have waited to tell you, but I didn’t want there to be any more secrets,” he admits.

I can feel my heart breaking for him, seeing the way the sparkle in his eyes that was there just a few minutes ago, dulls. I hate that this still causes him pain and probably always will because he was betrayed by the two people who should have loved and cared for him unconditionally. He was forced to live a life that was a lie and pretend to the world that everything was fine when really, he was looking for an escape.

"I get why you didn't tell me for so long."

Jake sits up and leans over, forcing me back against the soft bedsheets. His eyes bore into mine, his gaze never wavering. "I know now there's never a right time for anything. Life is about choices. The most important one is choosing if something is worth fighting for. Abby, I'm fighting for you now, the way I always should have. I don't want you to ever question that night back in high school when I told you I loved you. I did then and I still do."

The space between us disappears and his mouth moves against mine with a kiss that scorches through every part of my body. Unlike earlier, we don't screw the years of pent-up frustration out of each other. When Jake pushes inside me, he moves slowly, taking his time with every thrust, kissing away every painful memory we share replacing it with a better one.

He loves me harder than he ever has before, but there's a small part of me that still feels like there's one piece of the puzzle missing.

That's the reason why I don't tell him I love him back, even though I want to. He already has most of my heart in his hands, and the little part that's left, I need to guard carefully.

If he's going to have all of me, I need to be sure that this is it.

When I doze in his arms later, I hear him whisper against my hair, "Please be here in the morning. Don't run away from me again."

Sleep takes over before I get a chance to reply.

Chapter Twenty-Seven
Abby

I don't know how long I've been out, but I can hear my cell ringing down in Jake's living room. Gone are the days of ignoring such a call and drifting back to sleep now that we have Clara. I look at Jake sleeping, his face peaceful, then move carefully out of bed, trying not to wake him or he will be useless for his performance tonight.

When I manage to find my underwear and pull on one of his T-shirts, I slip out of the room and pad down the stairs. I find my bag in the kitchen, among the rest of our discarded clothing. As I pick it up my phone starts ringing, the sound shrill in the silent house, making me wince. I frown when I see I have fifteen missed calls and my mom's name flashes on the caller ID again.

I quickly answer. "Is everything okay?"

"Erm …"

"Blergh …" Down the line I hear what sounds like a monsoon of I'm assuming is vomit splashing in the toilet, then Clara begins sobbing.

"I think she has stomach flu," my mom explains.

Dammit. Remembering how important his performance tonight is and how little sleep he's already had, I decide it's not worth waking Jake. I'll call him later. "I'll be right there," I say, then hang up.

I rush through the front door of my parents' home and run straight up to the bathroom where I find Clara sitting with my mom on the tiled floor, whimpering in her lap. When she sees me, her eyes light up and she jumps to her feet before I have a chance to tell her not to.

There's no going back. Her eyes widen, and she turns green.

"Quick!" I shout.

Panicking, I try to spin her toward the toilet, but as I do, let go of my cellphone and watch in horror as it flies straight into the bowl. Any chance of salvaging it is lost when Clara empties her stomach directly on top of it. I watch as it bobs up and down, covered in what, I'm not quite sure.

It's soon forgotten when Clara starts sobbing and I pull her into my arms. We sit on the bathroom floor for hours. I stroke her clammy forehead until eventually the sickness passes and she falls asleep.

It's much later in the day. I've been dozing on and off with Clara in my arms in my old bed when there's a knock at the door.

"Come in," I call softly, being careful not to startle her awake.

When the door opens, I'm greeted with Dan's smiling face and my heart warms.

"How's she doing?" he asks softly, mimicking my voice.

"She's tired," I reply, stating the obvious. "Sorry, I'm tired too."

"I guess you had a rough night?"

I can feel the heat traveling across my cheeks. If only he knew how true those words were. God this is awkward.

"Yeah, it was hard." The warmth in my cheeks turns into full-blown flames.

Get your head out of the gutter, Abby. I remind myself that Dan doesn't have a clue where I was last night or what I was up to while Clara spent hours being ill, something I feel incredibly guilty about.

Looking down at Clara and deciding she's in a deep enough sleep that I can move her, I shift her little body with Dan's help, then climb out of bed and leave the room with Dan.

When we get downstairs, I walk into the kitchen and pour two cups of coffee from the pot my mom prepared earlier, then set them down on the counter and look at Dan.

"Are you ready to go?"

He nods. "All packed. My flight is in a few hours, so I don't have long."

My stomach tugs with guilt at the way he's looking at me, knowing how he still feels.

"I was with Jake last night," I admit.

He doesn't even flinch. "That's great."

I frown. That wasn't the reply I was expecting. "Really?"

He grins. "Really."

"Dan …"

He jumps in before I can say anything else. "Abby, I still like you. There's a bit of me that always will, but I know I don't stand a chance. I knew it the night we went on our first date and that asshole stood on stage and basically declared you were his."

"Why didn't you say anything?"

"Because I didn't want to admit to myself that you were already taken. The stubborn part of me wanted to believe that one day, maybe you'd change your mind."

I sigh and pick up my coffee, using it as an opportunity to think about what I'm going to say next. "He's not a bad guy."

"I know."

I laugh. "You just called him an asshole."

"Just because I want him to be an asshole, doesn't mean that he is. We've spent a bit of time together and I guess he's not so bad."

My eyebrows shoot up in surprise. Jake never even mentioned that he'd spoken with Dan before. At all. "Erm, when were you guys in the same room?"

Dan taps his nose playfully. "That's our business and no, I'm not going to tell you what was said."

I roll my eyes, but I'm unable to hide the smile that plays on my lips. I'll never be able to be mad at Dan.

"Want to know the real reason I know he's not actually an asshole?"

"Okay." I hold my breath waiting for his answer.

"Because if he was, you wouldn't be in love with him."

"I never said I was."

"You didn't need to. You can see it in your eyes every time you speak about him."

"Oh."

He steps in and wraps his arms around me. I relish the feeling of his hug. After last night with Jake, everything feels raw and this moment is what I need.

"Give him a chance, Abby," he says placing a kiss on my head. "Give yourself a chance."

"I'm going to miss you," I say, my voice muffled as I press my face into his chest.

"Don't be a stranger. Oh, and Abby …"

"Yeah?"

"You really need to shower. You stink."

Jake

She left. She actually left.

I woke up mid-morning, reached over to pull her into my arms, only to find the bed empty and the sheets cold. She left hours ago, and I haven't heard from her since.

The logical part of my brain tells me there has to be an explanation, but the sleep-deprived part wins and I'm left feeling uncertain about the whole night. What doesn't help is the number of times I've tried to call her only to be greeted with her voicemail every single time.

I walk into The Angel Orensanz early afternoon and the guys look at me skeptically.

"Fun night?" asks Sam.

"Dude, why do you have a dick on your face?" says Ryan.

Zach doesn't say anything, instead, he watches my every move intently, trying to gauge what kind of mood I'm in.

When I throw my guitar case down on the ground stroppily, he says, "So things didn't go well with Abby?"

"They went amazing …"

"What's the problem then?"

"Until I woke up and she'd left. I haven't heard from her since." Hearing it out loud makes it feel even worse and my stomach twists painfully.

"Oh," he replies.

"Yeah, big fucking oh."

"Are you okay?"

No. I'm not. I fucking hate this, I want to scream so that everyone can hear. I settle for, "I'm just tired. I don't know how long I can keep doing this."

Sam's about to say something else when Amanda walks over, clipboard in hand, with a serious expression. "Is Clara feeling better?" she asks absentmindedly, scanning over the papers in front of her.

The world stops and I feel like I can't breathe. "What's wrong with Clara?"

She looks up. "Did you not know?"

Starting to panic I stand taller and speak urgently. "I don't know anything, what's wrong?"

"She has stomach flu or something. She was really sick during the night. By the way, have you spoken with Abby? I haven't been able to get in touch with her all day and her phone's off."

My shoulders sag in relief knowing that Clara, although ill, is okay. "No, I haven't spoken to her," I reply vaguely as I pull my phone out and send Zoe a message, asking her to go to Abby's parents' and check on them both for me.

Amanda huffs and walks off. I turn back to the guys feeling unsettled at the news of Clara, but more positive than when I first walked in, now I have an explanation for Abby's disappearing act.

"Erm, I hate to be the bearer of bad news," says Ryan, clearing his throat awkwardly, "but that song we're meant to be releasing still sucks balls."

We all grimace, knowing he's right. We each stand awkwardly, not knowing what we're going to do when I have a light bulb moment.

"Change of plan," I say, bending over and unlocking the case that holds my guitar.

"Okay?" replies Sam.

I stand and shrug the guitar strap over my shoulder then begin tuning it quickly. We can't waste any time if we stand a chance of pulling tonight off. "We're doing it."

"What?" asks Ryan, oblivious.

"*It.* It, it."

He drops his drumsticks, and they clatter on the floor, echoing through the cavernous room. "Ohhh?"

"You're sure about this?" asks Zach.

"Yeah, it's time."

"Fucking finally," says Sam excitedly and walks to the mic ready to begin rehearsing the song that will now be our new release.

Before we start practicing, I tell the guys I have a call to make. Standing off to the side of the room, I raise my phone to my ear, listening as it rings, praying luck is on my side.

I'm about to give up when John West answers. "Hello?"

"I need your help."

"What do you need me to do?"

"I need you to get Abby to Orensanz tonight."

"Leave it with me," he replies, and the line goes dead.

Abby

Not long after Dan left to return to London, Clara woke up. The rest of the day was spent on my parents' couch with a never-ending stream of kids' TV.

My eyes feel like they're bleeding and if I hear one more variation of *Bah Bah Black Sheep* I think I might cry. I almost jump for joy when my dad walks into the room and smiles down at Clara. He lifts her up and sits her on his lap when he collapses beside me on the couch.

He stares at the screen, brows drawn together.

"Everything okay?" I ask when it becomes apparent, he isn't going to break the silence.

"I need a favor," he answers.

"Okay?"

"I need you to photograph S.C.A.R.A.B. at Orensanz tonight."

I shake my head. "No."

A long time ago I made it clear I wouldn't work with Jake or Dan. It made things too awkward and put the professionalism of our business on the line.

"Abby, please. Our photographer fell through at the last minute and we can't find anyone else."

"Dad. We live in New York. There are as many photographers as there are yellow cabs," I reply, calling him out.

He chuckles. "But none of them are you. You're the best, we both know it."

"Did your photographer actually cancel?"

"No," he admits. "I canceled them. I want you to do it."

"Dad …"

"You'll be on the books."

"This isn't about the money!" I exclaim and Clara looks around confused. I stroke a hand over her hair and lower my voice. "I don't need the money."

"I know you don't need this, but S.C.A.R.A.B. does. Tonight is a really big deal. This isn't just about Jake, it's about Sam, Ryan, and Zach too. Please."

He knows exactly what he's doing by lumping the guys in with Jake and I can feel my resolve starting to crumble. I hate this. This morning was supposed to be blissful. Instead, I have cold feet. I'm replaying and questioning everything that happened between me and Jake. I'm infuriating even to myself, but I can't stop doing it. Last night woke parts of me I'd forgotten were there and it scared the hell out of me. He told me he loved me, showed me how much, but there's still one tiny part of myself holding back, knowing that if I throw myself into this, that will be it. There will be no coming back.

I can't ignore Jake forever though, which is why I say, "Fine. Write down the details."

"No need. I have to be there too. I'll drive us." He removes Clara from his lap, stands, and starts to walk out of the room.

"Dad!" I call after him.

He looks back. "Yeah?"

"Don't think this is going to be a regular thing."

"Of course not," he replies, the chirpiness in his voice telling me otherwise.

I stare at the TV, not taking in anything on the screen. He's up to something, I know he is.

I'm just not sure what yet.

"Are you sure you don't mind doing this?" I ask my mom, as I look down wistfully at Clara.

"Abby, seriously? Get out of here. Now," she snaps.

"Bye, baby …" I say, kneeling and pulling Clara into my arms.

She shoves me away and looks up to my mom, the previous night forgotten. "Candy?"

I laugh and stand up. "I won't be late."

My mom shrugs, clearly not caring if I came back at nine, midnight, or next week. "Go, have fun, live a little."

My dad walks down the stairs in his standard suit fitting the role of hotshot record exec to a T. "Ready?"

I nod and turn to leave, but he clears his throat, stopping me before I reach the front door. "Abby …"

I turn back. "Yeah?"

"You can't take photos without your camera."

"Right," I stammer, leaning down and grabbing my kit bag from the floor, before running out to the car.

"It's going to rain," says my dad staring straight ahead, keeping his attention focused on the road.

I look out at the clear skies. "Right."

I start messing with the air con. Rain would be welcome right now if it meant an end to the relentless heat.

Dad clears his throat awkwardly. "I need to talk to you about something."

My eyes trail to his hands which are gripping the wheel tight. He's not a nervous driver, meaning he's nervous about whatever he has to say.

"Go ahead." I smile, trying to keep the mood light.

"It's about Jake."

Here we go, I think to myself.

"Just tell me," I say, exhaling.

"You're probably not going to like me after this." he looks over briefly then focuses his attention back on driving.

"Come on, Dad. Whatever it is, it can't be *that* bad."

"We'll see," he mutters. He takes a deep breath then the words come out so fast I'm not sure I hear him right. "Jake came after you when you left Brooklyn."

My mind goes blank. "Sorry, what?" I twist in my seat and stare, looking for any sign that he's not telling the truth.

"That first summer you came home, and you accepted the job in Cape Town. He came looking for you, but you'd left for the airport early."

A lump forms in my throat. "O—okay."

"He was going to come after you, but I told him not to."

Bile rises and burns as his words sink in. I try to figure out why he would interfere like he did but come up with no logical answer to why he would tell the love of my life not to chase after me. "Why would you do that?"

"For the same reason I told you to take the job in Cape Town."

"Remind me …" I snap.

"You both had so much going for you. If you'd stayed, if he'd followed, neither of you would be where you are now."

I can't believe what I'm hearing. The space in the car seems smaller suddenly and I have every urge to jump out, feeling like I'm suffocating from the truth.

Jake came after me. All along I've punished him partly because he didn't fight hard enough for us. Because he just let me walk away.

But he didn't. Not really.

He tried to fight for us and then he was told not to.

"That wasn't your choice to make," I say shakily.

"I know. I realized my mistake straight away, but it was too late. Then the tour happened and toward the end, Jake didn't know what to do. I knew then how much he cared for you, and I regretted telling him to stay away the first time. I told him to fight for you, but then there was everything with Clara and I'm assuming that's what muddied the waters …"

Staring out of the front windshield, I wonder how long we have left until we get to Orensanz because I don't want to be in this car anymore.

"Why didn't you tell me?" I barely manage to bite out.

"I tried, a few times, but then I feared what it would do for our relationship. I was being selfish. Baby, I'm sorry. Please know, I messed up, but I thought what I was doing was right."

I want to get angry. Hell, I want to scream in frustration. All along I've been punishing Jake for something that wasn't even his fault. This was just another obstacle that moved us onto separate paths. But I don't react the way I want to, because if everything hadn't happened as it did, then we wouldn't be here now.

I'm tired of living in the past. It doesn't matter how we got to this point. All that matters is that we're here.

"Don't get me wrong," I say quietly.

My Dad's shoulders tense.

"I'm pissed. But it's okay."

"It is?" he turns briefly, looking shocked.

"I'm tired of being angry and I'm tired of being sad." It hits me at that moment what I want. It's nothing profound or life-changing. It's really simple. I've spent years running away from the truth, too scared to admit it because I believed his actions didn't prove that he felt the same when really, they did. "I just want Jake."

My dad smiles. "Go get him then."

Chapter Twenty-Eight
Abby

An eternity passes before we reach The Angel Orensanz.

Actually, it's only a few minutes, but I feel like being dramatic.

Dad parks a couple of blocks away because apparently, it will be chaos. The world is waiting to hear S.C.A.R.A.B.'s first unplugged performance and they're excited.

Before I step outside, he looks at me sadly. "Are you still mad?"

"Yes," I answer bluntly and his face drops. I lean over and place a kiss on his cheek. "But I'll get over it. I know you thought you were doing the right thing."

His expression brightens and I climb out of the car. We walk the couple of blocks in silence, and when I look up at the darkening sky, I notice the dark gray storm clouds creeping over. Dad was right. It's finally going to rain.

I've been to The Angel Orensanz before, but it was never like this. The only way to describe it … carnage. People fill the road, running around frantically, while fans' screams fill the night. There are paps everywhere, the flashes of their cameras illuminating the two-story red gothic building. With every step we get closer, I brace myself for the chaos.

I try to block everything out when we find ourselves in the full throes, the noise deafening. I focus on one thing and one thing only, walking up the short flight of stairs and into the building before I lose my nerve. The camera flashes are blinding, and I hold my hand up, trying to shield my face. Halfway up the stairs, I glance up. The arch windows are lit in pinks and blues, glowing in the dusk. I quickly pull out my camera, raise it up and take a few snaps to show my mom and Clara in the morning.

When I make it inside with my dad close behind, the noise suddenly stops. It's a sharp contrast to the world outside, desperate to catch a glimpse of S.C.A.R.A.B. quickly becoming one of the biggest rock bands of the decade. My mouth goes dry, so before I do anything, I walk over to the pop-up bar stationed near the entrance to welcome the VIP guests. This whole thing is surreal.

I grab a glass of champagne and knock it back. When one of the servers gives me an odd look, I purposely grab another raise it up, and knock it back in quick succinct. Placing the glass down firmly on the bar, I give the server a tight smile then make my way into the main area of the old synagogue. It's breathtaking with its high, cathedral blue ceilings. The acoustics are perfect for live music, and I get now why they chose here. It's understated, low-key, cool. It screams subtle for the least subtle thing the band will ever do.

Tonight is going to take them even further up the fame ladder. Whatever song it is they choose to perform; it could be their biggest seller yet.

I move deeper into the room and head toward the stage. It's small and at odds with the cavernous ceilings. Unlike normal gigs, there are seats everywhere. This won't be mosh-pit central. Everyone is here to listen and absorb the music. Butterflies take flight in my stomach in anticipation of the guys.

I have a quick look through my bag, reorganizing my lenses and my memory cards so I have easy access to the ones I think I might need, and then I begin adjusting the settings on my camera. I spoke with Amanda briefly on the way here and she said the lighting would be dark and that's all I got. I don't have a clue what to expect, so I change them to what I think might be suitable.

Minutes pass in seconds and suddenly every chair has an owner. The room is filled with light chatter as people sit, waiting. Nervously I wipe my hands on my pants and my heart starts to race. I pull out my cell and glance at the time. There are only eight minutes until the band is due to come on stage.

Calculating I have just enough time to grab another glass of champagne, I power back to the bar and grab a glass, ignoring the frown of my server friend when I knock it back quicker than the first two. There's something to be said for Dutch courage. When I've discarded my glass, I walk back over to the stage, feeling ready to take on whatever the night has in store.

The final glass of champagne starts to flow through my veins, and I begin to relax. I watch as the stage crew quickly comes out and sets up seats alongside the instruments. A couple do a final tuning check then disappear. I glance down at my watch, there are only two minutes left. Even the champagne can't stop the butterflies from swarming.

The overhead lighting goes out and my heart stops.

The room falls silent apart from the sound of footsteps when the band makes their way on. I can't look, so I use the lens of my camera as a barrier. A small round of applause fills the room then it goes silent again.

A red-haired presenter steps out and moves under one of the dim overhead lights.

"Welcome everyone. Wow. Are we all excited?" The crowd cheers and when they quieten down, she continues. "S.C.A.R.A.B. are about to perform their brand-new single, unplugged! I hope you're all as excited as I am! This is going to be insane. Their new release will go on sale at midnight. Ladies and gentlemen, the world, I give you S.C.A.R.A.B."

Goosebumps cover my arms when she gestures back toward the band then makes her way off stage. The last of the overhead lights switch off and the crowd titters when we're plunged into darkness. Suddenly the walls of the room light up in a deep blue, the same color as the band's logo, then spotlights highlight the band.

I quickly adjust the shutter speed on my camera so the images will come out clear despite the darkness, just in time to hear Sam take a deep breath before speaking.

"Thank you everyone for coming and to everyone who's watching tonight," his voice doesn't falter. He sounds so calm, the complete opposite of how I'm feeling. High school is light-years away, there's nothing amateur about this. "This song is very personal and for such a special release in such an amazing place, it seemed only fitting that we go back to where we started. We're going back to our roots."

The room fills with clapping and cheers, which I barely hear. I hold my camera, my hands trembling, getting ready to capture the first moments of their performance. Jake plucks his fingers against the taut strings and the opening few chords fill the room. I suck in a breath when I'm transported back to that night in his room, seventeen years old, totally in love and watching as he played a video for me of the band playing one of their first songs.

There's nothing else I can do when the song kicks in, but walk back and forth alongside the stage, trying to capture as many images as possible. They need me to do this, and I can't let them down, even though my body shakes as the melody travels through my veins, stirring up emotions I thought I'd stamped down years ago.

After a few seconds, I manage to regain control. Just about.

Then everything falls around me. I feel like I've been sucker-punched when another voice joins Sam's.

Jake.

The crowd gasps as he sings the harmony of the song. His voice is breathtaking. I can't pull my camera away, I daren't. But as the song continues and I listen to the lyrics, I realize that each harmony he sings, the words mean something.

They've purposely chosen these parts for him to sing.

He's purposefully chosen them.

I slowly lower the camera, just for a moment, taking in the reality of what's happening. My eyes trail up to his face. Unlike the rest of the band who are staring out at the crowd taking everything in, he's staring at one thing, and one thing only.

When he sings, the lyrics are directed to me.

'Always you.'
'Always us.'
'Always.'

They're the only words I hear. The words he's whispered to me so many times I've lost count. S.C.A.R.A.B.'s new single is about us.

Get it together, Abby. I tell myself. Despite feeling nauseous, I carry on taking the images I need to support the performance. I do the best I can to avoid Jake's gaze, making sure to capture him in the images without looking at him directly. I can't look, because if I do, I'll fall apart.

The song gets closer to the end and the crowd starts to clap to the beat, cheering in utter euphoria because the song and the band's performance are outstanding. Sam and Jake battle each other with their lyrics, conveying the most emotion I've ever seen put into a song.

The atmosphere changes and what little air there's left in me is sucked out when Jake steps forward, right to the front of the stage. He crouches down and his eyes find mine, forcing me to look back, not caring that the world is watching. I stand in a trance as he sings the crescendo of the song.

The song ends and the room is so quiet you could hear a pin drop. Everyone has been stunned into silence. My eyes flicker to the left, then the right, finding the audience sitting with their mouths hanging open, shocked at what they've just witnessed.

Finally, one by one, every person in the room stands, and an applause that starts small, soon becomes so loud I fear the windows might shatter. The rest of the band move forward, their eyes shining. I make sure to capture every last second, every bit of emotion, not just on their faces, but on the faces of their fans in the room, who no doubt represent the faces of fans all over the world.

S.C.A.R.A.B. has proved their talent is like no other band.

The presenter comes back on stage. The cheering doesn't subside, it only gets louder and louder. She stands along with the band laughing. All the time I stare through my lens. Too scared to look back up in case my eyes catch with Jake's.

When the crowd finally quiets, the presenter says into the mic, "I'm at a loss for words," then laughs awkwardly.

Sam takes over and unlike earlier his voice falters. "Thank you all for coming."

The guys are whisked off stage toward the back of the building and I quickly pack away all my gear. My heart is still hammering in my chest when my dad walks over and stops at my side, staring at the now-empty stage.

"Well, that was something else."

I swallow and nod. "Yeah, it was."

He looks down and frowns when he sees I've packed everything away. "Where are you going?"

"Home. The set's done."

"Are you not going to celebrate with them?"

I tug the zip on my bag hard when it refuses to close. "I need to get back to Clara."

"Abby."

"Don't, Dad. I need to be alone. Tell the guys I said bye."

I manage to catch a cab surprisingly fast considering the crowds that swarm the streets. It crawls through New York in the late-night traffic, moving painfully slow to Brooklyn. I hear a steady *pat, pat* and look at the windshield. Rain. Finally.

The journey takes longer than normal when I request a detour to the closest store that opens twenty-four hours, to pick up some crackers for Clara.

When it pulls up outside my parents' home, the rain is falling heavier. I pay and climb out, the steam from the water hitting the scorching sidewalks causing sweat to break out all over my body. Shrugging my kit bag further up my shoulder, I look up and find a figure sitting on the top step.

Jake.

He stares down at me, his eyes hard. "Most people would kill to have a song dedicated to them …"

"I—"

He stands and walks slowly down the steps, the rain falls harder, coating my skin. When we're standing toe to toe, I lift my chin and hold his gaze. I might have walked away, but it wasn't for the reasons he thinks. I just needed a moment to catch my breath. My brain needed time to catch up with what my heart decided when he put his on the line tonight.

"Why didn't you call today?" he asks.

His eyes are full of uncertainty. It softens his face and makes him look younger, like the Jake I met in high school.

"Clara was sick, and I broke my phone."

He scowls. "Other people have phones, Abby."

"Last night was … amazing."

He rubs the back of his neck. "So, what was the problem?"

I go to say "nothing" but stop myself. This moment is pivotal for us and nothing, but absolute honesty will do. He's right, I could have found a way to call, I should have, but like after the performance tonight, I needed some space to digest everything.

"*That* was the problem. The years after high school before I came back were the easiest because I didn't know what it felt like, being with you. But then I did, and it hurt so much more. The last three years, I tried to convince myself I made it all up, that there was nothing there. But then last night happened and I won't ever be able to forget it."

He raises a hand and brushes his thumb against my cheek. "You don't have to. I'm not going anywhere."

"Why didn't you tell me you came after me when I left?"

His thumb stops moving and his brows draw together.

"My dad told me," I explain. "But what I want to know, is why *you* didn't?"

"I didn't want to ruin your relationship with him."

"Do you not think that was my choice to make?"

"You mean like Clara?" I purse my lips, knowing we could keep going like this all night, but then we'd be doing the same as we always do, and what would be the point in that? "I didn't have a relationship with my family like you do yours. What you guys have is special. I didn't want to risk ruining it."

"Why didn't you tell me about what you had planned tonight?"

He rubs the back of his neck again and stubs his toe against the wet ground. "It was kind of a last-minute decision, and I was nervous."

I smile and stand on my tiptoes, pressing a small kiss on his lips. "Thank you for my song." I kiss him again. He wraps his arms around my waist and pulls me in hard, making sure I can't run away. "I'm sorry for running off."

He grins and his eyes look clearer than I've ever seen them. "I expected you to. That's why I got here so quickly. I had an Uber waiting."

I throw my head back and laugh.

The rain falls heavily around us and within seconds it's pouring, hammering against the sidewalks, bouncing up and drenching us through to the skin. Jake raises his head and looks up into the night sky. When he looks back at me, water cascades down his face, and droplets cling to his lashes.

"We seem to have a thing for life-changing moments in the rain. It's a bit cliché."

"Nothing about us is cliché." Taking a deep breath, I say the words I've been too afraid to, since the first time they fell from my lips, "I love you."

"I know you do. I've known all along. I love you too. Always."

The breath is stolen from me when Jake drags his hands up my back, tangles his hands in my soaking hair, and pulls my head toward his, then kisses me like he never has before.

It's not just a kiss it's a promise.

No more running. No more hiding. No more lies.

Most likely a lot of fighting. But that's real life.

Our story isn't picture-perfect.

Our happily ever after didn't come easily. At times it was long, drawn-out, painful, and all the other stuff in between.

But it's our journey, our story, our kind of perfect.

And I know now, with every piece of my heart put firmly back in place, that it always will be.

Epilogue
Abby 6 Months Later

The rising sun stirs me from sleep, and I find myself settled in Jake's arms the way I have done every morning since the night at Orensanz. A part of me thought after a few weeks we'd settle into a routine and my feelings would calm. The opposite happened. It's like a pressure valve was released the night I told him I still loved him in the place where he broke my heart. Each day my feelings get stronger, and I love him with an intensity that takes my breath away.

He stirs and looks down at me disheveled with sleep. I reach over to the nightstand and grab my phone, snapping a photo, just for me.

"Morning," he says huskily, pulling me up and kissing me slowly.

I try to move away but he holds me firmly against his chest, his erection pressing against my stomach beneath his boxers. "Jake," I moan. "Clara will be awake soon."

"I can be quick," he replies, rolling us over and settling between my legs, nipping at my neck.

Pleasure takes over and I start to forget why we shouldn't start something we probably won't be able to finish. "Clara can be quicker. She's a ninja."

He lets out a resigned groan.

"I like waking up to you like this. I could do it forever."

"Good, that's how long it will take you to get rid of me." Ignoring my warning he starts trailing kisses down my neck then moves lower. My eyes flutter closed, the fight leaving my body when his fingers toy with my underwear.

"Why do that?" says a small voice from right next to me. My eyes fly open, and Jake's head snaps up. I throw him a look that says I told you so.

"We're cuddling baby," I reply, satisfied with my answer.

"Me cuddle!" she dives on the bed, then glares at Jake who still has his arms wrapped tightly around me. "Daddy, move."

We both burst out laughing when she pulls him off me and forces her way in-between us, cuddling into my side.

We lay for a while listening to Clara chatter.

"Are you okay?" I ask when he frowns.

His expression softens and he smiles. "I'm pretty fucking happy," he chuckles.

"Jake!" I exclaim, praying Clara doesn't start repeating him like she did the last time.

"Sorry."

"So, is it what you thought it would be? Us together, finally."

He looks out the window, contemplating his answer. "It's more than I ever imagined it could be."

He places a kiss on Clara's head and one on my cheek before climbing out of bed. My body misses his closeness instantly. "I need to get to the label to prepare for the interview this afternoon with the band."

"Good luck," I reply as he leaves the room to shower.

A couple of hours later I'm battling with Clara over some pens, contemplating whether to google if the Terrible Two's can turn into Terrible Threes, when my phone starts ringing. Normally I wouldn't answer with Clara screaming in the background, but Zoe's name flashes on the screen and my instant thought is that something is wrong at the office.

It's meant to be my day off, but I answer anyway. "Hey, what's up?"

"We have a problem. I need you to go to Orensanz today for S.C.A.R.A.B.'s interview, the photographer we booked called in sick."

"Orensanz? I thought the interview was meant to be at MTV?"

"The plan's changed," calls Sooz, from the background.

"It's an emergency, Abs," says Sophie, sounding a little closer. "We can't get anyone else."

"Bull. I can't I have Clara."

"Bring her with you," says Zoe.

"Yeah, right," I cackle down the phone. "You're funny. Sure, I'll just bring my screaming toddler along to one of the band's most important interviews to date for her to run riot and terrorize everyone."

"We will watch her. We just need someone to take the photos. Please, Abs," says Sooz.

I imagine them crowded around the phone together, waiting for me to say yes. They know me too well. "Fine," I huff, glancing around for my bag.

"Life saver!" shouts Sophie and I hold the phone away from my ear.

"I'll see you there. Make sure you bring candy and toys. You owe me."

I hang up and Clara's tantrum stops abruptly. She looks up at me brightly. "Candy!"

Locating her change bag in the kitchen, I start throwing in supplies haphazardly. Luckily, I find a small pack of sugary goodness at the bottom of my own bag which I keep for emergencies. There's enough to entice her out the front door until the girls bring more to keep her quiet. This is an awful idea.

The subway is packed, and it's painful carrying Clara and two bags all the way to Orensanz. Surely, they could have picked somewhere closer, I grumble to myself when I set her down. We run up the steps and I'm sweating my ass off even though it's Baltic and the sidewalks are frozen solid. When we get inside, I clutch Clara's hand tightly so she can't run off and quickly find the girls.

It's brighter inside than I expected, being that it's an interview not a performance like the last time I was here.

"Candy!" screeches Clara and everyone turns in our direction.

"Good luck with that," I say, passing her off to Zoe.

"No need," she replies, waving a giant bag in the air.

"She's your problem later." I laugh. The last time Clara ate a ton of sugar she was still running around the apartment at almost midnight.

I spend the next ten minutes, getting ready for the interview, so absorbed in what I'm doing I don't notice the band come in and get settled.

"Abby, we're ready for you," calls Sooz.

The atmosphere feels thick, and when I look around, I find only the band, the presenter with a notepad in hand, and the camera crew filming live for the television. Everyone watches me when I step toward them with my camera, but then focus their attention on the interview.

The presenter clears her throat and stares into the video camera, introducing herself and the band.

"So," she says when the formalities are over with. "Thousands of questions were submitted by your fans and drawn randomly, let's get going."

Half an hour passes, and I spend my time carefully photographing key moments.

"We have a few left," the presenter says to the guys, and they nod. "They link so we'll just work them together if that's okay with you?"

They nod again.

"Okay." She lifts a card up and carefully reads. "Who writes all your songs?"

The guys look between themselves and smirk. I expect Sam to answer because he always does, but he remains silent. My hands freeze, camera mid-air, and I watch Jake clear his throat and raise his hand.

"I do," he says, and his eyes find mine.

"Wow," says the presenter, taken off guard. "So, Jake. The lyrics you write are beautiful. When did you start?"

"In high school," he answers, his eyes still holding mine.

"Can you remember what inspired you to start writing?"

"Yes. I can." I feel like I can't breathe, waiting to hear what he has to say.

"Care to share?" asks the presenter, chuckling along with a few of the crew at his vague answer.

"It was one day, in a park, when I met a girl for the first time."

My stomach churns.

"She must be special."

"She is."

"Is there anything else that inspires your songs?"

"No."

She blinks. "Erm, okay? So, every song …"

"Is about the same woman. Every song we've released, every song I've written, is about Abby."

I glance around the room, trying to take in what's happening and the enormity of what Jake has just told the world. I thought he'd laid everything on the line the night they performed here, but he still had one card left to play, one he's been keeping close to his chest all along. My eyes move around anxiously, finding familiar pairs only staring back. Ones I didn't even realize were here with me.

To my left, I find my parents, Shaun and Amanda beaming. To the right, the rest of the girls are all standing their cheeks wet with tears, Clara bouncing excitedly at their feet. I gasp when I find Dan standing behind them and he throws me a wink.

Lowering my camera down to my side, I look back to the band, all staring at me mischievously. I clear my throat. "Erm, guys, what's going on?"

Nobody answers. Instead, the presenter shuffles her cards and says, "We have one question left. Jake, what's one thing you've always wanted to do?"

Jake grins and stands from his seat. I clutch my camera, holding on for dear life, feeling a little faint when he walks right up to me.

"What are you doing?" I ask in horror when he gets down on one knee.

"The one thing I've always wanted to." He slips a hand into the pocket of his denim pants, pulling out a little black box. His hands tremble when he opens it and a plain band shines in the light, a small diamond sparkling in the center. It's simple, understated, perfectly us. "Abby, will you marry me?"

Clara darts over and clings to my legs. I lean down and pick her up, using her as an anchor to stop me from floating away. I smile between the two of them. Two sets of almost identical brown eyes stare back, waiting.

For the first time in the history of mine and Jake's relationship, I don't second guess myself. The answer is easy.

"Yes."

Jake 2 Years Later

Abby and I moved into our own place one month after I proposed at Orensanz.

A week later she was known to the world as Abby Ross.

And now … we're here.

We didn't do things conventionally, we did them our own way like we always have, and I wouldn't change one part of it.

Sam's voice fills the arena with the first words of our opening song, and I strum the chords that I know better than

I know myself. Looking to the side of the stage, I find Abby beaming at me, rubbing her hand over the small bump sitting beneath her dress. Only visible if you know it's there.

I take a deep breath and my voice mixes with Sam's, dancing through the air.

It's a story about a guy that fell for a girl. From the moment he saw her he wanted her, then he knew he needed her, when they couldn't be together, he missed her, no matter how much time passed he couldn't forget her. In the end, all that mattered was that he loved her.

He told her it's always you.

He told himself it's always us.

The lyrics of our multi-platinum selling song reach the ears of every single person in the arena.

And the song … is called *Always*.

The End.

Acknowledgements

It's taken me a while to decide what to write here. Each time I think about the journey I've been on with these characters, I cry. No joke.

Just over a year ago I hit publish on the first part to Abby and Jake's story. Never did I imagine this is where we would end up.

I don't think I can say thank you enough to all the people in the background supporting me. The biggest of all goes to my family. There have been so many late nights, tears, and moments of self-doubt, but you've always been there, so patient and helping me to ride it out, right to the end. Mum, I owe you the world. So many times, you've dropped everything to help me do what I've needed to get here. You've helped me achieve my dreams.

My betas: Babs, Sarah, Bex, Kristin, Kirsty, and Cheryl. Once again you did a wonderful job of picking the story apart like no one else can. You're the people I trust to help take my stories to the next level and your passion for reading and the characters I create is infectious.

Every single person who has taken this journey, thank you, because that's what Abby and Jake became for me, a journey. To me they're not just a romance, they're a story about life, about finding yourself and all the messy bits in between. Thank you for putting your faith in me and reading right through to the end.

Finally, Abby and Jake. I haven't written the end. I can't bring myself to do it, I don't know if I ever will be able to. I couldn't have picked two better characters to start my writing career with. I grew right along with you. Thank you for being you. Your story will be a part of me, always.

Want to know more about Abby's Ex Michael Becket?

Keep reading for more information about Fool Me Once and Fool Me Twice.

Plus, an exclusive excerpt from Fool Me Twice!

Fool Me Once

I had it all: the girl, the home, the NFL career. The Life. I was living the dream.

Then I stepped off that goddamn plane. There are a lot of reasons I hate New York. Abby West ending our four-year relationship there has added another.

Then I met Britney Shaw.

My life is unravelling one mistake at a time for all the world to see and I'm about to hit rock bottom.

I'm learning the hard way that they're called secrets for a reason, and they should never be told.

Fool Me Twice

I have one regret in life: fooling Michael Becket, the most promising quarterback in the NFL.

He was supposed to be a simple job, a chance to put the past behind me. It turned into a media scandal which left him famous for all the wrong reasons.

They say keep your enemies close. Becket and I got too close, and something lurking in the shadows proved why we could never be together.

There were secrets.

Too many.

Whose were the darkest, only time will tell.

Britney

You can do this, I tell myself, watching Becket from a distance. He's sitting waiting to board the plane at the departure gate. He doesn't look like the asshole I imagined him to be, he looks hurt, broken. My heart tugs. Get it together, Brit. I bustle forward, making sure to catch his attention. He looks up in my direction. *Bingo.*

A voice from a speaker overhead announces it's time to board the flight. Becket's gaze breaks and he looks away from me. He probably thinks he won't see me again. Wrong.

Luck was on our side. The flight only had a couple of seats left. Thankfully, none of them were above economy, otherwise, Fiona would have gone berserk over the cost. Whatever it takes unless it costs a lot of money. My seat is conveniently next to Becket's. Coincidence? No. Another prime example of Leigh's skills when it comes to this job, and how far she's willing to take things to get the scoop.

Becket stands, picking up his bag and then gets in line to get on the plane. I walk over and join the line further down, so as not to make it too obvious I'm following him. I take a deep breath, it's game time.

"Excuse me. Sorry, sir. Excuse me," I say sweetly as I move along the center aisle.

I can see Becket sitting a few rows up from where I'm standing. The cap on his head is the only discreet part of him—he's well over a head taller than the rest of the people around us. Fleetingly, he looks up and his eyes find mine. Just as quickly he looks away. That's until his luck runs out and I stop at his row.

"Sorry. I need to get to my seat."

"No problem," he drawls out, a smirk on his face.

This is the asshole I expected.

He stands and I move past him to my seat, making sure my body brushes against his as I do. He freezes from the contact and when I look down, the bulge in his pants tells me everything I need to know. Pretending I'm none the wiser to his body's reaction to mine, I go about settling in my seat. He's still standing stock still, staring straight ahead. The bulge in his pants is now in my direct eye line.

Trying to ignore it, I look up at him and say, "Do you want the window seat?"

He shakes his head and looks down at me. His nostrils flare as he snaps, "I'm fine. I don't like the window seat."

Fluttering my eyelashes, I reply, "Everyone loves the window seat …"

"Not when it involves looking at New York City."

Not quite the answer I was expecting. New York is one of the most exciting cities in the world. What can he hate so much about a city everybody loves? I'm about to ask when I remember I have a job to do.

I raise an eyebrow. "Who shat on your parade?"

Internally I cringe at the words that have just spilled out of my mouth. They're not part of the plan, Brit. I'm meant to be wooing him not pissing him off. It's instinctive. I'm merely reacting to the few words he's shared and his body language, which has alarm bells ringing. He's brash and standoffish, like he couldn't care less about the person sitting next to him. The only person he appears to care about is himself.

He's an asshole basically. Just like the media says.

"Nobody," he sighs.

He's back to looking defeated and my heart flutters. I don't know how to take him. One second, he's hot, the next, he's cold. We've not been together more than a few minutes. The flight is over one hundred and twenty. I'm screwed.

I watch as he sits down slowly, not missing the way he shifts his crotch region away. Unfortunately for him, I've already seen the evidence of his face value attraction to me. He rests his head back against his seat and closes his eyes, very obviously wanting to go to sleep. Sorry Becket, that's not part of the plan. I can't woo you if you're unconscious.

"So …" I say bright eyed.

He ignores me and blatantly fakes being asleep. Nobody dozes off that fast.

"I know you're awake," I say, unable to hide the smile in my voice.

He opens one eye and looks at me. "Are you always this perky?"

He *did not* just describe me as perky. I bite back a snarky response, trying to remember the point of all this. "I'm not perky, just friendly," I reply. "Are you always this grumpy after a breakup?" The words are out of my mouth before I can stop them.

His other eye flicks open. "I never told you I'd broken up with someone."

Think on your feet, Brit. I roll my eyes, making it appear as though I couldn't care less whether he'd broken up with someone or not. "It's obvious," I say. "Nobody hates New

York that much, not unless someone's made them feel that way. I simply figured out the obvious."

He frowns, before closing his eyes and grumbling, "Whatever."

Another few minutes of back and forth, not very chatty, chit chat pass by before I try and push for more information.

"So, you did break up with someone," I say, after he almost bites my head off informing me, he's had the worst twenty-four hours of his life. A little dramatic if you ask me.

"That's none of your business."

My instant reaction is to narrow my eyes, but then remembering what the plan is, I plaster on the sweetest smile I can manage. We hold eye contact for a few seconds and my heart feels like it's about to burst out of my chest. When it becomes unbearable, we both look away.

"I'm Britney." It's the first genuine thing I've said since we met.

Of course, this is what sets him off. "How fitting," he says.

I frown. "What's that supposed to mean?"

He shrugs. "Well, you know …"

He is not about to go there. He can't be that much of an ass, surely. "No, I'm afraid I don't," I reply, shaking my head.

"It's fitting you'd be named after a crazy-ass celeb. Psycho comes to mind."

Do not lose your cool, I tell myself. I never expected the articles about his unlikeable personality to be true. Well, if that's the way he wants to play it, then I'll give him a reason to think I'm crazy. It's like flicking on a light switch and tears begin to well in my eyes.

"Excuse me?" I make sure my voice comes out strangled, as if I'm in physical pain by the comment he's made. "You think I'm a psycho?" I throw in an extra snivel just for good measure.

That's all it takes for him to start backtracking. "Maybe not *psycho* per se, but you're definitely some level of crazy."

So much for an apology. He really is a douche. I need time to rethink my plan, so rather than responding, I ignore him and turn to look out the window. I silently say goodbye to New York as the ground below disappears.

OTHER WORK BY LIZZIE MORTON

The Always Trilogy:

Always You
Always Us
Always

The Always Series:

Wanting You Always
Needing You Always

The Fool Me Duet:

Fool Me Once
Fool Me Twice
Fool Me Thrice

Summer Nights Series:

Just One Kiss
Just One Night
Just Once More